Rebel Treasure

Doris M. Lemcke

Published by
Melange Books, LLC
White Bear Lake, MN 55110
www.satinromance.com

Rebel Treasure ~ Copyright © 2017 by Doris M. Lemcke

ISBN: 978-1-68046-500-6 Print

Published in the United States of America.
First Edition

Cover Design by Shelley Schmit

I dedicate this book, as I do all my books, to the principle of persistence. And to my dear friends at Mid-Michigan Writers and my new friends at Southwest Florida Romance Writers. A special thanks to Mary Lou Bugh at MMW and my departed, but never-forgotten mentors, Norma Reinhart Price and Joyce Henderson, for their kindness, faith, and support. To my family and my writing partners Karen Auriti (writing as Kerryn Reid) and Karen Benson, for their patience and for encouraging me to write the Langesford/O'Grady family saga.

Chapter One

Jeffers, GA, 1866

Patrick O'Grady halted his stallion on a hill overlooking his destination. He leaned forward, listening. Nearly a year after Lee's surrender, caution was still second nature to him. Between renegade Confederates and Yankee deserters, it would be a long time before the South was truly safe—especially for a Northerner.

He leaned forward to pat the sleek, black neck of his impatient Morgan blowing gray clouds into the crisp March air. "Take it easy, Jupiter," he calmed the stallion. "Just let me enjoy this view while it lasts."

Under the vibrant, early evening sky, Langesford plantation house looked serene, untouched by the war. Early-budding magnolia trees formed a leafy arch toward a wide veranda with six massive white columns. Small glass panes on the front windows sparkled like so many twinkling stars in the last golden rays of the sunset.

"Perfect," he mused. *Like a painted backdrop on a stage.* Too perfect, instinct told him.

Still, unwilling to disturb the illusion of America's Camelot, he waited until the curtain of darkness descended before letting Jupiter go forward slowly. As usual, his instincts were right. The fairytale image faded with every approaching step, revealing the toll four years of war and one of "Reconstruction" had taken on the once brilliant symbol of Southern life. Now, wood slats covered windows broken by General Kilpatrick's rampaging troops and scars of abuse and neglect disfigured the once elegant façade.

He stopped short of the crumbling veranda to survey the property by

1

the light of the newly risen half-moon. You're a fool, Patrick Sean O'Grady, he thought. You could still be in Chicago, in front of a cheerful fire with a warm brandy in your hand, and a soft woman by your side. But some challenges were hard to resist.

If Anthony Langesford and his plantation were the biggest gamble of his life, they could also yield the biggest reward. And in spite of his Irish mother's advice to never put all his "eggs" in one basket, he'd sunk all his meager savings and a large amount of his partner's, into this venture.

He shrugged against the evening's growing dampness to approach a light glowing from a corner room in the front of the house. Looking forward to the warmth of a fire, he also hoped Colonel Langesford had squirreled away some of the imported brandy so plentiful in Georgia before the war.

~ * ~

"No!" Camilla Langesford's voice bounced off the battered plastered walls with a hollow ring.

Her father rubbed his temples in response to both her defiance and the constant clacking of her boots on the denuded floor of his study. He rose slowly from the lone, straight-backed chair in the nearly empty room and held his hands out to the heat roaring up the home's century-old fireplace, its hand-carved oak scrollwork now scarred by Yankee sabers.

"Tell me it isn't so," she implored, softer this time.

Instead of answering, he raised his eyes to the four-year-old painting of Camilla above the fireplace. She knew what he was thinking. At sixteen, she'd been painted as a model of Southern girlhood, wearing a white party gown with a wide hoop and a pink sash at her tiny waistline. Emerald green eyes sparked mischief from a heart-shaped face wreathed by auburn curls escaping her Madonna chignon.

She followed his gaze, knowing only too well how war and its aftermath had changed her. Too many years of a near-starvation diet had made her thin as a waif, and she stood before him dressed in a patched and faded dress made from clothes she'd once discarded to her slaves. But the most humiliating thing for her father, who prized beauty above

2

all, were the freckles from the hot Georgia sun now marring her once-creamy complexion.

No matter, she thought. She'd done what she had to do for them to survive. He'd spent two years reliving past battles and reviewing impossible plans for the future of the plantation. It was time for him to live in the present.

Hands on her hips, she spoke in a voice totally unbecoming of the genteel, Southern lady she was bred to be. "How can you become partners with a *carpetbagger*. After what they've done to us?" she accused more than asked.

Anthony left the fire to lean against the carpenter's table serving as his desk, arms crossed over his chest, his faded blue eyes narrowed. She took a deep breath. "Do you honestly think this can be good for us, Papa? He's a *Yankee!* Have you forgotten Sherman's barbaric march to the sea? Their war on innocent women and children, both white and colored? In the year since Lee's surrender, they've made and broken promises right and left, while we're drowning in debt, taxes, carpetbaggers, and scalawags. And now you would lease your precious, *ancestral lands* to one of them, just to live in what's left of this house?"

The breath used up, she took another. "The South and the conditions allowing Langesford to exist died in the war, Papa, along with Maman and Brent. Maybe it's time to let it go completely. She reached out to him, beseeching, "Please, instead of a partnership, sell the plantation to the Yankee. We can go somewhere else…"

"That is impossible!" Anthony growled in response, his eyes darkened in the growing gloom.

Her hands now clenched at her sides, she ignored the warning in his voice. "I've heard Brazil has a climate suitable for cotton, as well as low-priced labor. The Bartletts are planning to go there now that the tax collector has Havenwood. If we must continue being planters, let's sell out and put aside the ghosts of the past to begin anew."

Caught up in her dream of a life without war and slavery, she paced, punctuating her words with her hands. "Better yet, we can go west. Homesteads in the territories are free to anyone who will work the land. And Texas is not so far. We could be ranchers, planters, or go into the lumber trade. Or even New Orleans. Maman may still have family there

3

and since Flora is amazing with a needle and thread, and I'm a competent seamstress, we could open a business. You could retire to write our family history."

She reached out to him again, tears blurring her vision. "Don't you see? We're tied to a dead horse here, and no rich Yankee can bring it back to life. With the money from a sale, we could go anywhere and start over."

Her fingers never reached the thin arm inside the worn, tweed coat. Anthony stepped around her to approach the window. "A dead horse," he repeated, as if the words were dirty. "One does not pay fifteen thousand Yankee greenbacks to rent a dead horse, daughter."

Camilla gasped. "Fifteen thousand dollars? That is impossible. No plantation in the county has leased at such a price. Or sold for that matter." Frowning now, she asked, "Why did he pick ours to lease when he could have purchased—or leased—another at less cost?"

Anthony spoke to her reflection in the now-darkened window, explaining as if to a petulant child, "Selling is not an option for us. This land has been our home since your great-great grandfather and James Oglethorpe sailed to America and founded the colony. A Langesford served in the first Provincial Congress. We've fought the British, the French, the Indians, and now our fellow Americans, to keep our land."

He turned to her then, pointing a finger at her nose. "The blood of those brave and adventurous people is as much a part of this plantation as it is a part of me. *Of you!* As long as this land exists, a Langesford will live on it, or die trying."

Out of habit, he reached into his pocket for a watch he'd sold long ago. No matter, the sky had turned to sooty black. With the authority of a Colonel in the Confederate Army, he added, "This lease is a temporary agreement. Its terms will ensure the survival of our legacy. My new partner will arrive soon. Regional differences aside, you will meet him and be gracious to him. He has the manners of a gentleman—see that you behave like the lady you were raised to be."

His raised hand stopped her retort. "But take heart. Mr. O'Grady seems the city-type to me. I doubt he will spend much time here. And, since this is a large place, you should be able to avoid him easily."

He returned to the fireplace, rubbing his hands together above the

4

grate. "And at current cotton prices, even splitting the profits, one or two good crops should allow him a good return on his investment—and pay our taxes with some left over. In time, our life should return to normal."

A knock at the study door cut off Camilla's angry retort that nothing would ever be normal again. It opened a moment later to reveal a dusky-skinned woman standing at the threshold. Her bare, work-worn hands were folded in front of a starched white apron over a somber gray gown. Her eyes downcast in the way of all good servants, she announced, "There is a Mr. Patrick O'Grady here, Colonel. He sounds like a Yankee. What do you want me to do with him?"

"I won't—" Camilla began.

"No, you won't have to see him tonight," Anthony snapped. "He came to see me, not a wild-eyed hoyden just in from the field." He dismissed her with a wave of his arm. "I mustn't keep my guest waiting. You may go to your room. Time enough to see him in the morning, when you're presentable."

Camilla flushed with anger and tears threatened to spill from her eyes, as she looked from her father to Flora waiting at the door, the Yankee behind her. She had no choice but to obey. But rather than leave beaten, in a gesture she'd seen her mother do a thousand times, she pushed back curls that had escaped their net hours before, straightened to her full, five-feet, three inches, gathered up what she could of her narrow skirt, and swept out of the room into the wide, marble foyer.

If not for her old bloodhound, Scar, lying just outside the threshold, it would have been a magnificent exit. Instead, her haughty gesture ended in a humiliating stumble directly into a solid wall of a man in a white suit. Without his strong hands on her shoulders, she'd have fallen on her face.

Then those hands dropped to her waist and he lifted her over the barely startled hound. When she stood firm again, and Scar had relocated to a safer spot near the stairs, he said, "Pardon me," in a deep voice.

His big hands still circling her waist, Camilla stared at the top button of his vest. *Gold.* And his shirt was Chinese silk, with real pearl buttons. She hadn't seen clothing of such quality in years. When he released her, she stepped back, cheeks hot, the tears from her confrontation with her father still in her eyes. And when she finally dared to look at his face, steel-gray eyes wrinkled at the edges, glittering in amusement.

"You shouldn't be running inside the house, child," he scolded with a smile that took her breath away. "You could have been hurt. What would Master Langesford say?"

Child! Master Langesford! This...Yankee...took her for a servant! Rage choked her as she shrank from his pat on her head.

"Now, don't be afraid." He winked. "I won't say anything."

"Master," she choked. "He's not my master, he's..."

"Cammy!" Flora cut her off. Her mouth was set in a stern line, but her hazel eyes, more green than brown, in a *café-au-lait* complexion, were laughing. "Jes' look at you. Don' waste no more o' the fine gentleman's time. Go. Do like Master Langesford tol' you."

Camilla nearly giggled at the affectation in Flora's normally flawless English and continued the charade. She twirled her skirt, answering in a high, little-girl voice, "Yes, Miz Flora. Anything you sez, Miz Flora." She stooped to hide her laughter by patting Scar's head. The dog rose with a loud yawn, looked at the stranger, and followed her up the stairs.

The humor from the joke on the Yankee faded once inside her room. "Oh, Florie," she sighed, knowing the woman followed her with silent footsteps on the stairs. At the soft closing of the door, Camilla turned to her former nursemaid. "What are we going to do about the Yankee? He's not what I expected. He's not like the other carpetbaggers. He looks...."

"Competent," Flora answered for her. "And cultured and intelligent."

Camilla stared. Could Flora be going the way of her father? Had they all forgotten the last five years? She hissed, "There are no cultured and intelligent Yankees! They are all liars and thieves. This one is just better at hiding it than the others. I have to make Papa understand."

She unhooked the waist of her dress to hang it on a hook and stepped out of her skirt and petticoat to face Flora in the chemise that doubled as a nightgown. "It's his money," she announced. "Money clouds men's eyes. That's what tricked Papa."

And his deep voice and pretended manners. She could still feel the warmth of his big, gentle hands at her waist and blinked to erase the memory of a muscular chest straining against expensive pearl buttons.

6

Rebel Treasure

Feeling suddenly warm in the small room where Flora's husband Otis, had started a fire, she paced, removing the useless pins from her thick hair "And what happened to Scar? He's always been our protector. I didn't hear so much as a growl from him."

"With all the commotion going on in the study, I'm not surprised," Flora answered dryly. "He must be getting old, your Scar." She busied herself with the familiar tasks of folding down the ragged, bear's paw quilt and smoothing Camilla's dress over her arm to freshen it for the next day.

"Well, perhaps," Camilla conceded before climbing into the narrow, rope and straw bed Otis had made for her. "Thank you for saving me from embarrassing myself in front of the Yankee. I'm so tired I can't seem to think straight."

She lay back onto a bleached pillow made from a feed sack and goose feathers, staring at the cracked and peeling ceiling. Her sigh heavy with worry, she waited for Flora to sit beside her as she had done every night since she could remember.

As always, Flora sat in silence, her long, elegant fingers folded on top of her starched apron, waiting to hear the events of the day that Anthony didn't care to know.

"I spent all day with Leon and Cato today," Camilla began. "I returned late and didn't have time to freshen up when Papa called me to his study."

Flora brushed curls from Camilla's forehead, whispering, "Clothes do not make your worth, *Cheri*. You are beautiful—inside and out."

Camilla's answering chuckle showed her doubt. "Well, they convinced the others to refuse to honor our contract. We'll have to see that disgusting Federal Agent in Jeffers again, and another day's work will be lost."

She burrowed deeper under the faded quilt and touched an arm only a few shades darker than her own. "We will think of a way out of this, won't we, Florie? Talk to Otis. See what he thinks."

"Oui ma Cher," Flora whispered in a blend of St. Domingue and Creole French from her home in New Orleans. As she had since Camilla's birth, her work-worn fingers gently caressed the girl's forehead as she sang softly, *Au clair de la lune, mon ami pierot.*

When Camilla slipped into an exhausted slumber, Flora rose and whispered, "I will speak to my husband, *Cheri,* but I do not know what we will do with this man. I fear he is here to stay." Her steps slow and her back bowed, she snuffed the candle by the bed with her fingertips and left the room.

Chapter Two

Camilla woke before first light the next morning, lit her bedside candle and looked at herself closely in the cracked mirror above her chest of drawers. *Stupid Yankee.* How could he have mistaken her for a Negro? Though curly, her chestnut hair felt more soft than wiry, her skin only slightly darkened by the sun. Still shameful for any respectable Southern girl, she allowed, but tilling a cotton field while holding onto a hat made the work nearly impossible. Besides, all her bonnets had been ravaged to serve as patches and bindings for gowns and boots during the blockade.

Frowning at the tiny freckles dotting her cheeks, she touched her narrow, straight nose, noting her lips were full, but not wide, more like Flora's, who was only one-half Negro, and from Saint-Dominguc, in the Caribbean. *Certainly not like the Africans.*

And how could he have mistaken her for a child? She ran her hands down the thin chemise. Her breasts were small, but firm and rounded, the flare of her hips proportionate to her narrow waist. "I'm a woman," she announced defiantly to the mirror.

Now to the matter at hand: how to treat the treacherous Yankee in their midst. She determined a show of strength would be the best defense against his Northern arrogance. As a rich man, he no doubt considered an ailing aristocrat on a ravaged plantation, with a young daughter, an easy mark for his Yankee thievery. But she had no intention of being easy.

The Yankee needed to understand that one person saw through his deceptions and watched his every move. He needed to know the woman he'd lifted so easily last night was a woman to be reckoned with. A moment's doubt flickered in her mind. *You'll have to be if you want to keep him from stealing the home Papa refuses to sell.*

She washed from the basin Flora had filled during the night and looked scornfully at the pitiful array of clothing in her chest. Every one of them old, patched, mended, and literally turned inside out, top to bottom, and back to front. Flora's skillful stitching and eye for color kept them from being hideous, but none of them would serve her purpose.

She bit her lip. *Time is wasting!* She had to look the true Southern hostess and help Flora with breakfast before her father and *he* came down, or all would be lost. She'd made a fool of herself once and couldn't afford to do it again.

Not for the first time, she resented the extravagant gowns her mother had squandered their dwindling supply of cash and silver on, thinking what it could do for them now. Then her mood brightened. *Maman's room!* Even during General Kilpatrick's occupation, Flora had managed to keep Danielle Langesford's room and all her possessions intact. A shrine to the woman-child who had replaced her own stillborn son at her breast—and in her heart. Camilla hadn't entered the room since her mother's death, but desperate times called for desperate measures. There had to be something there.

She threw on a linen wrapper and peeked into the hall. Silence. *Good, Papa and the Yankee are still asleep.* Leaving her door open, she clutched her ring of keys and padded barefoot down the hall.

As expected, the door opened without protest. Camilla stood at the threshold, barely breathing. All the fine furnishings were still there. Danielle's mahogany canopied bed from Belle Rivière near New Orleans, a matching armoire, Louis XIV secretary, and the delicate vanity table, all stood exactly where her mother had placed them nearly thirty years ago.

She could almost see her at the vanity, brushing her moonlight-blonde curls. One hundred times, every night. During peace, war, death, and destruction, Danielle Trémon Langesford never missed her hundred strokes. That is, until her beloved Brent, her only son, died at the battle of Chickamauga.

As usual, thoughts of Brent were bittersweet. While Camilla always seemed a burden, Brent was the light of Danielle's tortured soul. He was also Camilla's only ray of sunlight in the shadows of madness surrounding their mother. When the news came of his death, the light of Danielle's life died too. She took to her bed, barely leaving it except for the necessities. Two years later, on the anniversary of the battle that killed her son, she took matters into her own hands.

Camilla hadn't set foot in the room since they found her Maman hanging from the sturdy canopy frame like a beautiful, broken doll, her long hair flowing down her back like silken threads. The image still haunted her dreams.

Now, standing in the doorway, ready to plunder Danielle's treasured wardrobe, she still felt her sad—no, mad—mother's disapproval, and almost turned away. *But this is an emergency!* She exhaled and took another deep breath before stepping toward the armoire.

The waxed mahogany doors opened at the slightest touch to reveal a white organdy day dress trimmed with yellow lace at the neckline, shoulders, and along the hem. It was the last gown Flora made for Danielle shortly before she died. Images of Danielle's once beautiful complexion mottled with red and brown spots, and deep creases alongside lips that had once smiled with gaiety, if not congeniality, flooded Camilla's mind. *Stop it! She's gone now.*

She pulled the gown out expecting it to be half rotted and smelling of mold. Instead, the fresh scent of lavender sachet greeted her. Another look inside told her all of her mother's gowns were maintained in the same condition. *Flora!*

A moment's resentment clouded Camilla's mind. She had suffered these five years, seeing the servants in clothes less worn than hers—clothes she'd foolishly given to them and couldn't bring herself to take back; while her mother's rich gowns of tarlatan, linen, silk, and wool were wasted in this shrine to a woman who'd been nothing in life but a shrew.

Now she was grateful for the small blessing that the gown had never been worn. Camilla took a deep breath, pulled it from the armoire, and dashed from the room. Once dressed, she struggled with hair that again refused to obey its pins, finally tying it back with a green ribbon before stuffing it into her last, ragged net. But as always, a few curls escaped, forming an unfashionable fringe around her forehead and temples. She shrugged, then looked down at bare toes peeking out from under the once-fashionable gown. *Shoes.*

Panic tightened her stomach. Her mother's dainty slippers wouldn't fit and her own were worn out long ago. She only had the boots she wore in the fields or riding, and her stockings were hideous, made over from a pair of Brent's drawers. She could only hope they wouldn't show under her half-hoop and petticoat.

She turned at the sound of booted feet on oak flooring coming from the room next to hers. *Brent's room!* How could her father put the Yankee in her dead brother's room? How could he allow his enemy to sleep only a few feet away from her, on the other side of a door with a broken lock?

Unbidden, thoughts of his chest without the fancy silk shirt, and his strong jaw with the shadow of a morning's beard invaded her mind. *Don't even think it! He's the enemy. And remind Otis to fix that lock.* She bolted from her room to dash down the back stairs before the Yankee opened his door.

When Camilla appeared at the kitchen door breathless, wearing Danielle's dress, Flora's hand left her knife buried in a warm loaf of bread, to cross herself and kiss the crucifix she always wore. And Otis, puttering over broken pot handles, whistled low. "Lordy, girl, look at you."

His wife folded her arms across her small chest. "So this is your plan to get rid of the Yankee? Frighten him away with your appearance?"

Misreading the laughter in her eyes as anger for wearing the stolen gown, Camilla threw her arms up in frustration. "I had nothing else decent to wear." Then she paced. "Maybe I should have just worn my work dress from yesterday. I'll probably ruin this one halfway through the morning."

She stopped when Flora's lips twitched upward, and Otis too, barely concealed his mirth. She stamped her foot. "Oh, you two. This is serious. I want the carpetbagger to feel the same embarrassment I did last night."

She primped her hair and twirled around, secretly enjoying the sound and feel of the expensive fabric. "Besides, I am a lady, you know. And no ill-bred Yankee is going to think me anything less." She reached for the few remaining good china plates. "We must show him we don't need him—only his money."

Flora moved quietly in the eye of her storm and Otis wisely left the house for his outside chores as she bustled around the kitchen sorting through the remnants of Limoges china her great-great grandmother had brought from England. Setting aside chipped or cracked dishes, she thought out loud, "If we show him how well we manage without his greenbacks, he may understand we don't need his all-powerful Yankee presence here when we do have them."

A flicker of doubt creased her forehead and she turned to Flora. "Don't you think?"

Her former slave and surrogate mother stopped mixing cornmeal and frowned. "I t'ink you t'ink you have all the answers and what I, or anyone else t'inks, means nothing to you." Then she turned her attention back to the bowl, molded the corn into cakes and put them in bacon grease to fry.

A moment later, the cakes sizzling in hot grease, she turned to Camilla. Her hazel eyes darkened to the color of amber and her voice grew husky. "No man is what he seems, girl. You know nothing of this man or his reasons for being here. Watch him. Listen beyond his words." A finger coated with flour again touched the cross at her neck. "Look to his soul before you judge him."

Gooseflesh rose on Camilla's arms. "What do you—?" The sound of male voices coming from the front stairs interrupted her. With a sidelong glance at Flora, who now concentrated on the morning coffee, she forced a smile and left the kitchen.

"Papa," she cooed, kissing Anthony lightly on the cheek. "Good morning. Breakfast is nearly ready."

Anthony stood open-mouthed at her transformation as she turned her attention to Patrick, who stood behind him, nearly a head taller. "Oh, and Mr...O'Grady, is it?" She smiled when his gray eyes widened and a flush crept up his neck.

To make up for her father's silence and avoid his increasingly suspicious stare, she held out a dainty hand covered by one of her mother's lace fingertip gloves. "I am Camilla Langesford. I trust you had a safe journey, and met none of those terrible renegades plaguing our countryside."

He nodded. "Yes, the new Pullman cars are quite comfortable. And no, I haven't met with any animosity. It appears I've been blessed in many ways since my arrival."

A big hand covered with butter-soft, calf skin gloves swallowed her small one, lingering a moment longer than necessary, and making her wonder how a coarse Yankee could have such a soft voice and gentle hands.

A Yankee, she reminded herself and forced her own voice to be cold. "Well, be careful. I believe the renegades call themselves the Ku Klux Klan. Being from the north, and a Republican I would guess, you should always be wary of them."

Anthony cleared his throat loudly. "Shall we be seated?" He squeezed her arm against his side to lead her into the dining room they hadn't used in nearly five years. His eyes narrowed when he pulled out her chair and whispered, "What are you up to, you little minx?"

~ * ~

Patrick wanted to laugh out loud as he chose the chair next to her. *She's magnificent*, he thought. She should have been Irish. He took the chair opposite hers. *But when it comes to playacting, my dear, you've met your match.*

Still, he'd gotten her message. He may all but own their plantation, but he was a guest in her house. *Pride.* He liked it. He smiled at his hosts. *This could prove to be a very interesting venture.*

They discussed the weather, the landscape, and all manner of mundane topics while Patrick ate heartily of the delicious corncakes, salted bacon, and fried grits. He blamed fatigue for his monumental error in judgment the night before. She was certainly no child. But not the pampered young debutante in the portrait either. *Which is the disguise?* he wondered.

He folded his napkin neatly beside his plate, declaring, "This meal was delicious." Pretending to notice his hosts had hardly touched their food, he added, "Please excuse me. I seem to have made a glutton of myself. It must be your fresh, country air." And since food and servants were always safe topics while dining with self-proclaimed aristocrats, he added "Your cook rivals the best I've sampled in Washington, New

York, or even Chicago."

Anthony nodded, dabbing his linen napkin needlessly to the corners of his lips. "Yes, Flora is from New Orleans. As my wife's nursemaid, she came with us when we married. I don't know what we'd have done if she and Otis had deserted us like..." He began to cough and excused himself, leaving Patrick and Camilla alone in the cavernous room.

Camilla explained the sound of choking coughs carrying to them from the kitchen. "It's a nasty winter cold still lingering. As soon as the weather warms, he'll be fine."

Patrick had seen the last stages of consumption more times than he cared to remember and had watched the only person he ever loved cough, gasp, and bleed to death in unbearable agony. Anthony was very likely hiding his bloodied handkerchief as they spoke, and the worried furrow in Camilla's finely sculpted forehead told him she knew it too. "I'm sure he will."

Her voice rose above the sounds of her father's suffering to ramble, "Papa fought in the Wilderness Campaign of '64, though he rarely speaks of the horrors he endured. But while it took a toll on his strength, I'm told the valiant efforts of our brave countrymen took an even greater toll on the enemy's strength."

She balled her napkin and tossed it on top of her uneaten food like a gauntlet of war. There was no apology in her voice when she added, "Oh dear, I suppose that was you...at the time. I'm afraid it's difficult to get used to a—a..."

"Damned Yankee in the house?" He wasn't amused anymore. Her father was dying, his plantation, except for Yankee money, all but gone; yet she sparred with him about a war that had been a lost cause from the beginning. "Please forgive me for the unfortunate location of my birth.

"The war itself was a great loss for the whole nation. It will take a long, long time for the wounds to heal on both sides of the Mason-Dixon Line."

Flora broke the ensuing uncomfortable silence to announce, "The Colonel is unwell, Mr. O'Grady. He has retired to his room and apologizes for not being able to give you your tour of the plantation this morning."

It suited Patrick just fine. He disliked being led around and told where to go. He'd much rather wander about by himself. Then he could see the flaws others tried to cover. The secrets they tried to hide. But Flora, like a soldier reluctantly obeying an order he detested, turned to Camilla. "Your papa wishes you to take his place as guide for Mr. O'Grady."

With a fierce look at Patrick, she said, "I will pack a lunch for you, and young Cato will ride along with it on a mule."

Patrick read the mistrust in Flora's eyes as she assigned Camilla a protector. He couldn't blame her, but had no desire to spend the day trotting behind a snooty Southern belle who obviously loathed him—all the while trying to hold Jupiter to the pace of a mule!

"No need to bother," he reassured. "I'm sure Miss Langesford has a full appointment book today. With just a few directions, I'll be fine. I never get lost."

Camilla surprised him by piping up a little too loudly, "No! I mean it may be dangerous for you to ride out alone until the neighbors know you're our...guest."

He understood. She didn't trust him. *Smart girl.* The most dangerous kind. He too forced a smile. "Why Miss Langesford, I do appreciate your concern for my welfare." He rose and reached out to help her stand. "I'd be honored to be accompanied by such a lovely bodyguard."

She rose from her chair without his help and stood less than an arm's length away, trapped between the table, the chair, and him. Before stepping back, his gaze assessed her, beginning with the yellow lace kissing her collarbone, to the tiny waist in no need of a corset, and the gentle flow of her hips.

An eyebrow raised when he saw the tips of worn work boots peeking out beneath the white confection of her skirt. "I am quite anxious to see the property. How soon can we leave?"

She followed his gaze down to the scuffed toes of her boots and flushed. "Oh this. I can change clothes and be down in just a few minutes." She darted around him and set off for the stairs, adding over her shoulder, "We have learned of late, to manage nearly everything on the spur of the moment."

Chapter Three

True to her word, she reappeared in a matter of minutes, wearing the riding habit she'd worn the day she tried to ride Brent's stallion at her mother's tournament picnic. She'd been a plump thirteen-year-old then, and now the tailored jacket and fitted skirt seemed horribly loose in some places and terribly tight in others. But a pair of Brent's old trousers were her only other choice.

She hurried down the stairs, pulling on short, kid gloves. All business, she asked, "Mr. O'Grady, what interests you most about our farm?"

His Cheshire-cat smile indicated she held that distinguished honor. "I'm just along to see the sights, Miss Langesford. What do you suggest?"

She stopped one step from the bottom, nearly eye-level with him and close enough to see gold flecks glittering like stars in the stormy gray gaze that seemed to drink in the length of her. She blushed at his scrutiny, suddenly feeling conscious of the places where the seams strained against her womanly curves. *If he doesn't approve, he can spend the day on the veranda.*

She tossed her head, testing the strength of her snood and the worn ribbons of her riding bonnet. Then she squared her shoulders, and side-stepped past him. "It's impossible to cover all of Langesford in a single day," she said over her shoulder on the way to the double oak doors.

"Oh!" she said when his hand covered hers on the latch.

"Allow me, Miss Langesford," he answered softly.

Her hand felt oddly warmed from his touch, even with gloves. She stepped back for him to pull open the door and usher her ahead of him with a courtly bow. They stood next to each other on the peeling, but solid wide planks of the deep veranda, inhaling the scent of spring in the air.

Camilla turned to him, surprised he was so close to her. She stepped back to sweep her arm at the flowering drive he'd missed in the darkness the night before. "We have more than two thousand acres of prime cotton land and forest." At the slight pop of a rotted thread in her sleeve, she lowered her arm to turn to their right. "The forest is much like any other one you may have seen in the north, except for the moss maybe. The river is quite commonplace as well."

Avoiding those strange eyes that seemed to look right through her, she unnecessarily smoothed her riding skirt. "We are, and always have been, primarily a cotton plantation, so I think the quarters and cotton fields might interest you. They're near enough to explore and return in time for supper."

As always, talking about the land strengthened her. She'd been a curious, roaming child all her life, and the real mistress of Langesford for more than four years. There wasn't a tree, rock or stalk of grain she didn't know. And none that she cared to show him. She turned back to him with a sly smile. "Shall we go?"

~ * ~

Patrick's breath caught when the shimmer of a mischievous Irish sprite shone from eyes rimmed by the long lashes of a French coquette. Remembering the painting, he allowed the artist, though passable, had painted her eyes all wrong. Instead of glittering green emeralds, specks of gold and amber surrounded the pupils like tiny kaleidoscopes within a ring of sun-dappled forest green. *A dangerous combination*

The die cast, he followed her gently swaying hips thinking, you're wrong about the woods. Lumber, turpentine, and pine tar were nearly as valuable as gold these days; while the demand for cotton had lessened due to hoarding and new competition from Egypt and India. *And it's unlikely I'll find the gold Brent Langesford stole from the Denver Mint stashed in a slave cabin.*

But he'd already gotten off to a bad start with this vexing young woman who both irritated and intrigued him. Simmer down, Boyo, he told himself. Stick to the plan. You have a crime to solve and a partner to pay. There's plenty of time to explore the mature timber later, and search the house after the tiny rebel and her father retire at night.

He caught up to her quickly and followed her gaze down the clay and shell paved drive. "A lovely view," he said, looking at her.

She flushed at the obvious compliment. "Yes, well, we're on a knoll, with the advantage of high ground. And this is a natural clearing. As you can see, it's a perfect place for my ancestors to build a fortress. Close enough to the pines to escape Indians, and open enough to make a sneak attack difficult. My great-great grandfather built the first log house on this very site. In some rooms, where the Yankees punched through the walls, you can see the original timbers, lath, and horsehair plaster."

Then, as if to make a point, she added, "Still, the Creeks burned most of it before he became an old man. This house arose from its ruins." Her voice took a vengeful tone. "No matter the disaster, Langesford always emerges stronger than before." *Without Yankee help* shouted from those expressive eyes before she stepped onto the drive.

Patrick liked how her voice softened when she spoke about the land and the history of her home. It reminded him of his mother's stories of her childhood home in Ireland. Except Mary O'Grady's ancestral home had been the stone hovel of a tenant farmer, no better than what he imagined Langesford's slave quarters were.

Less out of need for an explanation than a desire to hear more of her wistful voice, he pointed to several log structures nestled near the encroaching pines. "And those buildings?"

"The smokehouse and laundry. The distance keeps the heat away from the house. My Maman insisted my father attach the cookhouse to the main one, via a tunnel in the hillside below us, also enlarging the dining room for better entertaining."

Patrick noted an undertone of irritation in the comment. "How practical."

Her lips twitched at his sarcasm. "It seemed important to her at the time, I suppose." She stopped to meet Otis with Jupiter and her speckled mare in tow. When Jupiter pawed the ground impatiently and shied at their approach, she stepped back, turning a heel on a stone.

19

Doris M. Lemcke

Patrick again caught her by the shoulders, this time holding her against him until Otis got the big horse under control. "Jupiter's just a bit edgy," he said softly, "and doesn't care for the lead. He's usually quite gentle around women." He nodded for Otis to release the big Morgan, who approached Camilla with an apologetic nuzzle against her arm. "This is new territory for him." *And for me.*

Before she could refuse, Patrick knelt to check her leg for swelling. The slender ankle covered by hideous homespun stockings, hadn't begun to swell, but had taken what was certainly a painful a turn. He gave her credit for having the grit to keep from crying out when he pressed his fingers along the delicate bones.

"It isn't broken, but it must pain you," he said, giving her a chance to change her mind about the tour. "Would you like to go back inside? I'm certain I can find my way around."

Her "No!" sounded like a shot, tempered with, "I appreciate your concern, but I'm fine." She stepped away without favoring the twisted ankle, giving Jupiter a forgiving pat on his nose before mounting her horse without assistance.

Astride a battered, Confederate saddle, her frown dared him to comment on her unusual riding seat and gear. "And I'm not afraid of your horse. He just startled me." A heartbeat later, she whispered, "Run, Misty," and urged her mount to a gallop down the tree-lined corridor.

Jupiter overtook them with little effort, and they reigned in at the end of the drive, turning back to see Cato struggling with the old mule. It would take him some time to catch up and Camilla's frown showed she shared his own disinclination to wait.

She nodded at the trail. "The river is west of here, along with some fallow pastures." With a nod to their right, she announced, "The quarters and the cotton fields are to our north. The weather has been crisp, but they'll be ready to plant soon. We'll go this way." She turned Emily's head to the north and Patrick once again had no choice but to follow.

"Woman," he muttered. "You have a talent for knowing exactly what I want to do and doing the opposite."

Abandoned slave quarters didn't interest him. The rambling Ogemaw River flowing through the heart of Langesford would carry his crops and lumber to the ocean ports that would turn them into cash. And

20

worn out cotton fields were of no use to him. His fortune lay in the fallow ones—if he couldn't prove the Colonel had masterminded his son's daring raid on the Denver Mint four years ago.

Daring was an understatement. They'd done it in broad daylight, breaking into the old assay office through a walled-off storage room. In less than an hour, they'd looted the mint of a fortune in gold bars, hauling it away under a load of manure right under the nose of the Union Army. Then, they disappeared into thin air.

It haunted him until the end of the war and beyond, as the only case he couldn't solve. Two months ago, when Anthony showed up at the Chicago Gentleman's club looking for investors, Patrick convinced Allen Pinkerton to reopen the case and talked Dr. Clarke Johnson into bankrolling his fake investor scheme.

The timing couldn't have been better. It took five months to grow a cotton crop. Time enough to find either the gold or Langesford's plans for hiding it, and deliver them to Pinkerton. Failing that, he'd have enough profits from lumber, cotton, and the other crops he planned grow to pay back his old friend. A safe bet, the gambler inside him reasoned.

He hoped his share of either outcome would set him up in the horse-breeding business he'd dreamed of since running away from Boston's Orphan Home as a ten-year-old. But if neither scheme panned out, he'd be selling Dr. Johnson's Indian Blood Syrup from town-to-dusty-town for a long, long time. He frowned. With the little red-head sticking to him like a burr on a pant leg, things could get complicated. But, as his mother always said, "Time will tell."

Today, he only had to accompany a beautiful woman around her plantation under a sapphire sky with puffy clouds and a light breeze. As if overnight, early crocuses had poked cautious, multi-colored heads out of the ground, and yellow January Jasmine trees were already sprouting buds. The planting season looked favorable and for the time being at least, life looked good.

Minutes later, he brought Jupiter alongside Misty and leaned across the space between them. "Better slow down, Miss Langesford. Your boy's having a hard time with the mule." They both turned to see Cato and the stubborn mule nearly a quarter-mile behind them. "I'm anxious to see the place," he said. "But not at the expense of my midday meal. If it's half as good as breakfast, I'd ride the mule with it."

As if unable to bear being close to him for even a moment, Camilla turned Misty aside. "I'm sure it won't come to that, Mr. O'Grady. I'll have a word with him."

He patted Jupiter, watching her ride little Misty like an expert. He imagined her on the horse without a saddle, her burnished hair flowing in the breeze. He could even imagine her laughter.

Then he heard it. Clear and carefree, it's earthiness opposing the woman she presented herself to be. He wondered again about the Camilla in the portrait with a mischievous gleam in her eyes. *Which is the artificial likeness?* He smiled as the sound again floated to him on the warming breeze. Perhaps the morning wouldn't be a waste of time after all.

But the sprite inside her was gone when she returned. "Cato will meet us in the peach grove. Our tour should take us there at the right time for dinner." That settled, both horses set off at a leisurely trot toward the old slave cabins.

Misty stopped at the edge of a narrow lane. Where there had once been a dozen one-room cabins, each with its own chimney, standing in two neat rows on either side of the wide path, there were only ruins. Several were burned, the rest dismantled, the siding carted away. They stood like skeletons watching them as they rode slowly by.

Her voice tight, Camilla explained, "Before the war, these buildings were caulked, whitewashed, and inspected for vermin once a year. Families lived here, played here, and raised their children knowing they wouldn't be separated. It was quite a lively little place."

Patrick didn't answer. What would his mother have given for four separate walls of her own and a stove to warm the space in the middle, he wondered. Instead, she escaped the poverty of her Irish homeland to spend the remainder of her short life in an attic that froze her in the winter and suffocated her in the summer.

He bit back his anger that she accepted her place as a servant without rights, and swallowed his hatred for his own father. The lecherous Dr. Stainsby had used her for his own carnal pleasure until she became too wasted to interest him—all sanctioned by a social system based on, "freedom and liberty for all."

He stopped Jupiter near one of the sturdier cabins and dismounted. His back to Camilla, he said. "So this is where you kept your slaves."

She stopped beside him, but remained mounted. "They were never this bad when we had control over the Negroes."

"Is that so?" he muttered, stepping inside.

"Kilpatrick's men did most of the damage," she called from her saddle. Her voice sounded hollow in the little ghost town. "They quartered their horses inside and used the siding for cook fires." A bitter edge crept into it. "After the war, we would gladly have fixed them up, but most of the hands left for the *'riches'* in town."

He stepped onto the rotten porch and leaned against the lone beam supporting a sagging roof. Crossing one booted foot over the other and tilting his head to the side, he studied her. "You didn't really expect a newly-freed prisoner to return docilely to his old cell, did you? Even with a new coat of whitewash."

Her shoulders sagged and she made a pretense of stroking Misty's neck before answering softly, "No, I suppose not, but so many are ill-equipped to handle their new lives. We haven't bought or sold slaves in three generations and set aside funds for their care for when they became ill or couldn't work. Most of them stayed because this was their home, not their prison. Papa says they will soon learn the harsh realities of freedom and long for the security of their past lives."

He patted Misty's soft, pink nose before meeting her gaze. "And you believe that?"

The sadness in her voice told him she didn't. A heartbeat later, the sadness gave way to a bitter smile. "Why not? After fighting for survival for four years, Southern women are expected to slip right back into corsets that pinch the breath out of them; to worry about freckles ruining their chances of finding a husband, and to laugh insipidly at men's stupid jokes. In short, to return to their no-longer-gilded, but not-quite-whitewashed, cells."

The ice in her voice set him back. "Camilla, I didn't mean...."

She raised a hand and straightened in the saddle. "But worst of all, we're expected to sit idly by while the businesses we kept alive during the worst time in Southern history, are virtually ripped from our capable hands." Then she nudged Misty, leaving Patrick and Jupiter in a cloud of red dust.

She waited for him at the other end of the quarters and as they continued their ride in silence, Patrick watched the emotions play across her expressive features. He'd survived most of his life by watching other people, sensing their moods, finding their weaknesses, and using them to his advantage. But she presented a host of contradictions: childlike prankster, lady of the manor, zealous landowner, reluctant defender of slavery, and now rebellious supporter of women's suffrage. More and more, he wondered what really made her tick.

Now and then, Camilla slowed to pat Misty's smooth, golden neck. The movement stretched the rust-colored velvet jacket and Patrick saw the outline of firm breasts straining against seams made for a much flatter figure. At the same time, the short jacket raised to reveal a simple cord holding the waist of a skirt made for a much thicker middle. He smiled. *Even dressed in rags, she rides like a princess, sovereign over all the lands surrounding her.*

They stopped at the edge of the north cotton field. Six men worked where twenty had once labored. "Last year we got less than a third of our crop," Camilla spoke at last. "It promised to be an excellent year, but part way through picking, most of the hands quit and went to town."

She continued, one planter to another. "Flora, Otis and I picked what we could and managed to ship it to Savannah. Then, before the hands returned, the worms saved us the trouble of picking more."

It was difficult to follow her speech while drinking in the sight of her smooth cheeks flushed from the ride, and heavily-lashed eyes glowing with both passion and pride for her work.

"We nearly covered planting costs," she explained. "But most of the crop the worms didn't get, rotted. The freedmen have kept to the contract this year, but there have been problems." She pointed toward the huge field hand near the center of the field. "That's Leon. He and Cato are behind the more recent problems. I'll...I mean you...will have to visit the agent in Jeffers to settle the matter. I wasted two days doing the same thing a couple months ago, and a lot of good it did me."

Patrick stared as they dismounted. "You went to the agent?"

"Yes. Papa had gone to Chicago. To meet with you, I believe."

Touché. The pieces finally came together. Her work clothes the previous evening, her objection to his presence, and her exception to him riding alone on the plantation. It all made sense now. This land belonged to *her.* These people, slave or free, were hers. For the last four years, she'd cared for them and sweated in the fields with them. *She is the real master of Langesford!*

He watched her walk to the edge of the field. After pausing a moment to look at the rolling sweep of prime cotton land, she knelt at the edge of a plowed furrow. Ignoring the red clay clinging to her skirt, she scooped a handful of rich topsoil and watched it spill though her gloved fingers. When he joined her, she told him, "This is rich land, Mr. O'Grady. With proper rest, seed, and constant care, it can once again produce a wealth of crops."

She looked up, her eyes moist with emotions held in check. He imagined pulling her into his arms, pulling off her stupid hat and running his hands through the tangle of curls straining against its net. Instead, he squatted beside her.

He also scooped the topsoil into his hand. Even with no experience as a farmer, his Welsh blood stirred to the feel and smell of what made life possible. Next to her, with the fertile soil in his hand and the sun on his back, he felt...home. An unsettling feeling to say the least.

He hadn't come to Georgia to find a home. Home belonged to people who belonged—somewhere. He'd come to solve a mystery that had haunted him for four years, and to pay the man backing his mission.

Camilla's voice broke his reverie. "This is life, Mr. O'Grady. Our lives here on Langesford." Her voice was soft, as if in a place of worship. "For more than a century, we have farmed this land and until the recent...unpleasantness...we, and all of our people, have prospered."

She stood then, staring past him at the land her ancestors had carved from the wilderness. "But it seems all good things really do come to an end." She looked down at him, the sun a glowing halo behind her. "But understand this. It is only money we lack—because of that foolish war. We don't need a Yankee to tell us how to farm our land."

The ice queen once again, she frowned at his clean, white trousers. "Especially one afraid to get his pants dirty."

She brushed the dust from her gloves, her gaze wistful as she watched it dance in the breeze before returning to its place on the ground. Then she turned toward Misty, talking as she walked. "Cotton isn't our only cash crop. Since the beginning, the mission of our plantation was to see to the needs of the people here first. Before the war, we were totally self-sufficient. Over the years, we've grown nearly all the vegetables produced in the north, and besides cotton, have supplied Northern markets with fresh peaches. The grove is quite near."

Once mounted, she turned her back on the cotton field. "For lack of manpower, most of the plantation is fallow, though it may be a blessing. Cotton depletes the soil. A couple of years without planting should replace the lost fertility. She looked at him for the first time since leaving the field. "But I've talked too long. You must have questions."

"No," he lied as they moved on at a leisurely pace. He had a hundred questions, but gave her credit. "You've been an excellent guide, and what you haven't told me I've seen for myself." He thought a moment and added, "I do have one question, after all."

"And that is?"

"The young Negro you spoke of as being in cahoots with Leon to disrupt the work. Cato, I think is his name."

"Yes?"

"Is he the same fellow you entrusted with our dinner?"

She treated him to a sultry laugh he knew he'd never forget. "Yes, but since yesterday's trouble, it's better for him to be separated from Leon's influence. This is just the type of work he loves. He can ride in the sun and wait for us in the shade. And if we don't come, he can eat our food."

"I see. You do know how to handle your people."

She reined Misty in so hard the little mare reared. Then she fixed those magical eyes on him, dark now, and inexplicably angry. "Mr. O'Grady," sounded like a growl. "Contrary to Mrs. Stowe's fairytale, we did not whip our slaves at Langesford. Nor are they lazy. As you can see, without their hard work we'd have nothing. It is important to us that they be healthy and treated humanely. In fact, all my life so far has been spent caring for and anticipating *their* needs."

As if recognizing the absurdity of her statement, she added, "I mean, I understand their rush to seize their freedom, no matter the cost, but now, when the South needs their services more than ever, and is willing to pay for them, they refuse to work for us. It is hard to understand things the way they are now."

"I'm sure it is," he tried to console her. "Unless one has lived a life of forced servitude, the simple freedom of choosing your own employer can be taken for granted." *Wrong answer.*

"The last five years have taught us to take nothing for granted, sir." She nudged Misty again and they were off at a full gallop.

Both horses kicked up Queen Anne's lace in their race to the peach grove, a pink oasis on an open plain. Camilla dashed at a full run between the rows of blossoming peach trees, lowering her head to avoid the far-reaching branches.

Jupiter's height and girth prevented him from skirting through the trees like Misty, so Patrick pulled him up short at the edge of the grove. "Are you mad?" he called, half angry and half amused at the woman's recklessness.

"Not at all, sir," floated on the breeze as she led her horse back to him. She cocked her now hatless head. "You're cautious, Mr. O'Grady. I'd think a man like you would stop at nothing to win, especially over a woman."

He should have been angry at the taunt, but her hair captured his attention. It had finally fully escaped its net to become a wild tangle tumbling past her shoulders, the sun-kissed auburn curls framing her face. And her smile took his breath away with even, white teeth and a pink tongue that moistened lips meant to be kissed.

He smiled back. "You have no idea what kind of man I am, Miss Langesford. But for your information, I don't take foolish risks. Especially over a woman." He dismounted, drew her arm into the crook of his elbow, and with an untethered Jupiter following behind them, guided her to the spreading pink canopy where their luncheon awaited them.

Cato settled several trees away to eat his own dinner from a tin pail. With a truce called for the noon meal, Patrick ate ravenously of the cold chicken, grits, and biscuits with homemade honey, while Camilla nibbled on a small chicken breast and a biscuit. Careful not to look up, lest she run like a startled colt, he felt her staring at him. No, studying him.

"We've come a quarter-circle of the plantation, Mr. O'Grady," she told him after sipping from the jug of Flora's special lemon water. She handed it to him. "There's little else of interest within riding distance except the old gin and cotton house."

He nearly choked on the refreshingly sweet mix of lemon, water, and cane sugar and waved his hand. "Patrick."

"Pardon me?"

"Please call me Patrick. Mr. O'Grady makes me want to look around for an old man."

"Oh, I couldn't. We've only just met, and my own Maman called Papa Mr. Langesford or Colonel, until her dying day."

And I don't like you enough to call you by your first name, spit from her eyes. "Times change," he responded to both comments.

"Not that much."

"Time will tell."

She rose, refusing to let him have the last word again. "Well, there's not much point in seeing the gin and cotton house. They're ruins. Yankees burned nearly all our buildings, promising to return one day for the main house." Her voice low, she tested, "Fortunately Yankees aren't very good at keeping their word. They never returned."

He stood too, but instead of a caustic reply, smiled as if he recognized the fear behind her brave words. He stood over her, so close he could smell the scent of lilac soap in her hair. "Well, then there's no need to go there," he answered softly, sparing her the ordeal of reliving the moment her life and home were threatened. "And perhaps one day you'll find a Yankee you can trust."

She bit her lip as if biting back a sharp retort, then her shoulders relaxed in acknowledgement of his courtesy. She remounted and again took off at a run, this time back toward Langesford.

Patrick won the race. "A marvelous tour," he told Anthony who greeted them at the door, looking better, if not well. "Your daughter is a most knowledgeable guide and gracious hostess."

He pumped Anthony's hand while Camilla ran her fingers through her tangled hair and walked toward the stairs. She stiffened and turned as he told her father, "The plantation is truly filled with potential. I'd planned on staying only long enough to order supplies, but after today's tour, I'm afraid you're going to be stuck with a resident partner. I couldn't bear to be left out of this great adventure."

Chapter Four

Flora hissed through clenched teeth, "You set one foot in this room, and you'll never walk the same again." Her adversary towered over her and weighed three times as much, but he stood still as a statue, except for huge brown eyes rolling in a round, coal-black face.

He raised his arms in surrender. "But the new man tol' me to fix up all the floors an' walls in *all* the rooms."

Camilla ran up the stairs, calling, "Amos! Flora! What in the world is going on here?" She stopped short at the top, shocked to see the huge carpenter terrified of an old woman with a shawl over her shoulders and an antique gun pointed at his private parts.

Amos jumped. "Miss Camilla, Mr. O'Grady tol' me to—"

Flora's screech drowned out his baritone. "This is my Dannie's room! I won't have it dirtied by the likes of him."

"Put the gun down, Florie," Camilla ordered. "More likely it will backfire—if it fires at all."

The older woman did as her mistress asked, but kept her hard gaze on the workman.

Camilla then turned her attention to Amos. Her voice less threatening than Flora's, but just as firm, she warned, "I don't know what Mr. O'Grady told you, but there are two rooms in this house no one may touch without my approval. This one, and mine."

"But he tol' me all the rooms," Amos insisted. "Miz Cammy, A'hm s'posed to empty 'em out and check for loose boards, holes in the walls an' broken windows. He sent me here first 'cause' no one uses it."

Camilla's voice rivaled Flora's. "Well, he was wrong!" A month ago, Amos would never have imagined questioning her authority in her

30

own home; and for Flora to brandish a weapon was insane. But lately, everything at Langesford seemed insane. From the moment O'Grady stated his intention to reside at Langesford, the house had been in a state of constant chaos.

She'd barely seen her father in three weeks. He was either closeted in the study with Patrick, in his room resting, or off to Savannah on some mysterious "business" he wouldn't talk about. And Patrick rarely left the house while waiting for his new farm equipment to arrive.

He seemed to be everywhere at once, poking around cabinets, stomping on floorboards and rooting around cellars and attics. He told her he was checking the home's 'structural integrity' for needed repairs. She didn't believe it for a moment, and worried about why he took such an interest in a house he'd be leaving after the crop came in.

Now, with Flora's weapon lowered and Amos collecting his tools, Camilla vowed to take no more of the Yankee's interference. Determined to confront him, she turned on her heel—only to once again collide with his rock-hard chest.

Smiling at her determined frown, he asked Amos, "Is there a problem?"

Amos just stared at the toe sticking out of his worn boots until Camilla said, "I've taken care of the matter, Mr. O'Grady. Amos will find other work to do in the house."

He nodded and Amos stepped around them to take the front stairs two at a time. "He was following my orders."

It was the last straw. The man had moved into her home, bag and baggage, insinuating his way into her father's confidence. And now he assumed only his orders held sway in the house, as well as in the fields. "Your orders!" filled the narrow hall. "We have to talk, Mr. O'Grady. Privately."

When Flora stepped wearily toward the back stairs, Camilla stepped into the nearest room...Danielle's. Patrick followed and closed the door softly. With a low whistle, he walked past her to sit on the edge of the wedding-ring quilt atop a goose-down filled mattress. Arms crossed, his booted feet set squarely on the polished mahogany floor, he grinned. "Whatever do you have in mind, Miss Langesford?"

She realized the heat of her anger had caused her to choose her battleground unwisely. Even surrounded by silk and antique lace, the man exuded masculinity—no, mastery. But she'd gone too far to go back. Determined to ignore the frilly, French boudoir furnishings, she stuffed her hands in her apron pockets and paced. "We have to discuss what is going on here."

He caught her arm as she passed him. "I thought we were restoring the great Langesford Plantation to its former glory."

She pulled away at the sarcasm in his voice, clenched her fists and snapped, "I'm not a child. And I'm not stupid. Restoring this house has nothing to do with your partnership, unless you plan to live in it yourself one day." There, she'd said it.

"I am no sick, deluded old man, *Mr. O'Grady*. By urging my father to squander your rent money on luxurious furnishings and unnecessary repairs, we won't be able to pay our debts and Langesford will be yours for the taking."

She jabbed a finger into his chest. "Well I'm here to tell you I will not allow it to happen. Unless you complete your swindle, these people do what *I* say, and I expect to be consulted *before* any work is done in this house."

Her heart hammering in her chest, she turned and stalked to the door. But the handle wouldn't budge. "Damn," she swore, tears of anger and frustration filled her eyes as she yanked on the stubborn brass lever.

She felt, more than heard him step up behind her, and couldn't move when his breath warmed her neck. "There's no need for profanity, Camilla." A heartbeat later, he stepped in front of her. His calloused hand lifted hers from the door handle to raise it to his lips. "And you're wrong."

The unexpected caress sent shafts of heat up to her heart, and down to her belly at the same time, while his clear, gray gaze froze her in place. But her pulse still pounded in her ears as she stared at the gentle curve of his lips to whisper, "Am I?"

He nodded. "Yes, you are, lass. I've no desire to steal your farm. And even less to be Lord of the Manor." His hand firmly on her only means of escape, he said, "I know how important appearances are in the South. I'm paying for the renovations as part of my room and board."

He gestured at the decaying shrine to a beautiful…dead…fantasy.

"Perhaps I was wrong to order work in here."

For once, he sounded sincere instead of sarcastic or angry. She followed his gaze, suddenly embarrassed by her reaction to his powerful body so close to hers, his scent of cinnamon soap, and her own foolishness to defend this dreary, shabby room. *I should have let Amos gut it.*

Still, she couldn't excuse him so easily. "Yes...well, why should I believe you? Yankees have promised things before, only to loot our meager possessions like a swarm of locusts."

Perhaps because they were standing in her mother's room, or because their tour of the planation had rekindled memories of the horrible time General Kilpatrick and his officers occupied Langesford as if it—and all its belongings, were theirs, she explained. "Their stupidity in believing that my mother had a virulent disease spread by smoke, saved our home from their torches." Feeling strong again, she met his gaze squarely finding understanding instead of anger, in his eyes.

"I can't fault using a quick wit to protect a home," he told her. "But I shouldn't be blamed for others' broken promises." A little-boy smile lifted one side of his mouth. "Besides, this situation isn't entirely my fault."

"What do you mean?"

"I mean the wide berth you've given me since our ride made me think you had no interest in the work your father and I are doing." Then the door jerked open and he made the exit Camilla had planned.

Determined not to let him have the last word, she raced after him to the top of the stairs and shouted, "If it's my company you want, Mr. O'Grady, from now on I'm going to attach myself so close to you, you'll think you've grown an extra pair of legs." As soon as the words were out she cupped her hands over her mouth, and couldn't look at the curious workers peeking around doors and corners.

Patrick turned on the landing, smiled wide and bowed low. "I'm sure I'll be delighted with the situation. Perhaps we'll come to know each other well enough to use our first names...Camilla."

Without thinking, she reached for the hall table, wrapped her fingers around a delicate porcelain figurine and threw it. Her aim was true, but his reflexes were quicker. He ducked and it missed his head by a hair's breadth.

The little porcelain cupid in chards at his feet, he looked up and she froze at the intensity of his gaze. Then his face split into a wide grin and deep laughter rang through the house. A moment later, the closing of the front doors coincided with the slamming of Camilla's own.

Flora found her in her room, staring down at Patrick through the balcony windows. He stood with a wide stance in the drive now lined by blooming magnolias. The sleeves of his western-style shirt were rolled up to reveal tanned, muscled forearms as he instructed a new group of workmen.

"*Sa ena, Cheri?*" Flora whispered at her side.

Camilla understood and spoke the Creole language fluently. She and Flora often carried on entire conversations in her mother's native language—when her father wasn't present. But this time she answered in English, "Everything is wrong, Florie. And everything is lost. The Yankees won't stop until everything is theirs."

As if he'd heard, Patrick looked up. Camilla rubbed her arms against a sudden chill and turned from the window. "I've been taking the wrong tack," she announced, a spark of defiance lighting her eyes. "I can't fight him. I can only protect us if I'm near him. Watching him. Maybe then, I'll learn what he's really after."

The old woman pulled her into her arms. "Be careful what you ask for, ma petite. You may also find that you do not want to fight him."

Camilla stiffened. "Don't even think that! I know many women might find him handsome...in a barbaric sort of way, but to think of him...that way, makes my flesh crawl." Or did she mean tingle? She refused to think about it, returning instead to the original topic. "It's time I stood up to him. I know as much about this plantation as Papa, and I'm not going to mope in my room. The sooner we make a profit, the sooner this...interloper, will be out of our lives."

~ * ~

Before leaving for the field with his men, Patrick met her in the foyer, hat in hand, as she descended the stairs. "I must apologize for my boorish remark earlier, Camilla. I know you have a great deal to do and I do not intend to inconvenience you with my presence."

He was actually grateful she'd dashed off whenever they crossed paths after their ride. It allowed him to begin his systematic search of the house for evidence of the Langesford family's role in the gold robbery—maps, letters—anything to give him an idea where Brent and his men planned to hide the gold if they got into trouble.

But he'd underestimated Camilla. He should have remembered the glint in her eyes when she challenged him in the peach grove. He didn't need a hotheaded female shadowing his every move, especially one who heated his blood to the point of distraction.

Now, if he had to grovel to get out of the mess he'd made for himself, he'd do it. "In the future, I will not interfere with how you run your household and I will consult with you about any renovations I deem necessary."

Still, he couldn't resist a little barb. "So there's no need to attach yourself to me. Two legs are all any man needs."

She raised her chin, looking down at him, her suspicion evident in her posture, her frown, and those amazing eyes. With a sigh, she conceded, "Very well. I needed only to consider the source of the remark."

With Flora standing behind Camilla, the antique gun at her side, he bowed to the female advantage, and smiled. "Noted. Please feel free to remind me whenever I show my barbaric origins."

Turning away, he added, "By the way, you seem to have a deadly aim with a cherub. Do you shoot as well?"

"I don't think you want to find out, sir."

"Patrick."

"I don't think you want to find out...Patrick," she shot back.

He chuckled and put his hat back on. "No, I suppose I don't," he said, once again closing a door on their conversation.

Chapter Five

Anthony retired early to his room, leaving Patrick and Camilla to endure an awkward dinner alone together. After Flora cleared the plates away, Camilla folded her hands atop the table scarred by Yankee knives. Only its massive size and weight had kept it from their wagons.

"Now, Mr... Patrick," she began. "I would like to see the plans you and Papa have made for the house, as well as for the crops, hands, seed, and equipment. Also—"

He raised his hands. "Whoa. Hold on there. I don't need another partner."

She leaned toward him, her eyes reflecting the gold flames of the candelabra. "Another? Or do you mean a *woman* partner?"

His voice lowered to accept her dare. "I suppose I can adapt, Camilla. That is, if you are comfortable with a *Yankee* partner." He pushed his chair back and stood. "Please. Join me in my study and—"

"My father's study."

"Pardon me?"

"My father's study. I'll join you in my father's study."

He sighed, "As you wish. Your father's study. I'll brief you on the work so far."

"Good. I've heard the noise from the work, but...haven't been in there since the night...you arrived."

She stopped short just inside the doorway, her mouth agape at the transformation of the room where she'd spent most of her childhood. It was her haven from her screeching Maman, and the pranks of her noisy brother. A place where she could sit in one of the big leather chairs, read a book, and watch her father run the plantation.

Sitting in her little cocoon in a corner by the fireplace, she'd often been forgotten and allowed to hear negotiations and conversations about contracts. Even the terrible political mess leading to the war. While her brother rode horses and roamed the countryside, she read Machiavelli, Plato, and Shakespeare. And she learned how to run a plantation during good times and bad.

Now she stood at the entrance of a room very different, yet very similar, to the one she remembered. The massive bookshelves had been rebuilt, the floor polished to the silver-oak sheen they once had, now accented by a fine, Persian carpet. Even the old fireplace seemed to glow with pride.

"What...did...you...do?" croaked from her suddenly dry mouth.

"I know it isn't exactly as it was before, but your father didn't seem to care, so I improvised."

Stepping away from his offered arm, she entered the room slowly, caressing the refinished Georgia pine moldings, and stepping gently onto the gleaming, parquet floor. She twirled like a ballerina on the toes of her new satin slippers, stopping beneath a stunning chandelier.

Nearly as wide as the span of both her arms, two hand-painted porcelain domes depicted spring magnolias. A dozen polished brass candle settings reached out like tree limbs, dripping crystal prisms. All the candles were lit, their dancing flames reflecting off the inlaid tin ceiling tiles and wood paneling.

Forgetting Patrick was the enemy, she turned to him, her face warmed by the fire burning in a new, wrought iron grate. "It's beautiful," she whispered. "It's never been so beautiful. But how did you know to do all...this? Papa said you were a man who traveled a great deal in the West and only kept a small flat of furnished rooms in Chicago."

His pewter eyes warmed under the candles, his lips forming a mischievous smile. "Even a barbarian can have good taste."

She blushed at the memory of calling him just that. "I do apologize for my rudeness earlier. I was just angry...about the intrusion...in my mother's...."

"And rightly so, I have to admit. I shouldn't have imposed my 'improvements' without discussing them with you first."

As if the new room was neutral territory, he turned to the

bookshelves flanking the fireplace. "This is actually a replica of the library in a house I...well stayed in...for a while...in Boston. It held great appeal for me. I spent every moment I could in it."

"You remember a single room in such detail from just a visit?"

~ * ~

"It was quite a long visit." Ten years, as a matter of fact. From the moment Patrick could walk, he'd slipped out of his mother's attic room to sneak into Dr. Stainsby's library. Innumerable beatings followed those not-so-secret visits, but they couldn't keep him out—until his mother died and the good doctor sent him to The Boston Orphan Home.

Now he had such a room to use as he wished, at least until he had his answers about the mint robbery. Like the library in Boston, the only case he hadn't solved haunted him. He hated failure and rarely experienced it.

He pushed back memories of his past as the unwanted bastard son of Boston's oldest family, as the clever street urchin, wagon train stow-away, army scout, and relentless investigator, to smile playfully, "But you haven't noticed the pièce de résistance."

Suddenly, taking her hand seemed the most natural thing in the world to do. "Close your eyes, please," he whispered like a conspirator. "Just trust me this once."

She sighed, but didn't pull away when his fingers circled hers. He paused a moment to appreciate long, dark lashes resting on satin-smooth skin kissed by the soft candlelight. When his body proposed something his integrity wouldn't allow, he cleared his throat and nudged her forward. "Just a few steps straight ahead," he told the tension in her fingers.

True to his word, he stopped only ten paces away, reluctantly separating his hand from hers. "All right, you can look now."

She blinked at the huge desk nestled in the alcove between the fireplace and the window. "What on earth is that?"

Proud as a schoolmaster with a bright student, he pointed out the teak inlays set in polished mahogany. "It's a partner's desk. Quite rare, their size being rather impractical, I suppose. It's two desks fused into one top, with room for two chairs facing one another. Hence, the term partners' desk. I found it in a Savannah antique shop—before the war."

She walked around it slowly, gliding her fingertips over the luminous surface, bending to look at the ornately carved legs trimmed with brass claw feet.

"Please, sit." He pulled out a tufted leather chair on one side, surprised at how much he wanted...needed...her approval.

Once she settled into it, her hands neatly folded in her lap, he took the padded leather chair on the opposite side. He folded his own hands on the desktop and leaned toward her. The moment of truth, he thought. Enemies or partners? It would be her choice.

She broke his gaze to rest her palms on the smooth leather arms of her chair. "My father had a chair like this...once." Then she tested the swivel base to turn to the side, facing the refinished fireplace mantel. She looked up and met the artificial, green-eyed stare of her own likeness.

Patrick's hopes for a truce wilted as her shoulders stiffened. She raised a hand toward the portrait. "Why did you leave that? I'm sure it hardly fits with your remembered room."

"On the contrary, I find it brightens the room considerably, but only in your absence of course."

"It's hideous!" she exclaimed with a grimace and rose to look down at him.

Confused, he admitted, "Well, I'll admit it doesn't do you justice."

She leaned over the desk then, resting her weight on her palms, her face so close to his he could nearly count the tiny freckles across her slender nose and cheeks. But her voice sounded nothing like the genteel lady she pretended to be around her father.

"Don't you see?" she hissed. "Why can't any of you see? It isn't me! It never has been. I hated sitting for it. I hated it when Papa hung it here, and I hate it now. It's an image of what Maman wanted me to be, what the South said I should be, and what that fop of an artist, Monsieur Antoine, imagined me to be."

Pointing at the painting, she lowered her voice. "That girl never existed. And if she had, she'd be dead now. A weak and silly casualty of war." Taking a deep breath, she stared him down. "Don't confuse the painting with the reality, Mr. O'Grady."

Grateful she'd directed her anger toward the painting, Patrick partially agreed with her description of the artist. Arty Beecher may have been foppish, but he was also cunning, and as mean as any sharp-toothed possum in the forest. His fake French accent and mediocre talent as a portrait artist had gained him access into the homes—and boudoirs, of some of the most powerful Confederates in the South. The information he gained from those "sittings" made him very valuable to the union cause—until Langesford caught him hiding in Camilla's room a few weeks before the mint robbery.

He stepped around the desk to face her. "I would never mistake you for a painting Camilla, but I don't believe the shrew who threw a naked angel at me is the real you either."

Before he could give in to his desire to kiss those flushed lips, she sighed and fell back into her chair, fluttering a hand in the air. "It doesn't matter. The past is dead."

He disagreed. In his experience, the past never died. It only squeezed your heart with the pain of remembering until you either burst with anger, or accepted the pain. Still, he was grateful she hadn't read his intentions and wondered if he could have stopped at just one kiss? The risk was too great to test the theory.

When she asked, "May I see those plans please...Patrick?" he nodded and took his seat. "Of course."

Chapter Six

Camilla caught Patrick's enthusiasm during the hours they spent over sheaves of plans, proposals and schedules. She didn't agree with his plan to hire German immigrants from the North, and his proposed modern planting techniques baffled her, but for the first time in her life, she felt the excitement of a great adventure. And for her father's sake, she hoped he was right.

He and Anthony left the next day and had been gone nearly two weeks purchasing seed and arranging the delivery of the equipment. In their absence, Camilla had turned chaos into order in the house, collapsing into dreamless sleep every night.

On one sunny spring day, she brought her old rocker down from her room to share a sweet tea with Flora on the veranda. Scar, who had trouble finding a safe place to lay his weary bones during the past weeks, yawned and dropped noisily beside her rocker on the newly-painted plank floor.

"We shouldn't be doing this, Cammy," Flora insisted between sips of the cool tea. "Your Maman's room should be aired, and there's churnin' to be done, and preserves to be put up. And the new wood needs tendin'."

She shook a well-meaning finger at Camilla's smirk. "It's not good for women to be idle while the men are away."

"Don't be silly, Florie." She laughed. "This is our chance to rest up a bit." Seeing the amused twitch in Flora's lips, she leaned back, fluttered an imaginary fan, and drawled, "My, it is warm for early April, isn't it?"

They both giggled, and Camilla saw what a beautiful young mulatto

41

Flora must have been more than a half century ago. Her delicate, heart-shaped face and light eyes in a coffee and cream complexion, would have made her very desirable among men of any color. Not for the first time, she wondered how such a beauty came to be a servant on a dying plantation hundreds of miles from her home.

"Florie," she asked the woman who had been a constant presence in her life; yet about whom she knew so little. "Tell me about New Orleans when you were young."

Flora stopped rocking and turned to her. She repeated the words with an odd mixture of mystery and irony in her voice. "New Orleans when I was young?" She sighed and began rocking again, speaking slowly, as if the answer carried great importance. "So very different, I t'ink, from here and now. And yet not so very different, I fear."

Riddles. Her answer disappointed Camilla, but didn't surprise her. Try as she might, she could never get Flora to talk about her life before she became Danielle Trémon's nursemaid. All she really knew was that Flora's own child had died the same night Danielle's mother died in childbirth. From then on, Flora became Danielle's nursemaid and surrogate mother. But neither Maman nor Flora ever spoke of Danielle's father. All she knew was that his name was Philippe Trémon.

However, both women spoke longingly of the family plantation, Belle Rivière. Like the Langesfords in Georgia, the Trémon family was among the first to colonize the Louisiana Territory and literally carved the massive rice plantation from the wilderness. Danielle was the most sought-after debutante in New Orleans until Anthony Langesford whisked her off to Georgia. Camilla had often doubted that part of the story. Her staid and sober father didn't seem the kind of man to charm a princess from her castle, and her mother never referred to Langesford as anything more than a farm.

She had only pressed Flora once about the father of her dead child and how her life as a free woman of color had changed from slave and nursemaid to another's child. She regretted the question when Flora's velvet-soft eyes clouded with such grief Camilla nearly cried for the pain in them. But this time Flora surprised her by adding, "Do not seek the past, *cheri.* It cannot be changed; yet it can change the present and shape the future. It is best to leave it alone so it cannot harm you."

The clatter of a wagon coming down the lane stopped Camilla from pressing for more information. Both women stood to shade their eyes while Scar raised his head to growl menacingly.

Camilla recognized the driver before Flora's failing sight could make him out. "It's Cato."

Flora raised a hand to shield her eyes. "That crazy nigger'll get himself killed, drivin' other folks' horses like the devil hisself is on his heels." But her voice showed her excitement.

"He's just young," Camilla defended him. *Something I never had the chance to be.* Suddenly, she had to run, if only the short distance to the approaching wagon. She reached down to pull the back of her skirt hem up between her legs and tuck it into her belt. Then she jumped off the last two steps to the drive. "I'll go see."

Cato pulled to a stop some distance from the veranda and waited for the dust to settle before a broad smile split his wide, flat face. "Careful, Miss Cammy," he called.

She ignored him to hop up beside him and peek under the tarp covering the cargo. "What have you got in there?"

"A load from Savannah, Miss."

Frustrated at the darkness beneath the tightly wrapped canvas, she turned to Cato. She'd known him all her life, even played with him as a child until he grew strong enough to work in the fields. There was nothing sly or lazy about Cato then. He only changed after Leon came over from Rosewood. "I thought you'd left us once and for all," she scolded.

He put one big hand over his heart in mock surprise. "Miss Cammy, you all knows I won't do dat. Mr. O'Grady say to wait in Savannah for a load a goods and bring 'em right back here, and dat's 'zactly what I do." He pulled a wrinkled bill of lading from his pocket and flourished it in front of her. "Ever'thin' on the list, and not a thing broken, neither."

She laughed. "Just as I'd expect." Then an unsettling thought intruded. "Leon must not have known then."

Cato groaned and signaled the horse to move ahead slowly. "Now, don't go on 'bout Leon. He's a hard nigra, but he don't steal. 'Sides, he at the Redfern place with them new missionary folk what come down from the North. They's teachin' 'im the ways of the Lord."

43

Camilla frowned at the information. She never liked Leon, with his darting black eyes and oppressively powerful body. Since the war ended, he'd caused her nothing but trouble, but she preferred him where she could see him. Now, after several warnings to stop agitating the workers, Patrick had fired him.

"All right," she said, dismissing thoughts of Leon to take the bill of lading. "Let's see what we have here."

She whistled low as she read the list of items. China, linens, kitchen utensils, mattresses, draperies, and all manner of household items. *Everything the well-appointed plantation house requires.* Her mind reeled at the cost. More than enough to pay their taxes, she reasoned, though not enough to bankroll a cotton season. *Where is his money coming from?* "We could open a small mercantile with these things."

She forgot about the bonnet sitting on the shaded veranda to personally supervise the opening of each crate. An hour later, her face glowing from the sun, exertion, and excitement, she stood at the bottom of the stairs, directing Otis, Cato, and Amos from room to room, making sure they put each item in exactly the right place.

After, she sat on an ornate Chinese trunk propping the entry doors open, again trying not to think of the cost of this treasure trove. Cato startled her when he led three sweating field hands inside with an enormous crate.

She looked at the bill of lading. Each item had been checked off, yet there it stood, taller than she, and wider than the span of her reach. A yellow tag hanging on a nail read simply: "C. Langesford." Consumed with curiosity she told them to put it in her room.

It barely fit through her door, and rather than wait for the tired, clumsy men to fully uncrate it, she had them pull off the front panel. They all gasped at the exquisite rosewood armoire. Its double, hand-painted doors were decorated with dainty rosebuds and daisy chains while the legs curved into claw feet trimmed with shiny brass scrollwork.

Her heart filled with gratitude for her father's thoughtfulness. "Thank you," she told the crew. "Please see Flora for some food and drink, then rest a while." When they'd gone down the back stairs to the kitchen, she allowed tears of joy to spill from her eyes.

The armoire opened at the slightest touch and she caressed one of the lovely gowns draped over satin hangers. Except for her mother's rotting dresses, she hadn't felt silk in years. A pale-yellow gown with green ribbon trim and rose-point lace along the heart-shaped bodice, surprised her. Her father so often treated her like a child. Had he finally acknowledged her as a full-grown woman? She brushed her tears, and her doubts, aside to continue searching the rosewood treasure chest.

Lingerie filled one of the small drawers. Camisoles and pantalets made of Chinese silk and trimmed with Irish lace were folded neatly on top of one another. The second drawer held real silk stockings, and slippers to match her new gowns. And in the third, lay a white georgette nightgown. Its only accent was a pink ribbon drawstring at the neck and wrists. She held it to her body and faced the beveled mirror on the inside of the door, sighing as it fell in soft waves to the floor.

The crackle of paper drew her attention to the wide ruffles at her feet. *A note.* "Papa," she whispered and picked it up. Then she read, "To C. from P."

She fell back on her bed as if struck. The lovely things were from Patrick and not her father. She crumpled the note in her hand and made no move to keep her tears from falling onto the gossamer nightgown.

Moments later, she rose from the bed, folded the gown and tucked it back into the drawer. With a deep breath, she closed the armoire doors and turned to Flora who watched from the doorway with eyes wise in the ways of men. "Mr. O'Grady has excellent taste in women's clothes," Camilla told her. "But I'm afraid they won't fit."

Then an idea struck. "Let's have Cato and the men move this into his room. He bought them. He can wear them." She brushed imaginary dust off her hands, ready to give the order.

"No!" Flora's hand held Camilla's shoulder like a vise. Tears magnified her eyes, and her lips quivered. "The war has taken so much from you, *cheri*. Why not accept this as payment for your sacrifices?"

Camilla gasped, pulling free of the older woman. "What? Are you suggesting I actually *wear* these? I could never...It would be...indecent. He's a *Yankee!*"

Flora smiled through her tears. "Never say never, child. And what may seem indecent today may not seem so by tomorrow's light. Besides, I don't think you will find anyone willing to move this monster again."

Camilla conceded to her logic on the second point and shrugged. "Yes, well, you may be right about that...for now, but I won't wear those clothes. They can rot in there for all I care." A wary glance at the glass knobs winking in the afternoon sunlight called her defiant tone false.

Chapter Seven

The next day, Camilla threw the last set of draperies over the second-floor balcony to air and looked down into the yard at the sound of more commotion. Cato ran up to the house, craning his short neck as he shouted up to her, "It's Mr. O'Grady, Miz Cammy. He's comin' with 'nother wagon."

She recognized a cloud of dust as the wagon turned off the main road. Three days early, she thought, frowning. *Typical Yankee. Can't even keep his word about when he's returning.*

Blast him. He always managed to catch her at her worst. She pulled off her apron and yanked at her kerchief, sending damp curls falling around her face and shoulders. Well, she'd be hanged if she'd let him see her looking like a slave girl again. In one swift, unthinking moment, she stood in front of the rosewood armoire, her hand on the crystal knob, thinking only of the yellow dress. Then she gasped and pulled away. *What are you doing?*

She made a face at the offending piece of furniture. "I'll not give in so easily," she muttered and smoothed her brown calico skirt. *I'd rather wear rags than lower myself to wear clothes purchased by the blood of my countrymen.*

The wagon creaked to a stop at the front of the house. As much as she wanted to appear uninterested, her feet seemed to move of their own accord to race down the stairs. She reached the open entrance just as Patrick jumped down from the driver's box, slapping his panama hat at the patches of dry, red dust clinging to his white suit.

Men and women from all over the house and grounds clustered to gape and chatter at the strange looking machines stacked on the open

47

wagon. He looked up from the crowd to smile at Camilla. The smile faded like a flower wilting in the sun as his gaze traveled from her disheveled hair down the soiled work dress, to the work boots she'd promised to discard.

She fought the urge to clutch the small, white collar of her dress against his obvious desire to rip it from her. Instead, she raised her chin and approached him. "You're early."

His glowering expression brightened. "Yes. You're right. I should have sent advance notice. He waved at the wagon. "As you can see, things are moving right along. At this rate, we'll be ready to plant..."

But Camilla stared past him, down the lane, her lips pressed in a worried frown. "Where's Papa?" she interrupted. "He isn't well you know, and all this traveling can't be good for him. What fool errand do you have him on now?"

"Calm down," Patrick snapped. "Your father will be along shortly. He hired a carriage to visit the Bartletts on the way." Slapping his hat needlessly against his thigh again, he pushed past her with a disgusted look at her dress. "Now if you'll excuse me, I'll change clothes before seeing to the disposition of the equipment."

He turned with one dusty boot on the veranda step and arched a thick eyebrow. "By the way, did the household goods arrive safely?"

The now familiar twinkle in his eyes said he was playing with her. Well, she'd figured out his game. "Yes, it's all been unloaded and put away. I have the shipper's lading in the study for your approval."

"Anything not on the lading?"

Thinking of the nearly sheer white gown, she looked into smoky gray eyes that sent a rush of heat from her cheeks to her toes. "Nothing of any importance."

His, "I see," sounded genuinely disappointed. "Well then, please ask Otis to fill a tub. I need to wash off your precious Georgia clay before supper."

When the door to the house shut a little too hard, Camilla whispered to Flora, "I think I won this battle."

"Battle?" Flora spat in a tone she rarely used with Camilla. "What do you know of man/woman battles? This wasn't even a skirmish." She hugged an ancient, multi-colored silk shawl embroidered with tiny birds

48

and flowers, closer to her body. "Don't push the man too far," she warned, then joined the throng of curious people clustered around the wagon.

~ * ~

True to Patrick's word, Anthony arrived shortly before supper. In his honor, Flora prepared fresh goose with sour cream and mushrooms, his favorite of her Creole specialties. She and Camilla were in the kitchen and Patrick had gone to finish things in the barn when he strode into the house.

"Cammy. Flora. Where are you?" he bellowed loud enough to be heard in the kitchen. "A man leaves his home for a couple of weeks and his people desert it."

Camilla turned excitedly, nearly burning her arm on the oven where she basted the goose. "It's Papa," she shouted, throwing her apron on the work table and running from the room.

Prepared to greet an exhausted father returning from two weeks in the dirty, noisy city, she imagined Savannah to be, she skidded to a stop at the sight of him standing tall and impeccable in a new, tailored suit. Her sympathetic smile became an astonished gape. "Papa?"

"Who else would I be?" He chuckled, kissing her lightly on the cheek before turning to circle the foyer, touching his new possessions. "It's good to be home," he said, his back to her.

She could only stare at him. Before he left, he looked ten years older than his fifty-five years, his aristocratic features gaunt and lined. Now, color had returned to his cheeks and the haggard lines from years of worry were visibly smoother. His hair, though still more gray than chocolate brown, had been neatly trimmed and he looked…happy. She opened her mouth to ask the many questions flooding her mind when Patrick walked in and hailed Anthony.

"Welcome back, sir," he said enthusiastically, surprising Camilla with the respect—and affection, in his voice. "I have the equipment put away and Camilla has seen brilliantly to all the household items."

Anthony reached out to shake his hand. "So I see," he beamed and turned back to his daughter. His smile suddenly faded as he recognized the old dress she'd worn to breakfast after Patrick's arrival. His hard gaze then appraised her loose hair, freckled face, and the defiant set of her chin.

He stepped toward her, cupping her chin in his palm. As he might with a horse he considered buying, he turned her head from side to side. "You look tired, my dear. You haven't been working too hard, I hope. We have enough help now. You should spend more time with your books and fancywork."

He seemed to have forgotten that their treasured books had been fuel for Yankee campfires, as well as how much she considered fancy needlework a waste of time and effort. But it wouldn't do to argue with him on his first day home. Flushing under the Yankee's sympathetic gaze, she lowered her eyes and answered demurely, "Yes, of course, Papa."

She swept the outmoded skirt to the side and took her father's arm. "Supper is nearly ready. You can both wash up in the kitchen."

In an admonition to hurry, she added, "Flora spent most of the day cooking this goose and if it's overdone, ours will be roasted next."

The mood at the table was light as they ate the succulent goose with wild rice stuffing, mushrooms and green beans, all smothered in a rich cream sauce known only to Flora. For nearly two hours, the newly-furnished dining room once again rang with laughter as Patrick and Anthony related amusing incidents from their stay in Savannah.

Their descriptions of the people thronging there to "rebuild" the South, and the freedmen strutting the streets in fine suits with their women dressed up like saloon girls held Camilla spellbound. And tales about ships once again flocking to the famous seaport, with sailors from all over the world stumbling through the waterfront streets, both stunned and fascinated her.

Finally, Patrick leaned back in his chair and grinned. "Another stellar meal, Anthony," as if he'd prepared it. "And on short notice too. Flora is indeed a wonder."

Camilla ignored the omission of her role in preparing the meal to ask, "But surely the restaurants in the East surpass our simple food." She'd been too young to accompany Danielle on her yearly shopping trips to Philadelphia and New York. Then the war came, and the world changed.

Patrick leaned across the table toward her. "Simple things, well prepared, are always the best," he said quietly. "Much about the country is preferable to the artificial grandeur of the city."

Attributing her flush to the unaccustomed brandy, rather than his mesmerizing gray gaze, she addressed Anthony. "Papa, you look so well. The city must have agreed with you."

He cleared his throat. "I...ahem...,well, I let Patrick conduct most of our business. I became rather ill shortly after our arrival, and he kindly introduced me to a friend who is an accomplished, uh...nurse." He coughed and reached out for another sip of wine.

Camilla suppressed a shiver. *What if he'd sickened and died in Savannah?* Questions reeled through her mind. Had the Yankee planned all along to furnish her house to his own taste and then lead her father to his death? And why did her father not send word to her? Instead, he allowed a stranger to care for him.

Do they think I'm incapable of nursing my own Papa? She glared at Patrick. "You have a friend in Savannah who is a nurse?"

"Well..."

"A lot of Northern medical people have come south," Anthony interjected. "Miss Watkins has family there, and prefers the milder climate."

Patrick straightened in his seat, tenting his fingers under his square chin. "Yes, she used to be a...nurse...in Washington. I met her there when I was...wounded. After the war, she came south to care for an aging uncle."

He dropped his hands and smiled at Anthony. "She comes from a large family and has a number of uncles scattered across the country. They keep her quite busy."

The looks the two men exchanged made Camilla suspicious. "This Miss Watkins," she asked Patrick. "Is she young?"

"I doubt she was never young."

"I beg your pardon?"

"I mean, dealing with illness and injury as she does, and has from a tender age, tends to mature a woman quickly, wouldn't you agree?"

"Yes, I suppose so, but—"

"Enough of this talk of illness," Anthony announced. "Suffice it to

51

say the rest I received under her care worked miracles for my health." He leaned back in his chair. "I feel like a new man, thanks to her and Dr. Johnson."

Camilla caught Patrick's shift in his chair at the mention of the doctor and raised an eyebrow. "Dr. Johnson? Another friend of yours?"

Another shift in the seat. "Well, an acquaintance, actually."

Anthony launched into exuberant praise for the man. "An extraordinary medical practitioner, Camilla. Not like these fools here in Jeffers."

"But Dr. Samuels is a dear friend of yours."

"Friend, yes, but thanks to Dr. Johnson, no longer my physician. He slapped his hands on the new, Irish linen tablecloth. "Good heavens, Camilla, this sounds like an inquisition. A most unladylike trait, if I may say." He placed his napkin on the table to signal the end of the meal and stood. "Which brings me to my next topic."

Looking down at her, he told them both, "I stopped at the Bartletts on my way home. Young Chet was there helping his father and Eliza prepare to abandon their home."

"Papa, they're not abandoning their home. They're starting over."

He frowned. "Are you disagreeing with me in front of a guest?" An eyebrow arched. "It appears, Camilla, I may have left you to your own devices far too long. You have developed some most unseemly behaviors."

"Sir..." Patrick started to rise, stopping, when Anthony raised a hand.

"I'm simply noting that we've been isolated here for too long."

A sense of loss overcame Camilla's humiliation at her father's censure. It seemed her life had become a round of saying goodbye and waiting for someone's return. *And like Brent, sometimes they didn't return.* "But you've been gone for weeks, Papa, and only just come home."

He shook his head impatiently. "There's no time to waste, daughter. What I have in mind, is a gala. We haven't entertained since, well, a long time ago. And since many of our young men have now returned, I think it's time Langesford hosted another ball. In honor of our reunited families and the restored peace of our nation, as well as our newly renovated home."

Both Patrick and Camilla gaped in astonishment. Anthony hated parties and she didn't know the first thing about hosting one. She cringed as he dictated the guest list. Chet Bartlett was a bore and his sister Eliza, a waspish gossip.

At the mention of Mason O'Keefe, she looked up. "Mason?"

"Yes, young Chet said he's returned to Acadia Plantation. He's been recovering there from his injury in the Wilderness Campaign all this time. A bit of a recluse until recently."

"Mason wounded?" *And he's been home for two years? How did I not know?* She remembered how Brent's handsome friend kissed her on the lips when they left for the glory of battle. "Grow up and wait for me," he said with a wink. Now, she couldn't suppress a smile as she recalled his flashing black eyes and easy, flawless smile.

Suddenly, she didn't mind the idea of a party and agreed to begin planning it right away. Then she spoke without thinking. "But Papa, I've nothing to wear." She wanted to bite her own tongue at Patrick's sudden cough and triumphant smile.

Anthony looked curiously from one to the other. "But didn't Patrick's wardrobe arrive?"

She focused on her napkin. "Yes, it arrived."

"Well there should be any number of gowns suitable for the occasion in it. Lu...Miss Watkins has excellent taste."

Miss Watkins? Again? "I-I...suppose so." She couldn't face Patrick's gloating smile.

Anthony clapped his hands together. "It's settled then. In two weeks, Langesford will host a ball the likes of which Jeffers County hasn't seen in years. Now Patrick, let's retire to our study and go over those magnificent planting theories of yours."

Chapter Eight

After days of being trapped in the house, writing invitations, planning the menu, and preparing the neglected ballroom for Anthony's gala, Camilla felt like a prisoner. Even in the marble coolness of the third-floor, she felt suffocated. All morning, noise and activity from the yard below diverted her attention from the grimy walls and dusty floor.

The new plows were going into service today. They were smaller and lighter than the cumbersome slave hoe used in the South. She'd argued, "They look more like toys than tools," when they loaded them to take to the field. "They'll never cut through our red clay."

Patrick waved her off. "Earth is earth. Just because the slave hoe did a fair job, doesn't mean something else won't work better."

She mimicked his favorite phrase, "Time will tell," and stalked back into the house.

But all morning, she'd resented washing walls when she really wanted to be outside with the fresh, warm air on her skin and the smell of newly turned earth in her nostrils. Suddenly, the rag hit the pail of dirty water with a messy splash. Her red gingham kerchief landed on the floor and she ran down the stairs, stopping only to grab a straw gardening hat. She caught Cato hitching up another wagon and again tucked the back hem of her skirt into the front waist of her skirt to climb into the box. "Take me with you," she ordered, tying her bonnet with hemp cords instead of satin ribbons.

He shook his head. "The field ain't no place fo' a lady, Miz Cammy."

"Cato, have you forgotten how I worked like a hand in them myself not so long ago?"

54

"No, Miss," he stammered. "I mean, I know you bin there afore, but this tahm is difer'nt." Shuffling his bare feet, he looked at her wide-eyed, repeating, "Ain't no fit place fo' a lady."

He had her worried now. "What do you mean?"

Not one to keep exciting news, good or bad, to himself for long, he told her what she already knew. "Well, Mistah O'Grady, he hired on a bunch o' hands what come from the North and other countries. They's out there tryin' to run them new plows."

"Yes, yes, I know that. But what is the matter?"

"Well, they started jest after sunrise and now it's a terrible mess. Them for'ners don' even speak English and cain't plow a line. They's cursin' and swearin' goin' on in three tongues." He shook his head in bewilderment, explaining he'd been sent back for spare harnesses.

So the new men and equipment weren't working after all. As with the plows, she'd opposed hiring German and Swiss immigrants to replace the freedmen who worked erratically, even for Yankees. She leaned forward and took the reins. "Then you better climb up. They need someone out there who knows which end of the plow goes in the ground."

His description fell far short of the reality. The field was beyond a mess. The term bedlam fit the scene much better. Thickset German workers were shouting in their native language at each other, the mules, and the Langesford hands. Those who managed to hold on to the light plow for a little while were thrown off in different directions. Mules ran amok in the field, tangled in each other's lines, and injured men limped away, cursing.

Three plow-beams were broken, irreparable. The field, a gently rolling grassland a month ago, looked as if a herd of hogs had been rooting there. Only two straight rows in twenty acres of land had been plowed, and those by two of Langesford's experienced men and equipment.

Camilla and Cato stared in silence as one of the plowmen picked himself up from the mess, scraping wet, red clay from his face and what had once been a white shirt. His face was unrecognizable but she couldn't mistake the broad set of Patrick's shoulders and muscular chest beneath the muck.

He walked toward her, his white teeth gleaming in contrast to the clay drying on his face. "This is a surprise," he called out, limping a little over the uneven ground.

She jumped off the wagon, her skirt still tucked into her waist. *How can he smile about this?* A half-day's work and hundreds of dollars in equipment were lost. Animals and men were injured. A field was in ruin.

She met him at the edge of the ruined field. Standing with her legs apart, hands on her hips like a displeased foreman, she told him, "I'm the one who is surprised."

Smelling of damp earth, sweat, and sunshine, Patrick grinned. "A minor setback. I'm afraid I've a lot to learn about planting cotton."

She gave him an appraising look, from his smudged face to his crusted boots. "I'd say you've learned a great deal about planting cotton already, including how it tastes."

His laugh bubbled up from deep in his chest as he stood in the middle of the wreckage of his costly plans. But she couldn't appreciate the way his chest rose and fell under the shirt clinging like wet gauze to the dark mat of hair beneath it. Instead, she frowned and pointed at the scarred expanse of valuable cotton land. "You think this is funny? A joke?"

"Only on me, Cammy," he said. "Nothing is ever wasted. As you said, I learned a great deal here." As quickly as it had come, his smile faded and his voice took on a hard edge. "I may make mistakes, but I only make them once."

Following her gaze to the ruined field, he added, "This can be remedied in a short time, though I think our German farmers may be better off in some other line of work." He looked at her then, taking in her skirt hiked up between her legs, revealing the practical cotton stockings tucked inside her shabby boots. "I'm glad you came. It was a mistake to ignore your excellent advice. It won't happen again."

He stared past her then, at the ruined landscape. "It appears I'm going to have to hire some new workers. You wouldn't be able to give me some pointers, would you?"

Still blushing from his appraisal, she fixed her skirt and let her practical side take over. "Well, you can't do it from here and you can't go back to the house like that. Flora will never let you in."

As if for the first time, Patrick seemed aware of his appearance. He looked down at dirt already dried into crusty patches on his skin and clothes. He smiled like a young boy caught playing in mud. "You're the boss. What do I do?"

Suddenly, the urge to do something outrageous gripped her. Anything to avoid cleaning the ballroom. With Cato standing by his friends, laughing at the filthy, beaten foreigners, she climbed back into the wagon and took the reins. "Come with me."

He jumped into the box as she slapped the reins. "Where are you taking me?" he asked when she turned the horses off the main trail back to the house.

She smiled at him for the first time in days. "A place few people know about. It's not far and we'll have to walk some of the way, but I think you'll find it worth the effort."

He looked at her a long moment, shifting in his seat. "It better be." He flexed his right arm. "You're not planning on leading me astray are you? I think I've had all the exertion I can handle for one day."

Was he flirting with her? With a glance at his injured arm, she smiled knowingly. "Not at all. That's why I thought it would be safe to take you there."

"You think so?"

Knowing he'd never stop trying to have the last word, she didn't speak until they stopped at the edge of a thicket. This time he groaned. "After the day I've put in, you expect me to thrash through a jungle?"

Chuckling at his scowl, she jumped into the tall grass. "Trust me, it will be worth the effort."

She scurried around the edge of the wooded hill, her head down, searching for the entrance to the cave she hadn't visited in years. Not since she and Brent were children. She suddenly worried the little cave may have collapsed or grown impenetrable over the years. *What if I can't find it?*

As if in answer to her question, she saw the gnarled old pine bent over the barely visible opening to a wind-and-water hewn cave. She stood, waving her arms at Patrick, who had chosen to wait in the wagon. "Here. Come here."

He rushed to her side. "What's the matter? Are you crazy running off all by yourself? There could be snakes."

"The cottonmouths stay near the river," she pointed out with a smile. "But thank you for your concern. I just need help lifting this poor dead tree."

"Whatever the lady wishes," he teased with a dusty bow and easily lifted the dead limb. Then he stiffened in front of gaping hole behind the fallen tree, covering his surprise with a low whistle. "A secret cave. Camilla, you surprise me more and more."

Even a virgin could understand his tone, but for once, she didn't take offense. She was playing today, not afraid of getting dirty, or what adventure lay on the other side of the hidden passageway. "Don't flatter yourself, Yankee," she laughed. "Follow me."

Unlike her, he had to stoop to enter the cave. The rock floor was wet with slime, but Camilla's feet were sure. In a few moments, they stepped into…paradise.

At his startled, "Holy Mary, mother of God," she turned to see his swarthy complexion had turned ghostly pale, his eyes glittering like a trapped animal. "Are you all right?" she asked him this time.

He wiped his sweating brow with the back of his arm, took a deep breath, and evaded the question to step outside the cave. "This is the most beautiful place I've ever seen."

They appreciated the small clearing in the forest where a spring bubbled up from the ground to form a pool at the base of a rugged hill. Only gurgling water, humming insects, and the calls of birds disturbed the Eden-like peace until Patrick whispered, "I had no idea such a place existed here—or anywhere."

Pleased with his respect for her most holy of holy places, she smiled and took his hand, allowing him to keep his eyes open while she led him to the spring. They stood next to each other, still holding hands as the source of all life bubbled up from the earth in tiny ripples to smooth out against the mossy shore.

Satisfied she'd finally managed to surprise the world-traveling Yankee businessman, she picked up a flat stone and hopped onto a flat rock, her legs dangling inches above the water. The rock skipped on the water three times before sinking. "Not many people know this is here. It's too difficult to reach from the top of the hill, and the cave is quite forbidding. Don't you think?"

It didn't surprise her when he answered her question with a question. "How do you know about this place?"

"Brent and I found it by accident when we were children." She smiled at the memory. "We were playing hide-and-seek and I crawled under the tree to hide and fell into the cave. He heard my scream and when he picked me up, we saw the light at the other end."

Patrick nodded before lowering himself onto the soft grass at her feet, pulling up a long piece of sawgrass to chew on. *He moves like a cougar.* Graceful and sure of himself, yet powerful enough to keep away his enemies. *Perhaps this was a mistake.*

"Naturally, we had to explore," she struggled to focus on the conversation.

"Naturally," he agreed with a yawn.

Despite his tendency toward monosyllables, she continued, "We took an oath we would not reveal its location to anyone, as long as we both lived." Her eyes filled with tears and she didn't protest when he sat up to touch her hand.

"But now you've shown me."

She blinked, but didn't pull away. "Brent is dead. The childish oath no longer binds me. I thought that after your problems today, you would like—" *What?*

"You were right." He saved the awkward moment. His voice carried none of the arrogance she'd seen on their ride that first day. Today it was low, gentle even, his eyes so clear they reflected the clouds. He rose then and looked down at her, smiling. "I thank you for both your courtesy and your confidence, Camilla. I'll even take your oath of silence if you like." He turned to look at the fresh, bubbling water and then at his own filthy clothes. "The water looks inviting. I've never seen it bubble like that. Is it cold?"

Pleased to show him something he'd never seen before, she dipped a hand in the water. "It's one of the reasons I brought you here. It's a hot spring. There are others in the South and a few in the North I've heard. People pay great sums of money to visit them. They say the warm mineral waters have healing powers. It may do your damaged muscles some good, and you can rinse your clothes at the same time."

The question flickering from his eyes prompted her to add, "Give me your shirt and I'll wash it at the other end of the pool. You can soak with your pants on. They should all dry quickly in the sun and we can be back before supper."

His now-familiar chuckle added to the pleasant sounds of the glade. "I have to say this is the first time a beautiful woman has ever offered to do my laundry," he said, already unbuttoning his shirt. A moment later, he had pulled it and his boots off.

Something inside her fluttered at the sight of his naked chest. She'd seen men—Negro men—without shirts, but never up close. And certainly, never a white man with more than his forearms exposed. His muscles rippled like waves across his chest when he moved, mesmerizing her until she wondered if the fine layer of black hair tapering down the length of his torso was coarse or soft.

Shivering in the warm sun while perspiration trickled between her breasts, her mouth went dry. *This was a mistake!*

Recognizing her own hunger in his flinty gaze, she snatched the shirt and hurried to the other end of the pool. A loud splash told her he'd jumped into the water, but she refused to look up while he washed his magnificent body, and she washed his shirt. When she'd rinsed it, and hung it over a tree branch to dry, she returned to her rock, leaning against it with her back to the pool. While he hummed behind her and splashed around, she unhooked the top four hooks of her waist to catch the refreshing breeze on her skin.

He talked to her as he bathed, his deep voice sounding young and carefree. "I've heard of hot spring spas, but never thought I'd enjoy one in private with a beautiful woman washing my clothes." He chuckled.

His laughter made her skin tingle, in some places more than others, and she shifted her position on the ground to call out, "Your shirt, Mr. O'Grady, not all of your clothes." But she couldn't forget the sight of his bare chest, the corded muscles defining his strong arms, or the tone of his voice when he called her beautiful.

Suddenly, she ached to reach out for something…or someone. *But certainly not a Yankee.* This place was dangerous now. The position of the sun told her they'd missed luncheon and there'd be hell to pay with Flora. She stood to warn, "You better hurry, or we'll be late and my honor will be severely compromised."

His, "We wouldn't want to do that, would we?" felt like a caress against her ear, and her neck tingled from the heat of his breath. She turned to meet gray eyes now darkened to the color of a storm cloud.

She felt his arms around her. Of their own accord, her hands rested against the still-damp, curling hairs on his chest. *So soft.* Her breath quickened at the feel of his warm skin against her fingers, the damp cloth over his thighs pressing against her through the thin, cotton skirt and single petticoat.

His lips teased hers, the top first, then the bottom. She knew she should stop him, but she'd never felt anything so...natural. And when they coaxed for hers to open, she forgot he was a Yankee and let her body control her will.

Acting on instinct rather than experience, she wrapped her arms around his shoulders, and pressed against his chest. His hands cupped her face, his lips caressed hers until her entire body throbbed with heat. The path of his fingers along her cheeks, throat and shoulders burned until she ached to be free of her blouse, to cool her skin in the breeze as he had.

Her curious fingertips traced the landscape of his face, his shoulders, and chest. As the heat of his body touched hers, the tips of her breasts strained against their thin covering, and heat spread down through her belly to become a moist, throbbing pulse between her legs. Then she opened her eyes.

His eyes were open too, silver flecks flashing like lightning, pulling her into their storm. She pressed her hips against him, a surprised, Oh," escaping when she felt the extent of his passion pressed against her.

At the sound, the light returned to his eyes and his hands dropped to her waist to gently set her away from him. They stood inches from each other, her hand still on his chest, rising and falling with his uneven breath.

"Did I do something wrong?" she asked, disappointed, but also grateful for his restraint. Her virginity was all she had of value. If she gave it away foolishly, any hope for a proper Southern life would be gone.

He rested his forehead against hers. "No, Cammy, you did

everything right," he whispered, then pulled away and bent stiffly to fetch his shirt. "But we both know it's not right. For either of us."

She stood still, feeling weak, and somehow…empty. God, how terrible she'd been to enjoy, even hunger for his body as she had. Perhaps her father was right after all. She needed to find a Southern beau. She tried to remember Mason O'Keefe, and what he might look like after four years, but gray eyes and a crooked grin replaced Mason's glittering black ones and his practiced smile.

~ * ~

Patrick took his time with the shirt, cursing himself for staying so long at Langesford. But he'd never been able to resist a mystery, and even without the gold, they seemed to be plentiful in the Langesford family.

Anthony, the staid patriarch of the family, had succumbed to "nurse" Watkins' charms like a young pup. Though he now sat contentedly writing the family history, he'd been one of the Confederacy's greatest strategists.

Otis had told him the beautiful and tragic Danielle had married Langesford after a short courtship, leaving New Orleans for the backwoods of Georgia only weeks before her father died by his own hand. She in turn, hung herself after being unable to accept her son's death.

And Brent, one of many brave Confederate cavaliers, had died at Chickamauga; yet there were no records of him being in the regiments that fought the battle. Further shrouding the mystery of his disappearance, President Jefferson Davis, Secretary of the Treasury Meminger, and General Beauregard Rush, though busy trying to hold a dying government together, had attended the funeral.

And Finally, Camilla. The fierce and headstrong Daughter of the South had become master of the plantation while little more than a child. She'd outsmarted a regiment camped in her parlor and worked beside those who had once been her slaves. A virgin queen, he thought. Elizabeth I, born again in Southeast Georgia. Of all the Langesford family, Camilla presented the greatest mystery—and perhaps the most dangerous.

He'd never walked away from any mystery, but after weeks in Georgia, he'd found nothing to support Arty Beecher's story that Anthony had planned the mint robbery and charged his son to carry it out. Except for digging up Brent Langesford's coffin, he'd left no stone unturned in his search—and found nothing. Perhaps he should finally admit the one failure in his career and go back to Chicago with his tail between his legs. He'd find a way to pay Dr. Johnson for his failed investment...somehow.

Instead of facing Camilla, he looked up at the lowering sun. "You're right. It's getting late."

She faced him at the entrance to the cave. "I'll hold you to your vow about this place." Her eyes pleaded. "It's probably the only secret I have."

He nodded. "Though I doubt it, I'll take this one to my grave."

As if his word wasn't enough, she opened her hand and pointed at a tiny scar in the center of her palm. "Brent and I sealed it in blood."

He fought the urge to kiss the tiny white line. "Ugh. Isn't there another way?"

"Well, you could tell me a secret of equal importance to you."

Vixen. If only she knew how many secrets he had. From the day he ran away from the orphanage, he'd lived one lie after another, with one name after another, in one place after another. He sighed. "All right. How about this? I have a fear of small, dark places."

Gilded auburn curls bobbed in the breeze. "No. That was obvious in the cave. I have to know why."

This truth-telling business could prove difficult. "You drive a hard bargain. As a boy, when I disobeyed my father's rules, his servants locked me in the coal bin, under the stairs, and in closets, until I promised to behave. Needless to say, I spent a great deal of time there and dislike similar places enormously. Is that close enough to blood for you?"

As if recognizing the cost of the confession, she touched his hand—in friendship this time. "It's enough. I'm sorry."

He looked toward their only way out of the glen and chuckled. "Don't worry. With you leading me, I won't faint."

Both Flora and Anthony met them at the door. Camilla squirmed under the old woman's knowing gaze while Anthony said to Patrick, "I almost sent out a search party. Cato said you left the field before mid-day."

Patrick jumped from the wagon to help Camilla down. Diversion and half-truths had gotten him out of more scrapes than he cared to remember.

He always began with the truth. "Yes, I'm afraid I missed the mark on those new plows. Nearly all of them are damaged in some form and it looks like those German farmers aren't going to make the grade. We need a whole new crew."

Pointing to the stains on his shirt and pants as supporting evidence, he added, "I took a nasty spill. Camilla kindly showed me a place where I could clean up a bit before coming back."

"And where exactly was that?" Anthony questioned, staring at Camilla as if searching for signs of violation.

Now for the lie. "Down by the river near Well's Landing, I believe. I splashed my clothes to be presentable." He smiled at Camilla. "I'm afraid I got talking about my plans to rectify today's disaster and quite lost track of time. Camilla politely waited to interrupt me until absolutely necessary."

At her confirming nod and, "Yes, Papa. We're so sorry to be tardy," Anthony's jaw relaxed.

"I see. Well, let's go in and you can both change before supper."

As Patrick followed Anthony, he heard Flora ask Camilla, "Are you all right, *cheri?*" His conscience stabbed him when the answer came slowly. "I'm not sure."

Chapter Nine

Camilla took a deep breath before leaving her room. At her father's insistence, she wore one of the gowns from the rosewood armoire, a mauve moiré silk by Worth. It embarrassed her to wear the latest fashion in front of neighbors who hadn't worn a new gown in years. Still, she had to admit the rare color and fashionable narrow skirt swept to the back of the gown, flattered her tiny waist. Fish scale pearls sewn into a sheer white ruffle along the heart-shaped bodice reflected the candlelight, and a tiny smile curved her lips at the thought of Eliza Bartlett turning green with envy.

Flora hummed as she adjusted the hooks at the back of the dress, beaming. "It is as if the modiste had measured you from head to toe. Few men can describe a woman's form in such detail."

"Don't even think it, Florie!" Camilla flushed at the thought of *him* describing her proportions to the dressmaker even before he'd held her in his arms. *The gall!* She pushed the thought away to wonder how Mason would react to her now, as a full-grown woman.

Sensing her mother's eyes assessing her from the depths of the Cheval mirror, Camilla frowned and touched the base of her throat. "I look so...plain." Had she really, if only for a moment, resented selling Danielle's few remaining jewels? She turned from the mirror, reminding herself of the purpose for the evening's charade. To find a good Southern husband.

"Beauty such as yours needs no decoration," Flora assured, then put a finger thoughtfully to her lips. "Well, perhaps something simple." She pulled a black velvet ribbon from one of Danielle's outmoded dresses and tied it around Camilla's neck, letting two long black tendrils follow the low "V" at the back of her dress.

With a secretive smile, she pulled a linen napkin from her apron's deep pocket, opening it to reveal a lone, tear-shaped, pearl earbob. "The Yankees dropped this."

Camilla recognized it as one of an exquisite set of rare, perfectly matching Oriental pearls, so luminous she could see the color of her gown reflected in the creamy luster. She reached out an elegantly-gloved hand to receive the treasure. "Maman's wedding pearls," she whispered. "Though she never wore them, she forbade me to even touch them."

She looked into Flora's misty eyes. "Florie, the Yankees could have killed you for keeping this." Resentment welled for an instant when she realized that the sale of this one earbob—to the right buyer, could have covered the loss from the boll weevils.

She knew better than to ask why Flora risked her life and home to save the precious memento from her beloved Danielle. Instead, she kissed the old woman on the cheek. "But there is only one."

Flora's eyes now sparkled with mischief. "Not for your ears *ma petite,* but for your throat." She fastened the earbob to the center of the velvet ribbon around her neck and stepped back, gently turning Camilla toward the mirror.

They both smiled. Flora's expert fingers had managed to arrange Camilla's thick curls into ringlets from the crown of her head down her back, past her shoulders. A single braid strung with glass beads held the curls atop her head in place, leaving only a tiny fringe to frame her delicate face. She smiled again, daring that "nurse" from Savannah to do better.

Then the doubts set in. *I won't look good enough.* Maman was a renowned beauty. *The food won't be good enough.* Even Flora's talents could be thwarted by tainted meat. *No one will come.* It had been a long time, after all, and she'd never had many—any, close female friends. *Stop!*

Testing her "hostess" smile, she unnecessarily smoothed her gown to step into the hallway. A movement in her father's room caught her eye and she stepped back, her stomach tightening at the sight of him leaning over the chest beneath his mirror.

Only two short weeks since his triumphant return from Savanah, his skin looked sallow in the lamplight, dark circles again rimming his haunted eyes. Bottles clanked against one another as his trembling hands grasped an ugly brown one and raised it to his lips. A moment later, he shuddered and rested his head in his hands.

Shocked, and more than a little horrified, she held her breath, as his trembling stopped and the color returned to his face. A few moments later, he straightened his new, double-breasted jacket and forced a smile.

She stayed just a few steps from his door, hoping he'd see her and explain what had just happened. But Anthony gazed straight ahead as he descended the stairs, hands steady and his step firm.

The door to his room yawned open, daring her to step inside. She accepted the invitation, her steps slow and measured. Anthony's toiletries stood like tiny glass soldiers on the chest, each performing their own special function for the well-groomed gentleman. But the silver-topped glass decanters were violated by the presence of the large, brown bottle with a black and red label covering its flat front surface. Her hand wavered above it before lifting it to the light.

The crude label read, "Dr. Clarke Johnson's Indian Blood Syrup." The small print beneath it proclaimed it as a remedy for, "All diseases of the stomach, nerves and blood." She uncorked it, grimacing at the bitter odor.

"A lady's perfume would suit you better."

She jumped, nearly upsetting the bottle. *Patrick.* How did he always manage to come up behind her without a sound? Though startled, her discovery that the mysterious Dr. Johnson was a charlatan selling medicines made of God-knew-what poisons, concerned her far more.

She replaced the cork and held it out to him. "What is this?"

"It's Dr. Clarke John—"

"I know what the bottle says. I want to know what it is."

He stepped into the room. "Your father is a grown man, Camilla. He has the right to choose how to treat his own illness. He is gravely ill, you know."

"I know all about my father's health," she lied. "I asked you what is in the bottle you, your friend Dr. Johnson, and his nurse, whatever her name is, have given him."

"It's a patented medicine made from ingredients Johnson learned

67

from the Apache Indians. They used it as a cure-all. Its effects are short-lived, but harmless."

She'd stopped listening after the word, "Apache," Not caring who overheard them trespassing in Anthony's room, she raised her voice, "You have tricked my father into drinking *Indian medicine?*" She paced the tiny room until she finally turned back to point a finger into his chest. "You're trying to poison him so Langesford will become yours before our debt is paid."

He caught her arm when she tried to step around him. "The Indians, Camilla, had a civilization while our ancestors were beating each other with clubs. Many of our modern medicines are derived from so-called 'primitive' mixtures of herbs and roots. I told you it's harmless."

She stared at his hand on her arm until he dropped it. "It won't cure him, but if it substitutes for some of the laudanum—."

For a moment, she felt dead inside. Laudanum and brandy had led to her mother's madness—and death. *More secrets.* How could this man know more about her father in a couple of months, than she did after a lifetime? She wanted to call him a liar, but knew he'd told her the truth. "So now you're telling me Papa has been taking laudanum?"

She rubbed the circulation back into her arm and sat on the bed, heedless of the wrinkles it would cause. She'd never felt so alone. Of course, she'd known about her father's condition for a long time; the ever-present cough; the blood-spattered handkerchiefs, but she'd looked away, told herself he'd be fine. But now the sudden partnership with a Yankee. She had no control over anything in her life.

The bed sagged under added weight. She felt the heat of Patrick's body next to her. "The tonic won't hurt him," he repeated softly. "And if it gives him some relief during the time he has left, where's the harm?"

But she no longer cared about Indian Blood Syrup, or even laudanum. She turned, unaffected by his body so close to hers. Her voice sounded strange to her own ears. "Absolutely none, it seems. It's as you said, he's a grown man. What I think isn't important. You men seem to have all the answers in your own secret little club."

She rose and walked stiffly to the door before turning to face him. "After all, I am only a woman. What do I know of pain, illness or death? She smoothed her dress to step into the hall. "If you'll excuse me, I have guests to greet."

People she hadn't seen in years descended from refurbished and rented coaches, greeting each other as if a lifetime hadn't passed since 1862. But it had. The elder Charles Bartletts' thick, brown hair had thinned, turning white in the space of four years. And behind their smiles, the once gallant gentleman soldiers' eyes were tired, their backs bowed, steps slow.

The women seemed to have borne the horrors of war better, covering their wounds with remade antebellum gowns. But the scars showed when their laughter died at the mention of a lost loved one, and wariness replaced the sparkle of gaiety in their eyes. Once soft skin now bore freckles and tiny lines from the fierce Southern sun, and beneath their evening gloves, their hands were rough with the calluses and scars from hard labor.

Except for Eliza Bartlett, she thought bitterly, who spent the war in the Sea Islands, well out of musket range. As if thinking of her could make her appear, Eliza rustled up alongside of her.

"Oh, Camilla, darling," she exclaimed in her irritating blend of Georgia drawl and Boston-finishing-school twang. Fairly bursting the seams of her much too heavy, lime green taffeta gown, her buttercup-blue eyes assessed Camilla from head to toe, whining, "You're so thin."

She barely managed a polite smile. "But you're looking well, Eliza." *Fed.*

The girl waved a chubby arm. "Well, we do have to keep up appearances, don't we? I mean, with all the *strangers* around." Her gaze darted around the room as if searching for the infamous Yankee in their midst.

Camilla couldn't bear to listen to Eliza's trials and tribulations at her Uncle's island mansion and asked, "How is the move coming along?"

The question brought rose to Eliza's plain features and her lusterless, blue eyes shone with excitement, "Oh, I simply cannot wait until we embark. It has been such a nightmare here since..."

Camilla's patience finally snapped. "Yes, I hear the summer of '63 was warm on St. Simeon Island. And I understand good coffee was hard to come by unless you knew the right people."

Scalawags, smugglers and blockade runners. Rumors hinted the elder Bartlett and his brother had sold their honor to keep Eliza well supplied during the war.

Her face turned the color of an overripe watermelon. "Well, in Brazil, at least I won't have to sleep under the same roof as a Yankee."

Mutual dislike flashed like summer lightning between them. Camilla, outweighed by at least forty pounds, wanted to slap Eliza's sanctimonious face; and Eliza, well aware of Camilla's petulant nature and tenuous position in Southern society, dared her to try. They were spared a showdown when a splendidly dressed Otis opened the wide, double doors to admit the last of the twelve invited dinner guests. Another dozen couples would come later for the dancing.

Voices hushed as Mason O'Keefe entered the house. Eliza's eyes widened and she smiled coquettishly while Camilla stared in shock. Little remained of the handsome young man she remembered. His once tall, ramrod-straight frame now leaned over a cane. And the full beard hiding his chiseled features couldn't conceal a scar running from the center of his left cheek nearly to his chin.

But the disfigurement of war didn't cause her concern. Rather, her shock centered on his eyes and his mouth. His eyes had always sparkled with good humor, his lips quick to smile. Indeed, life had seemed a joke to Mason, and he smiled nearly all the time. Now, his full lips were drawn into a tight line, his eyes filled with anger instead of humor. She left Eliza to go to her father's side and extend her hand to their guest.

"Mason," she said, her heart skipping a beat when his eyes softened and his lips curved upward. But the smile faded when he leaned closer to kiss her cheek and noticed the dusting of freckles along the bridge of her nose. He pulled away and she pulled her hand from his before he felt the callouses through her lace evening glove. *What will he think when I remove them for supper?*

The warmth in his voice sounded forced when he said, "Ah, Cammy, darlin' you've grown to be quite a beauty." Then he wrapped her hand over his arm, took up his walking stick and stepped inside to greet his old friends and neighbors.

The male conversations centered on the restoration of the house, the pros and cons of new cotton farming techniques, as well as the wonderful food Flora and her hired helpers had prepared. Demurely quiet throughout the meal, the ladies, including Eliza, eyed Patrick curiously.

Mason also studied Patrick from across the table, only speaking when asked about his own renovations at Acadia. It relieved Camilla when Otis served the last course. She hoped the undercurrent of tension running through the gathering would ease when they retired to the drawing room for music, whist, and brandy. Mason had a marvelous voice, perhaps he'd sing for them.

But Mason refused to sing any of Stephen Foster's popular tunes. Instead, he sat in glowering silence on the settee in the now heavily furnished room, glaring at Patrick. "Who did you serve under?" he finally demanded.

Patrick turned from his conversation with Chet Bartlett to face Mason. Like an actor on a stage, he silently swirled the brandy in his snifter. "Burnside, for a while. And you?"

When Mason smiled, his face seemed younger by years, but his black eyes glittered with hatred instead of humor. "I fought alongside with Bobby Lee himself at Fredericksburg when we whipped you fellows clear back to Washington."

Camilla held her breath when the muscle in Patrick's jaw clenched before he took a sip of his brandy. She exhaled when he refused to take Mason's bait.

"Yes," he finally answered. "Lee certainly made the most of the twenty-day delay General Burnside so graciously granted him to set up his defenses in the sunken road."

Silence shrouded the room as men and women on both sides recalled the horrors of what many called murder itself. For even the Southern victors, memories of bodies frozen to the ground and to each other, three deep in places, would forever haunt their nightmares.

The older Bartlett broke the awkward silence. "Yes, Fredericksburg delivered a stunning blow to the Army of the Potomac, and was a terrible waste of young men's lives, on both sides of the battlefield."

Murmurs of, "Here, here," followed his conciliatory statement, as did silent toasts to dead comrades and family members on either side of the Mason-Dixon Line.

Camilla took advantage of the change in the room's atmosphere to ask Patrick, "is that where you were wounded?"

"Wounded?"

"Yes, the wound that sent you to Washington, where you met the…nurse." She still wasn't sure she believed the tale and hoped the brandy would entice him to share a little more of his secretive past.

He disappointed her by shrugging. "Oh, yes, Washington. Yes, I recovered there, but my wounds were quite minor, compared to the overall loss of life and limb."

Out of deference to the delicate ladies in the room, some of whom had opened their homes as hospitals for mutilated soldiers, no matter the color of their uniform, Bartlett interjected, "Indeed." He raised his goblet to the group to toast, "To peace."

Amid nods and murmurs of assent, Alan Fairchild from nearby Rosewood Plantation raised his own glass from an overstuffed chair near the fire. "Well, said—from a man about to abandon his homeland," he challenged. "Now, when we need level heads most of all."

Bartlett's face reddened, his angry step forward halted when his son stepped between him and Fairchild, owner of the only other surviving family-owned cotton planation in the county. "Perhaps the discussion of my father's decision is better suited for another time, Fairchild," Charles Jr. warned. "Especially since you are already fully aware of the reasons behind it."

To help ease the tension, the young lawyer offered, "But you bring up a good point, Alan. Level heads are desperately needed to meet the challenge of keeping the peace during our return to being one nation."

He glanced at his old friend Mason. "The rekindled popularity of the former Ku Klux Klan poses a considerable threat to our peace in their opposition to the Republican efforts in offering Negroes the vote. While the violence has been mostly to our north, it seems to be creeping our way. We must be vigilant and support peaceful measures to champion our cause during this transition."

As Charles convinced Fairchild that violence would only beget more violence in a region still grieving the loss of a majority of its adult male population, Camilla watched Mason O'Keefe. Though silent, Mason's agitation grew until his hands shook as he refilled his glass repeatedly, downing the contents quickly each time. She prayed the one man she hoped would save her from the life of a pitiful spinster was not one of the firebrands Charles referenced.

As the conversation wound to an unsolvable end, Patrick seemed to have earned acceptance as a fellow veteran of war, and an investor genuinely interested in helping the South rise from the ashes of war to its former glory.

"Now never you mind about those masked hooligans ridin' out after midnight," the elder Bartlett slurred. "It's only the darkies who need bide their ways. And that Republican scalawag Ashburn, who's stumpin' all over where he don't belong, tryin' to get the Negroes the vote."

On common ground again, Fairchild echoed. "Amen to that. He may just find hisself at the end of a noose one day."

The violent talk that would have once sent the delicate ladies to swoon, met with nods and worried whispers by both genders in the room, until Patrick held his barely touched brandy up in a toast. His gaze locked with Camilla's when he said, "Ladies and gentlemen, I don't presume to be able to judge the wicked and the good. I only wish this extraordinary country, North, South, East and West, peace and prosperity."

Who could argue with peace and prosperity? Patrick smiled as cheers of "Hear, hear," mixed with the occasional, "Amen," ended the dangerous talk of politics.

Chapter Ten

"Florie, do we have any more cut flowers? I want this room to bloom, just like in the old days."

Since the ball, Camilla had devoted herself to becoming the perfect Southern hostess, seldom leaving the house except to pick flowers from the garden. She hadn't even been to the cotton field since Patrick's fiasco with the German immigrants.

The change pleased Anthony tremendously, but Patrick preferred the old, feisty Camilla who constantly stuck her pretty little nose into things not her business. He'd begun to look forward to their breakfast discussions about planting schedules, lumber prices, and plans for a sawmill.

Now, she prattled unceasingly about clothes, flowers, and draperies. She was nearly as boring as that shrew Eliza who, while loudly voicing her loathing of Yankees in general, never stopped flirting with him at the ball.

He now rose earlier and took a basket breakfast with him to avoid Camilla's meaningless ramblings. But he'd risen later this morning after spending most of the night going over reports from Dr. Johnson about recent vandalism on plantations run by Northerners.

Two brothers in Mississippi had been killed recently. And in neighboring Ogemaw County, a whole crop had been burned. A renter from Ann Arbor, Michigan fled with nothing to show his backers but an empty bank account and a singed behind. Clarke couldn't pinpoint who planned the attacks, but the popularity of the resurging Ku Klux Klan threatened the ability of even someone as respected as Anthony Langesford to offer protection.

Since the nearly disastrous ball, Patrick had studied maps and made lists of hotheaded rebels in the area. But nearly any former rebel under sixty, young Chet Bartlett the one exception, could be termed a hothead. And though Anthony's neighbors had treated him with cautious civility, he'd seen the bitterness and distrust in their eyes. The so-called gentry of Jeffers County alone added more than a dozen names to his partner's list.

That, and his frustration with his lack of evidence indicating Anthony's involvement with the Denver gold robbery, had kept him up more than one night. And last night, the Irish whiskey he'd drunk to finally get some rest made him oversleep. Camilla's shrill voice demanding flowers assaulted his already frayed nerves.

"*Mon Dieu,* girl." Flora's voice felt like balm to an open wound. "You got so many flowers in here folks will wonder who died."

He stopped outside the parlor doors and watched the harpie Camilla had become wave her arms. "But I want it to be perfect. Mason is coming to see me this time, not Papa. I think he's changing, Florie. Each time he visits he's more like the old Mason."

So the wounded Confederate hero had begun calling on the beautiful princess of Langesford. The dignified master of the plantation, his lovely daughter—wearing clothes bought with Yankee money—and the Rebel war hero drinking himself to death on the rotting porch of his ancestral home, had tea while the despicable, money-grubbing Yankee sweated in the fields.

Long-buried resentment against the "upper classes" rose like bile in his throat. When he looked at Camilla, he couldn't appreciate her silk chignon and radiant complexion. He stepped inside the room, slipping into his mother's lilting Irish brogue. "So is it a weddin' you'll be plannin' with all this decoratin'?"

He slowly rolled up his sleeves. "And who, might I ask, is the unsuspecting bridegroom to be?" Then he slapped his forehead. "Wait now, could it be that bold lad O'Keefe?"

He swaggered up to Camilla. "Tell me lass, does the boyo know of his fate yet?"

Camilla's bright eyes darkened and her chin quivered for just a moment before she stepped behind a chintz-covered Queen Anne side chair. The fingers of her new kid gloves bit into the delicate, gold moiré silk upholstery. She lowered her voice. "I don't think my choice of flowers, or suitors needs your approval."

Instead of a cutting response, Patrick turned and plucked a tall white hyacinth from its crystal vase. "No, your taste in flowers is impeccable. What I question is your taste in men."

She left the safety of the chair to step up to him, a hellcat once again. "Odd? You have the nerve to call receiving one of my oldest and dearest friends, odd? You of the mysterious past, and Indian-remedy-peddling friends. How dare you question my friendship with one of Georgia's oldest and most respected families?"

Faith n' Begorrah, Marry O'Grady's voice whispered in Patrick's head. So the fairies hadn't replaced his stubborn Camilla with a simpering dolt after all. If it took needling to bring her to her senses, he'd do it all day long. She had no idea that O'Keefe's name topped his list of possible marauders. Perhaps it was time to tell her.

But she had a point. Her choice of suitors was not of his business. His Irish temper cooled as fast as it had heated and he leaned against a ceiling-high china cabinet to warn, "Old blood runs thin, Camilla. O'Keefe has been back for almost two years without coming to call. If he's such a *dear* old friend, what took him so long to come courting?"

Her renewed flush told him he'd sown a seed of doubt, but then her damned stubbornness won it over. "He's...he's been recuperating from his wounds."

"Pah. I've seen men hurt worse than that mount a horse, fight a battle, and ride all night to find a doctor." And since she was already angry, he pushed, "As much as I'm the last one to fault your charms, Camilla, there could be more to O'Keefe's sudden interest than meets the eye."

Tears suddenly melted the ice in those expressive green eyes and she turned away to face the window, her shoulders slumping in defeat. "So any man, even a crippled one with a disfigured face, would have to harbor ulterior motives to be...interested in me."

He cursed himself for going too far. Did she think he'd set her from him at the hot spring because she wasn't attractive? He swore he'd never understand a woman's mind—especially a woman as complicated as Camilla Langesford. But as much as he'd longed to go to her, pull her

76

into his arms and apologize, his mission came first.

Mason had been Brent's best friend, Anthony's, "second son." He could know something about the robbery. And until Patrick understood Mason's true intentions, he couldn't risk having him bolt. O'Keefe's interest in Camilla would keep him close. Still, she looked so...broken. "Camilla, I didn't mean it that way."

She turned back to him, not bothering to hide the angry tears on her cheeks. "Oh, yes you did. In fact, you're probably right. I have quite a reputation, you know."

She paced again. "I'm the girl who dared ride her brother's stallion at a Renaissance picnic. The one who wouldn't give up her father's plantation when the Yankees came through. And now I've lost any reputation I may have had as a virtuous woman because I'm living with a Yankee."

After an angry swipe at new tears, her beautiful mouth twisted and her voice lowered to a near growl. "And who could possibly want me except a crippled, penniless rebel?"

"But your father is here and you've never—"

"You fool," she snapped. "If you knew anything about the South at all, you'd know I don't have to *do* anything to become a pariah. I am guilty by association. Were you blind to the real purpose of Papa's ball?"

She took advantage of his surprise to step closer. "Only the price of a marriage certificate and the color of my skin differentiates me from a poor slave girl, before *and* after that damned war. And your fancy Worth gown helped me look good on the auction block."

Her reddened eyes boring into his, she cocked her head. "Am I to rot in this house like some delicate flower abandoned by the gardener? Mason O'Keefe is the only eligible young man in a hundred miles with the nerve to call on me. He's my last chance at a...life...in the South."

The truth of her words alarmed him, but her acceptance of it horrified him. He searched his mind for an alternative to O'Keefe. "But, but what about Chet Bartlett? He seems a decent sort. Not one to pass judgment."

In fact, he'd taken a real liking to the young, idealistic attorney. He reminded him of the man he might have become had he been born on the right side of the sheets.

A wry smile curved her lips when she answered, "You're new here. Chet will never marry. He's…different from other men. Besides, even if he did have the desire to call, he'd pay dearly for it. Eliza would make his life even more of a living hell."

"Eliza will be moving to Brazil shortly."

Her laugh sounded hollow. "If only you knew how ignorant you are. Let me enlighten you. Eliza may talk about moving with her father, but it will never happen. She's managed to delay the move for months and will, I expect, continue to do so until she finds a husband. Why do you think she flirted with all the unmarried men of any age, at the ball?" A finger pointed at him. "Even you!"

So she *did* notice. Alarmed, he entreated, "Camilla, you don't have to rush into anything with O'Keefe. He may not be the man you remember."

"What difference would it make? The war has changed us all."

He hesitated, deciding just how honest he should be with her. "What I mean to say is that he may be involved with the group of former Confederates vandalizing Yankee-operated plantations under the guise of the Klan. Innocent people have been killed, property ruined in their senseless rage. I fear he may be coming here to get information from you about our plans for the gin house and sawmill."

The room rang with the sound of her hand striking his cheek. "How dare you! Your mere presence here has ruined my life in ways the war never could. Now you are accusing my brother's best friend of using me to destroy Langesford. *You* are the one destroying it, heart and soul."

She circled him. "Oh, there may be a profitable plantation here one day, but it will not be Langesford. I only hope I'm not here when the last remnant of grace and dignity in the South dies."

Patrick raised a hand to his cheek and tested his jaw before answering, "Very well, Camilla. You were warned."

He strode toward the door, stopping at the threshold. Relieved there were no more cherubs within her reach, he turned to face her one last time. "But if O'Keefe should ask, we finish the gin house today and install the steam engine and press tomorrow. When the crop in the north field is picked, Langesford will again be a fully-functioning cotton producer—to make the profit you insist is so important to me."

"Ge milis am fion, tha e searbh ri dhìol," he added with a sad smile, thinking. *The wine is sweet, the paying bitter.*

She followed him to the front door. "What does that mean?"

Enjoying the opportunity to have the last word again, he raised the back of his hand to her. "Ask O'Keefe. He thinks he's Irish."

~ * ~

Camilla rose from the red velvet settee when Flora admitted Mason into the parlor. He stepped into the room smiling. "Cammy, you are absolutely radiant today. When I think of all the time I wasted recuperatin' up at Acadia, never knowing what a lovely young woman you'd grown to be, I could just die."

She smiled up at him, pushing the earlier scene with Patrick from her mind. It didn't matter if no other young men came to call. Mason had always held a piece of her heart. She sat down and tapped the seat next to her. "You asked me to wait for you, remember? A long, long, time ago."

She looked away when he awkwardly bent his misshapen leg to sit, hanging the crook of his cane over the arm of the settee. As he settled awkwardly into the small space beside her, the thigh of his good leg brushed hers, but she felt no heat. Not as she did whenever Patrick was near.

His voice husky, he answered close to her ear, "I remember, my sweet Cammy. I believe we sealed it with a kiss."

Smiling at his use of the old childhood nickname, and blushing at the memory of her first kiss, she offered him a plate of frosted cakes and a glass of Flora's sweet iced tea.

More than an hour passed in pleasant, meaningless conversation. Once, when Mason reached across her for another cake, his shoulder brushed against her breast. And later, laughing over a remembered prank with Brent, she touched his arm.

They both stopped laughing. Mason's black eyes fixed on hers and one hand enveloped both of hers. The back of his other hand caressed her cheek. He kissed her and she jumped at the strange coarseness of his beard, as well as the pressure of his dry lips on her mouth.

With Patrick's kiss as her only reference, she parted her lips, only to be invaded by a tongue tasting like cheap alcohol and Earl Gray tea.

When his teeth nipped at her lips and one hand squeezed her breast, she pulled away, wishing she had a handkerchief to wipe her mouth.

Breathless and clammy in the confined space, she pushed against Mason's thin chest to put a few more inches between them. "Why, Mason," she sighed, struggling to regain her breath and her wits. "I...I don't know what to say."

"My apologies, Cammy," he said, imprisoning her hands in his. But his set lips and dark brows knitted in a frown, called his apology false. "I may have misunderstood the purpose of your ball."

"The purpose?" To her disappointment, they'd barely spoken that night, and his injured leg had kept him from the dance floor.

His answering smile chilled her. "Well, it is no secret I have your father's approval—nay encouragement—to court you."

He dropped her hand then, leaving it sticky in the warm room. "But sadly, I could never ask a lady to become my wife and expect her to live in Acadia in its present condition. And with...the Yankee here. Well it makes things a bit awkward."

Southern pride. Camilla understood. Pride was all they had left. She lowered her eyes to hide her disappointment. "I see."

Mason's voice suddenly brightened. "Speaking of Acadia, I've come across a small amount of capital lately and would like to replant. Your father seems most impressed by O'Grady's ideas. Do you suppose your Yankee friend would share them with me?"

"He's no friend of mine."

"Oh?"

"Of course not." She said it so emphatically, his eyebrow raised. "Ideas are all he has. He's never planted a seed in his life."

Mason leaned back as if pondering this new information. "I had no idea."

It felt good to talk about something other than draperies. "He's just following my advice to plant a few of the fallow fields now, letting the soil rest a year between crops. He'll make up the difference by carefully culling the old growth forest."

"Your advice? Cammy, you truly are a wonder."

Taking his rare smile and raised eyebrows as interest, she continued, "Pine tar, lumber, and turpentine are profitable right now. The new gin house will give us the profits to begin the sawmill."

He whistled low. "A new gin house? Is that where our industrious Yankee has been all these afternoons when I've called?"

Patrick's parting challenge echoed in her mind. *Damn his sooty eyes and deep voice!* Either out of defiance to Patrick or to test Mason—or both, she answered, "Yes, he's finishing it today. The equipment will be installed tomorrow."

Chapter Eleven

Camilla couldn't sleep. The memory of Mason's sly smile when she told him about the gin house still made her flesh crawl. And Patrick's, "You've been warned," played over and over in her mind as she tossed in her suffocating bed.

The night songs of cicadas, mating frogs, and hooting owls, normally so soothing, kept her awake until fatigue allowed her a fitful slumber. A nightmare of Mason standing in front of her home with a lit torch, wearing the smug expression he'd worn when he bid her goodbye earlier in the day, woke her with a start.

She damned Patrick's Yankee hide for putting doubt in her mind, punched her crumpled pillow—again, and brushed her hair away from her sticky forehead and cheeks. *And why did I play into his hand by telling Mason about the gin house?*

Frustrated by her own confusion, she gave up the struggle for sleep and rose, crossing the room to look out her balcony window. The full moon still hung high above the trees. *Nearly midnight and I've not slept a bit.* She started at the sound of movement in the room next door and frowned, listening closely. Usually, Patrick retired early, the sound of his boots dropping to the floor just past dusk the last she heard from him for the night.

Fully awake now, she lit a lamp and set it on the chest. Then she crept closer to the door separating their rooms, listening to the steady thump of booted feet pacing the room. Her heart kept pace with his footfalls. *He's going out!* Without a thought about her appearance-or the light shining behind her, she pulled open the door she'd forgotten to ask Otis to bolt.

It squeaked and Patrick dove for the pistol on his bed to face her, the muzzle aimed at her heart, his finger on the trigger.

In the flickering light of a lone candle by his bed, he looked like a desperado in the penny novels she devoured whenever she found one. Shadows settled in the creases between his brows, his eyes glittered with deadly purpose, and deep creases alongside his mouth chilled her.

Then the gun's hammer clicked back into place and Patrick ran his fingers through his hair. "What are you doing here?"

"I-I...heard you pacing. Is something wrong?" she whispered, licking her suddenly dry lips. Her eyes widened as she became accustomed to the dim light. "And you're wearing a holster. What are you doing? Where are you going?"

"Shh," he whispered too. "I'm going out to protect my investment. I took your advice and let Leon come back to work to keep an eye on him. He's been just a tad too willing to help out at the gin lately."

His quicksilver eyes reflected the moonlight. "I suspect he may be working for the marauders I told you about, and since he disappeared today, I figure something is going to happen. Tonight."

Grateful he didn't suspect Mason, she pushed back a thick lock of hair and nodded. "Yes, Leon's always been trouble, but at least he's predictable." She touched his arm. "You can't guard the gin house alone."

He looked at her a long moment, then pulled away with a low moan and turned his gaze from her. "Don't worry, Otis will be there, and I have a couple of close friends right here." He patted the two revolvers slung around his waist. "I don't figure the renegades will do much if faced with armed resistance. They prefer to strike unguarded targets and victims who can't defend themselves."

"I'm going with you," she announced, turning toward her room.

"What? Are you cr—." She turned back to him, and put a finger to her lips. He looked away and lowered his voice. "Crazy? You're not going anywhere."

"It doesn't appear you have a choice in the matter, Mr. O'Grady," she answered his back as she tucked her chemise into a pair of Brent's trousers, pulled on one of his shirts, and bunched her hair up under an old work hat. Moments later, she returned to his room looking like a young boy.

She smiled at his surprise. "Don't forget, your investment happens to be on my father's property and my home. Brent would have gone with you, and my father too if his health allowed." Without waiting for his argument, she walked past him toward the front stairs.

He followed her to the study, where she took a key from under an azalea pot, and unlocked the gun cabinet, pulling down two Yankee Spencer repeating rifles taken from the Battle of Atlanta. With a grin, she tossed him one with a box of shells. "Actually, I'm rather fond of these old friends."

"Well, I'll be damned." Patrick matched her smile and left the room ahead of her this time, loading the carbine as he walked.

She hurried to match his long strides while loading her own rifle. "That is probably the only thing I've agreed with you about in weeks." Continuing to talk to his back, she argued, "But I think you're wrong about the danger to your gin. Leon's more likely just on a drunk. No one would hurt Anthony Langesford or his property, with or without a Yankee on it."

"Well, we'll find out soon enough, won't we?" He patted the rifle under his arm. "And if you're wrong, we'll have each other—and our friends Mr. Spencer and Mr. Colt, to defend it."

~ * ~

They rode in silence to the gin house, taking cover in the shadows of virgin Georgia pines. Clouds had rolled in to shroud the moon, the humid night air thick with the scent of the nearby Ogemaw River. The smell of money, Patrick thought. The river would float his ginned cotton to Savanah and bring back a return on Dr. Johnson's investment. If only he could solve his own mystery so simply.

With only the night noises buzzing, chirping and rustling around them, Patrick breathed deeply of the scent of pine sap and fresh-cut lumber surrounding the new gin house—of something he'd built with the labor of his own hands. It had been too long since his mind had hummed to the rhythm of a saw and the steady beat of a hammer. Not since his early days on the railroad—not since the war turned him into a spy and a hunter of human beings.

Over the last couple weeks, he'd sung along with the Langesford hands to make their labor easier. He'd felt—comfortable, for the first time in years. What his mother called a "fairy-mist" moistened his eyes when he looked at the sturdy, well-framed building that would likely stand long after his bones became dust. Pride filled his heart as he thought of the true meaning of the word, 'legacy'.

The euphoria died when he thought of Camilla spending her life with Mason O'Keefe. If he was wrong about O'Keefe, whatever feelings Camilla had felt for him at the hot spring would be destroyed forever. But after the failure at the cotton field, he was too proud of this success to lose it to the torch of a bitter, rebel sot. Time would indeed tell.

They settled under the canopy of a tall pine to wait, each of them too full of their own hopes and fears of how the night would end, to speak. All too soon, Patrick's senses sprang alert at the staccato call of what sounded like a great horned owl. The hoot repeated five more times, two seconds apart, from the direction of Otis' perch a quarter mile down the narrow dirt road. Six riders were coming their way from the south. *Good.* He could still save the cotton field.

He looked down at Camilla, dozing against his shoulder. Resisting the urge to kiss her smooth forehead, he whispered, "Wake up, Princess. The barbarians are at the gate."

Instantly alert, she reached for the rifle and obeyed the finger touching her lips to stay silent. Then, rising as silently as an Indian, Patrick used hand signals for her to follow him to the building. He posted her at the north end of the second floor. Hoping to give the impression of more men, he fixed one rifle at the other end, pointing down the ladder where bags of cotton would be raised to the gin.

He tied a rope to the trigger and handed the end of it to Camilla, motioning for her to lay on the floor above the hole where the presser would be installed. If the bluff didn't work and they set the building afire, she could climb down the rope ladder curled by the nearby window. When she was settled, he jumped down to peer through one of the small vent windows facing south.

The approaching men rode horses with hooves muffled by rags, unlit torches tied behind their saddles. Following their leader in military formation, they wore Confederate uniforms and black sacks over their

85

faces. Three of them fanned out at the edge of the clearing to check the perimeter. When the first one dismounted and entered the gin house with an unlit torch in his hand, Patrick knocked him unconscious and dragged him inside.

Raiders and defenders worked in silence until a second, and then a third marauder became a prisoner. As expected, Camilla refused to stay at her post, helping Patrick tie them up. She gasped as she pulled each man's mask off.

She didn't say their names, but Patrick knew them all, having entertained them at his partner's home only a short while ago: Dan Guilford from downriver, Casey Tildon from Belleford and Eric Chisolm from Greenbrier Plantation. They were all Brent *and Camilla's* childhood friends, leaving little doubt of the leader's identity.

"There's still time," Patrick whispered. He nodded toward the second-floor window. "Hide up there and no one will see you." It didn't surprise him when she shook her head and tightened the gags and ropes binding their unconscious prisoners.

Just outside the shadows of the forest, the leader on a gray Tennessee Walker shifted in his saddle as if easing the pain of an old wound, while his two companions complained that the building should be in flames by now. All three men drew their sidearms and moved forward.

"Waiting for someone, O'Keefe?" Patrick asked, his revolver aimed at the masked raider's chest. Drop your weapon."

Making no move to confirm or deny his identity, the rider signaled his men to hold their fire, and carefully holstered his gun instead of surrendering it. He slowly dismounted and approached Patrick with a limp. "Don't think you can stop us, Yankee," Mason's familiar voice sneered. "You and your money are not wanted here. Get out while you still have your skin and we may spare the building. It could be useful when it belongs to me."

"I don't take threats from a man afraid to show his face," Patrick taunted. "Did you Rebs lose your guts along with your glory in the war? Or did you never have anything more than glib tongues and grand schemes?"

It occurred to him that he may have trusted Camilla too much. His comments were intended to spark a foolish move on O'Keefe's part, but she could just as easily turn her rifle on him and reap the rewards of his death with Mason. He hoped he was right about her dedication to her home. After all, she'd made it clear that the plantation and her honor were all she had left.

"Curb your tongue, filthy cur!" Mason threw his mask on the ground, shouting, "You're a dead man."

Mason's obsidian eyes and the scar along his cheek glowing in the moonlight reminded Patrick of tales of Banshees roaming the Irish forests. But Mason O'Keefe was no myth. He was a flesh and blood threat to everyone around him, including the mounted men who leaned forward in their saddles, waiting for the order to shoot.

"No, you're the fool, O'Keefe," Patrick bluffed. "You didn't think I came alone, did you?"

Mason's laugh stilled the night sounds. "If you brought men they'd have shown themselves by now. Darkies never could follow orders without a whip, and no white man would come with you."

He raised his hand to order the murder of another Northerner. When it fell, Patrick would have one shot before he was riddled with bullets himself. He hoped it would be true and kill Mason before he could do any more harm,

"No white *man*, Mason," came from the darkness behind Patrick.

Mason's face went slack his arm frozen in the air. He craned his neck to see the person behind the voice he'd heard only hours before. "Camilla? What are you doing here?"

"Protecting my father's property from thieving renegades bent on destroying what little we have left." She left the safety of the gin house to stand next to Patrick, her rifle raised, her finger poised in front of the trigger. "Traitor!"

Mason fixed his hate-filled gaze on her. "Whore! You have the gall to call me a traitor for trying to run off our enemies. You sleep under the same roof, eat at the same table, and do God-knows-what with them—for what? A fancy house and pretty clothes."

His men, still hiding behind their masks, watched as their leader directed all his venom toward Camilla. "No, you are the traitor, bitch. You, your father, and your precious brother. He's probably living like a king in Mexico on the gold from the Denver Mint. While his countrymen starve, you peddle your body for your next meal, and your pitiful father pretends he can rebuild the South to its former glory with Yankee money."

Barely taking a breath, he continued, "And you're stupid as well, to think I'd ever want you. If not for Langesford, I'd sooner wed that horse, Eliza Bartlett than let you bear the O'Keefe name."

"Enough!" Patrick shouted and advanced on him. Mason drew his pistol.

The blast echoed in the clear night air, followed by the dull thud of a body striking the hard-packed earth, and the muffled sound of two horses running away.

Patrick approached Mason slowly, as he would a rattlesnake in the desert. First, he nudged what he knew was a corpse, with his boot, then knelt beside him to feel for a pulse at his throat. Finally, he looked up at Camilla and shook his head.

For a long moment, she stared at him, at Mason, and at her own smoking rifle. Then she fell to her knees with a cry that ripped through Patrick's heart. He left the body to take her in his arms. "It's all right, darling. You saved my life—and Langesford," he repeated over and over until she took a ragged breath and looked up at him with haunted eyes.

"Liar," she answered before collapsing against his chest, her body still convulsing from the effort to breath between cries of anguish and grief.

Patrick had known grief and seen suffering, but he could only imagine the pain this brave young woman had lived through. Her cries weren't from guilt over killing a brutal murderer. They were from the pain of knowing everything she believed in and hoped for was truly dead. No comfort existed for that kind of loss, and only time would tell if she'd survive unchanged.

She felt light as a bird in his arms when he carried her to the side of the gin house and sat with her, stroking her hair, rocking her until her emotions were spent.

He raised a hand when Otis arrived, gasping for breath from his long run. "She's fine," Patrick said softly. He nodded to Mason O'Keefe's body. "And he's dead."

88

Patrick had recognized Otis' uncommon intelligence the moment he'd handed Jupiter over to him the night he arrived at Langesford. There were secrets behind those coal-black eyes the man would take to his grave. He also knew Otis wouldn't hesitate to give his own life for Camilla—or take the life of anyone who hurt her.

Before judging Patrick, Otis picked up Camilla's rifle and sniffed the spent powder from the muzzle. At his questioning gaze, Patrick nodded toward the gin house. "She saved my life. Two got away and three others are inside. They're trussed up, but could use some minding."

With a wary glance at Camilla, now breathing evenly in an exhausted slumber, the faithful servant nodded and left to see to the prisoners.

She woke to the sound of three men, still gagged, their arms tied behind their backs, being prodded out of the gin house by Otis brandishing the Spencer rifle. Confused at first, she opened her mouth to speak, but no sound came out.

"Shh," Patrick soothed. "You'll be fine," he lied again. No one would be fine—in the South or the North, for a long, long while. As a son of Ireland, he knew the twin evils of greed and bondage. Together, they passed hatred on from generation to generation. If a thousand years of bloodshed had not ended the horrors between Ireland and England, he had no hope the conflict between countrymen in a nation less than a century old, would prove the cure.

"Please, let me take care of this," he said when she made a move to rise.

At her slow nod, he carried her back to an old pine rising above a thick carpet of soft needles, then joined Otis and their three prisoners.

"It ends here, tonight," Patrick told the sons of the South. "You men have families. If you don't want them to see you hang, you'll hang up your hoods forever. And that goes for your friends who left you to die."

At their nods, Patrick kept their rifles and Otis freed their hands, to wrap Mason's body in his blanket and sling him over his saddle. His horse, smelling death, strained against the tether in Tildon's hands.

Guilford approached Camilla, who now stood, her back against the tree trunk, her gaze riveted on the body slung over the horse. "This was madness from the beginning," he told them both. "We should never have followed him."

"No, you shouldn't," she answered, her voice hoarse from the ordeal as well as the damp chill of the night. "Now get off my land."

His head bowed, he told Patrick, "Mason's body will be found on the road to Acadia." A note of irony colored his voice when he added, "Ambushed, no doubt, by those raiders we've been hearing about. His gun will be emptied, and when they don't come back, he'll be a hero."

Then to Camilla, "Enough blood has been spilled. From this day forward, Jeffers County will be a safe place to live—no matter the color of a man's skin or his place of birth. I pledge this with my blood and the blood of my descendants."

Camilla nodded. "And mine as well." Tildon and Chisolm did the same before mounting their horses. Then the three men and the Tennessee Walker faded like specters into the rising fog along the river, Camilla slid down the tree. With no tears left, she wrapped her arms around her body, rocking back and forth, keening softly for the loss of all she'd ever held to be true.

Patrick again held her in his arms until the trembling stopped. Then with a worried gaze at the brightening sky, he told Otis, "You go on home. Ride Misty instead of the mule and if anyone is up, tell them she got loose from her stall. Leave the door to the back stairs open. We'll be along."

A bushy salt and pepper eyebrow rose as the former slave took a long look at Patrick and then Camilla. At her nod, he led Misty and the mule down to the road.

Camilla's eyes were nearly swollen shut, her dried tears a salty crust on her lashes and cheeks. Patrick lightly pressed his lips to her eyelids and whispered, "It's over. We can go home now."

But she made no effort to move, croaking, "But I committed—"

"No crime, Camilla. You saved my life." He stroked her cheek. "I should never have let you come with me. And I won't let anything like this ever happen to you again. I promise."

"Liar," she whispered back. "No one can make that promise." Her sad smile told him she knew he'd try. When he kissed her, she clung to him, her body molding to his, fingers combing through his hair. "Take me," she whispered. "Show me I'm still alive."

Patrick pulled away for the second time, knowing there wouldn't be a third. He wanted her. More than he'd ever wanted a woman. And something inside him told him he would have her—one day. But not like this. Not as a tool to prove she could feel. And not here, where the stench of gunpowder and blood still hung in the air.

He kissed her swollen lips lightly. "Later, my love. We've got to get you home." Smoothing her hair, he smiled and reminded her of the hot spring. "Or your reputation will be severely compromised. And this time, Flora will really have my hide."

She waved his supporting hand away. "You don't have to worry. I can take care of myself." Then the haunted look returned. "I only hope I can live with myself."

The moon had nearly given way to the sun when they approached the front of the house riding double on Jupiter's strong back. A strange horse was tied to the porch railing, the front doors open, and all the lights lit in the hall. Camilla frowned at Patrick. "You said it was over."

He shook his head. "I don't know Guilford well, but can recognize a man of his word. It has to be something else."

He dismounted, helping her to the ground. Hands steadying her trembling shoulders, he tried to hide his doubt. "But just in case, keep your mouth shut and remember, I shot O'Keefe to keep him from burning my building."

"You can't!"

"Why? Because it's a lie?" He chuckled. "I stepped over the line between truth and fiction a long time ago. Just keep your beautiful mouth shut for once and let me handle it."

Flora met them at the door with tears streaming down her face. "Cammy," she wailed, throwing her arms around the girl. "It is your Papa. He went out tonight too and is just come home." She wrung her hands. "Cammy, *cheri,* I think he is dying. Dr. Samuels is with him."

91

Chapter Twelve

Her world couldn't end twice in one night! Camilla swayed on her feet, but shrugged Patrick's hand off her shoulder to demand, "What happened?" as she pushed past Flora to race up to her father's room.

The insanity of the war faded in comparison to the events of this one night. Mason, a Southern hero, had become a cowardly renegade, riding under the cover of darkness, wearing a mask to hide his face and his hideous deeds; while Patrick, a soft Yankee businessman, handled revolvers like a frontier adventurer. And now her father, who hadn't stayed up past dusk in weeks, rode out after midnight. Her mind ran in a hundred different directions at once. *Where did he go? And why?*

But Anthony couldn't answer her questions. He lay in his huge four-poster bed, still and pale as a corpse. Rail thin, despite Dr. Johnson's 'medicine', he looked like a sleeping skeleton.

Patrick arrived at the door just as Camilla collapsed onto the hard pine floor. Flora arrived out of breath from her own run up the stairs to find him bending over her.

She pushed him aside, screaming, "Stay away from my Cammy!"

"Please, let me help," Patrick said softly to Flora. "Anthony is resting. Neither of you can do anything for him if you're exhausted or hurt."

After a long, appraising look, Flora nodded, stepping away to let him carry Camilla to the rumpled bed she'd left only a few hours ago.

Downstairs, Patrick met Otis pacing in the foyer and ushered him into the study. He lit a cigar and offered one to the old man.

Otis' eyes opened wide. Emancipation notwithstanding, a Negro did not smoke with a white man. He shook his head. "No, thanks suh."

"Suit yourself," Patrick answered with a nod. When he exhaled, Otis breathed deeply of the freshly-rolled Cuban tobacco. Risking stronger punishment than from smoking a forbidden cigar, he asked pointedly, "What you all goin' to do 'bout tonight?"

Unperturbed, Patrick withdrew the cigar from his lips, rolling it between his thumb and forefinger. "Why nothing, Otis, absolutely nothing."

"A man. A *white* man is dead," Otis observed. Shrewd intelligence lit his bottomless, black eyes. "That kind o' thing ain't so easy to ignore—'specially when two other white men saw it happen. If'n Ah was you, Ah'd be mighty nervous about a noose right now, even if Ah didn't do it."

Patrick hid his smile behind the cigar. So the old man would defend Camilla and have him hang, if it came to that. While it was true few would believe Camilla had shot her suitor in the middle of the night, two of the marauders had escaped with their masks still on.

Though he'd judged Guilford to be an honest man, they were his brothers in arms. How good was his word when it came to protecting them? He held another cigar out to Otis. "I'm nervous all right, but not about my neck. You know Camilla won't lie about what happened that night. She's riddled with guilt. We need to make sure she doesn't confess, and that Guilford, Tildon and Chisolm keep the others quiet."

The old man winced at the very real danger to Camilla. He reached for the cigar, allowing the white man to light it for him. He inhaled deeply, breathing out a string of smoke circles to float up to the candles in the chandelier. "What are you going to do?" he asked without affectation, his usually wide eyes narrowed in speculation.

"No one will harm Camilla," Patrick assured him with more confidence than he felt. "They have more to lose by revealing what happened than we do." He took his own deep breath of the soothing tobacco and changed the subject. "What I want to know is why Master Langesford ventured out after midnight."

Otis' shoulders relaxed as he watched the ashes grow fat at the end of the thick, rolled tobacco. "Flora say a little niggra boy bring a note right aftah supper."

"Go on. And you can drop the field hand act around me if you want to. You're good, but I can hear a Boston "A" a mile away." It seemed both Otis and Flora were hiding more than an uncommon intelligence to play the roles of houseman and nursemaid. Why, he wondered, deciding to save that mystery for later?

Otis's dark face blanched from dark cocoa to fresh tea, but offered no explanation as he considered the offer. Then he sighed. "She didn't know the boy. Too many new folks around here now to keep track. She gave him a sweet and watched him run away before taking the note up to the master's room."

He paused a moment, his dark eyes rolling in his effort to remember what his wife had told him. "Just past midnight, she heard a noise outside and looked out the window to see Colonel Langesford riding off on Cap'n—south, toward the swamp."

Patrick's eyebrows raised. He'd only been in Georgia a short time, but knew the dangers of being anywhere near the swamp at night, especially in the spring. The insects were thick enough to choke you, and if they didn't get you, the cottonmouths would. Yet the evidence in Anthony's room had supported he was there: the wet floor and his discarded clothes all smelled of the rank, fetid swamp.

Why on earth would a man as sick as Anthony Langesford risk suicide by going to the river in the middle of the night? And why did it coincide with the marauders' attack on my gin house? Life at Langesford got more interesting each day. He crushed the half-smoked cigar in a cut-glass tray and shook Otis' hand. "Thank you for…everything…tonight."

~ * ~

Anthony's illness spared Camilla the ordeal of attending Mason's funeral, which was attributed to an unfortunate meeting with the notorious renegade nightriders. For the next two weeks, she avoided Patrick by spending all her waking moments caring for her dying father. But both good and bad luck run out eventually.

Rising a little after dawn instead of before sunrise, Patrick caught her coming out of her room. Visibly shocked by her appearance, he lightly touched her arm. "Camilla, you look terrible. Are you sick, as well?"

She couldn't bear to look at him after...that night. She had murdered a man—an old friend—to save Patrick's life. No, to save Langesford, she told herself over and over, until she almost believed it. And even now, the mere touch of his hand through her sleeve, reminded her of how she'd begged him to take her—like the whore Mason accused her of being.

She shook off his hand to answer sharply, "I appreciate your concern, but I'm well, thank you. Now, if you'll excuse me, I have more important things to do than listen to your compliments."

"Like what? Martyring yourself for your father? You're more help to him alive and healthy than a walking skeleton." He took her arm again, more firmly this time, and gave it a tug. "Come with me. You need to eat something. And we need to talk."

This time, her efforts to twist out of his grasp were ineffective. Too tired to fight, she implored, "Please leave me alone. I don't want to talk and I'll eat when I'm hungry. I don't need you dragging me around the house."

But he wouldn't release her arm until she confessed, "Don't you understand? My father is dying and it's my fault. Nothing else matters."

He dropped his hand. "You matter, Cammy. A great deal, to a lot of people, but especially to your father—and to me. I haven't known Anthony long, but I do know he'd be repulsed by what you're doing to yourself in his name."

Before she could protest, he scooped her into his arms and settled her on her feet in front of the mirrored door of the armoire in her room. "Look at yourself. Do you want Anthony to see you like this when he wakes up?"

She'd stopped looking in the mirror the night of the attack on the gin house. Now, she gasped at the vision of a haggard, hollow-eyed, near-corpse who somehow managed to mimic her every movement. Bloodshot eyes rimmed by dark circles stared back at her as thin fingers with splintered nails, ran down a parchment-pale cheek.

"No," she cried, blocking the vision of the disgusting specter facing her. Then she pulled her ragged shawl over the shoulder blades poking through her calico gown, nodded and followed him down the back stairs to the kitchen.

"She'll eat now," he told Flora when they entered the kitchen.

Though Flora didn't answer, Camilla recognized a softening of the older woman's features when she nodded to the Yankee. *When did this happen?* While Flora had never spoken against him, she'd always treated him with icy respect.

Camilla felt a flush of jealously creep up her cheeks. After her mother's death, she'd only had to share the woman's respect with Otis, who adored them both. She wondered if Flora knew she saved Patrick's life by killing a childhood friend. *A childhood friend who'd gone mad.*

Suddenly feeling like a stranger in her own home, she accepted a plate of warm grits sweetened with honey, a small piece of warm ham, and one of Flora's signature corn biscuits.

Patrick watched her take her first hesitant bite, then picked up his own breakfast basket from Flora. He touched Camilla's shoulder. "With your father's...illness, we'll need to work together. From now on, we'll meet here at dawn to discuss the plans of the day, and again at supper, if you can leave the sick room."

She could only stare into those slate eyes. Apparently, much had changed in the household since the night her father took ill. The Yankee was now in charge, and she wasn't sure she liked it. But she hadn't the time or the strength to fight him and owed him a debt for his restraint when she'd abased herself at the gin.

"I won't leave until you agree."

His smile sent a shaft of heat through her bones. she hadn't felt in weeks. At her nod, he looked to Flora. "You'll see to it?"

Camilla gaped when Flora answered, "Oui, Master O'Grady. I will take good care of her."

"And a good hot soak in a salted bath," he added.

Camilla flushed at the inappropriate reference to her hygiene, but it felt so good to be idle for a few minutes in the sunny kitchen, and she couldn't fight them both That would be her father's task when he recovered.

Still, she could only eat half of her first full meal in weeks. In little more than an hour since meeting Patrick in the hall, she emerged from a lavender-scented bath softened by Carolina sea salts. Wrapping herself in the thick cotton towel Flora held for her, she admitted her legs felt stronger. Now the reflection in the armoire mirror looked less haunted, more human. Without complaint, she accepted Flora's offer of a green linen gown from what she still considered Patrick's wardrobe.

Though roomy on her shrunken frame, it felt good to be out of worn homespun smelling of lye soap. After a deep breath, she believed she'd survive yet another day of nursing a man who'd barely been conscious for weeks.

"A blessing," Dr. Samuels had said. He felt no pain and it allowed his heart to rest.

Still, she approached her father's room with heavy steps. The tapestry curtains were shut to keep the room cool during the increasing heat of early summer. Flora had set fresh-cut flowers around the room, but it still smelled of camphor and the soiled bedding they changed whenever needed.

Someone stayed with Anthony constantly. When Flora and Camilla had other matters to attend, Otis sat sentinel from an overstuffed reading chair. This morning, he was dozing when Camilla touched him lightly on the shoulder.

"It's all right, Otis," she whispered when he jumped.

"What? Oh, Miss Cammy." His lined face reflected the weary sadness in Camilla's soul when he answered her unspoken question. "Not a move, Miss, and nary a sound."

Her nod dismissed him and she went to her father's side. She could look at him now with compassion and pity instead of overwhelming grief and guilt. As much as she hated to admit it, Patrick was right. Her father had no use for slovenly women or martyrs. If he dreamed of bringing Langesford back from the dead, then so would she. And when death came for her father it would end his pain and sorrow. The vise gripping her heart told her it would only prolong hers.

With a cheery, "Hello, Papa," she sat next to him to warm his cold, waxy hand with hers. "I'm here," she whispered into his ear. "And I'm willing to do whatever you wish. Please, just wake up."

Did his head move slightly, or was it just her weight on the feather-tic mattress? She leaned over him, her pounding heart drowning out the sound of his uneven breathing as she willed her own life force into his body.

Doris M. Lemcke

Again, she sensed, rather than felt, a movement. This time weak fingers squeezed hers. She held her breath and dared not blink for fear of missing some sign of life. "Oh, Papa," she whispered. "Please come back, if only for a little while."

So much time had been lost between them, so much left unsaid. Anthony had virtually ignored her as a child, focusing all his attention on Brent, the hope for future generations. With a mother who inexplicably loathed her, and a father who doted on his only son, acting outrageously seemed the only way to capture their attention. Even their anger was better than indifference.

Then the war came. Brent volunteered and her mother took to her room. General Lee, her father's classmate at West Point, coerced him into taking a commission in the Army of the Confederate States of America. Anthony hired Mssr. Antoine to paint her and her mother's portraits, along with miniatures for him and his son to take with them into battle. Then they rode out of her life—Brent forever, her father to return a sad shell of the man he'd once been.

His few visits home during his three years as one of General Lee's officers, had more to do with the state of the plantation, than his wife and daughter. To him, she was either the mischievous little girl who continuously tried his patience, or the imaginary one wearing a stupid white frock with pink ribbons. Now, she desperately wanted to tell him how much she loved him, and even more desperately, for him to say he loved her.

She froze when another squeeze on her hand was followed by the flutter of one eyelid, and then the other, until Anthony's cloudy blue eyes met hers. She leaned close to kiss his withered cheek, barely hearing his hoarse whisper, "Cammy."

After weeks of caring for him, fearing his death, her blood warmed and tears of happiness flowed from her eyes. *He's awake and can speak. He'll be well again!* She wiped at them with her sleeve and choked, "I'm here, Papa."

Thanking the God she thought had abandoned them, she rubbed his hands, sending heat into his body and urging blood to flow through the spider web of blue-green veins beneath his opaque skin.

Moments later, his tired eyelids fluttered as if the struggle to keep

98

them open took more strength than he could bear. His hand left hers long enough to point to his bureau. "The brush," his dry throat rasped.

"Brush?" Was his mind addled from the fever? He'd never used a brush, preferring to finger-comb his fine, straight hair. "No, Papa, you need water—and food." She started to pull away, but his weak fingers curled around hers.

"No…time. The brush." Her hopes dashed when his chest rattled against the struggle to speak.

She risked taking her eyes off him to yank open the dresser's top drawer, There, winking at her in the rays of light peeking between the closed draperies, lay her mother's silver hair brush. Memories of Danielle beating her with it clenched her stomach until she mustered the will to pick it up.

It lay heavy and cool in her palm as she carried to her father and pressed it in his hand. His eyes still closed, he caressed it like a blind man tracing the lines of his lover's face.

"Oh!" she gasped when the tarnished oval engraved with the Trémon crest, opened and Anthony reached trembling fingers inside.

Camilla's own heart tightened in her chest waiting for whatever evils might be released from her mother's cherished brush. But it was only a piece of paper folded into a tiny, thick square. Tears spilled down her father's cheeks when he reached out for her hand.

"Brent," he whispered, pressing it into her palm. "Not a traitor." He coughed then, spattering the newly washed sheets with blood. With his last breath, he gasped, "Beecher knows. Stop him."

Chapter Thirteen

She was too shocked to cry. Maybe it was selfish to hope for some word of affection before he died, some acknowledgement of her strength, her sacrifices, but it hurt that his last words were reserved for her bother. Despite Mason's insane accusation about Brent living like a king in Mexico, everyone knew he gave his life to save three men trapped by crossfire at Chickamauga. General Rush described his heroism in a letter. And she'd never heard of anyone named Beecher.

Tears flowed at the realization that like Mason and her mother, her noble father had gone mad. Eyes burning, she opened her palm and slowly unfolded the parchment. The Langesford watermark identified it as stationery she hadn't seen in nearly five years.

Ink and paper were expensive, even before the war. She wasn't allowed to touch the family stationery until she could write legibly, and then only for letters and invitations. She recognized her father's hand in the curving lines, inverted "V"s, and random letters written in the blue-black ink he favored. But this, like all the events since Patrick entered their lives, made no sense.

She rubbed her eyes, refolded it and shoved it deep into the pocket of her apron before leaning down to give her father one last kiss. It was time to once again begin the ritual of burying a parent next to her brother's empty grave on Memorial Hill.

Flora was with Otis in the kitchen when she entered, saying only, "He's gone." *And I am the last surviving Langesford.* If not for Otis' arms around her, she would have collapsed under the burden.

He helped her into a chair while Flora smoothed her hair, whispering, "These things will pass, *cheri.* And they will only make you

100

stronger."

"But I don't want to be stronger," Camilla protested. She only wanted to curl up into a ball and sleep—then wake up to find the last five years had only been a bad dream.

She'd be a child again. A *good* child who obeyed her parents. Her mother and father would cherish her. She'd marry the handsome, charming Mason O'Keefe, not the monster of her dream. There would be no war, no death, no illness in her life; and they would all live, happily ever after."

"We are never given more than we can bear," Flora answered. "Come *petite*, the weather is hot and there is work to be done."

Camilla took a deep breath. Though sometimes the burden of simply being alive seemed too much to bear, Flora was right. Summer had come early. They had to prepare Papa's body for burial or it would rot under their very noses. The work, the worry, and now even the weather kept her from mourning her dead father. *Time enough for that later.*

~ * ~

Patrick quit early and mounted Jupiter. Things were going well. The first tender crop had sprouted flowers and if the warm temperatures held, they should see bolls in less than a month. Depending on the weather and the price of cotton, he and Anthony stood to make a healthy sum in just this first year. His share would at least cover Dr. Johnson's investment, if not the house renovations intended to disguise his search for evidence.

While Mason had confirmed their information about Brent leading the raid on the mint, it appeared that Anthony had carefully hidden—or destroyed, any evidence of his involvement. If the old man died, any hope of finding a map to their hiding place would die with him. His record as a detective would still be flawed, but Langesford—Camilla, would have a future. He could live with that.

He decided he'd stay on until the crop was in and his debts paid. Then he'd cut his personal losses and move on. *To what?*

He remembered Camilla's laugh on the trail to the slave quarters, the sadness in her voice when she settled to be courted by O'Keefe. And finally, the haunted eyes he'd seen this morning. Langesford had proved difficult in too many ways. Staying in one place too long trapped a man, and each time he looked at Camilla, the trap tightened a little more.

He was considering Allen Pinkerton's offer to join his new civilian team of investigators when Otis, mounted on Misty, approached the field at breakneck speed. The memory of Camilla riding recklessly through the peach grove gripped Patrick's heart, while a chill his mother insisted foretold a death, raised bumps on his arms. As the shudder passed through him to Jupiter, the big stallion shook his head and blew.

Otis slowed Misty enough for Patrick to catch her bridle. The frantic expression on the old man's face told him something terrible had happened.

"Camilla," Patrick choked. "Is she...?" He couldn't say it.

Workers appeared out of nowhere, closing around the two men and the spent mare as Patrick held his breath. Otis slipped into his slave dialect. "She fine, Suh. Though she surely seen bettah days. It's Mastah Langesford. He gone now. Jest a little while ago. I got to git Doc Samuels so's we can git him ready for the buryin'." He eyed Misty's heaving withers. "But Ah's gonna need a new horse."

Patrick volunteered Jupiter, who'd shown a rare fondness for the kind servant. Any doubts he had about Otis' ability to handle the spirited mount disappeared as he fairly bounced onto Jupiter's back and they sped down the path as if they were one body.

"Well, I'll be..." Patrick slapped his hat against his thigh. Once again, he wondered how Otis ended up a slave on a crumbling plantation. And even more, why both Otis and Flora stayed after emancipation. If ever two people did not belong in servant roles, it was the two of them.

He felt no rush to return to the house, knowing it would be shrouded in eerie silence. It had been since Anthony became ill. He took his time readying a draft horse, pondering the many mysteries surrounding Langesford.

The new servants had been dismissed lest they disturb the comatose master. The sunny drawing room's doors were closed, the dining room abandoned, as they all ate their meals on the run. The kitchen, study, and his own room were the only ones he used, while Camilla kept to her own path leading to and from the sickroom.

The sound of footsteps descending the stairs stopped him in the gloom of the shuttered foyer. As if his thoughts had conjured her,

Camilla stood in mid-step on the stairs, a large washing pitcher in her hands, a soiled towel tossed over her narrow shoulder. She stared at him a moment, her delicate features pinched by grief and determination.

He felt like an intruder in the home he virtually owned. "I met Otis on his way to town."

Under her silent, glassy stare, he brushed his hair back and buttoned the collar of his shirt. "I'm so sorry, Camilla," sounded empty to his own ears. "Is there anything I can do?"

"Thank you, no. There is nothing more you can do for, or to, us." Her voice could have been cut from a block of ice, increasing the gloomy chill of the room. "If you'll excuse me, I have a great deal to do before the funeral." Then the stranger she'd become said, "With my father gone, I'm afraid your current living arrangement here in the house is quite impossible, Mr. O'Grady."

His eyes narrowed at the use of his surname, but he let her play her hand.

"I'm sure you will be able to make something quite comfortable out of the old overseer's cabin until the legal matters are resolved and you return north."

She's bluffing! He wanted to shout for joy. She hadn't given up. Though they both knew she'd lose, she'd go down fighting.

"It is a shame things didn't work out better for you here, but I'm sure this first cotton crop should cover your investment. And as you said, the renovations were part of your room and board."

So she hadn't ignored the operations of the plantation while seeing Mason, or even nursing her father. Of course, Otis and Flora would have kept her informed. He wanted to applaud, but it would have been inappropriate. And cruel. She obviously didn't know the terms of his partnership agreement with Anthony. *Time enough for that later. Let her have this hand.*

He held his hat to his heart and bowed as he backed away from her. "Of course, Miss Langesford. I'll have Cato and a few hands start on the cabin and move my things over this evening." He met her red-rimmed eyes, willing her to understand. "I never intended to compromise you in any way."

Her flinch told him she understood his reference to their embrace at the hot spring, and his tenderness at the gin house. She nodded, but couldn't hide her trembling chin. "Thank you. I really must go."

He let her have the last word this time, but couldn't resist a smile at her rod-straight back. "Whatever you wish, Cammy," he answered and left the house.

Chapter Fourteen

After wearing mauve silk, Camilla frowned at the old-fashioned black bombazine mourning gown her mother had worn to Brent's funeral. Her nose wrinkled when she pinned on a black veil smelling of dust and the lingering scent of Danielle's musky, *eau de toilette*. Still better to wear these ugly old clothes than starve from the lack of money spent on new ones, she told herself.

With a final tug at the veil and pull on her mother's black kid gloves, she lifted her chin and left the room. The time had come to lay Anthony Langesford between his wife and his only son's marker.

Patrick stood on the veranda, waiting by the rented funeral carriage to follow the hearse to the burial plot. His warm hand on her elbow steadied her recoil from the heavily curtained conveyance. "Would you care for me to ride with you?"

She looked up at him, then back at the mourners lining up to follow her. *Yes!* But she didn't intend to throw away what was left of her reputation by riding alone with a Yankee in a curtained carriage, even to a funeral. "No. Thank you."

He followed her gaze to the curious mourners, then helped her up the step and backed away. He needn't have worried, she thought. In the short ride to the century-old Memorial Hill, Camilla felt the presence of her entire family. Brent next to her, ramrod straight in his gray Confederate uniform. Danielle on the other side, the spicy scent of her vetiver root perfume growing stronger with every turn of the wheels. And on the worn seat across from her, the sad, loving presence of her father. She bit her lips and closed her eyes to keep from seeing the disappointment on all their faces that she had survived them.

As the carriage slowed to approach the hallowed field of the dead, Camilla parted the curtains to view five acres of manicured lawn. The perimeter was fenced by hand-wrought iron gates brought from New Orleans after Danielle's marriage to Anthony nearly twenty-five years ago.

Rows of white stone crosses, tall obeslisks, and stone baskets testified to the long relationship between the land and the Langesford family. Only a fresh mound of dark Georgia clay covered by a tarp marred the perfect landscape.

Anthony and Danielle Langesford's eternal resting places shared a tall pedestal topped by a delicately carved marble angel. And next to the angel, a simple stone marker commemorated the birth and heroic death of their son.

The few of Anthony's old friends still left in the county came to pay their respects; however, his best friend, the elder Bartlett, was sorely missed after he and a distraught Eliza departed for Brazil shortly after Mason's untimely death. In testimony to Anthony's humane treatment, the knoll outside the iron fence was lined with his freed slaves, including Flora and Otis, who Camilla would have welcomed at her side.

The brief ritual of burying the dead was performed by a visiting parson who had never met Anthony, accompanied by the former slaves' low hum of, "*Swing Low, Sweet Chariot,*" in the background. Camilla sighed when a final, "Amen," finished the hollow ceremony and the only thing left to do was feed her father's body to the gaping hole at her feet.

The soloist from the Anglican Church they rarely attended, honored their English heritage with, "*Amazing Grace,*" but Camilla didn't hear the words. Instead, she wondered how, after shedding so many tears in the last four years, she had none left to shed for this man she'd worshipped; yet failed to please all her life. At the end of the song, she laid a single white rose, symbolizing her family's lineage to the English House of Tudor, on the gleaming cherry casket.

Fewer visitors than attended their ball, stopped by the house for the funeral meal. Camilla dutifully played her role of brave, grieving daughter, shaking hands, smiling, enduring sweaty hugs from overdressed mourners, and shallow condolences from petty officials. And through it all, she did her best to ignore the whispers of those betting her failure would be their gain.

She could see their thoughts in their eyes. *Surely the Yankee will return home with his tail between his legs. Camilla will be forced to sell what she can. But where will she go? Who will marry her after living in scandal with a Yankee?* And in the greedy stares of those who'd managed to hide their money in England or France before the war, the certainty that they could pick up pieces of one of Georgia's founding plantations for mere pennies an acre.

They were all gone by early evening, leaving her alone with only Chet Bartlett and Patrick in the gloom of the mourning mansion. Patrick looked tired, and was oddly quiet, while Chet paced the drawing room in wide circles, running his fingers through his sandy hair and muttering to himself.

When Chet cleared his throat for what seemed the twentieth time, followed by the fifteenth clink of Patrick's teacup against its saucer, Camilla wanted to scream. She'd known Chet all her life, and knew more of his secrets than he thought. He had something on his mind. And Patrick never drank tea. She looked at him from lowered eyes. *Why doesn't he leave?*

"Chet," she finally spoke. "Is there something you want to say? Or shall we call Dr. Samuels to treat your throat disorder?"

The tall blond lawyer fingered his collar. "Actually, Camilla. I know how exhausted you must be and all, but ah…well, when your father came to me last month—"

"He saw you last month?" *Why are you surprised he never mentioned it?* She cast a resentful glance in Patrick's direction. Then again, Papa seldom told her about things when they affected her profoundly.

"Yes. Yes, he did. *Ahem.* Well, anyway, he left me clear instructions to make you aware of the contents of his will immediately after his funeral. So you could be prepared."

Her stomach knotted. She'd never seen Chet so upset. "Prepared?"

He coughed dryly and drained his cup. "Well, it's just, well, orphaned daughters such as yourself…and, and widows too…have few legal rights. He didn't want to worry you with his plans for your future."

He droned on, but Camilla's mind focused on, "few legal rights". She was painfully aware that those few rights, while allowing unmarried women to own property, gave them few opportunities to participate in

Doris M. Lemcke

business, especially the business of running a plantation. She knew of one or two widows in the area with sizeable plantations who attempted to balance the dichotomy by marrying again, only to lose all they owned to their philandering new husbands.

But it won't happen to me, she reminded herself. She had no husband to bilk her out of Langesford and would remain unmarried if it meant fulfilling her father's wish to keep it intact—if only until her death. *I am the sole heir. No one can keep it from me.*

She fought a shiver in the warm room. "Do you mean to read me his will now, Chet?" *How could he?* She doubted she'd even comprehend what he said.

The young lawyer stared at the new carpet covering the scarred drawing room floor. "I'm only following your father's wishes."

"It sounds unpleasant."

"He had only your wellbeing in mind."

An auburn eyebrow arched. "Papa's idea of my wellbeing and mine often differed greatly."

"Please," Chet implored, his voice rising with his distress. "It won't take long. Shall we all go into the study?" He took Camilla's arm and nodded at Patrick, who set his half-full teacup on the trunk by the stairs to follow them.

Chet sat on one side of the partners' desk, with Patrick and Camilla sitting in two leather reading chairs flanking the fireplace. He adjusted his reading glasses and opened a folio in the center of the massive desk.

With one last, "Ahem," he raced over the nearly unintelligible legal phrases until he reached the last page. He paused then, took off his glasses and pinched the bridge of his nose. Folding his hands over the document, he explained to Camilla what Patrick already knew.

According to the partnership agreement between your father and...Mr. O'Grady, in the event of Anthony's death, you will inherit the plantation in name only..." He nodded to Patrick. "...while Mr. O'Grady will control of the land and assets, excluding the house and five acres surrounding it."

Camilla sat in dry-eyed shock, her fingers shredding the antique lace edging her handkerchief. Her mind raced. It was clear that while Langesford Plantation remained in the family name, she had no say in how it would be run. *I'll be a boarder in my own home!*

With the allowance Patrick would pay her, she'd be well fed and clothed—just like the slaves—until he sold her land, leaving her alone in a rotting mansion. She glared at him. *And what will he ask in return?*

Patrick's jaw tensed at her heated stare. He swallowed hard and stood, looking down at her. "I never thought we'd use the clause, Camilla. And I didn't know you when we signed the…"

"Partnership," cut him off.

"Yes," he admitted. "When I realized the extent of your father's illness, I couldn't risk Dr…my…investment on a young gir…woman I'd never met."

He knelt on one knee in front of her, covering her cold, unresisting hand with his. "I realize now how capable you are, I'm sure we can work something—."

"Please, Mr. O'Grady," Chet interrupted. "Be seated." His voice cracked when he said, "There is more."

Rebuked, Patrick obeyed and listened as, from the grave, Anthony Langesford made his plans to leave impossible.

Chet read more slowly this time, his orator's voice wavering now and then. "Knowing there are few unmarried young men in our community with the high moral standards and means to support my beloved daughter; and to ensure my descendants continue to possess Langesford in its entirety, it is my hope that Camilla will marry my partner, Patrick O'Grady."

Camilla jumped to her feet, shouting, "This is outrageous!"

Patrick stood too, echoing her outrage. "He can't make me—her—I mean us—marry."

Chet raised a hand. "Of course, you can't be forced to marry, but in the succession clause of your partnership agreement, Mr. O'Grady, your attorney neglected to insert a time-period for you to control the assets in the unfortunate occurrence of your partner's death. Please be seated, both of you. There is still more."

But they remained standing, Camilla's face blanched with shock and Patrick's dark with anger. Chet removed his spectacles again and rubbed his eyes before putting them back on to read: "If my daughter is not wed within thirty days of my death and continues to believe her heritage is a 'dead horse', Langesford plantation will be sold. Proceeds from the sale will first go to tax liens and other creditors. The remainder, after reimbursing Mr. O'Grady's investment, will go to Camilla, to begin the new life she so desires."

Patrick and Camilla both sank back into their chairs as the meaning of the will became clear. If they didn't marry, Langesford would be sold; yet the money would go to the tax collector. They both knew there would be no 'remainder'. She would be penniless as well as homeless, and Patrick would be out of business and up to his neck in debt to Dr. Johnson.

Camilla wondered if she'd prefer penury to being the wife of the enigmatic Yankee whose powerful body radiated suppressed violence—and whose touch made her lose control of her own senses. She couldn't think about it now and wished again to wake up and discover the whole experience was a bad dream. And if not, a clear enough mind to find a way out of her father's trap.

She looked from Chet to Patrick. "I simply cannot comprehend this...this...obscenity proposed by my father. I am going to retire. We can discuss it in the morning."

Turning to Chet, she added, "It's late. You're welcome to spend the night." Then to Patrick, "Good night. Please join us for breakfast in the dining room at seven o'clock." She ripped the mourning snood from her hair and tossed newly-freed curls to stride from the room.

"I still have a few things in my old room," he called after her. "I'll stay there." Though they all knew it was unnecessary, he added with a sly smile, "You wouldn't want to compromise your reputation by spending the night alone in your house with an unmarried man. I'll be your chaperone."

~ * ~

Camilla and Patrick arrived in the dining room at exactly seven o'clock the next morning. She almost smiled at his tired and mussed appearance. A new beard shadowed his usually clean-shaven face, his normally clean and pressed suit was wrinkled, as if he'd sat up in it all night.

She, on the other hand, had taken great care to dress, controlling her hair as much as possible, even using some of her mother's powders to cover the dark circles under her eyes. She'd thrown the black bombazine into a corner of Danielle's wardrobe, ceasing to mourn a father who had sold her to her enemy.

Patrick spoke first. "I doubt you'll believe me, Camilla, but I knew nothing of your father's marriage plans. Whether he lived or died, I planned to leave Langesford after the first crop and go back to Chicago. An annual meeting with Anthony—or you, would have been all the contact I needed for the remainder of our agreement."

She saw the truth in his tired eyes, but it didn't matter. Chet said the will could not be broken. They could either abide by, it or consider Langesford a total loss. "But now if you leave, you'll lose all your investment and have no profits. How unfortunate for you. I, on the other hand, will be put onto the street, a penniless woman with no marketable skills."

"No, no...not at all..." He paused to meet her accusing stare. "Well, yes, I suppose that could be the worst case. But I'm sure you have many marketable skills."

At her raised eyebrow, he added, "I mean. Don't you sew?"

She shrugged. "Strictly utilitarian."

"Cook?"

"Passably."

"Well, I know you're amazing with figures."

"And where would you suggest I secure a position adding and subtracting in Jeffers County? I know cotton, Mr. O'Grady. It's *all* I know."

He sighed. "But well, don't you have family...somewhere...to take you in?"

She gave him a long, disgusted stare and turned to the lawyer who had just entered the room looking as tired and rumpled as Patrick. Feeling no sympathy for either of them, she fluffed her aqua taffeta gown noisily and allowed Chet to seat her at the table already set with fresh linens, coffee, and steaming buttered croissants.

She ignored the food and drink to lean forward and fold her hands on the table. "Well, gentlemen? What do we do now?" And with a sidelong glance at Patrick, "Aside from me becoming a bookkeeper in an

111

---

impoverished county."

Chet shifted nervously in his chair, his expression somber. He looked from her to Patrick and found no relief. After one more annoying clearing of his throat, he said, "Well, you could follow the...letter of the will...but not the intent."

Silence prevailed as both parties considered the objectionable option. Patrick took a deep breath as if to speak, but Camilla's interest was piqued. *Could there be a way out?* "Go on."

Chet brightened. "Well, the letter of the will requires you to marry within one month of Anthony's death."

"I remember what it said," Patrick snapped.

Camilla gave him a sharp look and Chet sipped his coffee before going on. "Well, in the legal world there are two interpretations of documents such as these. As I said, the marriage is the literal interpretation. However, knowing the Colonel as I did, I believe the intent was to produce heirs to the plantation." He raised his hands as if to ward off blows. "But no one can force nature in that respect."

He flushed and coughed. "What I mean is that a quick and simple ceremony will comply with the ownership codicil of the will. Whether or not there are heirs would be, ah, well...up to you."

Camilla stood. "Chet, are you suggesting we actually abide by this dictum?"

"Arranged marriages have been common throughout the centuries," he answered hastily. "And a marriage, even in name only, is the only thing that will keep you both from financial ruin."

Camilla clung to the words, "in name only" and narrowed her gaze. "You mean only on paper. Once signed and sealed, we could go our own ways?"

It appealed to her. A marriage on paper would give her social respectability. *But can I trust the Yankee to keep from exercising his conjugal rights?* She credited the tingle she felt in her belly to hunger and sat down, avoiding Patrick's gaze by reaching for a croissant.

Then Patrick stood, his mouth set in an ominous line, his eyes nearly black with suppressed anger. He looked at her first, then Chet, his disgust at the proposal obvious. "Chet, do you know how many of these arranged marriages *throughout the centuries* have led to despair, disease and even crime?" Then, as if he'd read her thoughts, he said to Camilla, "And aren't you afraid I'll ravish you as soon as our agreement is 'signed and sealed'?"

Camilla licked a tiny bit of warm butter from her fingertip. "Can you deny it has occurred to you?"

Successfully baited, Patrick raised his voice. "As you well know *Miss Langesford*, I have never forced a woman into my arms. And I do not plan to begin now. If it is a marriage in name only you want, a marriage in name only is what you'll get." This time, it was his napkin that hit the table like a gauntlet. "But you may live to regret it."

"I doubt it."

"Time will tell."

Determined not to show her fear that he may be right, she put down the French pastry and faced Chet. "It's settled then. Arrange it. But not a day before necessary." And to Patrick, "I cannot rush from mourning black to wedding white. It would be too much, even for me."

Chapter Fifteen

Nearly two weeks after a private wedding with only Flora, Otis and Chet as witnesses, Camilla dressed for her torturous evening meal with her husband. She frowned at the nightly ordeal. They would enter the dining room by separate entrances and sit at opposite ends of the long table. Except for a few comments about the cotton crop or household business, they barely spoke and their eyes seldom met. When they did, Camilla always looked away first.

At first the game seemed to amuse him. Now, his long, brooding looks and the tightness in his voice when he said her name, spoke of passions growing more impatient by the day. And her own body often betrayed her to flush with the same impatience.

Both Patrick and Flora had warned her of the danger of fighting the ways of nature between a man and a woman. And just this morning, after she and Patrick exchanged barbs over how best to handle a conflict between the new hands, Flora told her, "Don't test the man. His patience is running thin."

He'd caught her arm later in the day as they passed each other by the stable, and forced her to look at him. "We need to talk, Camilla," he said. "If we're going to be partners, we can't keep up this charade. Our *situation* may not be of our making, or to our liking, but to get out of this with a few dollars in our pockets, we need to trust each other."

Trust? She doubted an ounce of trust still existed in her body. Anyone she'd ever loved, excluding Flora, Otis, and Brent, had used her for their own selfish purposes. And she refused to sell her body for room and board, no matter how tempting the offer.

Still, Patrick had a point. Even their own people seemed to notice their tension and had begun to play them against each other. Perhaps she and Patrick could better define the terms of their partnership and reach some common ground—for Langesford's sake.

She'd already chosen to protect her heart by resigning herself to spinsterhood, but it seemed unfair to impose a celibate life on a man as virile as Patrick. He'd made no secret of his desire for her. And since she feared her own weakness to his obvious charms, concluded it may be time for a change in perspective.

Perhaps, if she took a more active role in the operations, she could encourage him to leave Langesford in her hands, freeing him and pursue other entertainments. At the very least, it could divert any amorous intentions he had for her.

Her head suddenly throbbed at the thought of Patrick with Miss Watson, the mysterious nurse, in Savannah, but saw no alternative. *Well, there's no time like the present.* She steeled herself for her first step into Anthony's bedroom.

Other than fresh paint and varnish on the floor, as well as a new draperies and bedding, the room hadn't changed. Anthony's old bureau still stood in its corner, as if waiting for her to sort out his belongings. His mirror and all the familiar decanters from his toilet still stood on top of it—including the hideous brown bottle of Dr. Johnson's Indian Blood Syrup.

Her eyes blurred with sudden tears recalling her father standing at that same bureau on the night of the ball, the vile concoction in his hand. She also remembered his nearly instant transformation from a weak and worn out gentleman soldier to a proud and dignified survivor. Shakespeare's tragic Hamlet whispered in her head,

> *"Diseases desperate grown,*
> *By desperate alliances are relieved,*
> *Or not at all."*

Like her father, Camilla's strength was spent. If this savage elixir would give her the strength to form an alliance with her enemy, so be it. Her feet moved swiftly across the room, where she separated the nearly full bottle from the others. She uncorked it and held her breath to take a long swallow. But instead of simply shaking her head as he'd done, she dropped the bottle, barely missing the new Isfahan rug as she held onto the bureau, the liquid burning its way down her throat, setting her stomach on fire.

She stood there a long moment, gasping for breath, unable to even call for help. Then as suddenly as the pain began, it ended. Her head felt clear, unburdened by worry, grief or anger, as if she'd not a care in the world. She looked down to see her once trembling hands calm, and a face in Anthony's oval mirror that looked—young.

She touched her suddenly warm cheek and smiled back at the glittering reflection of her eyes. A miracle, she thought. *But for how long?* No matter, she felt strong for the first time in months, maybe years—finally ready to battle her, "partner."

As usual, they sat at the table in silence. But this evening, she felt suddenly gay and drained her glass of wine before Flora served the entrée. Patrick walked the length of the table to refill her glass, which she raised to her lips before he'd retaken his seat.

Patrick stood again when Flora arrived bearing a tray laden with bowls and a steaming tureen. He offered, "Let me help you, Flora. It's only the two of us, no need to walk the distance with this burden? I'll take this and you can bring my setting closer to my wife."

Camilla looked up at his emphasis of the word, "wife" and caught the worried frown on her maid's face. For weeks, they'd had a practice of dining as far away from each other as possible, as quickly as possible. Flora's rush to follow his order, rankled.

Patrick settled into his new seat on Camilla's right and Flora served him a steaming bowl of Cajun stew made from oysters, fresh off the boats from New Orleans. Her eyebrows raised when she turned to Camilla. "Are you unwell, Miz Cammy?" she asked, love and concern softening her voice.

Camilla finished her second glass of wine and smiled up at her. "I'm wonderful, Florie. You know how I love oysters."

Flora looked at her a long moment, then carefully set Camilla's bowl in front of her, saying, *"Bon appétit."*

The sounds of their spoons against the old English china punctuated the uncomfortable silence at the table until Camilla grimaced and dropped hers noisily back into the bowl. She frowned disapprovingly at Patrick, his spoon halfway to his lips. "How can you sit there and gobble this obviously tainted food?"

He looked up, one eyebrow raised. "What are you talking about?"

"Just what I said. The stew is bitter. Unfit to eat." She grimaced at his nearly empty bowl. "You apparently have the discerning taste of a field hand." Energy surged through her veins and she sprang to her feet, upsetting the chair in the process.

The room grew suddenly warm, the walls spun around her, while the floor rose and fell like an ocean wave. She opened her arms but found nothing to steady her until Patrick's chair also hit the floor, his hand wrapping around her forearm and pulling her toward him. He held her against him until the room righted again.

"Cammy, what's wrong?" he whispered against her cheek.

Afraid the vapors would return if she shook her head, she slurred, "I'd...don't know. I've never felt...like this before." But she'd seen it often enough with her mother. She'd passed her mother's spells off as ploys to refocus the waning attention of her guests on her.

Still woozy and more than a little frightened that her mother's madness had passed on to her, she didn't protest when he scooped her up and carried her to the horsehair sofa in the study.

She closed her eyes against the sight of his strong chin, the evening beard darkening his cheeks. When his hands withdrew and she felt the firm cushion beneath her, she opened them, happy to find the study right side up. Then she risked turning her head and met Patrick's worried gaze from where he sat upon the tufted footstool at her side.

Genuine concern replaced the sly, secret smile he usually wore. "It must have been the stew," she whispered, her mouth suddenly dry. *But he ate the same thing and looks perfectly fine. More perfect than fine.* She almost giggled.

Her heart racing, she turned her gaze upward, suddenly fascinated by the candlelight bouncing from the chandelier's crystal prisms against the pressed tin ceiling. *So beautiful. Like dancing fairies.*

Suddenly, the shining prisms grew brighter and she saw herself dancing with Patrick under the same sparkling ceiling, twirling...and twirling...within his strong arms. She closed her eyes. "Are you certain

117

your food…?"

A soft voice she barely recognized answered, "Delicious, as always."

The fairies dancing in her mind quieted and she risked opening her eyes again. The chandelier was just a chandelier, the flickering lights on the ceiling, simply reflections from the hearth and candles. She struggled to sit up but thought better of it when the room began to shift again, though more like a ship rolling on a gentle sea this time. "How strange. There must have been something wrong with it. Perhaps only some of the oysters were tainted."

Then her fingers went numb, and she felt light….no, weightless, like a feather caught in the breeze. Only his hand holding hers kept her from rising off the couch toward the fairies who had returned to dance above her head.

"Perhaps your system is just upset. You have been through a great deal, darling."

His voice sounded strange, as if it came from inside her head instead of from lips that were…so close to hers.

"No, I was just fine, before…" *No, you haven't been 'fine' since you first fell into this man's arms.* "It must have been the wine. I stood up too fast, and lost my balance."

He chuckled, low and seductive, "Well, you did hit it a little hard…and fast." A warm hand touched her forehead. "And you don't seem to have a fever."

How could that be? With only embers in the grate, heat seemed to consume her body. Her cheeks burned. The heavy taffeta gown with its layers of petticoats, weighted her down, and her legs felt like sausages in silk-stocking casings.

Gentle fingers touched her eyelids, closing them. "The best thing to do when this happens is close your eyes and sleep for a bit. You didn't drink a great deal. Let it wear off, and you'll be…"

She woke with a start after what seemed only a moment, but was nearly an hour according to the mantle clock. Patrick was still holding her hand. "Welcome back, Sleeping Beauty," he said, his fingers caressing her now cool forehead.

"I don't know…what…happened." she said, pushing his hand away.

"I'm fine now. Really."

It was a lie and they both knew it. Her heart beat fast and her skin tingled down to her toes. Still, she struggled first to sit up and then to stand, succeeding only with the aid of Patrick's arm around her waist.

Once on her feet, she froze in the circle of his arms, fascinated by the rise and fall of his chest beneath the white silk shirt he'd worn the night he first came to Langesford. But now, he'd removed the cravat and unbuttoned the top two pearl buttons.

Her fingers ached to open just one more button and touch the tanned skin and soft black hair she knew lay beneath it—again.

His eyes glinted like polished silver beneath the candles and his lips, their color, shape, the way they moved, fascinated her when he spoke, "Do you want to go to your room?"

"My room?" The thought of her tiny bed and another lonely night tossing with disturbing dreams, repelled her. As quickly as the surge of energy had come, it deserted her, until she suddenly felt exhausted.

She leaned against him feeling his heart beat against her cheek, its rhythm matching her own racing pulse. She looked up to read a new expression in his eyes. It wasn't anger, or amusement. Not sympathy or sorrow. Just...something...else. Her breath disturbed a small black curl at the nape of his neck. "I don't know."

He cupped her cheek with his palm, caressing it with his thumb. His lips close to hers, he suggested, "Let's take a little walk to clear your head. Then we need to talk."

"Why?"

One arm still around her waist, he sighed. "I mean we have danced around each other long enough. I didn't favor this farce of a marriage to begin with. It's time we sorted some things out."

The fogginess in her brain began to fade and Camilla's legs felt stronger. She pulled away, shaking her head. "I can't. I'm confused. Since the night I ki...Mason died, and then Papa... I've barely felt alive. And now I'm a married woman."

She looked up at him, surprised to see the sharp angles of his face relaxed, the set of his mouth softer, sympathetic. "I know I've made mistakes, but I don't know where to turn. What to do. Who to trust." Then the tears came.

With a low moan, Patrick wrapped her in his arms, rubbing her back and resting his chin on the top of her head as she cried into his shirt one more time. "Turn to me Cammy," he whispered. "Trust me."

The tenderness in his voice slowed her sobs and her fingers spread across his damp chest. Then she raised her head to meet his waiting lips with her own. This kiss was different from their brief encounter at the hot spring, and his tenderness the night she killed Mason. This time they were husband and wife. But it mattered little. Her body controlled her mind. She could no longer fight her heart, no matter that he would surely break it.

She pressed against him as he showered kisses on her eyelids, her cheeks, her ears, and again claimed her lips until they opened for him. Their tongues touched and a shudder rippled through her body in response.

He broke the kiss. Stepping back, his eyes shining with both passion and pain. "I won't force you, Camilla. Are you certain?"

Her mind had never seemed so clear. She ran her fingers across his brow, along the side of his cheek, the curve of his jaw, to rest on his lips. "You are my husband."

He kissed those fingertips and smiled. "I've been your husband for weeks. Why the sudden change of mind? If I'd known my kisses were so good, I'd have done this long ago."

She stiffened in his arms. "Are you mocking me?"

"Not at all." he chuckled, pulling her close again, his hand tracing lazy circles up and down her back until she relaxed against him. "I just don't want to be accused of rape in the morning."

"Nor I of seducing a Yankee for his money."

He chuckled against her neck. "Welcome back, Cammy. Agreed. No accusations—and no regrets?"

"None." She smiled, guiding his hand to the base of her breast. "Just hurry."

After another long, slow kiss, he smiled. "No, my darling, the one thing you don't want me to do is hurry."

She felt like a kitten in his arms as he carried her upstairs. When he reached her room, she stopped him. "No."

To the sudden cloud darkening his eyes, she pointed down the hall to the master bedroom. "There is where we belong."

~ * ~

Early rays of the sun peeking through the lace curtains woke Camilla. She stretched, feeling rested for the first time in months—no ever. She closed her eyes to savor the moment and opened them to meet pewter-gray eyes glittering with…what?

Patrick's mussed hair made him look more like a boy than a man nearly ten years her senior. He leaned on one elbow and brushed aside her own wild curls. "We'll have to keep our children's hair short or they'll never be able to see." He smiled and kissed her forehead. "Good morning, Mrs. O'Grady."

His jaw set at her silence.

Caressing the dark stubble on his cheeks, she smiled. "Don't be angry. I can always tell, you know."

He lay back on his pillow, hands behind his head. "You can? How?"

She sat up, making no effort to cover the breasts that had pleased him so thoroughly the night before. "Is something wrong? There shouldn't be secrets between husbands and wives. Tell me what you're feeling."

She straddled him then, her tongue circling his brown nipple as his had hers, until he pulled her down on top of him. "Enough talk, woman. Let me show you what I'm feeling. Now." His big hands circled her tiny waist and settled her over his erection like a sheath covering a blade.

This time, with no barrier to be broken, no tightness as her body adjusted to his size, she moved with him, rocking slowly, her hands kneading his chest as his steadied her on the huge four-poster bed that had known the births, marriages, and deaths of four generations of her family.

This time, with the sun streaming in the window, she appreciated the beauty of his body and saw his appreciation of hers in his eyes. We were made for this, she thought, arching her back to accept his release.

But he delayed his own pleasure to pull away, and roll her onto her back. His arousal caressed the nub of her femininity while his tongue and lips traced a line from her pouting mouth to the puckered tips of her breasts; across the ridges of her ribs, down the slope of her soft belly to the moist, musky oasis of her femininity.

"Oh," she gasped as his teasing tongue entered her—there.

"Shh," he whispered, cupping her buttocks in his big hands as he slid into her again. This time her legs wrapped around his waist and they rocked together to the beat of the blood pumping through their veins.

He moved slowly inside her, touching a place she never knew existed until she couldn't identify where his body ended and hers began. Then it came, the wave of pleasure she never imagined a human could feel. A light brighter than the shining prisms of the lamp in the study pierced the darkness behind her eyelids. Her legs and arms tightened around him, imprisoning him until he stiffened and she felt the heat of his soul pouring into her.

When their bodies relaxed, she opened her eyes to see tears in his. He lowered himself to press his lips between her legs, returning a moment later to her mouth, letting her taste them both on his tongue. Then he shifted his weight, leaning on his elbow beside her. "Did I hurt you?" he asked, concern deepening his voice.

His big, tanned hand moved across her breast, settling over it like a perfectly fitting glove. She remembered the way the muscles in his arms quivered as he'd balanced his weight above her; the way he moved over her like a panther, his tongue soft, soothing words purring from deep in his throat; and the satisfied sigh at his release that had quickened her blood. "No, only the first time."

She laughed, smoothing her fingertips over a sudden furrow in his forehead. "Don't worry." She imitated Flora's Creole accent. "Eet ees only the barrier of childhood, *cheri*."

He smiled and winked. "Oh, you're a woman, all right. What else did your wonderful French slave teach you?"

She tossed her hair back and leaned into him. "We'll just have to see what I can learn from you."

"Well, my dear, I seem to have no plans for the rest of my life. How about you?"

She giggled against him, "I'll have to check my calendar, but I think I'm free."

Chapter Sixteen

After living so many years in a nightmare, the next two months seemed like a dream. She and Patrick rode out together early each morning to oversee the maturing, picking, and ginning of their cotton. Next to him, dark and masterful on his black stallion, Camilla felt like a fairytale princess with her knight in shining armor. Even the rehired, former slaves smiled and waved in greeting when they passed by. But it's better than a fairytale, she mused. Because the people waving at them were free.

Now they stood together at the gin house they'd saved from their neighbors' torches what seemed like a lifetime ago. "Well, we're done," Patrick said soberly when the last of the ginned cotton bales were loaded, ready to be floated up the river to Savannah for shipment.

Camilla leaned against him, wishing her father could be there to see it. But perhaps he did, she thought. Through her eyes. "You don't seem overly happy about it," she said.

"I'm more relieved. I'll be happy when this is sold and the money is in the bank. I don't know how you planters stand the worry of producing this crop. So many things can go wrong in this business and ruin you."

"Typical Yankee!" She laughed. "You want guarantees. Don't you know we Southerners are all gamblers at heart?"

He kissed the palm of her gloved hand. "Mayhap, but this thing isn't over until the bank is credited and the bill collectors are away from our door."

She primped her netted hair and drawled, "Money is your area. Ah am just a farm girl."

"I don't expect you were ever 'just' anything." He chuckled, then nodded toward the wagons. "I'm going with them to Savannah. With the new ocean cable, our factor there will get the best prices from London in a short time."

The sudden chill at being separated from him reminded her that all dreams end eventually, and not all fairytales have happy endings. She rubbed her arms against a sudden chill, remembering Flora's warning, "Gooseflesh in the sunlight means someone just walked over your future grave, girl—never good news."

"Must you go?" she asked. "Can no one else handle the business in Savannah?"

He leaned over to kiss her. "Never trust another to do what you can. I'll leave at first light and be back within the week. In fact, why don't you come with me? We never had a wedding trip."

The offer tempted her, but the new hands needed oversight and there were her father's papers to assemble. "No, I have too much to do here. We can honeymoon later, when the money is in the bank."

"You're more Yankee than you think, my darling."

His smile took her breath away and she knew she'd never get tired of him calling her darling. "It must rub off, *my* darling." She laughed and accepted his help mounting Misty.

They made love enough that night to last the separation, but Camilla couldn't escape the sense of gloom she'd felt at the gin house. Even with Patrick's arms around her, the scent of his body filling her senses, she worried.

He'd traveled extensively, lived in exciting cities, did exciting things with lovely, well dressed women. *Like the nurse in Savannah who has such wonderful taste in clothes.* How long, she wondered, before he became bored with her?

She couldn't deceive herself into thinking she could keep him interested forever; though she couldn't imagine a better place to be than wrapped in his strong arms until she turned into a wrinkled old lady. She kissed his shoulder without waking him, praying he'd finish his business in Savannah early and come back to her so they could live happily ever after.

~ * ~

From the moment Patrick disappeared down the magnolia grove, Camilla drove the new and rehired house workers to clean the mansion from top to bottom before his return. She planned to use the last few days to empty the sacks of her father's old papers into leather pouches for storage in the empty linen room next to the study. The tunnel to the old summer kitchen was closer, just behind the newly-restored bookcase, but she disliked the damp and gloom where her ancestors had hidden from the Cherokee who burned the original house.

She could think of her father now without the heart-wrenching grief she'd felt at first, or the angry resentment following the reading of his will. He'd loved her in his own way and she would miss him when she and Patrick fulfilled his wish for heirs to his family's legacy.

His clothes and toiletries (excluding the discarded bottle of Indian Blood Syrup) had already been sent to the little-used ballroom to make room for Patrick's things. The rosewood armoire now stood where Anthony's battered old chest of drawers had been. When Patrick returned, the heavy, dark furnishings of the master suite would be replaced with lighter colors more suitable to a feminine lodger.

But when she opened the double doors to the study, memories of arguing with her father the night Patrick arrived assaulted her. Her father's voice repeating her own words, "A dead horse," whispered in the silent room.

He'd never spoken to her with such a tone of disappointment...no, *disgust,* and now it seemed all she could hear. It accused her of being a traitor to her own family. A coward who preferred to run away rather than pick herself up from the ashes of her way of life.

I am neither traitor nor coward, she told herself. I am as much a soldier as my father and brother. It ran in her blood. She'd faced marauding soldiers carrying torches, outsmarted occupying troops with plunder on their minds, and she'd kept Langesford in one piece—along with those who depended on it, while her brother and father were away.

Now, Papa, Maman and Brent were gone. Though she'd never have chosen the path of a forced marriage, she believed fate had led Patrick to her for a purpose. Together they would take the reins of Langesford Plantation and make it a success—without the curse of slavery.

But without Patrick, the sad mist of her father's ghost seemed to linger in the room. She left the doors open behind her and approached the partners' desk warily, frowning again at the portrait still hanging above the hearth. "Your time is over," she whispered to the imaginary sprite on the wall, vowing to banish it to the cookhouse cellar as soon as Otis could manage it.

"There's no point in putting this off," she told herself, adding Flora's favorite scold, "Thinkin' don't get it done."

With a deep breath, she tied a kerchief around her head and smoothed what seemed to be the only clean apron in the house. The one she hadn't touched since Anthony died. The tiny lump of paper deep inside the pocket reminded her of his last words, "Brent is not a traitor." And finally, her father's last breath of life, "Beecher knows. Stop him."

She reached into the apron, pulling out her father's last bequest—the unintelligible note hidden in her mother's brush. Pulling the tiny square parchment from the apron, she again felt the warning chill of someone treading on her grave, but ignored it to open the note and lay it on the pristine surface of the desk.

Lowering herself into the chair on her side of the partner's desk, she wondered why her father used his last moments of life to give the note to her. Who is Beecher, she again wondered? And what am I supposed to stop him from doing? She leaned over the note, placing Anthony's magnifying glass over the tiny script. Nothing had changed. The symbols, lines and random letters still made no sense.

She rationalized the fever, laudanum, and weakness in his lungs, along with the horrors of war, had addled her dear Papa's mind. But the memory of his eyes, so clear they seemed to peer into her soul, the warning in his voice, and the pressure of his hand on hers, had shaken her to the core.

Admitting the waste of time and energy in asking questions without answers, she turned from the note to pull open the first of two deep drawers on the side of the desk her father had used for such a short time. It fought her, jammed nearly full of folded and crumpled receipts, letters and notes. She piled them on top of the desk. At the bottom of the drawer, like a treasure buried beneath the trash of generations, lay a neat stack of ledgers.

Pushing the loose papers onto Patrick's side of the desk, she started with the most recent. Her fingers glided over her father's precise, Spenserian script. The whorled capitals, flourished endings and precise numbering spoke of the man her father had once been. Lord of his domain and master of his world. A world he'd watched die in front of him. The ledger entries ended the day Patrick arrived.

Tears blurred her vision when she closed the drawer, knowing the pile of messy papers belonged to Patrick and not her father. So where was the Langesford History? She opened all the drawers, finding nothing of Anthony's dated after Patrick arrived. What had he been doing all these months? Perhaps he only dreamed of writing the colorful history of his family that settled Georgia with James Ogelthorpe. Somehow, it didn't surprise her.

She carefully set the ledgers back into their drawer, finding an old journal tucked among them. One of her mother's, she noted. There were several up in her old room, all written in her own hand, in High French. Something she'd never taught her daughter to read.

Something I never wanted to read, she thought. She tossed it back in with the ledgers and returned to separating the more recent receipts and bills from the older ones. While it would take all day to sort it into her own system, she smiled, thinking how pleased Patrick would be with her efforts.

She'd barely noticed the growing shadows, or the stiffness settling into her shoulders when a thump against the open oak door startled her. "Find anything interesting?"

Scar, after seeing so many strangers coming and going, had ceased being a protector, settling happily for companion on a soft rug at Camilla's side. But at the sound of the stranger's voice, the old dog stood and growled menacingly.

Camilla's hand settled on Scar's neck. "Down," she ordered and with one last growl, he settled back to the floor. She looked up to see a thin silhouette of an old man bent over a walking stick blocking the afternoon light from the hall. She shaded her eyes.

The voice sounded familiar but she couldn't match it to the oddly shaped creature in her doorway. A wounded veteran, perhaps. A cripple. After nearly two years, wounded and maimed soldiers were still trickling back home from Yankee prisons or hospitals. She happily offered aid or

127

Doris M. Lemcke

refuge, and never turned anyone from their door.

From the foul odor carried on the breeze from the open doors, she guessed him to be an out of work vagrant needing a job. She rose to step around Scar and greet him. "Is there something I can do for you?" she asked. "I'm Mrs.—"

"I know who you are, Cammy." He stepped into the room without invitation, pausing only when Scar stood again, bared his teeth, and growled more menacingly. "Call him off!" filled the room.

Surprised at the force behind the voice of such a small, crippled body, it took a moment to realize he'd called her by her childhood nickname. She ordered Scar to stay, but he disobeyed to stand by her side, the hair on the back of his neck erect in warning.

Camilla's body tensed when the little man came within an arm's length of her. Reeking of alcohol and the swamp, he cocked a head sparsely covered with clumps of greasy, graying hair and appraised her with an almost toothless grin. Spittle ran down his chin when he spoke, "Don't play the innocent with me. The gold. Tell me where it is."

She recoiled, fighting the revulsion churning her stomach. She didn't recognize his scarred face, distorted by anger and hatred, but the ice-cold, pale blue eyes assessing her, and the disapproving leer were all too familiar. She backed up against the desk. *It can't be!* "Mssr. An...toine?"

A familiar laugh chilled her in the warm room. She'd heard it often enough, along with Danielle's giggle, drifting from her mother's room following a portrait sitting.

"Arthur, actually," he sneered. "And the last name is Beecher. Though none of you 'aristocrats' give a rat's ass about a servant's surname."

Camilla ducked when he waved the gnarled cane close to her face. "But the French name and phony accent got me into all the best mansions in the south—and some of the best Southern tail too. I especially enjoyed your mother's."

She cringed at the image of him with her mother. But while he had revolted her as a child, as a woman, she now understood her mother's attraction to him. Barely taller than the diminutive Danielle, he'd been trim and elegant then. His wavy blond hair, though long by normal standards, fell neatly to just above his shoulders. And he turned nearly all the female heads with his haughty strut, sensuous smile, and French accent.

But even then, he made Camilla's flesh crawl, albeit for entirely different reasons. Now, she couldn't look away from the beast he'd become. The once straight patrician nose twisted to one side and rough, poorly-healed burn scars covered his high cheekbones. His back bent oddly forward, tilting to the left, as if healing badly after a break, and his leering smile was now a jack-o-lantern grimace.

Beecher! She remembered the fear in her father's voice when he'd said the name. And he wanted gold. Mason's voice accusing Brent of, "living like a king in Mexico on the Denver gold," taunted her. *What were they talking about?*

But she couldn't worry about gold now. All the servants were assigned to work in other parts of the house while she faced a lunatic who blocked her only exit. Her father had once kept a Colt revolver in the middle drawer of his desk. *His old desk. The one the Yankees burned.* She prayed he'd transferred it to this one.

She edged around the side of the desk, back toward the drawer. "I don't know what you're talking about Mssr., I mean *Mister Beecher*. If that's really your name. Do you think we'd still be here if we had the Denver gold? I...mean *any* gold."

His grin at her slip of the tongue displayed broken and blackened teeth. "I never mentioned Denver, you little slut. I knew it! It's real. Give me the map. I know you have it."

"I don't know what you're talking about." This time she meant it.

His twisted hand reached for her wrist, stopping only at Scar's snarl and bared teeth. Beecher stepped back, giving her time to step within reach of the center drawer. But it was only a moment before he stepped closer exhaling fetid breath into her face from the other side of the desk.

"Oh yes you do. I listened from the grate in your room when your father and his Rebel friends met in this very room to plan the robbery. They were about to discuss their escape route when you found me and ruined it all."

She remembered the night only too well. Her mother's farewell ball for Brent. But it's true purpose was to showcase her portrait to Jeffers' elite. Beecher had only painted Camilla's likeness at Anthony's insistence, and Danielle forced Camilla to wear the ridiculous dress from the painting.

Shortly before midnight, she'd broken a champagne flute and her mother banished her from the ballroom, sending her to her room. She'd found her door ajar—the artist couched in a corner by her bed, an ear pressed to the floor vent. She screamed in surprise and he lunged at her, tearing her skirt. Then her father, two generals, four lieutenants, and the Secretary of the Confederate Treasury burst in, dragging him away.

They never told her where they sent him, but looking at the abuse his body had taken, Camp Oglethorpe came to mind. The greatest shame of the noble Confederacy and the greatest fear of any Yankee prisoner.

Now, fully understanding his madness and her danger, she tried to calm the beast he'd become. "They said you left out of shame for trying to steal my virtue."

His body contorted in hysterical laughter. "Your...virtue? Why would I want the fat little princess when I had the queen?" he bellowed. As quickly as the mania came, it ended. "Oh, I left all right, straight for Camp Oglethorpe in Macon. Two years later when the Hell-hole filled up, I got *promoted* to Andersonville—to be further starved, tortured, and beaten, until I became this disgusting creature you see before you."

He cocked his head again. "But I survived. And now it's time for you to pay for the sins of the father and of the son."

"What do you mean?" covered the whisper of a well-oiled drawer opening.

White, foamy spittle dripped from the corner of Beecher's mouth. "I mean your brother looted the Denver Mint of a fortune in gold bars. They planned to stash it along the way if they got in trouble and marked the place on a map. Your father agreed to give it to me at the swamp if I spared your life, but the fool died first. I know he gave it to you and I want it. I earned it. It's mine."

He stepped forward, stopping only when Scar barked and leaped to stand between them, teeth again bared. Beecher grinned and pulled a two-shot Remington derringer from his jacket pocket, pointing it at Camilla. "Give me the map and I may let you and your nasty dog here, live."

Her fingers closed around the Colt in the drawer. To divert his gaze while she hid the gun in the folds of her skirt, she looked up at her portrait. "Maybe it's hidden behind the portrait. I don't want anything to do with it. If there is a map there you can have it."

"Whore," he shouted and stepped forward. "You're lying...ahhh."

He fell with a crashing thud under the weight of a massive, brown body with snapping yellow teeth. The tiny gun flew from his grasp and Scar, stood on his chest, looking at Camilla for further instructions.

"Scar, release," told the old slave catcher he'd done his job. He jumped off Beecher to sit proudly in front of his mistress.

Beecher raised a hand to his bleeding cheek and stared at Camilla, pointing a six-shooter at his face.

"You're a liar," she hissed. *And Mason too.* "My brother and father were honorable men. If they robbed the Yankee vault, they did it for their country. And if Brent never returned, then he died a hero."

She kicked a soiled rag toward him to staunch his bleeding. "Now, leave my house. If you're even in the county when my husband returns, he'll have you jailed—or worse."

Beecher sat up, pressing the calico rag to his battered cheek. "Your husband," he laughed, eyes bulging. "You don't expect me to believe the so-called marriage of yours to Inspector O'Grady is real, do you? He's either duped you or you're in cahoots. He needs you for the map and you need him to get the gold out."

"What...?" Her voice shook, but her hands remained steady on the gun.

"Oh, poor thing," he crowed. "You mean you don't know your husband worked for Allen Pinkerton as a spy during the war?"

He struggled clumsily to get up, frowning when Camilla kicked the cane out of his reach. "Then you don't know he led the investigation to find the gold. But he failed...until I told him about your family of thieves and murderers."

"What are you saying?" Her voice cracked, and he smiled as he crawled like a crab on one knee and one hand to retrieve his walking stick.

Finally standing upright, he faced her. "What I'm saying stupid cow, is that O'Grady never gave up on the case. He came here based on information I gave him. We're partners and he's not going to cheat me out of what's mine."

His smile turned sly after placing the seed of doubt in her mind. "If you don't believe me, ask him about Miss Watkins. I believe she retired to Savannah some time back. They were quite the pair of spies. Nearly as good as me in getting into all the best balls."

He started toward her, hesitating at the renewed rumble in Scar's throat, and the pistol in Camilla's now shaking hands. "What pitiful fools you Langesfords are. Your mother, lost in fairytales. Your brother who fancied himself a knight in shining armor, and your father who dared think they could rob a Federal mint across the continent and get away with it. But you are the biggest fool of all, *Cammy,* for marrying the man who's been obsessed with finding it for years."

He backed out of the room, a grimace of a smile on his battered face. "But it's mine. You won't keep me from it."

"Liar!" she cried through angry tears flowing down her face. Her arm ached from the weight of the gun as she followed him out the front doors to watch him climb awkwardly onto a worn out nag. "And you're insane." she called after him. "My brother and father were heroes and my husband is a businessman."

She watched until the horse turned from the magnolia-lined drive. The weight of the gun still in her hand and the stiffness in her shoulders told her she hadn't dreamed the bizarre encounter. *No, the nightmare is just beginning.* Closing the doors to the office behind her this time, she lit a lantern rather than lower the chandelier.

She wiped at the crust of her drying tears, finally understanding her father's dying words. Beecher had just accused Brent of being a traitor and a thief, and while Papa had denied he was a traitor—he hadn't denied his son was a thief.

The ache in her heart told her Beecher's story held some truth. If so, he may also have told her the truth about Patrick. But she needed proof. Turning to the littered desk, she swept the loose papers onto the floor. They meant nothing now. Langesford meant nothing. *She* meant nothing. Her fingers reached down to the fraying note in her apron. Shaking fingers carefully smoothed it out, holding it up to the light of the lantern. The curving lines and markings made sense now. *It's the map!*

If Beecher was right, it was a map of the Western territories. Twisting it in her hands, she admitted some of the inverted 'v's could be symbols for mountains, and the wavy lines, rivers. They looked familiar, but she couldn't decipher the hash marks and 'x's scattered singly and in clusters.

With the energy of a mad woman, she tore through the books lining the new shelves until she found a geography primer with a folded map inside titled, Indian Territories. The thin page ripped out easily and she spread it out next to Anthony's map, pulling the lantern closer to the pages.

The markings were nearly identical. Her lips pursed as her fingers traced the maze of rivers and trails on her father's note, and again on the larger map detailing an area of Northeastern New Mexico.

Her heart beat fast with both excitement and dread. Instead of sacrificing his life in battle, her brother had given his life for a pile of gold. And her father, by refusing to give Beecher the map, had done the same. How many more lives would it take?

She thought bitterly of her brave brother proudly setting out on his adventure to save a doomed cause with Yankee gold. He'd died somewhere in the wilderness drawn on the map. She considered asking for Patrick's help—until she remembered Beecher's cruel accusations.

Her legs suddenly gave out and she sank back into the chair to retch into the dirty mop water bucket. Her mind reeled as violently as her stomach. The man she'd trusted to put her life back together had used her to find a hidden treasure! In many ways, he was more a monster than Beecher. He'd stolen her trust, her virtue, and her heart, leaving nothing left of her to live. Yet she continued to draw breath without an actual desire or reason to. God could indeed be cruel.

Wiping her eyes on the soiled apron, she accepted logic over the screams of denial coming from her breaking heart. *Inspector O'Grady.* The hatred in Beecher's voice and his words, could not be dismissed as madness. He'd already sunk too far into the lowest level of humanity to bother lying.

She thought then of Patrick's insistence on renovating the house—*obviously a ruse to search it from top to bottom.* Of his long conversations with her father about the war—a *ploy to learn about*

Brent's secret mission. Of introducing her father to Lucille—*using feminine wiles to learn his deepest secrets.* And finally, of convincing him to use Dr. Johnson's Indian Blood Syrup. *Drugging (or poisoning) a dying man to weaken his will.*

And she'd drunk it too. But Patrick didn't know that. Had he also put something in her food the night they first made love? *Surely, he wasn't so cruel.* While her heart denied it, logic told her that where there is greed, anything is possible. His love for her was simply a performance to expose her brother's crime—or, if Beecher was right, to claim the gold for himself. *And Miss Watkins?*

Why hadn't she listened to her instincts? She'd seen the anger hiding behind those stormy eyes. *The danger.* But she'd ignored it, thinking her love would heal the pain she also saw there. Good Lord, she was as pitiful as her mother; waiting for a knight in shining armor to save her from the meaningless monotony of her life. But it appeared that love didn't conquer anything. She cursed herself for being the stupid fool she was.

Sitting in the lantern's tiny circle of light, her anger turned outward. She may have lost…everything, but *he* hadn't won. She could see to it he never found his gold. With one last look at the map, she stepped over to the empty fire grate, lit one of the long matches and set the tiny flame to a corner of the fine parchment. She watched it burn until the flame threatened her fingertips before tossing it into the ashes from the night before. The map from the primer followed, obliterating all trace of her family's shameful legacy.

She ignored Flora's call to come to supper, pleading work. But instead of neatly scribing receipts into ledgers, she stirred the ashes and sat at the desk, a ghost in the deepening gloom. Precious hours passed, but time didn't matter. Neither did past sadness or brief happiness.

Only the present mattered. She had no family. No money. No property. In satisfying her father's will to marry Patrick, he now owned Langesford, including the clothes on her back. He'd even taken away her family name.

She'd been granted the wish she'd voiced only months ago. The tether to the dead horse called Langesford was cut. The freedom she'd so vehemently wished for awaited her. Empty now of all emotion save survival, she rose. Time was critical. Patrick would be back within the week.

Chapter Seventeen

She met Flora in the kitchen, where the older woman sipped coffee in the waning light. Her voice hoarse, she asked, "Florie, please come to my old room," and turned, knowing the faithful servant would follow her up the back stairs.

Flora froze in mid-step when she saw a worn satchel on top of the bed. Tears filled her eyes. "Looks like someone is about to take a trip."

Camilla nodded to the woman she loved more than any member of her family, and held her hands. "A man came to the house today and told me some terrible things about Brent and Papa and…" She swallowed hard, "And…Patrick."

"Don't believe these bad things, *cheri*," Flora cautioned. "Your father and Brent, they were good men. They did what they felt was right—even if for the wrong cause." Her voice lowered. "And your Yankee, he loves you. More than I think he even knows. You are healing him. Who is this man who told you these t'ings?"

Camilla wanted to believe her, but Beecher knew too much about her family—and Patrick. Her father's map confirmed it. "No. A lie is what I've been living for the last six years. The man was Mssr. Antoine. Remember, he came to paint the family portraits?"

Flora's face puckered. "*Mon Dieu*, I remember him only too well."

Camilla wrapped her arms around Flora's shoulders. "He came here today. I barely recognized him," she explained. "He's insane, but I know with certainty that what he told me is true. Because of it, I must leave."

"What are you saying, child?" The old woman pulled away, her hazel eyes hardened to the color of amber. "You cannot run away from the home and the man you love because of lies from the depraved man

136

who ruined your parents' marriage." Her fingers bit into Camilla's shoulder. "Now you tell me what this...this monster said to you."

Beyond tears now, Camilla's voice cracked. "His real name is Arthur Beecher and he told me they—Beecher and Patrick—and the...the nurse from Washington, were spies for the Yankees. During Maman's going away ball for Brent, Mssr...Beecher hid in my room, listening through the floor vent to Papa and the others planning a raid on the Denver Mint. They caught him and sent him to Camp Oglethorpe."

Flora touched the crucifix at her throat and dropped heavily to the bed. Camilla sat beside her, suddenly calm after retelling Beecher's horrible tale. "He said Patrick was an investigator for the Federals and is here to find it...the gold...for himself."

Eyes wide, Flora whispered, "Eske se vre," in her mother's Haitian dialect. "This cannot be." But Camilla understood enough of the old tongue to know the lie. "No, it is true, isn't it?" Camilla whispered. "About Maman and that...beast. And what father and the other men were planning that night."

Flora's silence confirmed it. Unable to look at the grief on her face, Camilla turned to begin her packing. "You don't have to lie any longer, Flory. Even as a child, I understood things were not right between Papa and Maman. When I was older and...the artist came, I saw the changes in her. When he left, I thought she grieved for Brent, but it was for Antoine...Beecher. I found her journal after she died. She planned to run away with him.

"But they caught him and put him in prison. When he got out, he went to Patrick with what he heard that night. They're partners and they think I have a map that can lead them to the gold."

"No!" Flora squeezed Camilla's hand. "You must not believe this monster over the man who loves you. He has longed for you from the first day, when he realized you were not a child. And you felt it the moment you fell into his arms. You must wait until he returns. You must hear him out."

Camilla's eyes also filled with tears. "No, I can't Florie, because I've seen the map. It's all true. I must leave before he returns."

Flora removed the tiny crucifix from her neck and kissed it, whispering, "The sins of the fathers are visited on the children to the third and fourth generations." She fastened the antique silver chain around Camilla's neck. "This will protect you. What do you want me to do?"

"I am leaving tonight."

She gasped, "Mon Dieu, qu'est-ce, que c'est? What is this plan of yours? Where will you go? What will you do?"

Until speaking of her mother, Camilla had no idea where to go. Though Danielle had spoken longingly about her, "beautiful city," she'd often said without grief that her father was dead. She also spoke of a rice plantation outside the city, *Belle Rivière.* Perhaps it survived the war and there were family members, old friends, neighbors...someone who could help her create a new life in the ancient city.

She suddenly felt strong again. "I'm going to New Orleans." Puzzled by the look of horror on Flora's face, she explained, "The Trémon family is one of the oldest in Louisiana. There must be some cousins there who will help me find work. I know it's been a long time, but can you recall anyone?"

Flora swayed, steadying herself on the footboard of the old bed. Her breathing shallow, she shook her head at the hope in Camilla's eyes. "No, *cheri.* There is no one. Your Maman was the only child of an only child. The line is...dead. No one will help you there!"

But Camilla had set her mind on the plan. She shrugged off her disappointment to answer, "Well perhaps someone will recognize the name. And I remember Maman receiving a letter once, from a New Orleans attorney. The stationery and script were so beautiful, I remember it still. The firm of Marchaud et Marchaud, Esquire." Hope glittered through her tears. "I'm adept at figures. Perhaps he can help me find work in a shop."

She again took Flora's hand, pleading for understanding. "But for you and Otis, I have nothing left here. It all belongs to Pat—the Yankee. Maybe it will be enough for him and he'll let my brother's memory lie in peace." Then with a weak smile, she added, "I feel as if I am going home. I know someone there will help me start my new life."

A new life. How long had she wished for it? Dreamed of it? As much as she wanted to comfort Flora, there was no time to waste. It was past midnight and she had only a few hours to reach the Omer station before the only train to Savannah left at six o'clock. She could purchase a ticket to New Orleans there.

She hugged Flora. "Please, help me. We need to hurry. I'll finish packing if you ask Otis to hitch up the buckboard."

Red-rimmed eyes blinked at her. "La volonté de Dieu," before leaving left the room.

Not God's will, Camilla thought. *Mine.* She was finished allowing other people to control her life with lies. She stuffed her old tapestry bag with practical, if worn, clothes from her old life—before Patrick.

Grateful she hadn't shredded the black bombazine dress from her father's funeral, she retrieved it from the floor of Danielle's chifforobe to examine it. It was old and wrinkled, but still quality. And roomy enough for her to wear all three of her petticoats under it, without a cage.

What she couldn't carry in the bag, she would wear, and the extra layers would add matronly girth to her slender waistline. She'd also wear a weeping veil and carry her heavy black shawl. New Orleans would be warm, so there was no need of anything heavier.

She counted the few dollars she had left in the house. A little over twenty. Not much more than train fare. She'd have to be careful where she slept and what she ate.

"Do not worry 'bout money, child," a resilient Flora told her from the hall. She stepped inside the room carrying a plain muslin underskirt with a ruffle at the hem. "Put this on."

"But I'm wearing three petticoats now. I won't be able to sit with all this padding."

"Yes, but this is worth the weight."

Camilla took it from her, noting it weighed more than her bag. "What is this made of?"

Flora deftly slit a small length of seam along a ruffle, reached inside and fished out a Double Eagle twenty-dollar gold piece. Camilla gasped and bent to feel the rest of the ruffles. Each of ten ruffle pockets held an identical gold piece. "How—?"

Flora closed Camilla's fingers around the coin. "Never mind. They are yours, *ma petite*. And the petticoat is safer than the purse or corset." Pure love replaced the sadness in her eyes. "Now put it on, or you will be late for the train."

Otis drove the matched pair of draft horses in silence under a full moon in a sky so clear the stars seemed close enough to touch. She wondered if they would look the same in New Orleans, or if the smoke from the city would dim their light.

The depot stood silent in the grayness between night and day. She was unable to meet Otis' eyes when he helped her from the wagon. "Thank you," she said against his neck before willing her feet to run the long yards to the station. She stopped to catch her breath as well as her courage beneath an ancient oak dripping with Spanish moss. A glance at the brightening sky told her it was an acceptable time for a widow to purchase a ticket for Savannah.

She knocked on the sill, waking the napping attendant. Her breath caught when her childhood playmate wearing the station manager's uniform, picked up a crutch to limp over to her. She breathed easier when his once lively blue eyes glazed over at yet another woman in widow's weeds. "One ticket to Savannah please, no return," she asked with a husky voice.

He shrugged, exchanged her gold piece for the ticket and turned away, adding over his shoulder, "Train only stops a couple minutes, ma'am. And leaves at six o'clock on the dot. Don't get many passengers this time o' day, so it won't wait if you ain't ready."

Camilla smiled behind her veil. Alan Hadley wouldn't remember selling this ticket at all, much less to her. She wished the young man who had left a leg at Fredericksburg, sweet dreams, and sat on the bench under an old Georgia pine to await her train.

Chapter Eighteen

The train scheduled to leave for Savannah promptly at six o'clock didn't arrive until half past the hour. Camilla smelled the sulfur and saw the huge column of black smoke long before the train came into view. Old, ugly, and dirty, with only two passenger cars attached to the coal car, it approached the platform with an ear-splitting scream of the steam whistle.

The conductor, a lean, string of a man, tossed a bag of mail off the steps of the first passenger car, calling, "Board," in a hoarse voice. Whether disinclined to lose his head of steam or to simply toy with the few boarding passengers, the engineer never came to a complete stop. A carpetbagger in a suit too large for his bony frame rushed ahead of Camilla to board and she missed her chance to reach the step.

With the last car approaching, she struggled with her skirt and bag to make the life-threatening leap. Teetering with one foot balanced on the moving step, her free hand grasping for the railing, a strong arm scooped her up onto the safety of the vestibule, holding her until she was steady on her feet. When Camilla looked up to thank him, the warning screech of the locomotive's whistle covered her cry of alarm.

"Easy ma'am," Patrick said softly. "O'Connor likes to play with his passengers, but he wouldn't have left you behind."

A look at the gravel roadbed told them the train had picked up speed. If he didn't jump soon, he'd risk his neck. Still, he hesitated. "Are you all right?"

"Y-yes, I'm fine," Camilla stammered, her voice barely a squeak. She certainly didn't need her husband on the same train she'd planned for her escape.

Patrick cocked his head to the side as if studying her, then tipped a finger to his hat, grabbed his leather bag, and disappeared into the steam.

Still standing on the vestibule, she watched him disappear into the past as the train hurled her into the future. She touched the place on her arm where he'd steadied her, and turned to enter the car. Grateful for the layers of padding under her dress, she settled into the only available seat on a hard wood bench.

She wondered how a tall man like Patrick could possibly endure sitting in such a cramped manner. Then she noticed there were no men in her car. Only women and children. One, about her own age, nursed an infant while a toddler pulled at her skirts. Suddenly her own breasts ached from the milk she'd never give a child, and her arms to hold the babes she'd hoped to give Patrick. She tore her gaze from the woman she envied most in the world, raising her veil to brush a clean white handkerchief at the corner of her eye.

"There, there, my dear," came from across the narrow aisle. "You mustn't continue grieving." A heavy woman with blonde hair and bright blue eyes leaned toward her. "It's bad for the digestion and the blood."

"Pardon me?" Camilla scooted back toward the grimy window when the young mother rose and the plump raven in rustling black silk crossed the aisle to sit beside her.

"Judith Carter." She introduced herself, holding out a hand covered with black lace finger gloves. She touched Camilla's worn black kid glove. "Please pardon me. I sometimes forget how reserved Southerners are and speak as though I have already been introduced.

"My husband and I have recently come down from Boston to do missionary work among the Negroes. We have been preaching in the area near Langesford Plantation. Do you know the place?"

She laughed before answering her own question. "But of course you must, if you are from around here, I suppose."

New at lying, Camilla answered warily, "Yes, I have heard of it."

Judith smiled. "I thought so. Poor tragic family those Langesfords. I understand the only son died early in the war and both master and mistress have now passed as well." She patted Camilla's hand. "But I hear their daughter is newly married. Perhaps prosperity will come back to them now."

Judith's honest gaze fixed on Camilla's exposed face. Then she finished, "But often the worst tragedy results in the greatest blessings."

Camilla adjusted the veil as a shield against the woman's knowing gaze. "Thank you, Mrs. Carter," she answered coolly. "But in my experience, one tragedy simply leads to another."

The older woman wouldn't be put off so easily. "You may think so now, but one day you may realize otherwise. I have buried two husbands and three children, and seen the suffering of countless young men in the war." Tiny lines under her eyes and mouth appeared when her smile faded, but she recovered quickly. "I assume you are newly widowed?"

How bold! But Camilla couldn't refuse her. *After all it is my disguise.* "Yes," she answered writing her story as she went along. "My husband has only recently died after years as an invalid...from the war."

Judith's eyes narrowed as Camilla again reached up under the veil to dab at an imaginary tear this time. "I see."

The doubt flickering across her expressive features prompted Camilla to clarify further. If she could convince this chatterbox of her fabricated situation, perhaps she'd leave her alone. "It happened about a month ago," she began, looking out the window at the familiar countryside she'd likely never see again.

"I...lost our...farm after my husband died," she continued, "So I have decided to seek relatives in New Orleans and perhaps find work there." She gasped. *I just told her where I'm going.*

Mrs. Carter smiled and again patted her hand. "Good for you, child," she said rather too loudly for Camilla's comfort. "So many young widows have resigned themselves to mourning the past forever. It is marvelous to find someone with the spunk to pick up and start over."

"Yes. It will be good to start over." Camilla sighed, hoping the wish would make it true. When Mrs. Carter made no move to go back to her seat, she asked, "You mentioned your husband, Mrs. Carter. Is he traveling with you?"

The woman's smile took years off her face. "Why land, yes, Mrs....what did you say your name is?"

Understanding that some grain of truth lent credibility to a story, while other facts could be changed, Camilla lowered her gaze to the bag in her lap. There, delicately carved in the gilded clasp, were the initials

"C.L." "Carrie" she said, adding with emphasis, "Carrie Lange."

One blonde eyebrow raised. "Well, Carrie, this train has separate cars for men and women. The children stay with the women of course." She winked. "The men say it is out of deference for their comfort because of the cigar smoking, crude language, and bad manners of some men; but I am certain it's because they wish to be left to their pursuits without the burden of conscience women would put on them."

Camilla nodded. It did seem men had the power to relegate women to whatever position or place they deemed suitable—in the name of their own welfare. Yet she'd read of pioneer women in Texas who had fought off Indians while the men were gone to war. *They expect women to bear children and fight Indians, but don't think they can tolerate a little cigar smoke.*

Her mood brightened as they approached the Savannah station. She'd always imagined it as an enchanted place with tall buildings and parks, and shining brick roads. The reality disappointed her as the train rolled up to what looked like a hastily constructed wood depot not much larger than the Omer station.

Judith tapped her arm. "Better hurry dear, if you want to get a decent room and some food before the others beat you to it."

Camilla realized she hadn't eaten since breakfast the previous day. She accepted Judith's logic when the passengers pushed and shoved like children in their hurry to book a room at the tiny hostel behind the station.

Despite her hunger, she hung back, sickened by the smell and crush of so many bodies crowding into such a small place. Her comfort could come later. First, she had to secure passage to New Orleans.

She approached the ticket window, speaking above the din. "Excuse me, I would like to book passage on the next train to New Orleans."

The clerk looked down at her. "Ain't no train goin' to New Orleans from here."

Her heart fell, until she noticed his smirk. She straightened her back and raised her veil to show the insolent creature his remark didn't amuse her. "Then please tell me the routes available for me to get to New Orleans."

After a long look at her stern expression, he blushed. "Sorry,

Ma'am."

Ma'am? Do I look so old? So used up?

He shuffled papers off to the side of the counter to spread out a map. "Let's see, now." He placed a finger on their current location. "There are two routes you can take, ma'am."

She tapped her foot impatiently as he explained in a slow monotone, "One is by way of Macon, changing trains in Columbus, Montgomery, and Mobile." He paused to let her digest the information before continuing. "An' at Mobile, you kin take a steamer to the Pontchartrain railroad, which is only an hour from New Orleans."

He peered at her delicate build. "But sometimes the passage from Mobile is choppy and people become seasick, especially those without much experience in water carriage."

"And the other route?" she snapped.

He slowly refolded the map and opened another. "The other route is by rail via Chattanooga, where you board the Memphis and Charleston Railroad, stopping at Grand Junction and Canton, and then right on into New Orleans."

He tapped his dull pencil on the paper to conclude, "This route is longer, but there ain't so many changes." Then, as if understanding her disapproving glances toward the now-crowded hostel, he added, "They also have bigger benches and sleeping cars for an extra fee."

She kept a sweating man in a plaid waistcoat and soiled cravat waiting as she weighed the advantages of both routes. The cheaper, more circuitous one via Mobile with a change to the steamer sounded exciting, but it would give her more exposure at various stations. And she didn't like the way this clerk stared at her, as if memorizing her features. What if others did the same and were asked later if they recalled a young widow traveling alone?

The simpler route on one railroad without complicated transfers or expensive public lodging sounded the better of her two choices. She smiled. "I'll take the longer trip then. There's no need for a sleeping compartment. What is the fare?"

The clerk looked around at the emptying station and winked. "The same for both. Ten dollars." He nodded toward the no vacancy sign posted on the door of the hostel. You can be on your way at half past eleven tonight and arrive in New Orleans not long after the Pontchartrain."

She'd only have the rest of the evening to wait, eliminating her need to buy a bed for the night. Judith had hinted many of them had vermin in the sheets. Now, she could simply rest her head against the back of one of the waiting benches under the awning of the busy station until her train boarded.

A few hours later, Judith found her there and offered her a sack. "Fresh turkey and rice pudding," she announced. "Guaranteed to build your blood and put meat on your bones. You'll need it for the next leg of your journey to the steamer. Did you find an available bed?"

Camilla accepted the food gratefully. "No, I'm not staying over. There's a train out tonight. It will take me directly to New Orleans. It's a little longer, but I'll have an earlier start."

Answering Judith's worried expression, she explained, "I have never been able to abide travel by water." It wasn't really a lie, because she'd never traveled by water—or anything else, truth be told. The war had imprisoned her within the Jeffers County lines.

Judith considered the wisdom of her choice and finally nodded. "I understand, my dear. Water passage takes a strong constitution." Then she brightened. "We are meeting several other families at Mobile, but should be in New Orleans for a week or so, at the St. Charles Hotel. From there we embark on a riverboat to St. Louis and Independence, where we'll form a wagon train headed west to minister to the Indians near Santa Fe, New Mexico."

A worried frown clouded her features as she pressed a piece of paper into Camilla's hand and closed her fingers over it. "This is the address of the St. Charles. If you need—anything—you come to us."

"Thank you, but I really don't—"

"Child," Judith interrupted, sounding much like Flora—with a Yankee twang instead of a Creole drawl. "It's easy to see you've never been to a big city. And New Orleans is different from any other big city in the world. It is important to know someone there. Promise me you'll come to us if you need help."

She rose and squeezed Camilla's hand. "I'm sure there will be no need. But humor me and take the address." She waved across the platform at a tall man with bushy dark hair and a full beard. "Father gets impatient when I wander." She winked. "Go with God...Carrie."

Though Judith's hovering presence was a little unnerving, Camilla felt strangely alone without her. Suddenly sticky in her heavy clothing, she parted with another portion of her coin to purchase a small bucket of water and took it to the outhouse for ladies behind the station.

There, she removed three of the unweighted petticoats and sponged her chest and underarms, emerging slightly more refreshed for the exciting last phase of her journey to freedom.

The evening passed quickly on the bench as Camilla breathed deeply of the fresh ocean breeze and enjoyed watching the people come and go along the busy thoroughfare. Still, when someone approached, she pretended to focus on the book she'd taken from Patrick's new library. *Gulliver's Travels* seemed appropriate as she embarked on her own trip to a strange world called New Orleans.

She boarded the train at precisely half-past eleven. This locomotive, much larger and cleaner than the Omer train, included several passenger cars and a dining car. Families sat together on leather upholstered seats with button tufting for comfort.

Eyes wide, she took in the polished wood paneling and wide windows, as well as fashionable couples chatting on the enclosed vestibule platforms between the cars. Her mouth watered as vendors walked up and down the aisle selling cakes and breads before they rolled out of the station. This was no ten-dollar passage. Her heart thanked the attendant who had apologized for his rudeness by giving her the more comfortable trip at a discount.

She found a seat near the rear of the car and sacrificed part of her ticket savings for a large piece of gingerbread to nibble during the trip. Since she'd be sleeping in this car as well, she looked forward to a decent breakfast and settled back in her seat.

After the final, "All 'board," echoed through the station, the mammoth beast rolled out of the Savannah station. She slept to the gentle sway of the car, waking to find the countryside had turned from lush coastal grasses to verdant forests and rolling, green hills.

"Well, good morning," a cheerful, female voice greeted her.

Camilla blinked to focus on a young woman roughly her own age, with the kind of flawless beauty even other women noticed. A plumed, sky-blue hat matched her eyes and accented her blonde hair; but the woman's blue satin gown featuring a scooping neckline and short sleeves dripping with lace, shocked her. Where she came from, such fashions were for evening wear only.

Camilla's gaze drifted to the loosely woven white lace finger gloves showing long, slender fingers tipped with manicured nails painted…red. Her breath caught to see a harlot's hand on the body of a woman dressed like a princess, with the face of an angel.

"You've been sleeping a long time," the girl continued, her eyes sparkling with mischief. "I had to check now and then to see if you were breathing. I don't want to be responsible for a dead body next to me."

"Oh." Camilla pulled away from the scent of the woman's spicy toilet water—a scent she recognized on her father's shirts when he returned from Savannah. But she couldn't hold this friendly young woman's poor choice of perfume against her.

"I'm sorry. I'm afraid I must have dozed off a while."

"A while?" the girl chirped. "You missed breakfast and luncheon."

Camilla's face fell. The gingerbread in the napkin on her lap would have to last for hours until dinner. She moaned. "I so looked forward to the dining car."

"Well, no fear," her companion winked. "I thought you might be hungry when you woke up so I bought a little extra cornbread and saved you some of my chicken."

Camilla warmed to the kindness in her eyes. "How kind of you, ah…."

"Lucy," she responded. "Just call me Lucy."

"Lucy," Camilla repeated. *Just first names.* She liked it. She held out her own rough hand with broken, unpainted nails. "And my name is Carrie," she said with a note of finality that made Lucy smile.

Chapter Nineteen

Three days later, right on schedule, the train crossed the marshes of Lake Pontchartrain on little more than rails built upon earth mounds in the swamp. Camilla stared in speechless wonder at white and pink birds flying in a cloudless blue sky above a lake reflecting the greens and browns of the surrounding Cyprus marshes. The tropical paradise enchanted her. *This is what Eden must have looked like before the Fall!*

After a five-mile trek across the lake serving as New Orleans port to the Gulf of Mexico, the Pontchartrain Railroad pulled into its station on St. Peter's Street. There, the tropical paradise gave way to a city teeming with human life.

Her senses filled with the earthy scents of silt and fish, along with coal and wood smoke from the huge stacks on both river and ocean-going ships. Nearly every dock was filled with giant paddle-wheeled steamboats resembling floating mansions. She even saw an ironclad, lurking low in the water outside the mouth of the river like an ancient sea serpent.

The train slowed to a noisy stop in the heart of the old city and the aroma of exotic spices from cooking pots sitting right out in the street replaced the smell of the waterfront. Vendors hawked the quality of their crabs and shrimp in languages she'd never heard, sounding like a symphony. She didn't need to understand the words to know it was the sound of *real* life, not the romantic fantasy of plantation life. Hope swelled in her heart for the first time since she'd faced Anthony Beecher.

Now and then, Camilla recognized a mixture of the high French Danielle spoke in public, and the soft, Creole patois she and Flora slipped into when they thought they were alone. It mixed with the other languages of sailors and laborers from around the world, holding Camilla motionless in wonder.

After forty years, The View Carré looked exactly as Flora described it. She now understood why the old, "Creole-of-Color" referred to her home city as a "queen." Then as quickly as it came, wonder turned to fear. Once again, she'd been given what she asked for. And once again, she had no idea what to do with it.

Panic cramped her stomach *Where now?* If she left the train, she'd surely be lost. But if she didn't, where would it take her before the conductor realized she didn't have a ticket?

Lucy nudged her. "Carrie, if you don't get off here you'll have to pay more passage at the next station. I thought you wanted to find your Creole lawyer?"

Her new friend's voice pulled her out of her fugue. "Yes, I mean, no. I mean I don't want to pay more. My Maman's family had a home here." She rose to pick up her bag, leaving the mourning veil on the seat as she followed Lucy off the train.

The girl disappeared quickly into the throngs of workers, passengers and vendors until Camilla walked alone in the middle of the bustling, dockside street. With each step, the din grew louder until she stopped in mid-step, with absolutely no idea what direction to go. She turned in tiny circles, the noise, colors, and jostling pedestrians made her head spin until she closed her eyes to keep from fainting.

"Bel pain pa-tate, bel pain pa-tate, Madame. Ou-eou le bel pain pa-tate?" The voice came from a tiny, brown-skinned woman next to her. In her hands, she offered a "lovely" sweet potato pie from a wicker basket.

I understood her! Grateful for the little interest she'd taken in her mother's native tongue, she reached into her purse and handed the woman a nickel in exchange for the fragrant pastry wrapped in a white napkin. It tasted as delicious as it smelled.

"Oh, good, you're still here," came from Lucy's now familiar sultry voice. An older, heavier woman dressed in an outlandish, multi-colored striped silk dress accompanied her. Her jet-black hair glistened in the sun and despite her girth, she carried herself like a queen in the jewel-toned gown with white feathers rimming a daringly low bodice.

"Carrie, this is my Auntie Kate," Lucy introduced the woman. "She has a house here in the Quarter near Basin St. I'm going to be work...er, staying there. I thought perhaps she could help you locate your long-lost solicitor." She beamed. "Auntie Kate knows anyone in New Orleans worth knowing."

Once again giving thanks for the guiding hands leading her to her new life, Camilla wiped crumbs from her fingers onto the napkin before extending it. "How do you do, Mrs.—"

"Holliday, dear," the older woman replied in a deep, raspy voice. "Kate Holliday. Just call me Kate." Violet-colored eyes smiled, along with perfect teeth and dimples at the corners of her ruby lips. Then she went to the point. "Lucy told me you are from Georgia, searching for members of your mother's family through a Creole attorney."

The amount of information Lucy shared with Kate rankled, but she allowed the girl's good intentions. Perhaps Kate Holliday could help her find her grandfather's attorney, as well as an inexpensive place to stay.

"Yes..." she answered, pausing at the shrill whistle of the departing train.

When it quieted, Kate covered Camilla's hand with one bearing rings of different jewels on all her fingers. "Come now, girls. Let us get away from this dirty place to somewhere more suitable for genteel conversation."

They followed her the few blocks into the heart of the French Market to sit comfortably under a bright umbrella while the city fairly flowed right by them. Kate ordered *cafe-au-lait* for all of them.

Camilla rarely drank coffee, mainly because of its scarcity. But before the war, Flora and Danielle had enjoyed a deep, rich blend each morning. Later in the day, they paused for this lightened, half-coffee, half-cream mixture that looked more like dessert than a beverage.

Kate settled on a sturdy hand-wrought iron chair similar to the abundant iron lacework on the merchant buildings and homes. She held the tiny cup in her plump, ring-covered fingers, her brilliant eyes fixed on Camilla. "Just who is the attorney you seek?"

Camilla met her gaze squarely. "It is—Marchaud, I think. It was the surname of a witness on her parents' marriage certificate folded inside the Langesford family Bible.

She was fascinated by the fancy script and musical pronunciation of

151

the name Marchaud. For a time, he played the role of Prince Charming in her little-girl fantasies, riding up on his steed to whisk her away to his castle in the magical city called New Orleans.

"A Mssr. Marchaud witnessed my parents' marriage. I'm hoping he'll have some knowledge of my grandfather, Philippe Trémon, or any remaining members of my family."

The older woman coughed as if the smooth drink had gone down a wrong pipe. Her hand trembled slightly as she put the demitasse down and took a deep breath. "Philippe Trémon was your grandfather?"

Camilla put her own cup down, wincing when it clattered on the hammered glass tabletop. "Yes. Have you heard of him?

Kate cleared her throat. "Yes, I have heard of him. It is the name of one of the premier Creole families."

She covered Camilla's hand with hers, the sun glinting off a blood-red ruby on her third finger. Her husky voice turned soft, "I'm afraid, my dear, the years have taken a toll on your family. Your grandfather died many years ago by his own hand, shortly after his daughter, your mother…" Her smile faded to say the name, "Danielle…left the city." She lowered her lashes, hiding her beautiful eyes. "I met her once. A beautiful…girl. So you tell me she lives in Georgia." Looking closely at Camilla, she added, "What an unlikely place for her to go."

"I suppose so," Camilla offered. "She and my father met when he visited Belle Rivière on business. They fell in love at first sight and married before he returned home."

"Love at first sight," Kate echoed. Then softer, "So unlike Princess Danielle.

Hope sprang into Camilla's heart. "Did you know my mother? What was she like when she was young?" A hundred more questions threatened to erupt. How she longed to know the kind of girl her mother had been in her cherished home.

She stopped at Kate's raised hand. "I met her once or twice," was all she offered. "A beautiful young woman. She could have had anyone, young or old, in the city. And how is she now?"

Camilla's romantic picture of her parents' courtship faded. "She's gone. A few years ago." To Kate's raised eyebrow, she lied, "Of a fever. Medical supplies were in short supply at the time…"

"Dear, dear," Kate shook her head and patted Camilla's hand. "What sadness you have survived in your short life. I am so sorry, but like your grandfather and your poor Maman, René Marchaud, is also gone. Yellow Fever back in…'57, as I recall. He and I were briefly… oh my, it is getting late. That is perhaps a story for another time."

Camilla's heart fell when Kate rose. Marchaud was her only hope to find her family, but Kate seemed familiar with other Creoles in New Orleans. Perhaps she could recommend her to a dressmaker or shop owner needing a clerk. But she still had one last hope Is there perhaps a son of the senior Marchaud?" *Could he have taken over the practice?*

A shadow crossed Kate's features as she addressed the hope brightening Camilla's eyes. "Yes, *cheri*, there is a son. Delmont. But he is not the man his father was. He cares only for the dollar and isn't inclined to help people unless it benefits him—greatly."

She leaned back, taking a long sip of her cooling coffee before shaking her head. "I do not recommend soliciting him for information. Perhaps, as you said, it is best to start over—fresh, so to speak"

But Camilla shook her head. "You don't understand. I must know for certain if there is someone even close to my family. I cannot believe Mssr. Marchaud is so mercenary as to withhold such important information simply because my family is no longer wealthy." Heat rushed up her cheeks and she set her lips. Nothing would keep her from locating the attorney, Delmont Marchaud.

Kate sighed in the face of her determination. "As you wish. His office and home are nearby. The address is 129 Rue de Royale. Known as Royal St. to non-Creoles." Her eyes narrowed. "But, pardon my saying so, shouldn't you find lodging to prepare yourself for such an important meeting?"

Camilla flushed with embarrassment this time. She'd been on a train for three days, sleeping in her clothes, and had been forced to use her skirt as a napkin.

She couldn't look at Kate, the bright-colored peacock, or the radiant Lucy, who looked like she'd just stepped from a salon in a yellow frock that highlighted her sunlit hair. "Of course. I would like to rest a short while. And a bath would feel heavenly."

Kate smiled as shrewd violet eyes met mischievous blue ones across the table. "My dear," she told Lucy. "You arrived early, and I'm afraid your room isn't quite ready. I had planned to put you up at the St. Louis for a few days, but worried about your reputation, staying there unaccompanied. But now, if Miss…"

"Mrs." Camilla interjected. "I'm married…I mean I used to be married. I'm a widow…now. My husband died." *Of course he did, you ninny, or you wouldn't be a widow.* She wanted to die of humiliation right there, but kept on babbling, "Lange. My name is Lange. I'm Carrie Lange."

Kate's smile never wavered, but those expressive eyes narrowed slightly, a superbly etched eyebrow rose. "Yes, well, Mrs. Lange, would you be so kind as to share a suite at the St. Louis Hotel with my…niece until my house is ready? With a widow as her companion, dear Lucy will have no worries about her reputation, and you will be assured the safety of a companion who is familiar with the city."

"Well, I don't know," Camilla hesitated. "My funds are rather limited. I'd thought more a rooming house of some sort."

Kate waved a fleshy arm. "Nonsense. You are a descendant of the early Creoles. What better place for you to stay than the magnificent French hotel. And since you will be doing me a favor by chaperoning my niece, I will show my gratitude by making it a welcome gift for you."

She winked conspiratorially. "Besides, you mustn't let Delmont suspect you are not wealthy. A room at the St. Louis will make him all the more willing to help you…and collect his fat fee."

Lucy's angelic face glowed when she touched Camilla's arm. "Oh, please say yes, Carrie," she urged. "This way I won't have to stay in my hotel room the whole time for fear someone would think me the wrong type of woman."

Practicality trumped Camilla's pride. Everything in this city cost money. Her meager purse and the coins in her petticoat couldn't keep her long if Delmont Marchaud took his time locating her family. She smiled at the two generous and kind women. "Well, I suppose it does make sense. But I will repay you when I'm able."

Lucy squealed in delight and Kate hailed the waiter for a plate of luscious croissants.

The St. Louis Hotel, built in competition with the American, St. Charles Hotel two squares above Canal St. was only a short walk from their cafe, but Kate insisted they take a cab. She complained her expensive kid-skin slippers, not her girth, prevented her from walking any distance.

Only a short time later, the fine, chestnut gelding stopped in front of six graceful columns with ironwork galleries overlooking the busy thoroughfare. Five stories rose from the street level with a gracefully curving rotunda extending from the second floor. The wonder continued when a splendidly liveried Negro came outside to open the cab doors and help them onto the shaded tile, *banquette.*

Stepping onto the slightly raised walk that remained dry even during the many storms of summer, Camilla realized how her mother must have missed her home. It was so unlike anything Georgia had to offer. Her mouth formed an astonished, "O," when they stepped inside the hotel, where the interior thrilled her as much as the outside.

Velvet and silk draperies hung in a lobby as big as Langesford's house. Giant oil paintings hung on tapestry-covered walls, and chairs of pure, white damask invited the weary to rest in them. Merchants, planters, bankers, and women dressed in silks, strolled through the lobby. And while Kate registered them, she saw richly furnished parlors with giant bars and tables where both men and women consumed liquor, even at this early hour.

She was still trying to hide her shock when Kate approached them. "Well, my dears, here are the keys to your adjoining rooms. Rooms 221 and 223," she explained. "I have already ordered up baths for you both.

"She cocked her head at Camilla's battered, tapestry bag. "I see you travel light, Carrie dear. There is an excellent modiste here in the hotel. A Creole of color. Quadroon, I believe. She can copy even a Paris gown for a modest price. And if you are short on funds, I can offer—"

This kind woman had done enough for her already and hopefully she wouldn't have to take advantage of her generosity for more than a day or two. At the risk of sounding ungrateful, she answered, "No, I'm fine thank you. My mourning period is well over and I have a dress that will suffice nicely for my meeting with Mssr. Marchaud. I'll freshen it today."

Kate's doubt showed plainly in her brief frown, but she recovered quickly. "As you wish. I'll leave you two to your ablutions." Then to Lucy, "I've set up an account for you until you come to my house. Feel free to use it for whatever you need—within reason of course."

Lucy nodded. "Of course, Auntie Kate," she oozed. "I understand perfectly. And you know I'm good for it." She tossed her curls, took Camilla's arm and started toward the staircase.

"Good for it?" Camilla repeated with a sidelong glance at Kate, her arms folded across her nearly-overflowing bosom.

For just an instant, Lucy's face hardened and her eyes narrowed. "Nothing is free, Carrie." Then she laughed. "We just have to decide if the price is worth it."

"I'm afraid I don't understand."

Lucy smiled again, a little ruefully this time. "When I go to Auntie Kate's, I'll be at her beck-and-call, so to speak, and will have to follow her rules." She let go of Camilla's arm to place a dainty hand on the banister of the grand staircase, adding, "But for now, we're free. Let's enjoy it."

Chapter Twenty

By late afternoon, Camilla had finished bathing and freshening up her only other dress besides the bombazine with potato pie stains on it. No longer in mourning, she put on a cooler, light blue linen dress with a sensible yoke neckline and wide, dolman sleeves. Her chestnut hair shone under a light coating of scented vegetable oil provided by Lucy, who also magically secured it on top of her head with only a few curls tickling her neck.

Her reflection showed her looking more rested than she had in years. *Except when Patrick and I were together.* Pushing aside the pain those dangerous thoughts caused, she turned to Lucy. "Well, I'm off to my meeting. Are you certain you'll be all right without me?"

Lucy stopped brushing her own long, silky tresses to smile. "Of course. I'm just going to change and go down for an early dinner Any time before six o'clock is perfectly acceptable for a woman alone in the city," answered Camilla's raised eyebrow.

I have so much to learn about city life, she thought, taking a deep breath. "Well then. Wish me luck." She smoothed her skirt for the short walk to Royal St.

She walked slowly, shielded from the sun by Lucy's parasol, staring at the many-storied houses, all connected to each other by the most beautiful and intricate ironwork she'd ever seen. Now and then, she peered through an open gate to catch a glimpse of lovely gardens, serene and cool amidst the afternoon confusion.

Finally, the number 129 appeared on an enormous iron gate with a huge, "M" inter-woven with iron grapevines. It moved with the slightest touch of her hesitant hand and she stepped into a cool, flagstone-lined passage.

It could have been a fairytale setting, with ivy covered walls, and sweet-smelling tropical flowers scenting the path. She paused at an archway that opened onto a sunny garden surrounding an ancient fountain. The bright yellow stucco exterior of the home looked more like a private residence than a place of business, and she had no idea whether to approach from the garden, or to climb the curving iron stairs to the upper floor.

Choosing the ground level, she approached another wisteria-covered archway leading to an engraved bronze plaque inscribed with, "Marchaud et Marchaud, Attorneys at law," above a dark green door. She climbed the two steps to the entry, gently raised the heavy brass knocker and let it fall, stepping down to wait for a response.

As if he'd been standing on the other side waiting for her, a young man opened the door a few inches and looked at her critically. *"Oui? Ce qui vous veulent?"*

What do I want? What an odd question to ask a person calling on an attorney. She answered, *"Je voudrais voir Mssr. Marchaud,"* then tested his English, "About a business matter."

He squinted at her from a face too pretty to belong to a man. Then he opened the door, stepping back only enough for her to cross the threshold. "What is your name please, and your business?"

His high, nasal voice and button-small brown eyes both annoyed and unnerved her. *What kind of creature is this?* Perhaps if she answered him quickly he'd go away. "My name is Carrie O'...Lange. I have come to speak to Mssr. Marchaud about locating members of my family here in New Orleans."

The diminutive young man nearly a head shorter than her, sniffed like a spoiled puppy and turned from her to sit at an antique French writing desk. Taking a quill pen from its well, he held it poised over a clean, parchment sheet. "The family name?"

She took his position as an invitation to follow him and stepped inside the white, red, and gilt-colored room. "Trémon. My grandfather's name was Philippe Trémon. He owned a plantation near here named Belle Rivière. Mssr. Marchaud's father was his attorney."

With only a slight twitch of his thin, bloodless lips, the boy wrote the information down, blotted the note and folded the paper into a square. Then he rose to stand,

"Mssr. Marchaud, *père*, has been gone a long time. The records have been put away. And Mssr. Marchaud, *fils,* has not returned from luncheon." He appraised her simple dress to sneer, "And he is not in the business of locating missing persons."

When Camilla didn't move, he turned his back on her. "However, I will see to it he hears of your inquiry. Perhaps if you call sometime around mid-morning tomorrow, he will find time to see you." He raised a small, almost feminine hand to dismiss her.

She fought the urge to bat it away, instead saying firmly, "I'm sorry, but this is extremely important. I will wait here for him to return." She turned and sat in a silk tapestry-covered chair.

The secretary tossed unfashionably long black curls and puffed through pursed lips, "It could be some time."

"I have come all the way from Georgia. I can be patient."

Moments later, the door flew open and a tall, slender gentleman about her father's age bounded inside. "I tell you, Georges," he exhaled. "It is a gorgeous day for a promenade. I just ate an exquisite feast at *Madame Begue's* and I don't know if I shall ever have to eat again."

He spoke fast, but his patois so mirrored Danielle's, Camilla easily followed his praise of the Bistro she'd passed on her way from the hotel. It gave her the confidence to smile.

He stopped in mid-stride when he noticed Camilla. "But, ho, what is this?" he asked in English, bowing low, appraising her with dark, almost black eyes until Georges stepped between them to hand him the note.

The older gentleman's brows knitted and his smile faded as he read it. His right hand unnecessarily smoothed thick, black hair lightly dusted with gray along his temples. He nudged Georges aside to greet her with a wide smile. Carelessly tossing his hat on Georges' desk, he reached out to help her to her feet, gently sliding his gloved hand beneath her elbow to guide her into his office.

"My, my," he breezed. "I haven't heard the name Trémon in nearly twenty-five years. I was but a lad then, apprenticing under my father. Of course, I never did any Trémon business. Yours was a far too important family to be handled by a novice."

Camilla relaxed at his easy manner and smiled into his dark eyes. "But you are no longer a novice."

He laughed heartily, and slightly longer than necessary before answering, "No, I most certainly am not. But now, let us talk about your quest."

He led her to another silk and tapestry-covered chair, this time facing an enormous, rosewood desk. A glass paperweight topped by a brass cupid sat between a sheaf of watermarked stationery and a row of silver-tipped ivory pens on the gleaming surface of the provincial desk. Behind him was an entire wall of bookshelves filled with both antique and new, leather-bound books

He settled gracefully into an ox-blood leather chair, tenting his fingers beneath the cleft in his strong chin. "Now, *s'il te plait,* tell me, how it came to be, after all these years, the granddaughter of Philippe Trémon appears at my doorstep?"

Impressed with his interest, but a little surprised by his use of the more intimate and informal phrasing of the word, "please," Camilla told him more than she planned, including her ruined plantation and her parents' deaths. She replaced Patrick with a fictitious, dead, war-hero-husband named Beauregard Lange, finishing with her desire to locate members of her mother's family.

He leaned back in his chair, smoothing the evidence of his dark-haired Spanish ancestors back from the fair skin of his French ones. "So you are Danielle's child?" he said softly, his hooded eyes glittering in the afternoon sunlight. "And she is dead?"

At her nod, he asked, "What caused her death?"

What odd questions for him to ask a client? She understood he would have known Danielle, and as the son of her family's solicitor, perhaps even been friends; but she didn't care to share her mother's humiliating and tragic death with a stranger. "A fever."

He watched her a few moments, from beneath heavily lidded eyes. When she had nothing more to offer, he stretched like a cat after a nap, rising in one fluid motion that barely stirred the humid air in the over-furnished room.

One long step brought him to her side. "My condolences on your many losses, Mrs. Lange," he purred. "Or may I call you Carrie, in deference to our long family relationship?"

She accepted his outstretched hand and rose. "Of course."

"Marvelous." He smiled and clasped her hand warmly between his palms and with a hand on her elbow, escorted her to a door facing the garden.

How odd to be shown a side exit from a business meeting, she thought, but appreciated the blessing of avoiding Georges' venomous stare again. Delmont placed a warm hand low on her back and reached across her to open the glass-paned door, inhaling deeply of the scent of Lucy's perfume.

His breath disturbed the wisps of curls along her neck when he sighed into her ear, "I'll let you rest from your travels tonight. But I simply cannot let you spend days at your hotel, waiting for word of your next of kin. You simply must join me for dinner at Galatoire's tomorrow night, and an evening at the French Opera House.

"The marvelous soprano, Adelina Patti is returning to recreate her debut role in Meyerbeer's *Le Pardon de Ploermel*. The woman has a voice second to none and promises to become the finest soprano in the world. It is a rare opportunity to see such a talent and I would be honored to share it with you."

Blocking the open door, he bowed low and kissed her hand. "And of course, the Opera House is a wonder to behold. A sight anyone visiting the Crescent City should see."

The scent of his musky hair tonic mixing with Lucy's spicy scent, or maybe her infrequent meals, made her queasy. She pulled away and stepped across the threshold, grateful for the breeze wafting from the garden fountain. Her mother had told her about the opera. The opulence she described went beyond anything Camilla's prosaic experience could imagine. Women wore original Paris gowns with ropes of pearls around their necks and glittering jewels on their wrists and fingers. And patrons drank champagne in private parlors, watching the performances from gilded boxes.

But a new gown for the evening would deplete the pockets sewn into her petticoat. "I am so sorry," she answered, taking Kate's advice to keep her financial situation hidden, she lowered her gaze. "But we've only just met, and I am alone here. I must concentrate on the search for

161

my family."

A long finger lifted her chin. "But that is work, Carrie dear," Delmont crooned. "And work is to be done during the daylight hours. You are in New Orleans now, and the night is for music and laughter. I simply cannot allow my old friend Danielle Trémon's daughter to miss the opera."

Refusing her refusal, he dropped her hand and stepped back into the room. "I will call for you in my carriage at your hotel at six o'clock." He turned then, his eyes narrowing as he took in her modest gown. "And what hotel is that?"

"The St. Louis," she answered, thanking fortune for presenting her with Kate Holliday and Lucy.

Lucy. She'd completely forgotten her promise to keep her company. What would she do now? Delmont had already closed the door behind her with a gallant bow and, *"Au revoir."*

Left with no other choice, she returned to the now-thronging street and formed a plan. She'd see if the modiste Kate recommended had something finished, or slightly used, for her to buy at a reasonable sum. Confident her future would soon be secure, she risked parting with one of Flora's gold coins.

"The French Opera House!" Lucy exclaimed when Camilla told her of the invitation. "Your family must have been very important. People literally have to inherit boxes at the French Opera. It's like a temple. You simply must go. Auntie Kate will be so pleased for you."

"But I promised I would keep you company."

Lucy's eyes suddenly turned cold. "I've been taking care of myself for some time now, Carrie. I think I can manage one evening."

Then the impish smile returned. "Auntie Kate will understand. Besides, this is a rare opportunity. I want to hear all about it when you come back. Now, what are you going to wear?"

Camilla shrugged. "I have no idea. I brought nothing appropriate, have limited funds, and only one day to acquire something." She frowned, "If the hotel modiste has nothing ready to wear, I really don't know what to do." Then an idea struck. "No, wait. I can claim illness."

"Oh, no you can't." Lucy laughed. "I'm not going to miss a firsthand account of the French Opera because you packed unwisely.

Now, are we going to waste more time, or are we going to get you ready for the ball, Cinderella?"

She strode purposefully to the chiffonier where the maids had hung the lovely dresses and gowns from her trunks. Tapping her foot while studying the array of finery, she stabbed inside the soft, colorful mass and pulled out a gown. "This will suit you perfectly."

Camilla had never seen such a stunning gown, including the Worth Patrick brought from Savannah. She stepped back at the memory of that night. "No, I can't wear your—"

"Of course, you can." Lucy held the gown up to her and confessed., "It's not actually mine anyway. It belongs to a...friend of a friend."

To Camilla's questioning glance, she added, "I, ah...left home rather suddenly and packed it by mistake, but I'm sure she won't even miss it. She's a bit of a country mouse, I'm told. Stuck on an old farm somewhere. It would be wasted on her." Shaking her impatient arms in the air, she ordered, "Now unbutton your bodice and let's see how it looks with your skin and hair."

Curious, Camilla ignored what was a completely accurate description of herself to pull the shirtwaist and chemise off her shoulders. Then Lucy held the deep purple silk in front of her in the mirror.

They both gasped in surprise. The shimmering fabric glowed against her skin, bringing out the gold highlights in her hair. Her green eyes shone like emeralds against it and when she moved, the depths of the pleated folds on the skirt darkened, while the outer ones glittered in the sunlight. *What will it do in candlelight?*

Both women stared at Camilla's transformation. Lucy rested her hand lightly on her bare shoulder to lean close and whisper. "Carrie, this dress could have been made for you. You simply *must* wear it tomorrow night." Then she giggled. "If you do, you may not have to worry about finding your family. I understand Marchaud is filthy rich."

"Lucy!" Camilla exclaimed. "The man is old enough to be my father."

Lucy's guttural laugh contrasted with her angelic features. "All the better. Rich widows fare better than poor ones, don't they?"

163

Chapter Twenty-One

Camilla soon realized the gown was only the beginning of excruciating preparations necessary for an evening out. Lucy was a master at hair and cosmetic artistry, forcing her hair to do things she never thought possible. She had no idea her wild curls could be tamed into tight ringlets at her brow and coiled into smooth ropes at her neck. But when Lucy produced a box of powders and creams, she consented only to a touch of pale rose on her cheeks and mauve on her eyelids to bring out the green of her eyes.

"Enough," she laughed when Lucy lifted a stylus from an ornate copper vial filled with kohl. She moved just in time to avoid having a beauty mark painted on her cheek. Lucy sighed disapprovingly, but put it away and turned to yet another pot, applying a hint of rouge to Camilla's lips.

A messenger announcing the arrival of the Marchaud carriage put an end to Lucy's torture. Camilla rose to pull on short white silk gloves and adjust Kate's contribution—a filmy white shawl embroidered with shimmering, gold threads. Finally, with Lucy's beaded bag dangling from her wrist, she set off for the stairs.

Her breasts strained against the plunging, diamond-cut bodice, and the fitted hips of the skirt made each small step a fluid, torturous movement. She held her breath the entire length of the stairway, praying she wouldn't trip in the unfamiliar heeled pumps and end up a purple heap on the lobby floor.

Delmont stood at the bar with his drink halfway to his mouth when their eyes met. His handsome face lit with pleasure. Graceful as a leopard, he crossed the lobby to offer her his hand when she reached the bottom stair.

"Carrie," he oozed with charm. "You are the most beautiful woman I have seen since your...well, before the war." He adjusted the gossamer shawl around her shoulders, brushing his hand lightly across the back of her neck and smiling at her flush.

Her arm in his, they strolled toward the hotel doors, enjoying the envy and attention of both men and women in the lobby. "It is such a lovely evening, my dear," he spoke close to her cheek. "Why don't we dispense with the carriage and stroll to Galatoire's? It's on Bourbon Street, only a square from here, and near the theater."

Her stomach rumbled in protest because she'd been too nervous to eat all day. Walking several blocks in heeled pumps would take forever. She breathed deeply of the warm, night air. "I would love to."

The interior of the famous New Orleans restaurant disappointed her. Instead of unparalleled opulence, the walls were rough red brick, void of even one painting under the meager light of simple gas fixtures. Only the quiet conversations of patrons disturbed the eerie quiet of the nearly-full restaurant.

Delmont leaned in to explain, "Decor should never compete with one's dining pleasure, Carrie. And music is for the Opera. A gourmet meal is to be enjoyed thoroughly and quietly, punctuated by intelligent conversation and sophisticated laughter."

Nodding as if she understood, she was relieved when he ordered for them both. For him, *filet de truite almandine*, a fine trout covered with melted butter, almonds, and seasoning. And for her, *poulet chanteclair*, a plump chicken soaked in claret, then baked with mushrooms, bacon, and other ingredients known only to Chef Jules Galatoire.

The moment she tasted it, she understood the reasoning behind the lack of decoration and entertainment. Here, each course was a work of art and deserved the same respect. It wasn't a meal. It was an experience to be savored. It took nearly two hours to finish, though in her tight-fitting gown, Camilla did little damage to the lovely meal; while Delmont ate heartily, partaking of the several wines offered between courses.

Afterward, they strolled at an easy pace across the street to the most magnificent building she'd ever seen. The four-storied, Greek revival building towered above the others on the corner of Bourbon and Toulouse Streets. Its grand entrance was bathed in the glow of dozens of gas lights and decorated in traditional Creole colors of white, red and gold.

She turned to Delmont, too excited to notice how closely he held her to him. "Oh, Mssr. Marchaud." She sighed. "So, this is the opera. It's just as Maman described. Look, I can see the chandeliers and the great mirrors even from here."

"This is only the beginning," he assured her with a pat on her arm. "Come let us join the throng." He helped her step up to the banquette in front of the entrance and shortened his stride to match hers. Once inside, her legs nearly buckled from wonder. Finding strength in his strong arm, she smiled demurely as Delmont greeted elegantly-dressed Creoles.

He introduced her as Madame Carrie Lange, from Georgia. The men bowed low, and the women murmured, *"Charmante,"* rustling their fans until they regained their escorts' attention. Finally, Delmont whispered, "Come, Carrie. We don't want to miss a moment. He guided her away from the others, saying, "We are in *Les Loges,* surrounding the orchestra seating. We'll have an excellent view of the stage."

He smiled. "We may even glimpse the lions roaming the stage box opposite our *esteemed* Customs Collector Mssr. Cuthbert Bullitt." He leaned in to whisper, "I always hope for one of those young lions to cross the parquet and enjoy him for dinner."

A chill ran through her body at the hatred in his dark eyes at the thought of a government official being eaten by lions in an opera house filled with nearly two thousand people.

They left the giant *Salle* to pass the gilded double staircase and enter the "dress circle" on the main level. Four seating tiers rimmed the enormous stage like a giant horseshoe. Her gaze quickly took in the parquet flooring and comfortable seats that extended into the orchestra pit, along with neat rows of curtained and netted box seating surrounding it. She felt light-headed when she gazed up past *les seconds*, the second level of boxes, and further up to the *le paradis*, the inappropriately named highest tier, where non-white patrons crowded together on hard benches.

Flora had told her about the suffocating closeness endured by the people of color who occupied the benches. The shadow population of free people with mixed blood and few rights, consisted of tradesmen, small business owners, and the secret families of the city's elite. Where Flora, with one-half Negro blood, had squinted to recognize the actors on the stage.

"But we could hear the music," she'd explained, her voice soft with the recollection. "And though we felt as if we were in the flames of Hell, the music rose to us like the songs of angels."

"Be careful," Delmont's voice broke her attention from the gallery while his hand on her elbow kept her balance. He smiled patiently. "Come, my...ah, partner had to leave the city suddenly. On business. We're fortunate to have the box to ourselves the entire evening."

He led her to a carved, gilt-painted box with velvet draperies tied back to present an unblocked view of the stage and surrounding theatre. Once settled into their tufted velvet chairs, Camilla thrilled at the sounds of so much humanity in a single building.

Shouts of recognition carried from all levels in the giant cavern until eight o'clock, when a bell sounded from below and the lights dimmed. As if in one breath, the din went silent, and the first notes of the overture welcomed Camilla to the timeless world of the opera.

Though sung in an antiquated High French dialect, she easily understood it's meaning in the haunting strains of the young soprano's arias, and the tenor's serenades. Like the other women in the audience, Camilla nervously clutched the railing, her emotions ebbing and following with the joy and sorrow of the characters.

During the first intermission, Delmont smiled broadly. "I knew you would appreciate Miss Patti's talents. "You seem flushed, perhaps a libation will restore order to your heightened emotions." He turned to a silver bucket on the Syrian Tabouret table next to him and poured French champagne, iced to perfection, into a crystal flute.

Like so many other things in her life, by the time she'd reached the age to enjoy good coffee, New York shopping trips, finishing schools, and fine champagne, the opportunity to do so were gone. Admitting how dry her throat had become, she drank the entire flute, finishing with a little cough and a tiny giggle.

She looked up at Delmont's deep chuckle, surprised to see his black, fathomless eyes glinting with amusement at her expense. "No, no," he corrected and refilled her glass. "Good champagne must be sipped. Else the bubbles get into your nose and cause the most embarrassing sneezes."

They both laughed and she tried again, developing a taste for fine champagne, as well as for the opera, gourmet cuisine, and fine clothing. The only thing missing was a crooked smile, and gray eyes glinting with starlight.

Stop, she told herself. *The Patrick you loved never existed.* As if in agreement, the lights dimmed for the second act and she didn't pull away when Delmont's strong, smooth fingers covered her hand.

Chapter Twenty-Two

Several days passed in a blur of shopping and sightseeing with Lucy, and evening dinners with Delmont. Despite Lucy's insistence that all their hotel expenses be put on her generous account, Camilla had parted with dangerously many of Flora's coins.

She justified them by telling herself it would only be for a short while. Delmont assured her he would have news of her family soon. And she had to look presentable when she met them.

But now, shopping and *café-au-lait* had become tedious. She paced in her room, wondering why Delmont's search took so long. It didn't make sense her family would hide themselves in the same city they helped settle. The questions made her head ache.

She turned impatiently at a knock on the door and opened it to meet the effeminate face of Delmont's secretary, Georges. As usual, she suppressed a chill when she met his unfathomable dark eyes. "Hello, Georges," she said, without inviting him in.

"Madame Lange," he answered, his voice echoing her revulsion. "I have a message for you from Mssr. Marchaud."

She took the linen envelope but refused to open it in front of him. "Does it require a reply?" she asked, wondering why he still plagued her with his churlish presence.

When he made no move to leave, she reached for the door. "Well, thank you for delivering it. I'm sure you are busy with many errands to run." A little ashamed of her rudeness, she bid him good day and closed the door in his face.

The Marchaud seal opened easily beneath her manicured fingernail. She read: "My dearest Carrie. Finally, I have some news for you. I am busy this afternoon and prefer to present it to you this evening at my home. I am having a small dinner party. Please join me as my hostess and we will celebrate together. Ever yours, Delmont."

He's found them! She sat on the bed to catch her breath. Perhaps he'd introduce her to them at his dinner party. The postscript said his carriage would arrive at nine o'clock.

There were only a few hours to prepare for her debut as a member of New Orleans royalty, but she took the time to write a note to Flora. To share this joy with the one person in the world she could trust.

After posting the letter with the hotel concierge, she found Lucy bidding adieu to a new gentleman acquaintance in the lobby. When he left and Camilla shared her news, Lucy hugged her, saying, "I'm so happy for you."

Then she backed up to arm's length. "I think the cream and gold satin for this occasion. A descendant of the Trémon family and hostess for a prominent Creole attorney must look truly exceptional."

Hours later, Camilla felt as radiant as a bride descending the hotel stairs to board Delmont's carriage. Lucy's modiste had sold the finished, but unclaimed, gown to her at a ridiculously low price. And this time, she borrowed Lucy's embroidered, silk cape to ward off the evening chill. Just before leaving, she dabbed on a drop of the rich, patchouli perfume Delmont had given her after the opera.

The lights were lit in Delmont's living quarters above his office, spreading a golden sheen over the brick and cobblestone drive. Camilla stepped down from the carriage into the welcoming glow and lifted the hem of her dress to climb the curving, iron steps.

But a sullen Georges intercepted her at the office door, only stepping aside when she showed him the invitation he himself had delivered. Refusing to let him dull her joy, she followed him into Delmont's office to wait for her host.

At the sound of the closing door, she dismissed Georges from her mind and hung her wrap on the hall tree in the corner. Delmont entered quietly from the garden, touching his lips to her bare shoulder She turned, "Delmont, you startled me."

"Pardonnez moi" he whispered kissing the palm of her open hand before stepping back to assess her. His smile spoke of his appreciation of

the golden, *fleur de lis* pattern stitched into the sheer lace modesty panel above the gown's deep, diamond neckline. Both hands now on her shoulders, he placed a light kiss on each cheek. "You are truly *charmante, ma petite oiseu.*"

But Camilla wasn't a little bird, and her patience, as well as her money was running low. She held back when he offered to escort her upstairs. "Delmont," she breathed, "I simply cannot wait. Please tell me your news now, before the guests arrive. I really must know of my family."

He patted her hand and ran an elegant finger along her cheek. "In due time, *ma cheri.* In due time."

She hid her disappointment behind a frozen smile when he introduced her to his four guests, all of them men. Business associates, he said. Rather more like the Yankee scalawags who invaded the South with their little carpetbags than attorneys and financiers.

They wore cheap, ill-fitting suits and smoked cigars without asking her permission. Still, she smiled pleasantly, laughing modestly at their ribald jokes. And when the interminable meal ended, she retired to Delmont's office while he finished his business with them in the drawing room.

Hours later, she woke on the settee to find him sitting behind his desk, his silk cravat loosened. He stared at the half-filled glass of wine next to a tattered book on his desk.

She rose and approached him. "Delmont," she asked, growing more concerned by the moment. "Is something wrong? Were those people really business associates? They were so coarse. Must you deal with them?"

He stood, meeting her on the other side of the desk. The waning light of the fire made him look older, the glint in his eyes a reminder of his comment about the lions at the opera.

A *frisson* of fear prickled Camilla's arms when he sneered drunkenly, "And if I do? What say do you have in the matter, *Madame*?"

She stepped back at the anger in his tone, the edge of the desk biting into her hip. He reached out to stroke her flushed cheek. "I am afraid, degrading as it is, I must deal with them, *cheri.* They, and others like them, are now in control of our beloved Queen."

Doris M. Lemcke

Leaning closer, the wine fresh on his breath, he explained, "You can see why I had no wish to be seen in public with them; yet it is expedient I entertain them. They have friends at City Hall who can do a great deal for my business." He smiled then, his hand sliding from her cheek, along her neck, to rest on the hollow of her throat. "But you were wonderful." His wine-soaked lips covered hers.

She was surprised at the sudden advance from a man who had thus far been the epitome of a gentleman. She'd begun to think of him as a kind uncle. But this was no kiss from a kind uncle. She tried to step away from him, but was trapped between him and the desk. "Delmont, please."

He ignored her to wrap his left arm around her waist while his right curled behind her neck to where a silk ribbon tied the lace bib of her gown. A second later, it ripped, baring her décolletage to his hungry gaze.

"Beautiful," he mumbled, this time forcing his tongue into her mouth and his fingers down the front of her dress.

Shocked, terrified, and bent nearly backward while strong arms and legs imprisoned her, Camilla pummeled his shoulders and chest with her fists. But no amount of pushing, pounding or wriggling did any good. "Delmont, stop," she screamed when the hard length of his sex pressed against her. "Don't do this, please."

He paused then, lifting his head to focus on her tear-filled eyes. But the curve of his lips couldn't be described as a smile when he answered, "This is what you were born for *ma bichette*." While his body pressed her against the desk, one wide hand pushed her skirt up above her thighs, following the line of her leg to reach through the opening in her drawers and cup her bush.

This can't be happening! He probed a finger into the part of her that belonged to only one man, turning her shock into fear, and as quickly, her fear into anger. "No!" she screamed, pulling her knees together and twisting her body to the side, her hands pushing against his chest. "*Bichette?*" she snapped. "I am not your little doe. Not an animal to be used at your will. Release me. Now!"

Her spirit only heightened the determination in his eyes. His finger still inside her, he cocked his head. "So you wish to fight me *chou chou.*" He removed his hand, only to tighten his grip around her waist.

172

He now stared at her as if he didn't recognize her. He was mad, she realized. One didn't reason with madness. "Delmont," she whispered as if in surrender while bracing her hands on the edge of the desk to risk one last push against him. "You don't have to do this."

As she'd hoped, he took it as a sign of acceptance and stepped back, allowing her to stand upright, though still blocking her escape with his body. Breathing hard, he slowly tucked a stray curl back into place and licked a shimmering tear from her lips. She shivered, folding her arms over her exposed breasts.

He snickered at her futile attempt collect her modesty. "You are so right. I most certainly do not have to do this." But instead of stepping aside, he pinned her hands to her sides, suckling and biting her tender nipples until she bled. Then he raised his head to savor the taste of her blood on his lips. "But I do enjoy it so, my little Camilla."

He grinned at her shock. "Yes, I know who you really are. And what you really are. And because of who *I* am, I can have you whenever I want." Smirking, he watched her try to repair the tattered bodice of her gown.

"You're mad."

He threw his head back and laughed. "You are not the first to say so. But after I give you the news you have waited so anxiously to hear, you will be quite happy to accept my affections, mad or not." Imprisoning her legs between his strong thighs, he reached into his breast pocket to wave a crumpled paper in front of her nose. "I promised you news of your long-lost family, did I not? Well here it is."

When she turned her head away, he pinched her jaw, turning her head to face him. "Oh, I'm so sorry. You speak French, but I doubt you read the language of your ancestors." He cleared his throat. "*Alors,* allow me to translate."

As he turned his attention to the paper, Camilla pushed against him hard enough to loosen the vise-like grip of his legs. She took barely two steps before his foot stepped on her gown, ripping away both her cream and gold skirt, and the cage beneath it.

Her scream filled the room when he grasped a loose tendril of the thick hair Lucy had so artfully arranged, pulling her back to him. Her skull felt like it had been ripped open and she saw her own, brutal death in his eyes.

He wrapped her hair around one hand and pulled her closer. "Do I have your full attention now, Madame?" Perspiration beaded on his forehead and upper lip, but his hand remained steady as he again looked at the yellowed paper.

"This is what is left of your family," he growled. "The birth record of your grandmother, Flora DeBoucher, the mulatto daughter of Mssr. Charles DuValier and his Negro mistress, Cesarine DeBoucher."

The accusation confirmed his madness. While Flora had been Danielle's surrogate mother at birth, and they shared a bond that transcended age and race, Danielle was the epitome of the Creole French *demoiselle*, physically and emotionally, from her fair skin to her blue eyes and blonde hair.

Though Delmont's wild accusation could explain Flora's devotion to a woman who treated her as barely human—and the reason she and Otis stayed long after they had the freedom to leave, it could not be. After Patrick's betrayal, her Maman's madness, and father's deception, this could *not* be true. If it was, she'd abandoned the only person left in her family—for a dream that was about to kill her.

She met Delmont's eyes squarely, without fear. "So you have Flora's birth record. Her Creole father is no secret, or her mother. Perhaps your advanced age, too much wine, and too many women have addled your mind. Your certificate means nothing." She bit back a cry at another painful tug on her scalp.

"Stupid little bitch," he snarled, spraying her with wine-tainted spittle. "You doubt my words? You need more proof?" His hands bit into her waist, again pressing her back against the desk. Winding another handful of her hair in his fist, he pressed his nose against hers.

"Then perhaps you will be interested in the chronicles of my sainted father. Because of his friendship with your grandfather, he kept Philippe Trémon's terrible breach of both God's law and man's, a secret."

He grinned at her gasp. "Yes, my pére. The most honest man in the city, confessed his sins in his diary. A diary I found among his personal papers after his death. I keep it close, to remind me of the perfidy of women."

He pulled away to reach for the tattered little moleskin journal behind her on the desk. He waved it in front of her. "A journal proving that all women are liars, seducers, and evil at heart." He cocked his head. "The truth will be your ruin."

Chapter Twenty-Three

One hand circling her throat, he read an entry dated June 24, 1822.

"I have this day, repaid the terrible debt owed my dear friend Philippe Trémon. When he saved my life at the battle of Orleans so long ago, I pledged mine in his stead should the time ever come. Alas, if it had only been so simple. For in the end, the price of Philippe's life became my honor, not my blood. I have now become a thief, a forger, and worst of all, a digger of unconsecrated graves.

He paused for dramatic effect and licked a finger to turn the page.

"This night, during one of the worst of our raging summer storms, a messenger arrived from Philippe, begging me to come to Belle Rivière. All Hell was breaking loose, young Otis said, and the master sent him for me. Amid crashes of thunder and flashes of deadly lightning, I knew my note had been called due. No matter, I would help Philippe defend his home from whatever enemy threatened.

But when I arrived, I heard no gunfire. I saw no enemies charging the stately home. But as Otis had said, chaos ruled the house. I shall carry to my grave the sight of my friend's face when he met me at the door. Philippe's face was gray and lined by fatigue. His blond hair hung limp along cheeks, greasy with sweat. I crossed myself against the living ghost he'd become.

I recoiled from his hands, covered with blood while he thanked God for bringing me to him. Then just as quickly, his halleluiahs ceased. Shoulders bowed, he escorted me upstairs as wailing house servants ran from us with terror on their heathen faces. When he drew me inside the master bedroom, what I saw will haunt my nightmares forever. Philippe's lovely wife Eloisa lay dead on a bloodstained sheet, a scream of unbearable agony etched forever on her soft, young face.

But the horror had just begun. Next to her in the bloody sheet, lay the still form of a dead man-child, his life cord tightly wrapped around his tiny throat. I thought I had seen horror in war, but mon Dieu, I had never seen anything like this. My stomach lurched and I wanted to run from the room, back to my family and my cheerful fire, but I stayed for the sake of my friend who wept like a child as he explained to me the events of this horrible, bloody night."

Camilla's captor again leaned close to her horrified face, pressing against her as he sipped his wine. With a satisfied sigh, he returned to the diary.

"Little Eloisa had chosen this violent and stormy night, of all nights, to bear her child. Still two months from her time, she collapsed in a gush of blood from her loins. As stubbornly as the child fought to be born, her tiny body held it back. I held Philippe as he grieved over the deaths of his wife and child, still wondering why he had called me instead of the priest. Then, he led me along another corridor to a servant's room.

There, in the soft glow of a lamp, I felt serenity amid insanity. A woman with doe-colored skin and luminous hazel eyes sat in a rocker in the corner by the fireplace. She cradled a newborn infant with downy blonde hair, to her breast.

As Philippe's closest friend, I knew he kept a placée in the French quarter, and from the love in her eyes when she saw him, I knew it was she. A free woman of color, he had taken Flora DeBoucher into his home as menagére when she approached her time. And on the same night his wife and son died, she gave him a healthy, golden-haired daughter.

What cruel ironies life plays on us, allowing the girl-child with no name to come into the world healthy; while the man-child with the noble birthright strangled in his mother's womb. But not only irony would be heaped upon us for the rest of our days; rather deception. No, sacrilege.

This night, as the heavens raged in fury over our sin, we buried the unbaptized soul of a white boy in an unmarked grave, while a bastard girl with tainted blood, sleeps in his cradle."

Delmont stole a glance into Camilla's horror-filled eyes, purring with pleasure as he read his father's last tormented words.

"For this, Philippe and I are doomed to eternal torment, to be joined one day by Flora DeBoucher. And to compound my sin, in the

stead of Dr. St. James, I have falsified a death certificate saying Elouisa Trèmon died after giving birth to a healthy infant girl. It is beyond me how Philippe will endure living in sin with the Negro mother of his child, who pretends to be her nursemaid. My debt is paid. My friendship is dead."

Camilla jumped when Delmont slapped the book on the desktop. Then she slumped forward, no longer holding the edge of the desk for support; no longer worried about her modesty, her virtue, or even her life. But Delmont showed no mercy.

"Something always seemed different about your dear and protected mother," he sneered. "My father never let me court her. Too good for me, I thought. And the way the darkie nursemaid of hers watched over her," he rambled. "Always too uppity for her station. Yes, it all fits now."

As if to a stupid child, he droned on, "You see, Danielle and I were secret lovers, and before I could defy my father to propose marriage to her, Philippe announced her engagement to a...peasant from a backwoods plantation in Georgia."

Still blocking any way of escape, he stepped back and thumbed through the worn journal. "Let me see. Yes, here it is. June 12, 1840.

"Philippe Trémon has again approached me to add more lies to the web of deceit laid so many years ago. It seems my own son is enamored with his quadroon daughter. Philippe, fearful his house of cards will come crashing down on him; and I, out of love for my son, have added another crime to our list of unforgivable sins.

There is a young man visiting here hoping to entice investors in his new horse breeding enterprise. He is quite smitten with the beautiful and dangerous Danielle. To keep my son from marrying a person of color without betraying my vow to my friend and bringing dishonor on myself, I will complete a marriage contract before young Langesford comes to his senses.

Oh, how I pity him, for Danielle has grown from a willful and selfish child into a malicious and calculating woman whose soul is as tainted as her blood."

Camilla moaned. Her world had ended. *Again.* It was true. Flora, whom she had always seen as a loving servant, was her grandmother. No longer concerned about her own life, her heart broke in sympathy for the lie her dear Florie had been doomed to live.

What agony she must have borne to give up her freedom for a shadow life as the slave to her own daughter. How she must have loved Philippe Trémon, as well as Danielle, to do it. And how Otis must have loved her to go keep her secret all these years. *And how stupid I was to run from that most unselfish love into a world where just one drop of colored blood marks you as an inferior being.*

But worse, she'd left her last remaining family in Georgia, and she couldn't go back because of the deceitful, fortune-hunting Yankee. She raised her defeated gaze to Delmont's.

He smiled, his fingers toying with a curl he'd ravaged so efficiently earlier. "So, my pet. I have given you the information you sought. Now it's time to pay me for my services."

He frowned at her lack of response. "The sins of the fathers," he repeated Flora's words from what seemed so long ago. "It seems they truly are visited on the children—at least to the second generation."

A mad smile lit his face. "But good things do come to those who wait. After being denied my beautiful Danielle, I am now to have the pleasure of her daughter, without the legal responsibilities."

He crushed her lips with his again, forcing her mouth open to receive his invading tongue. Frustrated when she gagged, he slapped her. "Surrender to your fate, Camilla. I will keep you well. You will have the finest clothes and jewels, and live in an elegant flat in the *View Carré*, while you wait to serve me."

A gilded cage. Camilla's mind snapped and she screamed into his hideous face, *"I am not a slave!"* Her stomach lurched again at his taste, his touch, his smell. She had to get away. It didn't matter if she died trying.

With as much dignity as she could muster in her nearly naked state, she faced him. With strength she didn't know remained in her battered limbs, she pushed his repulsive hand away and hissed, "You will not 'keep' me in any way, you filthy beast."

Loathing now reddened his face. "Oh, yes I will. Whether you enjoy it or not will be entirely of your choosing. You see, the doors are all locked now, and the servants gone—even Georges. No one will answer your pitiful little cries." A long, elegant finger, raked her cheek.

"Now, I am tired of these games. It is time you accepted your destiny. As my *placée*—mistress if you prefer—you will enjoy a certain amount of social position in your world.

"A world of slaves and whores," she spat. "And thin-blooded degenerates like you living off the family name and old money." She ignored his darkening face. "I would rather die."

He took his time wiping the spittle from his cheek. "I will be happy to grant your wish, but not until I've had my fill of you. And if you change your mind, any one of my colleagues at dinner this evening will be happy to place you in the tent of an Arab sheikh or Chinese dignitary. American women of color claim a high price in the far East."

He pressed her back over the desk. "Which will it be, my green-eyed African Princess?"

This time she knew better than to fight. Instead, she pushed herself onto the desktop and lay back, her arms out as if to receive him. And while he unbuttoned his trousers, she groped for shears, a letter opener, even a quill pen to defend herself. His sigh at releasing himself from his trousers distracted him just as her fingers touched the base of the glass paperweight topped by a brass Cupid.

Hoping to distract him, she tried to reason one more time. "Delmont, this is not the golden age of the Creoles and I am not my mother, or a slave to be used at your will."

As she knew he would, he laughed, bending low to take another bite of her breast and tear her pantalets open. As his head dipped between her legs, she plunged Cupid's arrow into the base of his skull.

His head rose in reflex to the blow, a flicker of surprise sparking from his black eyes before they lost their brilliance and his mouth hung agape. He fell against her to slide down her body to the floor—his last living sounds a sigh, followed by a gurgle.

Shaking uncontrollably, but too exhausted to cry, she steadied herself on one arm to look down at him. Embers in the fireplace sputtered behind her, and the grandfather clock ticked away the minutes, as she waited for him to rise up and kill her.

The clock striking five times broke her paralyzing numbness. Georges came in at six o'clock to set up the day's schedule. *I have to get away!* Slowly, she stepped around Delmont's body, noting that the tiny hole in his neck emitted little blood. Then horror and panic surrendered to reason. *Maybe I can make it look like a robbery.*

She gathered up the remains of her skirt and threw them into the glowing embers in the fireplace. Then she pulled open the desk drawers and dumped them onto the Persian carpet. But he'd taken the birth certificate and journal with him to the floor, his body on top of them.

She couldn't bear to touch his body to retrieve them. And in the time it took her to upset the room, the last of the embers had gone out. The clock struck the half-hour. She didn't dare start a fire again and burn the book, even if she could lift his weight. She turned to the hall tree where she'd hung Lucy's cape and the velvet reticule holding the last of Flora's coins.

"Oh, no," she gasped, raising a bare foot pierced by glass from the shattered paperweight. Realizing her slippers also lay beneath Delmont's body, she prayed the folds of the cape around her numbed body would hide her bare feet and slipped out through the garden doors.

Chapter Twenty-Four

Patrick tried to pry Camilla's whereabouts from Flora for nearly a week after he returned from Savannah. She told him his wife had gone to Redfern Plantation to tend a difficult birth. It was less than a day's ride one way and after three days, he sent Cato to check on her. But when the ex-slave returned alone, he confronted Flora in the kitchen.

She looked like she hadn't slept in days and her hands shook as she turned the morning's bacon. "Where is she?" He croaked through a lump of worry the size of an apple in his throat.

Flora's eyes, a soft green in the morning light, reminded him of Camilla's, but instead of mischief and determination, they were filled with pain—no, panic. "Gone," the old woman whispered.

"Gone?" It couldn't be. She hadn't spent more than one night away from Langesford in her entire life. The plantation was so important to her she married him to keep it. She couldn't be...gone.

"Where?"

Her voice trembled, but her chin held firm—like Camilla's. "First you must tell me something."

Guessing games? Is she playing guessing games with me? Now?
"What?"

"Why did you really come here?"

He crossed the room, looming over her tiny, bowed shoulders. "To be driven insane I think, by you *brave* Southerners. Do you have something to tell me?"

"What will you do when you find her?" The tears in her eyes belied the set of her chin, telling him the importance of the answer—to both of them.

Rebel Treasure

"That's two questions, and what the hell do you think I'll do? Bring her back of course."

"Why?"

"Why what?" carried into the yard, sending chickens fluttering to a safer pecking spot.

"Why do you want to bring her back? Is it because of the gold from the Denver Mint?

"What?" The hard look in her eyes, told him she knew why he came to Langesford. He'd intended to tell Camilla when he returned from Savannah, so they could begin their new life together based on the truth. Now it was too late. *How on earth did she find out?*

It seemed the old woman held all the aces. Her eyebrows arched as she waited for him to either bet, or fold his cards. But as good as she may be at answering questions with more questions, he could match her all day. But he sensed there wasn't a lot of time to waste.

He rested his hands on her narrow shoulders. "Don't play games with me. Is Camilla's disappearance because of stories about the lost "Rebel Treasure? How did she even know about it?" He shook his head. "Never mind, it doesn't matter. Just tell me she didn't take off after that wild goose."

He left her then to pace. "I'll admit I first came here check out a story someone gave me that Anthony and his son were behind the Denver Mint robbery back in '62, but I've found nothing to support it. It was stolen all right, but it disappeared somewhere between Denver and the old New Orleans mint."

Tears clouded his eyes as he took Flora's hands in his. "Flora, you have to believe me. I stayed because I believe in what Anthony wanted for this plantation. For the future of the South. But most of all, I stayed for Camilla. As far as I'm concerned, *she* is the Rebel Treasure. Mine anyway."

Tears coursed down the old woman's cheeks and her tiny hands gripped his. "But do you love her?"

"More than life itself," he whispered. "On my mother's grave."

Satisfied, Flora freed her hands and moved the smoking bacon from the stove. They both sat at the chopping table. "On the day before you returned from Savannah, the man we once knew as Mssr. Antoine came

183

here. He said you are his partner."

Beecher? It couldn't be. *But oh, yes it could.* The man was desperate, brilliant—and deranged. Patrick cursed himself for underestimating the crippled shell of a man. *I should have known he'd follow me.*

Anger with himself made his voice harsh when he ordered Flora, "Tell me all you know, what you think you know, and everything between. Beecher is a lunatic. He's maintained the story of Langesford masterminding the lost gold because of his hatred for Anthony." *And I took his bait.*

He again paced the tiny room. "Believe me, I ate dust for nearly two years looking for that gold and I've searched this place from top to bottom. If I can't find it, nobody can."

Ignoring the renewed horror—and contempt, on Flora's face, he leaned in. "The case is closed. If Anthony and Brent were involved, they carried their secrets to the grave. I'm a planter now. I thought Camilla understood."

Flora's trembling lips set in a thin line. "Did you tell her?"

No, I never did. But hadn't he showed her in a hundred different ways? Women were such a mystery. Mysteries were his business, but since coming to Langesford, he'd become a dismal failure at solving them. He looked down at Flora, again thinking how much alike she and Camilla were, despite their obvious differences—so small, yet so strong. "Did she go with Beecher?"

His heart both soared and broke when she shook her head. Beecher hadn't taken her, but Camilla believed a monster over her own husband. And why not his conscience told him. After all, Beecher hadn't lied. And only Patrick knew the game changed the moment he held her at the hot spring. *If only I'd told her.*

But life was full of 'if-onlys'. And worrying about what might have been, could have been, should have been, would eat up a lifetime. Only action could change a regret into a new beginning. He leaned over Flora. "Tell me where she went. Because as sure as the night follows the day, Beecher followed her. And if she doesn't tell him where the gold is, he'll kill her."

She shook her head again. "She did not go in search of the Yankee gold. She searches for a far more dangerous secret." Head bowed, she told him, "She left to seek the solicitor of my...her mother's family. His name is Delmont Marchaud. She wore widow's weeds to take a train to New Orleans on the same day you returned from Savannah."

Her fear chilled his bones when she said, "And if she finds him, he is far more dangerous than the crippled artist. His evil is more powerful than greed because it is a hatred born of love. And it has been growing for more than twenty-five years."

"What do you mean?"

She shook her head. "There is no time to explain. You must find her quickly. She has entered a dark place where evil from...the past will destroy her. You must leave now or it will be too late." The rest of her words were an unintelligible torrent of French and Creole patois, muffled by sobs into her shaking hands.

"Flora, tell me—"

"There is no time!" she shouted and stood. "*Pressé!* Hurry. Go. Now. Quickly." Pushing him out the door, she repeated, "Hurry. *Vite, Vite.*"

While he packed and Otis readied his horse, she explained, "The devil once lived with his father at 129 Royal Street, in the Vieux Carré, what Anglos call The French Quarter." Cammy thinks he will help find her family." Her voice lowered. "Instead, she will find hatred and betrayal."

Again, she reached for Patrick's hand. "It may already be too late. The circle is closing. The sins of the fathers!" she cried and ran from the room.

A widow! He cursed himself with every brutal word he knew, in Gaelic, English and Mexican Spanish. She'd run right into him, looked at him from behind a hideous black veil! He knew something was familiar about both the woman and the veil, but he was so bent on surprising Camilla with his early return, he'd shrugged off his instincts—again.

~ * ~

He missed the train from Damon and rode Jupiter hard to get to Jeffers by the time it stopped to refuel, making it to Savannah by evening. Unlike Camilla, he chose the faster route via the steamer across the Pontchartrain. His Irish luck held and he arrived in New Orleans less than forty-eight hours later.

Midnight had long passed, when he stepped off the, "Liberty Belle." Despite the late hour, he hired a hack to take him to 129 Royal St. The open gate told him the man was entertaining and one light still glowed in the office wing. Trusting he could confront the man in the morning, he set off to look for Camilla at the St. Louis Hotel, where a note from Camilla had been posted more than a week ago.

"Paddy!" halted him as he approached the still-busy front desk. Turning toward the familiar voice, a blonde woman in royal blue waved at him from the bottom of the staircase. She lifted her skirt to run toward him with a smile. "I knew you'd find me."

His hands gently holding her at arm's length, he kissed her on the cheek. "Hey, Luce. Things get too hot in Savannah?"

She shrugged. "Bad timing. One of my uncles passed away—in my bed."

"I'm sorry for your loss," he answered dryly. "But I'm in a bit of a hurry." He turned toward the desk, asking, "I'm looking for a widow who may be staying here." He flipped a five-dollar gold piece into the air. "She may be registered as Camilla Langesford. Or O'Grady. Or Trémon."

The clerk raised an eyebrow at the strange request, but snatched the gold piece in mid-air. Then he shook his head to all three questions. Lucy touched Patrick's arm. "Don't blame him. There are a great many widows in the South, Paddy. I'm even sharing a suite with one now, before I go to Kate's House."

He raised an eyebrow at the intriguing coincidence, and led her to a secluded table behind a potted palm. "Well my widow looks like this." He produced a diamond-studded gold broach from his pocket and opened it to reveal a miniature of a lovely, russet-haired woman with green eyes.

"I had it made in Savannah." He coughed as if something had lodged in his throat. "It's...was...a wedding gift."

"Wedding gift?" Lucy's eyes narrowed and a rare frown marred her beautiful features. "You married the little farm girl? Patrick, you disappoint, but I suppose even the mighty do fall—for a fortune in gold, as I recall."

When Patrick didn't share her humor, she ordered a wine and took the locket from him. After a long sip of the exquisite Chardonnay, she laughed.

Patrick showed his ill humor at her reaction by taking the locket from her and standing. She caught his hand and laughed again. "Paddy, you are still the luckiest son of a bitch I know. This is Carrie Lange, my companion."

Fatigue and worry forgotten, he looked down at his old partner in espionage to demand, "Where is she? Take me to her. I don't care how late it is."

She stood too. A soft white hand with red-painted nails caressed his stubble-covered cheek. "Hold on. She's not in her room."

He pulled her hand away. "Lucy, so help me God, stop playing games. Where the hell is she?"

Her smile grew sly, her voice silky. "What's the rush? She's with another man, and I'm right here."

His hands fisted at his sides. "Another man? Who? Where?"

She put a finger to her lips. "Shush. All right. Patience never was your strong suit. Your sweet wife is hosting a dinner party tonight for one of New Orleans' most prominent attorneys."

"What attorney?"

When she told him, he swore, "Goddamnit, I just left there. A light was lit in the office, but I didn't see any carriages."

"Well there you have it." She smiled at a waiter and ordered a bottle of the hotel's finest champagne. "Just wait. She'll be back soon."

Two hours later, Patrick grew impatient. At five-thirty in the morning, even Lucy's bright eyes were dulled with worry. "Maybe we missed her," she offered. "Let's check her room."

They entered it through Lucy's room, hoping to find Camilla sleeping peacefully in her bed, but there was no sign she'd returned from her dinner engagement. Still, Lucy tried to reason, "Have you forgotten?" Parties in the Vieux Carré often last until dawn?"

They both knew Camilla would never drink until the sun rose—or spend the night at a bachelor's home—willingly. Patrick opened the armoire and parted the gowns to find her old carpet bag still tucked in a corner. *She's still here!*

187

He hugged Lucy. "You're right. Are you up to some late-night revelry, my love? I've heard there is a party just breaking up at 129 Royal Street."

Laughing brightly, she took his arm and lifted the hem of her dress to quick-step down the stairs with him. In the lobby, she tugged on his arm. "Slow down, darling. I don't want to twist an ankle and miss your reunion."

Impatient to have his arms around Camilla, his answering chuckle showed little humor. "Always the romantic, Luce. Try to keep up or we'll be too old to enjoy it."

Chapter Twenty-Five

Grateful the streets were nearly empty in the hour just before dawn, Camilla limped on the wounded heel, crouching low to peek inside the doors of the St. Louis Hotel. *Nearly empty.*

Thanking the god she no longer trusted, she pulled the hood forward to hide her face and entered the softly-lit lobby. Lucy's familiar laugh came from the direction of the stairs. With the instinct of a hunted animal, Camilla dove for a secluded table in a corner behind a potted palm. The hood still over her head, she sat with her back to the grand lobby, but the low, slow-building chuckle, so close it could have been meant for her, caught her breath and made her heart leap. *Patrick!*

The part of her still hoping he'd follow her and prove that Beecher had lied, forced her to risk a turn in the direction of the voice. But they'd already passed her by. Lucy's dainty hand held her close to a tall man in a well-tailored white suit who bent low to whisper something in her ear.

In another heartbeat, they disappeared through the hotel doors into the pre-dawn darkness. Stop imagining Patrick in every white suit you see, Camilla scolded her foolish heart. *He doesn't care about you.*

She rose to run quickly up the stairs, knowing she had less than an hour before Georges found Delmont's body and sent the police to her door. Dropping the cape on the floor, she tore off the remaining shreds of her clothing and threw them into the room's tiny coal stove, lighting the coals to stave off the chill she feared would never go away.

Afraid to stay, but more afraid to roam the streets before dawn, she used the time before her capture to scrub wherever Delmont had touched her, salving the oozing wounds he'd inflicted. Then she sat naked in front of the warm stove and cried like a child, hugging her knees against her savaged breasts.

When the tears were spent, she rose to watch the pink Louisiana dawn. *Time to go.* She took the few remaining pins from her hair and ran her fingers through the tangles. Stretching her sore muscles and rubbing a forearm already a deep shade of purple, she crossed the room to the armoire.

She ignored the lovely dresses fashioned by the hotel modiste to reach into the back for her battered bag and the black bombazine." This time she took comfort in the worn fabric and old-fashioned style. It would again help her melt into the background of society.

The sun had fully risen by the time she'd battled her hair into a chignon, closed the bag, and wrapped her shawl over her arm. Georges would likely have already found Delmont's body. The police would come any time now. She opened the door with one shaking hand on the handle, the other gripping the valise, ready to hurl it at anyone who stood in her way.

Her knees trembled with relief to find the corridor empty. Then, step by cautious step, she descended the stairs, exhaling only when she melted into the growing throng of early morning pedestrians, horses, and street cars. *Where now?*

Judith Carter's kind face came to her mind, her tender voice saying, "We'll be at the St. Charles Hotel. If you need anything, come to us." At the time Judith extended the invitation, she'd been so certain she'd find her family she'd barely listened. Now the invitation became her lifeline.

It would take time for news of a crime in the Vieux Carré to reach the American quarter. And if it did, it might not be given as much importance as in the French Quarter. She climbed onto a street car going north, praying the missionaries would still be in the city.

~ * ~

The gate to 129 Royal Street still welcomed visitors when Patrick and Lucy arrived. "Odd," he muttered, pushing it open. Unless things had changed a great deal since his last visit, the people of New Orleans locked their gates when the last guest left.

"Wait here," he ordered as Lucy hiked up her skirts and took off her slippers. "Sorry, Paddy," she whispered. "I love Carrie—I mean Cammy, too."

He knew better than to argue with the woman who had saved his hide more than once during the war. His boots and Lucy's stockings were silent on the stone path. He whispered, "I saw a light in the room off the garden earlier. What is it?"

"His office, I think," she whispered. "There's a garden entrance to the right. He lives upstairs."

Every nerve in Patrick's body tightened. The bastard may have been in there trying to seduce Camilla—and he went to the hotel instead. He knew only too well how strong the underground white slave market had grown in the South since the war ended. Northern and European factories were screaming for cheap labor, willing to pay a premium for hardworking women and children.

Even China had entered the arena, populating their brothels with Anglo women. Camilla's untamed beauty and spirit, along with her intelligence, would bring a good price anywhere in the world. He reached for the derringer in his boot. "Stay here," he ordered, knowing Lucy would be right behind him, no matter the danger.

They moved quickly and silently toward garden doors standing open to the courtyard. Only one dying taper on a side table and the smell of fresh ashes in the grate spoke of recent occupants. A cloud moved from the fading moon to reveal the dark outline of a body on floor.

Patrick stopped in mid-step, with Lucy bumping into him from behind. His heart slowed in his chest and Lucy stifled a cry. Then, silent as shadows, they crept inside. Tears clouded his vision. He couldn't survive if it was his beautiful wife's body crumpled on the floor. Lucy knelt beside the body and rolled it over. "Marchaud," she whispered.

When his blood started flowing again, he wanted to shout for joy and scream in frustration at the same time. Camilla had obviously saved herself from the danger Flora predicted, but she'd also slipped by him twice. *What is wrong with me?* Had love and worry softened his brain so much he couldn't even find a little slip of a woman running away from home for the first time?

He squatted beside the body, touching the dead man's face. "It's still warm," he whispered. "At least the devil had the courtesy to die face down on the rug." He picked up the base of the cupid paperweight only inches from the dead man's ear and smiled. Camilla's exceptional aim had sent the arrow directly into the stem of his brain, rather than an artery, leaving little blood to clean up.

"How resourceful," Lucy observed. They both jumped as the clock struck six times. "Georges," Lucy whispered, panic in her gaze.

"Georges?"

"Delmont's assistant, and...pet. He made the arrangements for Carrie...Cammy, to be picked up at the hotel. He hates her, and he knows where we're staying. He'll be in soon to prepare Delmont's morning toilet. He'll send the police to her door as soon as he finds the body."

Patrick stood. "Then we have to get rid of it." He stuffed a handkerchief into the small wound in the back of Delmont's neck, telling Lucy, "Help me prop him up."

"What?"

"He's still soft. We can move him."

Using the quick mind that made her such a successful spy, Lucy said, "I know a place."

"Where?"

She smiled. "There was a Negro funeral procession on Basin Street yesterday. They won't seal the crypt until sunrise. We have about a half-hour. St. Anthony's isn't far and there's no one sober on the street yet. We'll fit right in."

Patrick lifted the bulk of the man's weight, and stooped to pick up a document and what looked like a journal, stuffing them both into his pocket. Lucy stuffed Camilla's slippers into her reticule. She answered Patrick's look with a wink. "Cinderella's slippers."

But making a corpse look like a drunk wasn't as easy as they thought. It took nearly the full half-hour to find the new tomb of Haney Jones, a free man of color who had been run down by a carriage. Delmont lay face down again, this time in the spongy loam of the Colored cemetery while they pushed the heavy stone lid wide enough to push his body inside, and close it back up.

The pink dawn had turned blue with the promise of a cool, September day when they slipped through an open delivery door in the back of the hotel. They ran up the maids' staircase to the suite, but were too late again.

Warm coals in the grate told them Camilla had come back to her room after all. Tepid, pink-stained water in a basin testified she'd taken the time to bathe. Was it her blood? "Damn him to Hell!" Patrick shouted, slamming a fist into his palm. "If he wasn't dead already, I'd do it myself, slowly, the Comanche way."

"Hush," Lucy warned. "You'll wake the neighbors." Her comforting hand on his arm, she said, "I know it looks bad, but we've only been gone a short while. And if she could clean up this quickly, she's not injured badly."

Patrick grudgingly accepted her optimism and opened the armoire. He pointed to the empty space where her bag should have been. "And it looks like she's gone back to being the widow Lange."

Knowing sleep wouldn't come for either of them until they found her, Patrick told Lucy to scour the Vieux Carré, while he left for the American Quarter with the miniature in his hand. He returned at two o'clock in the afternoon with only rumpled clothes and three days' growth of beard to show for his efforts.

"The quarter is quiet," a sleepy Lucy told him as she rose from the settee in Camilla's room. Her lustrous hair hung loose around her worried face, her dress stained and muddied from walking the streets all day. Still, there were no reports of a missing Creole attorney, and no one had noticed that poor Haney Jones had been sealed for eternity with one of the most active Ku Klux Klan members in the parish.

Patrick hired the off-duty desk clerk to watch the trains and riverboats in case she decided on a hasty exit from the city. Until the clerk returned, he had only one hotel left to check. He'd left the St. Charles Hotel in the American quarter for last because he figured Camilla had to be low on funds. Though Marchaud's office looked like it had been ransacked, he knew her honesty would never allow her to steal, even from a dead man who had most likely ravaged her.

Flora had told him about the two hundred dollars she'd sewn into Camilla's petticoat, but after a look at the gowns in the armoire there couldn't be much left. And since she'd left the new clothes behind, he knew she wouldn't squander the rest on a fancy hotel. The St. Charles was a long shot for sure, but it was also his last hope.

Too tired to think straight, he collapsed on Camilla's bed, and breathing her scent lingering on the pillow, fell asleep. He woke with a start as Camilla's voice called out, "I don't know where it is." He reached out for her. Then he remembered. *She's gone and it's my fault.*

He rose slowly to face his guilty reflection in the vanity mirror. Gaunt, hollow-eyed and with a sinister looking growth of beard, he'd more likely terrify a desk clerk than inspire his confidence. He took the time to wash, shave, and change his clothes before checking with his versatile daytime investigator and nighttime concierge.

The young man shook his head. "No, sir, she didn't show up at the docks or the train station. You said she'd be dressin' like a widow and I gotta tell you, a widow woulda stood out in the crowd." He pushed Patrick's ten-dollar gold piece across the counter. "I'm sorry, sir. I didn't earn this. I hope your find yer girl."

"Wife," Patrick corrected him. "And I *will* find her."

Losing faith in himself with each passing moment, Patrick hired a cab to the St. Charles. The evening clerk didn't recognize the face in the locket, or a widow seeking a room, but then, he'd just arrived for his shift. If Camilla had come straight here from the St. Louis, the day concierge would have been on duty.

"When does he report for work?" Patrick asked, scowling at yet another night's wait to inquire. In that time, she could be anywhere.

Chapter Twenty-Six

Camilla floated in darkness, waiting for her judgement. Heaven or Hell? Demons chanting perverted versions of, *"Au Clair de la Lune,"* and Flora whispering, *"The sins of the fathers,"* made her head pound.

"No," she called out as Mason O'Keefe's scarred face sneered at her, and Beecher's rheumy blue eyes judged her. "I don't know where it is."

Finally, a familiar voice whispered, "There, there, Carrie," and she remembered—everything. She opened her eyes to feel Judith Williams' cool hand on her forehead, concern and worry furrowing her brow. "Are you awake now, dear? Can you hear me?"

Camilla could only groan.

"It's good to have you back," Judith said cheerfully. "We were worried about you. You collapsed at our door yesterday morning and slept the entire day and night through. "You were quite feverish, mumbling about something you couldn't find."

Judith's hand cooled her cheek. "But you seem much better now. Whatever could have happened to you to put you into such a state, dear? You seemed so happy to find your family."

Camilla sat up a little too fast, closing her eyes until the room stopped spinning. She remembered Judith answering the door on her second knock. Her buttercup-blue eyes had widened, but quickly warmed with concern, pulling Camilla into her arms and helping her inside. It was the last thing she remembered. *Yesterday? I've slept an entire day away. They must be looking for me by now. The trains and docks will be teaming with police!*

"You didn't call a doctor, did you?" she asked more sharply than she meant. She'd surely be identified and taken directly to the gallows—without a trial. "I...I mean, thank you so much for helping me. It has been a whirlwind since I arrived. I must have been overly stimulated. I do feel so much better now." She looked at the gray sky outside the window. *Is it morning or evening?*

"No, dear." Judith answered her question about the doctor. "We didn't need a doctor. I'm a nurse. And you're right, there is nothing wrong with you some rest and good food won't fix."

She offered a tray with a steaming bowl of chicken broth and fresh sourdough bread with warm butter. "Eat some of this. Chicken soup cures almost anything and the bread will help put some meat on your bones."

While Camilla devoured her first meal in more than twenty-four hours, Judith asked, "At the risk of being a poor hostess, dear, are you able to be up and be about? We're leaving for St. Louis today."

"St. Louis." *I nearly missed them!* She began to doubt her doubt in God and looked around the small hotel room with a curtain separating the little sitting room from the bed and washroom. Guilt for imposing on this generous stranger, made her want to run to the door, but she doubted she'd make it.

Instead, she stared at her hands, unable to stop them from shaking. "I'm so sorry to bother you, Mrs. Carter, but I needed some help and you were so kind...to offer..." She moved to stand. "I apologize for my interruption. You must have a great deal to do, I won't keep you any longer."

Judith's hand on her knee stopped her. "No need to thank me...Carrie," she answered. "We are all God's creatures and need the help of other humans along the road of life." She leaned closer to add, "And truth be told, I missed you. I took little comfort leaving you in Savannah, but we must each walk our own path."

She poured rich, dark coffee into a bone china cup and offered it to Camilla. "Drink it black," she suggested. "It will give you the strength to tell me what happened to you. When I opened our door, you looked like the hounds of Hell were at your heels. And frankly, St. Louis can wait until I have the answer." She folded her arms across her bosom and rocked back in her chair.

The brew had a bitter edge to it but it did seem to strengthen her still-numb body and calm her shaking hands. And as much as Camilla wanted to spew out the whole hideous story to this woman of God, she couldn't burden Judith with the consequence of her own stupidity. And yet, she couldn't lie to her.

She drained the cup and set it carefully on the table between them. Her own voice sounding strange in her ears, she avoided Judith's all-seeing gaze to tell her what truth she could manage. "So, I have no family left alive in New Orleans. I spent most of my money on the search and haven't found a position. There is nothing here for me now. I've been thinking of going to St. Louis, but..."

She hesitated, remembering Kate's comment about Lucy. "I'm afraid if I travel alone, well some people might get the wrong idea about me."

Judith sipped her own sweetened coffee slowly. "There, there," she comforted, patting Camilla's hand. "Don't worry about a thing. I'm so glad you found us. We have plenty of room and would love to have you join us."

"No," Camilla surprised herself by answering. "I didn't come to impose myself into your group and I'll not take charity. That is meant for others more in need. I simply wanted to see you again...before you left."

Judith looked hurt when she answered, "Oh I'm sorry to hear that."

Afraid she'd offended the woman who likely saved her life by sheltering her, she reached out for Judith's hand. "But if I can be of some help to you, I would love to accompany you to St. Louis. I have a little money toward my passage and will pay you back for any other expenses when I find work there."

Judith's knowing smile returned with her patient nod. "There's no need for repayment. Our expenses have been paid in advance. One more soul on board won't increase our cost."

"But I'm not one of your...group," Camilla protested. "She couldn't let them harbor a...murderess any longer than absolutely necessary. "I'll be leaving you in St. Louis."

Judith's eyes narrowed again. "I see. Well, I had hoped you would want to join our marvelous endeavor." Then as if inspired, she clapped her hands. "But if you insist on repaying a debt I refuse to accept; I have many things to organize for the expedition."

Her soft smile showed Camilla the beautiful woman Judith must have once been—no, still was.

"And I'm only recently coming into the realization that I don't have the stamina I had twenty years ago. You would be of great assistance to me. And once we're in St. Louis, you may even decide you want to complete the journey with us. I will pray on it."

She reached over to embrace Camilla. "Oh, please say yes. It would ease my burden considerably."

Camilla didn't have the strength to weep, even for joy. "Oh, yes," she breathed. "I would be honored to be your assistant. Thank you so much."

Judith adjusted a stray shock of fading blonde hair and took her kerchief back from Camilla to wipe the sudden tears in her eyes. "No thanks are necessary. You remind me of....well, let's just say you make me feel young again."

She rose and touched Camilla's arm, frowning at her wince. "You still seem fatigued. Why not lie down again? Charles will be busy this morning and we don't depart until after mid-day."

"Did I hear my name?" came from a bearded face suspended in the opening of the drapery divider.

"Charles, dear." Judith parted the curtain and took the arm of a man shorter and slighter than she, drawing him into the room. "I want you to meet the lovely young widow I told you about from the train to Savannah. Mrs....oh really, let us not be so formal. Carrie Lange from Georgia, this is my husband Charles Carter, from Boston."

Camilla stood to meet the preacher, whose thick, untamed mop of gray, black, and white hair seemed to have a mind of its own. His small, muscular body radiated energy, but his eyes were the kindest, warmest brown she'd ever seen. When he set them on her and smiled, the tension holding her together released. And when his strong hand touched hers, she collapsed.

This time Judith revived her with smelling salts, and after suffering yet another embarrassing display of weakness, she again sat on the settee, this time to drink tea. "Oh, I'm so sorry. Thank you—again. I am quite fine now. *No, I'm not, but I must get out of New Orleans.*"

She waved off further contact with Reverend Carter's hand to rise on her own, but her legs trembled with the effort. With a deep breath and a strong grip on the arm of the couch, she asked, "Do I have time to freshen up?"

"Of course, my dear." Judith smiled, tucking her arm through Camilla's to show her the way. "The bath is through the curtain, on the left. Do you need help?"

And have her see my bruises? "No," she answered too quickly and too loud, but managed to walk steadily to the tiny washroom. Alone in front of a fresh basin of water, her mood brightened.

St. Louis! The jumping off place to the Western territories. The very place she'd dreamed of exploring as a child. Where she'd begged her father to take her what seemed a lifetime ago. There, she could put the war, Mason, Patrick, and Delmont all behind her and begin again. Excitement pumped new strength into her battered limbs as she focused on the future.

"My, you do look refreshed," Judith told her when she emerged. "Charles and I are so pleased to have your help. And the fresh air from the river cruise will surely make you feel like a new person."

Camilla smiled back and picked up her bag, ready to follow Judith out of the hotel room. "A new person is exactly what I'm hoping to become."

The rented hansom cab didn't compare to Delmont's gilded carriage, but for Camilla, it could have been Cinderella's magic coach on the short ride to the Mississippi River wharves. Stepping into the sunlight, she lowered the brim of her hat to look for uniformed men searching the most obvious escape route for a murderer.

Instead, she saw people of all colors and descriptions hurrying among the loads of cotton, wood, and other merchandise to be loaded onto the waiting boats. The busy throng dodged horses, carriages, pedestrians, and each other in their rush to finish their tasks before the boats sailed. Scanning the busy docks lined with steamboats and barges of every size for over a mile, she turned to Judith. "Which boat is ours?"

Judith held onto her broad yellow hat in a sudden breeze. "Why, the Robert E. Lee of course." She gestured with her free hand to a giant stern-wheeler only a few boats down from them.

Camilla's mouth went slack at the sight of the giant floating hotel that would be her home for the 1,300-mile trip to St. Louis. The largest of the river cruisers, its bright red hull contrasted with sparkling white pillars and gleaming black smokestacks. She laughed, comparing it to a giant raft with wedding cake tiers going up three levels.

Judith touched her arm, frowning when Camilla jumped. "I have to find Charles, dear. Will you be all right? Can you meet us there?"

Camilla appreciated her concern, but bristled at being treated like a child. Still, she risked another look up and down the wharves before forcing a smile. "Of course."

"Wonderful."

As if she'd noticed Camilla's furtive glances around them, Judith added, "If you're still fatigued and want to board, just tell the mate you are with us. Charles has billeted you with Emma Pruitt and her young son, Sam.

"Emma's husband has gone ahead to meet us in St. Louis," she explained. Little Sam is a handful, but theirs is the only cabin with space for another person." Her eyes searched Camilla's. "I hope it won't be too much for you."

Relieved to not be staying with the Carters, whose wise eyes saw too much, she answered quickly, "Oh, no. It will be fine. I'm quite well now and I love children. It will be like having a family for a little while." Her stomach quivered with the pain of knowing she'd never know the pleasure. "You go on and do what you have to do. I'll settle in and be ready to work when you get back."

"Work." Judith laughed. "Time enough for that in St. Louis. For the next four days, we simply eat and stroll the deck. Meet us in the salon after we leave the dock."

Without Judith's protective presence, she felt conspicuous standing on the wharf alone. Doubts set in. What will I do in St. Louis when they move on? I'll be totally alone. And what If they ask me again to join them? The thought both excited and terrified her. Then Flora's voice whispered in her mind, "Be careful what you ask for, *cheri*. You may just get it."

The truth of those words nearly set her to bolt when a voice boomed from the Robert E. Lee, "All dat goin' please to git on board and all dat ain't going please to git ashore."

Camilla took it as a sign. She had to make a choice. Without looking back, she walked up the narrow plank to the broad deck of the riverboat, looking forward to recovering her courage and planning her new life on the way to St. Louis.

"Excuse, me ma'am," came from behind her and she stepped back as a young crewman in a blue coat rushed past her. One brown eye winked as he passed her with a two-finger salute to his fisherman's cap.

Frowning at again being called "ma'am," she stepped out of the way of other boarding passengers to lean against the rail. They made their way to the staircase at the rear of the boat, ascending to the second-tier cabins, promenade, and what surely must be the salon Judith mentioned.

It pleased her that only the one crewman noticed her. Once again, she was invisible in her widow's weeds. None of the missionaries, pilgrims and adventurers had any idea she'd killed a man. She felt free for perhaps the first time in her life, choosing to carry the sights, sounds, and smells of New Orleans, rather than its horrors, into her future.

With plenty of time to find the room she'd share with Mrs. Pruitt and her son, she strolled the main deck, pausing by the giant paddlewheel that would push the behemoth through the Mississippi River's thick, muddy water. She craned her neck to see the giant black stacks rising well above the third tier of the boat, belching black smoke as the stern wheeler built up steam. "Samuel James Pruitt," startled her from behind "You stop this minute or I'll have your hide for the skinning."

She remembered Danielle's ugly threats to shave her head when she came home with muddy skirts after playing on the forbidden riverbank. *No child should fear having their head shaved OR their hide skinned.*

"Don't let her get me," accompanied a tug at her shawl.

She looked down to find a small head of bright red hair buried in the folds of her skirt. Five or six years old, she thought. She placed a protective hand on his head and turned toward his attacker. But instead of an angry shrew, she faced a tiny, elfin-faced young woman with huge blue eyes and red hair nearly as bright as the boy's.

A couple inches shorter than Camilla, she stood with her hands on her hips, her small bosom heaving from running with bags nearly half her size. But instead of anger in the set of her jaw, her lips quivered with a smile and her eyes sparkled with laughter.

The little boy risked a glimpse from Camilla's skirt, an impish grin lighting up his pixy face. "Well, Samuel," the woman scolded. "You've managed to scare me and this lady nearly to death. What have you to say for yourself?"

She surprised Camilla by reaching out, not to strike him, but to take his hand. And even more surprising, he bowed his head and went to her quietly, saying, "Sorry, Ma."

His mother cuffed his ear lightly. "You certainly are. Now apologize to this nice lady for nearly knocking her over and messing up her skirts."

The impish smile disappeared when he stared at his shoes and shuffled his feet. "I'm sorry ma'am."

The young mother echoed his apology. "And so am I. It's...just with all the excitement and all, I'm afraid Sam got a little rambunctious. This is our first riverboat trip. First trip away from home. That's Gadsen. Alabama. Sam's father has always been the disciplinarian and he's gone now. Ahead, I mean. To St. Louis. We're meeting him there and then going west to carry the word of God to the natives."

The young woman's smile was infectious and Camilla smiled back. She could have listened for hours to the musical, Irish brogue, so much like Patrick's when he drank too much brandy. "Not to worry. It's quite all right," she assured the woman. "He just did what everyone else is too grown up to dare."

She knelt to the boy's eye-level and took his hand. "It is nice to meet you, Samuel James Pruitt. I am Carrie Lange." The name came easier each time she said it, perhaps because there had been so little time to become used to Camilla O'Grady.

"Oh, my gracious," Sam's mother exclaimed. "I forgot my manners." She laughed and held out a hand. "I'm Emma Pruitt. You'll be staying with us."

She caught Emma's excitement. "I thought so. Judith told me this morning. I hope it won't inconvenience you. I've only lately joined your group."

"Certainly not." Emma grinned and bent to pick up her two bags. "There is plenty of room and I would love the..." She rolled her eyes to a disappearing Samuel, "adult company."

Nodding toward the railing, she said, "The mate over there told me we're on the second level. Our room is on the end of the port side of the corridor. That's the left. Or is it the right? Anyway, it's number 22."

Camilla followed her glance to the crewman with the blue jacket who had bumped into her. Again, he tipped a finger to the brim of his hat and winked. She turned away quickly to take one of Emma's bags. "Let me help with those."

"But you have your own."

"Only this." She held up the carpet bag. "It's almost nothing." She'd purposely taken only the most necessary items—again. "Please let me help."

Emma bowed to her need to be needed, letting her take the bag. At the end of the corridor, they were pleasantly surprised at the stateroom they shared. Roomier than Camilla had expected, there was a large bed with a trundle underneath for Sam. The single round window allowed enough light inside to make the red furnishings and dark wood walls seem inviting. The basin and washstand were in a small, curtained alcove. Two oil lamps on either side of the bed and a small chair in the corner added the comforts of home.

"This is better than our cabin in 'Bama," Emma exclaimed, dragging her bag to the side of the bed nearest the alcove. She bounced like a child on the mattress to test its softness, squealing, "A real feather bed! I may never want to leave this boat and just sail up and down the river forever."

Her laugh trilled, like the fairies Patrick spoke about in bed while her fingers traced circles in the mat of black hair on his chest. *Why does everything make me think of him?*

Emma patted the spot next to her while Sam played peek-a-boo from behind the curtain. "Please sit down. It's a long trip. We should get to know each other. Tell me about your family and how you came to join the Carters."

Camilla did as she asked, aching to stretch out and sleep until St. Louis. It seemed to her that a lie told often enough can sound like the truth. "There isn't much to say really. Like so many others, I'm a widow starting a new life. I met Judith on the train to Savannah. But my story has no interest, tell me about yourself."

A shadow crossed Emily's guileless face. "Before the war, my James was a lawyer. He served the Confederacy as an officer, and survived the terrible slaughter at Gettysburg."

At Camilla's sympathetic nod, she went on. "When the war ended, he couldn't practice law, or even vote. We became tenants on our own farm and couldn't eke out enough money to pay the taxes. In despair, he took to drinking and it changed him from a kind and gentle man, into a..."

She swiped at tears suddenly filling her expressive eyes. "Well, one evening, about a year ago, we went to town and saw Reverend Carter preaching." Her warm hand grasped Camilla's. "We were so moved. Most of the people were in tears by the sermon's end. Even my Jim."

Like a preacher herself, she paused for effect. "We listened to the Reverend's stories of how much the Indians need God's word, and how we can heal our own wounds by helping them. We suddenly didn't feel so sorry for ourselves anymore and Jim put down the bottle for good."

Leaning in closer, she whispered, "The Reverend Carter saved our lives."

Camilla smiled. *Finally, a story with a happy ending.* "So you joined the Carters' expedition?"

Emma shook her head, red curls bobbing every which way. "Not right away. We felt sorry for the poor savages mind you, but were not inclined to seek them out until Reverend Carter approached my husband with a proposition."

"A proposition?"

"Well, yes, in a way. Besides being an attorney, Jim is a skilled carpenter. Reverend Carter needs those skills to help build the mission and school while he tends to the souls."

So, the Reverend offered a poor drunk and his family salvation and purpose—in exchange for their labor. Suddenly Judith's husband didn't seem so mesmerizing. Camilla gently pulled her hand away. "I see."

"No, I don't think you do." The hard edge in her voice belied Emma's fragile exterior. "We all serve the Lord in our own ways. Some preach, some teach, some heal, and some build. We teach others the love of God by showing it in our own lives. And we honor ourselves in how we treat others. We'll show them God's love by living side by side with them peacefully. It will help us all heal the wounds of war."

In Camilla's mind, it would take more than a few buildings and being nice to end more than a century of hatred with the original inhabitants of this land; but she'd just met this woman and wanted to like her. "I wish you well," she said, patting Emily's dainty hand.

Emma's eyes widened. "But aren't you one of us? Judith said..."

"Judith is a dear woman," Camilla interrupted and stood. "She saw I needed help and offered to let me accompany your...group, but I am only going as far as St. Louis."

She anticipated Emma's next question. "My family is...dead. I hope to begin again there."

Her new friend stood too, wrapping her arms around Camilla's shoulders, pulling her close. "Yes, we are all beginning again, aren't we?" She smiled through fresh tears. "And I wish you well too."

Emma began unpacking her bags into the little trunk under the window, chattering, "It will be so exciting seeing St. Louis, don't you think? I've never been out of 'Bama, and I miss Jim. He's been gone nearly a month now, organizing the train and getting supplies ready.

"He went to find a wagon master and have things all prepared before we arrive so we can go right on to Independence. We're leaving late, but since we're taking the old Santa Fe Trail, if we make good time, we'll avoid the bad weather in the mountains."

A whistle cut off the sound of her voice and all three occupants of the stateroom covered their ears to the shrill sound. It died a moment later and the floor lurched beneath their feet. The Robert E. Lee was pulling away from the dock!

"Ma!" Samuel screamed, his little hands still pressed against his ears. "We're moving!" He climbed on top of the trunk to look out the round window. "You should see. All the people on the docks are yelling and waving at us." He jumped down and tugged at his mother's arm. "Let's go out and wave at them too."

Emma smiled at Camilla. "I'd better go or I'll lose my arm."

Sam reached out for Camilla's hand. "You come too, missus. You don't want to miss it."

Caught up in the excitement, Camilla held the little boy's other hand and they joined the throng on the promenade deck. A space opened for

205

them at the rail so they could watch the people on the wharves shrink as the Bobby Lee pulled away from its berth.

Camilla watched as men who only moments before had been sweating over cargo, now lounged on the empty wagons and carts, waving along with the friends of passengers. Emily and Sam happily waved back, but Camilla couldn't bid a fond farewell to a city that had brought her only pain.

Her heart skipped a beat. A dark-haired man in a white suit stood with his back to her, talking to one of the draymen. She held her breath when the huge laborer pointed at the retreating riverboat. But just as he turned, another passenger shouldered her aside to take her place at the rail.

By the time he moved, the boat had gained steam and she no longer saw the man in white. Fool, she scolded herself again for hoping Patrick loved her enough follow her. After all, he was a detective. How difficult would it be for him to find her?

She backed away from the crowd. It didn't matter now. Even if he did follow her, she was wanted for murder. She wasn't the first woman betrayed by someone she loved. And wouldn't be the last.

She frowned at the reflection of her plain black dress and pinched face in a stateroom window. *I'm alone now and can never go back. So be it.* A moment later, she pulled off the hateful chignon, freeing her hair to tumble down her back. Camilla Langesford O'Grady was dead, and Carrie Lange had officially finished mourning.

Chapter Twenty-Seven

The four-day trip aboard the Robert E. Lee seemed like an enchanted voyage. She spent mornings strolling the three decks of the boat, afternoons conversing in the main cabin furnished with ornate sofas and chairs, and decorative ceilings etched with gold. In the evenings, she enjoyed cool river breezes and the moonlight reflecting off the mysterious river's dark water.

At night, she slept soundly on the gently swaying boat. The powerful steam engine humming below decks reminded her of the night sounds at Langesford, the home she would never see again. Oddly, it comforted her. She could never go home again, but it would always be with her.

Emma Pruitt spent considerable time in the main cabin with Judith and Reverend Carter, leaving Camilla and Sam free to roam. She acknowledged Sam was a handful. His fascination with the forbidden paddlewheels, gave her frequent excuses to be on deck, where she was awed by the lush Mississippi shoreline and the many mansions that survived the war. She wondered if they'd passed her Manan's beloved Belle Riviére.

Spending so much time on deck, she couldn't escape the mate who flirted with her the first day. They called him Sandy instead of his real name, Sherwood. His ever-present, gap-toothed smile charmed her, along with light brown eyes glowing with life and a love for the river. On their second evening out, he gave her a tour of his floating home, his strong hand on her arm helping her navigate the narrow steps up from the promenade deck to the "hurricane" deck above the passengers' cabins.

"This is the real heart of the Bobby Lee," he told her from three stories above the water. In the cloudless night, only the smokestacks and the crew's quarters seemed to stand between them and the constellations. He leaned over the railing to peer at the black water two stories below. He touched her arm and pointed. "Look, a planter."

Camilla leaned against the waist-high railing for a better look, while he held elbow. She gasped at what looked like a giant tree growing right out of the river, the top branches nearly scraping the side of the riverboat.

Sandy chuckled "Ol' Cap'n Baker knew about that one. They're the worst, planters are. You never know how big they are under the water. But they don't move around much. Once you know where they are, an' if the river's clear o' barges, you can skirt 'em." He lowered his voice to add, "Not at all like sawyers."

Camilla remembered reading about riverboat fires and entire ships sinking after hitting trees in turbulent waters. Suddenly her voyage didn't seem so magical. But rather than her own safety, she worried about Judith and Emma—and Sam. "Oh, dear," she replied. "It must be doubly dangerous at night. How does your pilot know where they are in the dark?"

He shrugged. "It gits into yer blood, and comes with time on the river. Cap'n Baker, says his bones tell him when to jig and when to jog. He's been doin' this since he's a youngster, so I guess, he's got good bones."

Camilla laughed. Imagine bones guiding you through life. Forgetting she was a fugitive for a rare moment, she lightly touched her new friend's arm. "I feel so much better knowing our pilot has such experience. But what is this sawyer, you mentioned?"

He smiled and patted the hand on his arm. "Sawyers ain't big, just snags of fallen trees and logs, but they move with the current and can be a problem in low water. Not to worry. A sawyer won't blow you up like a planter, but it can poke a good hole in the hull so you're dead in the water a while."

She again pulled the shawl closer. Suddenly, her bones were telling her the faster, more expensive train may have been the better choice. "I had no idea river travel could be so dangerous."

"Not to worry," he repeated, puffing out his chest. "It was plenty dangerous in the early days when we burned pine knots for lamps. Their light don' carry worth spit. But Cap'n Baker knows all the still water and when to cross back an' forth. An' he knows every bend in the river in daylight and dark. The Bobby Lee is safe as your granny's carriage."

He covered her hand with his. "And I won't let anything happen to you." He bent toward her and kissed her lips.

For a moment, she imagined other lips, other arms, pulling her close, and allowed the dream to become reality. But when he nipped at her tender lips, the dream became an all-too-familiar nightmare. She pushed him away, nearly losing her balance when Cap'n Baker's bones told him to swerve around the planter—or was it a sawyer?

"I'm so sorry," Sandy groveled. "You're just so beautiful under the moon and you looked so sad. I figured with the time we spent together, I could...I just wanted to..."

Knowing only too well what he wanted to do, she stepped away from the railing, wanting to slap him and run. But she also knew the futility of fighting a man, especially a young one capable of throwing her into a raging river. Wiping the taste of old tobacco from her mouth, she looked into his eyes. They held no malice or hatred, as Delmont's had at her refusal. Only confusion and a little shame. But ...well I am not ready to replace my...husband."

Relieved to see sympathy in his gaze, she asked, "Perhaps in time...if we had a chance to better know each other...we...could become friends." She turned then, feeling guilty for the false hope she'd sown.

Two days later, on their last morning on the river, Judith observed, "This trip has done you a world of good, Carrie. You positively glow. It appears you've overcome your tribulations with water travel."

"Tribulations?" Camilla remembered the lie she'd told Judith in Savannah, and looked out at the river. "Yes, it appears so. I do feel quite well, and I'm so grateful for your generosity. "But I don't know how I'll ever repay you. I haven't earned any of my passage as we agreed."

"No need, child. Seeing your smiling face when you were walking with the nice young crewman is payment enough, and of course the help you've given Emma with little Sam is beyond measure." Her voice lowered and she leaned in close. "The girl is so delicate. She'll need all her strength for the journey. And Sam needs a strong hand."

At Camilla's answering nod, they faced the river in silence, lost in their own thoughts of what the future held. Judith spoke first. "What will you do, Camilla, after we get to St. Louis?"

"I have a plan—" She stopped when she realized Judith had called her by her real name.

"I've known since the train," answered her gasp. Judith's eyes were kind as always, but her mouth had set into a serious line. "Remember, I told you we were preaching near Langesford plantation? Well we were very near. You and I passed at the Omer market now and then, and when we heard of Anthony Langesford's death, we came to the service to pay our respects. We would have introduced ourselves, but your young man spirited you away quickly, and we didn't want to force our presence at your home."

Camilla's blood chilled as she searched for an escape from what had been a haven for four days, but Judith's strong, work-worn hand held her fast. "I don't mean to pry," she said. "Lord knows I've made my own mistakes, but I've learned that running away is no answer to life's difficulties. I'm also an excellent judge of character. I met Mr. O'Grady several times during our stay, to discuss your man, Leroy. And after your wedding, you both looked so happy together. For the life of me, I can't imagine what would have caused you to leave both him and your family home as you did."

Camilla turned away, her tears joining the river's muddy water. "You don't understand and I can't share the awful truth I discovered about my husband. I only ask you to believe that I couldn't stay."

More to convince herself than Judith, she added, "When I left my home I left to go *to* something. A better life. But what I sought wasn't there, so now I'm starting fresh, in St. Louis."

She covered Judith's hand with her free one, imploring, "Please don't tell anyone who I am. Just know I can't go back." As much as she wanted to, she couldn't say why.

To her surprise, Judith didn't press. "So be it," she sighed. "Your secret is safe with me. But you must know that a new name won't turn you into someone else." Now she looked out over the river. "The past never dies."

Camilla heard Flora's voice when Judith added, "All we can do is make peace with it and determine how much it will shape our future." After a long silence, she smiled. "Now, tell me about this fresh start of yours, Carrie Lange."

Relieved, Camilla smiled too. "Well, Sandy, I mean Mr. Sutcliff, has a friend who owns a boardinghouse near the docks. He says it's reasonably priced and the owner needs good help. He thinks I could get a job there. Maybe even a room."

Judith crossed her arms over her bosom. "Do you really want your new life to be washing dishes and serving food in a riverfront flophouse?" Her eyes narrowed. "If Sandy knows the owner, you must realize it is a place where rivermen stay. They can be a rough lot unless you're under the protection of one of them." She touched Camilla's arm. "Do you know what that means?"

She nodded, answering Judith's second question first. "Y-yes, I know what 'protection' means, but Sandy has been a perfect gentleman." *Except for that one stolen kiss on the hurricane deck.* "He understands I am not interested in...that," she added with a shake of her head. "And no, of course I don't want to wash dishes forever, but it will keep me safe while I look for another position.

"Such as?"

Is she purposely being difficult? "Well, I could run a small dress shop or keep books. Tutor, perhaps. I'm fluent in two languages, three if you include Creole. I'm sure in a big, bustling city like St. Louis, I won't have a problem finding a place."

"And if you don't?"

"Oh stop!" she cried out. "I will be fine because I have to be. Don't you see? I wasn't lucky enough to die, so now I have to go on."

Judith's features softened. "I just want you to know how difficult it will be for you alone. You would be much safer with us. You can still be my secretary and record our epic adventure for posterity. In two, or three languages, if you wish," she added with a wink.

The offer was almost too tempting. "Thank you. But you have done too much already. It's time I took control of my own life." She smiled then. "Truth be told, I'm not sure wild Indians are safer than city folk— or even river men."

Judith's answering laugh was as large as her heart. "That judgement will be yours, dear." Then, as she had in Savannah, Judith offered, "Remember, we will be at the Planter's Hotel for two weeks. There is always a place for you with us."

While Camilla blinked back tears of gratitude, a deep voice called out, "There you are, woman," and Charles Carter ambled up to them. "We dock shortly, and here you are, river gazing." Despite his stern voice, he smiled when he looked at Camilla. "Unless you're recruiting another worker for the Lord."

As always, Camilla couldn't meet his gaze. *He is a man of God, and I am a murderess.*

Judith saved the awkward moment with a wink at Camilla. "Time will tell, Charles." She took his arm, patting it affectionately as they strolled away. "Time will tell."

Camilla's heart raced at Judith's turn of Patrick's favorite phrase. When it calmed, she determined to fill the emptiness inside her with activity, and set off to check on Emma and Sam in their cabin.

While Emma repacked her few belongings, Camilla played with Sam. "Ain't you comin' with us?" he asked trying to tie a knot Sandy had shown him.

"No, Sam," she answered, taking the rope from him. "You do it this way." She took one end of the rope from him, saying, "This is the tree." Then she picked up the bottom end. "And the rabbit goes around the tree to get to his hole, like this." She undid her knot and returned the rope to his small hands. "And it's aren't, not ain't."

He frowned. "But I thought you liked us."

She touched his soft, red hair. "Oh, Sam, I like you so much, you and your Maman. But I cannot go with you."

"You goin' to marry Sandy?"

The precocious child apparently didn't miss a thing. "Whatever made you think I'm going to marry him?"

"I seen you an' him walkin' and holdin' hands, and once I seen him kiss you. My ma says only married people and folks who is gittin' married kiss."

She blushed. Apparently, Sam had escaped his room to follow her and Sandy to the upper deck. What could she say? She'd spent two lovely evenings with Sandy, taking comfort from his strong, warm hand at quiet moments. Only once had he stolen a kiss.

"Well, Sam," she said after a deep breath. "Sometimes friends kiss too, and Sandy is a good friend. I might not see him again for a long time." She pulled the boy into her arms and tousled his hair. "I'm going to kiss you too when we leave the boat this afternoon. Does that mean we'll get married?"

Sam quieted for a rare moment, his mouth set as he considered his answer. Then, smiling wide, he announced, "I don't like kissing, but I'll marry you if you wait for me."

Chapter Twenty-Eight

After the goodbyes, Camilla adjusted her bonnet, smoothed the skirt of her shapeless calico dress, took a firm hold of her little bag and repeated the directions Sandy gave her to the "River's Rest" boardinghouse. A short walk down Market Street, a few blocks to the east of the wharves and just past the Mercantile Exchange, he'd told her.

Though nearly noon, she'd have plenty of time to meet with the owner, Hiram Woods, and hopefully gain employment before supper. Her spirits lifted. This time she had a place to go. The exhilaration of freedom made her want to skip like young Sam. But the docks were still near and police from New Orleans could be waiting for her.

The riverfront smelled of fish, steamboat fumes, sweat, and horse piles. This is real life, she thought. Not the fairytale she'd been raised to believe. Not even the soot-stained clapboard siding, sagging steps, and dirty windows of the River's Rest, dampened her enthusiasm.

Still, standing in front of the rambling building she hoped would be her temporary home, she thought of Flora and prayed for her grandmother's strength. Remembering her mother's weakness, she also prayed that courage skipped a generation. Then she climbed the creaking steps and opened the ripped screened door into the dining room.

It took a moment for her eyes to adjust from the bright sunlight of the street, to the dim, smoky interior of the "Rest." In the weak light penetrating the only window's grimy surface, she saw a cigar-filled tray on a filthy table, and a tarnished spittoon next to the table. Horseflies feasted on scraps of bacon and ham still sitting on plates from breakfast.

She froze as her hopes for the future again crashed against the craggy wall of reality. *This is my only hope? My new life?* Then anger replaced despair. *How can someone with a thriving business allow such filth?* The stench of old cigars, spoiled food and sweat suddenly turned her stomach and she made for the spittoon.

Humiliated at her body's betrayal during such an important time, and perspiring from the oppressive closeness of the room, she rose, pressing a lavender-scented handkerchief to her mouth. Then she turned to face an apron-clad giant of a man frowning down at her.

"This ain't no hospital," he said in a gravelly voice, his black eyes looking from her to the spittoon in disgust.

Would he prefer I used his floor? Though, from the look of the sticky, rubbish-covered planks, no one would notice. And she'd certainly clean up after herself. "I am so sorry," she apologized as the man wiped dirty hands on an even dirtier apron. But she couldn't resist a barb in her defense. "I felt fine until I came inside. Perhaps you could let some fresh air in here to—"

"An' I 'spose you want some herb tea too, Miss, to settle yer insides."

The jowls under his massive side whiskers wobbled when he shook his bald head. "Well I ain't got none. This here's a hotel for rivermen. The Planter's caters to women-folk. You kin catch a cab at Market and River to take ye there." He ignored the now swarming spittoon and turned away. "I got a noon meal to make."

Her stomach cramped again. She had to get away from the spittoon, but she needed a job more than her dignity. "Wait." She followed him into the kitchen. "I'm looking for Hiram Woods. Sandy Sutcliff from the Robert E. Lee said he might need some help for the kitchen or the rooms."

When he turned, she looked at his eyes to avoid retching again at the sights and smells of the disgusting kitchen. Arms the size of tree limbs crossed over his barrel chest as he scowled and looked her up and down. "Sandy sent you here? I don't believe you."

Progress at last. "Oh, yes, he did. I met him on the boat." Talking nearly as fast as Emma, she explained, "I accompanied some missionaries. I'm a...a widow. I'm starting over in St. Louis. He said you were looking for someone to help you here."

She stopped suddenly and cocked her head. "You *are* Hiram Woods, are you not?"

"Aye. But I still don't believe Sandy sent you here. How kin a little chit like you help me?"

She struggled to find a way to convince him while he watched her from hooded eyes. *Sandy's real name!* He said few people knew it. If he and Hiram were friends, he might. She folded her arms across her own chest and raised her chin. "I know Sandy's real name."

Two bushy eyebrows raised from a straight line across his forehead. "Which is?"

"Sherwood," she nearly shouted. *What a strange interview for a job as a scullery maid.*

Hiram Woods silently appraised her again, focusing this time on the lace-trimmed handkerchief she twisted in her hand. Then he dropped his arms. "Aye, so you know Sandy. But you don't look much up to feedin' and cleanin' up after a dozen river men." A glimmer of humor sparked in his dark eyes when he tested, "Ye look like a soft Southern lady-type to me. Won't last a week."

My turn. She enjoyed the sparring. It made her feel strong again, like when she ran Langesford during war—and afterward, when she and Patrick... *Stop!* She tucked the dainty hanky up the wrist of her sleeve.

"I'll have you know, Mr. Woods, during the War I managed the largest plantation in Georgia with only a few freedmen to help. I have picked cotton until my fingers bled, helped birth cattle and babies, fed twenty people on next to nothing, and cleaned pigsties no worse than this place."

She risked stepping closer to the burly, beast of a man to boast, "I may be small, but I come from a long line of..." Had she nearly said slaves? "Hard workers."

Suddenly, Hiram's jowls shook and a roar much like the bellow of a cow, followed his face-splitting grin. "I bet you did it all in the mornin' and gave fancy dress balls at night."

Sensing she'd somehow passed his test, she curtsied, extended a hand and drawled, "Of course. The best in the South." She only flinched a little when he squeezed her hand and raised a ham-sized paw to slap her bruised arm.

"Well yer gonna need all yer spunk for this job, Missus. My woman left a few years back. Things have got a little behind in the housekeeping chores. I got a young boy, but he ain't never 'round when there's serious work to be done."

She stepped further into the room to survey what had once been an efficient kitchen, large enough to cook for many more than Hiram's twelve boarders. The large twin tubs could accommodate dishes from a full house and she found a solid wood chopping block buried beneath a pile of garbage.

"No worries," she answered with false bravado. "I can get even the laziest hand to work." She smiled up at him. "My name is Carrie Lange. I can clean this mess—and bring you more business."

Still doubtful, Hiram shook his head and addressed her formally, "Well, Missus Lange, havin' a lady here might make some the rowdier roomers behave. But it ain't gonna be easy."

She took another disdainful look around her. "I agree, but first things first." Sensing him warming to her proposal, she pushed, "Sandy mentioned you would provide a room."

"Are you mad?" he roared. "You cain't stay here with all these randy river rats, pardon the language."

She didn't try to hide her crushing disappointment at having to beg for a room to stay. Judith's offer would still be valid, she thought, but she couldn't live on the kindness of others for the rest of her life. She would survive on her own, or she would die.

Looking up at the man who had just dashed her last hope, she swallowed hard, forced her back to straighten, and met his gaze. "You're making a huge mistake Mr. Woods. "I am adept at all business practices. I know how to run a house, can cook High French cuisine, Creole specialties, and American wild game fit for a king. I can also clean this place up and bring you respectable clientele and an income you can't even imagine, for little more than the cost of a room." With the arrogance of a Delta demoiselle, she picked up her simple skirt as if to protect a priceless gown from the filth on the floor, shook her head in disgust and spun on her heel. With a small wave of her hand, she dismissed the River's Rest owner with, "I guess sometimes, you can't even give the golden goose away."

"Wait!" stopped her, but she took a moment before turning back.

"Yesss?" she drawled and turned slowly to face him again.

She suppressed a smile. He reminded her of an actor in a play at the French Opera House, with his booming voice and forbidding size. His head, bald above salt and pepper eyebrows bobbed and a gold center tooth flashed from under a black, handlebar mustache. He waved his arms and planted his feet, posturing as he tested her resolve. But for some reason, he didn't frighten her.

"I must be goin' soft, but I got a house a block down the street," he said. "It's empty. Not a bad neighborhood, neither. I guess I could let you live there, as your pay o'course."

"Slavery has ended, Mr. Woods," she pointed out. "But I understand such an accommodation would come at a price. Just how much of my pay do you propose to withhold?"

"Well..." He smoothed the drooping corners of his mustache with one hand while rubbing the other over his smooth skull. "I suppose I could manage a dollar a week and room and board."

A dollar a week! She recalled how quickly Flora's twenty-dollar gold pieces had disappeared in New Orleans. How could she possibly survive on such a paltry sum? *But it does include a house and food.*

She didn't miss the irony. Except for the dollar, it mirrored exactly how the slaves had lived on Langesford. Perhaps it was divine retribution for her to endure this period of indenture. *The sins of the Fathers.* Philippe Trémon's sins were now being visited upon the second generation. Perhaps if she suffered enough, her children would be spared—if the joy of children was ever to be hers.

"Well, Missus," Hiram said, "What say you?"

She'd watched her father do enough horse trading to know the game. Mr. Woods wouldn't respect her if she didn't counter his offer. "An additional dollar for other essentials, Mr. Woods, with conditions."

His eyes narrowed. "What conditions?"

"In one month, if I manage this place well enough, my pay will be doubled and I'll receive five percent of the rent paid for any boarders above your current eight. If not, you may let me go with just my room and board."

He rubbed his chin as he considered what looked like a sure thing in his favor. Finally, the mustache twitched. "Agreed. Anything else?"

"Yes," she said and left the nauseating kitchen for the fetid-smelling back porch. "The boy you mentioned. How old is he?"

"Thirteen. Fourteen maybe."

"How do you pay him?"

"Meals and a bed in the woodshed."

She stared at him. "Why does he stay?"

He shrugged. "He's a half-breed. His ma's a Comanche Injun. He ain't worth much, but he sweeps up all right and helps with the wood."

The term half-breed stung Camilla, making her answer sharp. "And I thought your Mr. Lincoln ended slavery."

"Injuns don't count."

The set of his jaw told her he meant it, but she pushed her new employer's patience to respond, "I see. Well, I'll need a room made for him inside. In the attic, perhaps. And he should be paid for his work. Fifty cents a week, I think. Take it from my pay if you must. He'll earn it. And I want complete control over his duties. I'll need him for the heavy work."

Careful to leave him no chance to recant, she changed the topic. "Now if you'll give me directions to my house, I'll settle in and start working today. Please have the boy ready in three hours." Before he could refuse, she turned again toward what passed for a dining room.

Hiram Woods followed, still shaking his head when he reached behind the scarred oak counter for the key to his house. "It's on Market Street," he told her. "Just down the block." He handed it to her. "Third house on the left. Blue, it is, with a fine oak out front."

Then he left her to yell, "Jesse, where you hidin' out this time? Git yer filthy red ass in here now!"

Chapter Twenty-Nine

The faded old blue house with an ancient oak in front stood a little slanted on its foundation, but the key turned easily in the lock and the door opened without protest on well-oiled hinges. It surprised her to find it clean inside, with three little rooms and sparse, but serviceable furnishings. Stepping inside, she set her bag on a stool by the door. For a month anyway, it would be her home.

Pleased to find a clean, feather tick mattress in the bedroom and that she didn't have to scrub her new home before going to work, she changed into one of two gray muslin work dresses she'd purchased on the way from the Rivers' Rest. Then she secured her willful curls with a wide strip of muslin wound around her head, Creole style.

"Oh, my stars," she sighed, when the cracked mirror above the bedside table confirmed her bloodline. Her fingers traced her face as if it belonged to a stranger. *How did I never notice?* She didn't bother to stem the flow of tears as she recognized the grandmother she'd thought a slave, in her own eyes. Then she said another prayer for even a tiny bit of Flora's strength and wisdom.

When she returned to the Rest, Hiram stood with a giant paw clamped on the shoulder of a dirty, skinny young boy with greasy, straight black hair covering his eyes. One look at the boy's large, raw-boned build and hooked, Roman nose told her he was Hiram Woods' son.

She frowned at Jesse's skinny legs extending well below the fraying hems of his trousers, and his filthy bare feet shuffling nervously on the rough floorboards, until Hiram finally spoke, "I told him I'd whip him good if he ran away from you."

The word "whip" also held more meaning for her these days. Poor Jesse was a slave in his father's house. She looked up at Hiram. "Did you tell him about his pay? And the room?"

"You mean you was serious?" he bellowed, and led her away from Jesse's wide, hopeful eyes. "'Bout putting him in the attic an' payin' him out o' yer own pay?"

She settled her hands on her hips. "Mr. Woods, you need a lot of help around here. This boy and I are all you have. And we're wasting time. Now, if you'll see to his room, Jesse and I will get started."

She assessed the boy from top to bottom, just as his father had regarded her. The kitchen would have to wait. This child-man hadn't bathed in months, maybe longer. His clothes fairly crawled on his body and he added yet another sour odor to the cloud of stale air overpowering the boarding house.

She spoke softly as she met his dark eyes. "Jesse, I won't hurt you. I only need your help. In return, you will have a decent place to sleep and regular food." She took his filthy brown hand and led him into the kitchen, her gaze searching the yard for something large enough to serve as a bathtub.

"Light the fire in the stove," she told him. "Heat as many pans of water as you can." Trusting him not to run away, she said, "I will be right back," returning a few minutes later with two men carrying a copper watering tub. The men grinned as they happily helped the young missus tote Jesse's bathtub.

The bigger one with a bushy white beard joked, "Injuns are afeared o' baths, missus. Think they'll melt." He and his scrawny partner laughed uproariously, apparently unaware they smelled as bad, or worse, than Jesse.

"Kin we watch?" the smaller man asked. "We're takin' bets on which one o' you'll end up in the tub."

The one with the beard leered at her. "Yeah, I wanna see that."

Clearly, if she didn't put them in their place now, she'd never have a moment's peace. She pulled the meat cleaver from its hook on the wall, raising it and stepping toward them. "And what are you willing to pay for the sight, sir? A hand? Your good right arm perhaps. Or your tongue." Then she smiled wickedly at the buttons of their pants. "Or

Doris M. Lemcke

something else that shouldn't be allowed to wag loose."

Terror registered in the eyes of the two jaded, Mississippi rivermen. Both sets of arms went up in surrender. "No. No. No need for violence, ma'am. Jest jokin' 'bout the Injun, is all," they chattered at the same time.

"And me," she hissed back. "And I don't like it." She raised the cleaver again. "Where I come from, men who disrespect a lady pay for it. *Did I really say that?* But she'd gone too far to stop. "The war taught *Southern* women how to protect our honor in many ways." She abandoned the heavy cleaver in favor of a carving knife. "Now get out of here while I do my job."

Mouths agape, they turned, both trying to fit through a door meant for one. She chuckled, calling after them, "And thank you so much for your help." She turned then to see Jesse staring at her, wide-eyed with wonder and admiration. Then admiration turned to terror when she pointed to the tub.

Betting a superior intelligence lay behind his mask of imbecility, as it often had with slaves, she told him, "You know it has to be done. You cannot hide under filth forever. With me, you will earn a wage, have a room like a human being, and be treated as an employee, not a slave or an animal."

He stared at her a moment longer, then shrugged in wary acceptance of his fate, and began pouring the first of the pots of hot water into the tub. At half-full, she handed him a bar of lye soap and a vegetable brush. "Put your clothes on the floor over by the stove and get in the tub. Scrub until your skin turns red. When the next batch of water is done, wash your hair. I'll help you rinse."

She busied herself at the pump until she heard a splash and a gasp at the unfamiliar hot water. She scooped up his soiled clothing with an ax handle, to dump them into a boiling cauldron.

A few minutes later, "Please ma'am, I am ready for more water now," came from behind her. When she turned, a clean, handsome young face grinned at her from a head white with soap lather. She put her hands on her hips. "Well now Jesse, aren't you the one." She dumped another pail of warm water over his soapy head, releasing years of grime and drowned vermin into the tub.

222

He dressed in the one set of work clothes Hiram provided from his stack of unclaimed clothing. Then he sat quietly on a kitchen stool while Camilla cut more than 10 inches from his pitch-black hair. Like a sculptor with a chisel, each snip of the shears revealed more of his high, proud forehead, well-formed ears and what would be a strong, thick neck when he grew into his bones.

Suddenly, "Now you done it," raged from the doorway, nearly making her cut Jesse's ear.

The boy cringed and she felt his fear. Knowing the older man could batt her away like a fly if he wanted, Camilla pointed the shears like a sword, shielding the son from his father. But Hiram kept his gaze on the boy while ranting to her. "Cleanin' 'im up. Dressin' 'im in white man's clothes. Givin' him a bed and pay, for God's sake. It won't be a week afore he runs away."

Now she understood. Hiram had lost his "woman" and though he wouldn't acknowledge Jesse as his son, didn't want to lose him too. "He won't run away," she assured him with more confidence than she felt. "He will work harder and better than before. You'll be proud of him." Then she appealed to his cash box. "Don't forget our bargain. If it doesn't work out, my labor will be free. You can't lose."

She knew she won when the mustache twitched and he nodded to the two river rats peeking through the ripped screen. For show, he waved a fist in the air. "And don't think I won't hold you to it."

~ * ~

In only a few days, the kitchen almost sparkled. Tasty meals with a Cajun flavor, served by a pretty woman on clean dishes—the constant washing of which left Jesse's hands little time to get dirty—attracted more than rivermen for the food.

At the end of the week, Hiram beamed. Camilla's meals had brought in more money than a month of boarders. Jesse hadn't run away, and she'd spruced up his old wreck of a house, recruiting idle roomers with just a smile or a promise of peach pie.

Sandy stayed at the Rest and walked her home at night. On the night before he left to return to New Orleans, he put his arm around her shoulders. She didn't pull away this time. It felt comfortable to be with him, almost like a brother, if she pictured darker hair and blue eyes.

But as they approached her door, his arm tightened. "This is my last night here, Carrie," he said. "I'll be gone three whole weeks."

She stepped away to retrieve her key from her bag. "You make it sound like a lifetime."

"It seems like it when I'm away from you," he breathed, pulling her into his arms. Then he kissed her, his hands pulling her hips against him.

She'd learned from experience that a struggle would only encourage him, and fought her revulsion to his wet, sloppy kisses by not responding. When his hands loosened their grip on her buttocks to roam upward along her ribcage, she brought her elbows down on his forearms as hard as she could, and ran up the steps.

Holding her key in front of her like a weapon, she wiped his spit from her face with her other arm. "What do you think you're doing?"

But the Sandy who had been such a gentleman, such a friend, now glared at her. His breath came heavily, his trousers bulging with his intentions. He took the two steps in one leap while she backed against her door. The impotent key still in her hand, she looked past him for help, but the hour was late, the street empty.

He stopped just in front of her, holding his hands out. "Carrie, I didn't mean to scare you, but you have to know how much I want…care for you. After all the time we spent together and because I'm leaving tomorrow, and, well…you being a widow and all, I figured you were ready. You have to admit I been a patient man."

At her silence, he stepped closer. "I know you want me. You don't need to pretend. Women like me. Just give me a little somethin' to remember while I'm gone. So folks'll know you're mine."

"Yours!" echoed down the empty street, as well as the sound of her slap. "How dare you! I do not *belong* to anyone."

His face reddened from more than the mark of her hand, and he lunged for her at the same moment her knee met his groin. He doubled over, tears flooding his eyes. "Jesus H. Christ," he swore and backed down the steps, clutching his crotch. "You little whore," he screamed. "No, you're worse than a whore. You're a tease. A damned little Southern Belle tease. I'm gone at first light tomorrow, but when I get back your teasing little ass better be out of St. Louis, or I'll show you what you missed tonight—in spades."

Halfway down the block, still bent over, he turned and waved a fist. "You kin bet on that."

She waited until he was out of sight to turn the key in the lock with a shaking hand. Once inside, she relocked the door and leaned against it. A slow-moving shadow in the darkness, she dropped her shawl and apron on the stool and went to her bedroom.

Still trembling with fear and anger, she closed her window curtains against the full moon and starlit sky, lit the lamp and dropped to her knees on the braided rug. For the first time in four years, she folded her hands and bowed her head. "Make it stop," she whispered to the darkness.

Time will tell, whispered through her mind, followed by the sounds of the old house creaking under its own weight. She sighed, tossed her head cloth onto the floor and went to the tiny kitchen. Too tired to heat a bath, she pumped cool water into a bucket and brought it back to the bedroom. A sponging would have to do.

She spread a thin white towel over the woven, rag rug and stepped out of her clothes before dipping a sponge into the bucket and rubbing it across her one luxury, lavender soap. Its soothing scent calmed her mind as she rolled her head from side to side, easing the kinks and letting the cool water flow down her back and between her breasts like fragrant, liquid silk.

Finally, she raised her arms to stretch and lave soapy water under her arms and down her belly, singing softly, *"Au clair de la lune, mon ami Pierrot."* The song began with a man begging for a door to be opened, pleading, "for the love of God." It ended with a dark-haired woman opening hers, "for the God of love." She'd loved the tune as a child, but now realized the old French folk song echoed the confusion in her own heart.

At the end of the last verse, when the man is finally admitted into the light of the woman's kitchen, a whisper floated to her from the darkness. "You're a difficult woman to find alone, Cammy."

At first, she thought she'd dreamed his voice, as she so often had, imagining Patrick searching the ends of the earth to find her. He'd tell her Beecher had lied, Marchaud had lied, and she hadn't killed two men.

But the reality of the now-chilly trail of water dripping down her legs called her hope false.

She turned, clutching the sponge to her breasts, following the voice to a shadow in her doorway, it's face hidden beneath the wide brim of a Panama hat. But she didn't have to see Patrick's flinty gray eyes to recognize him. Her entire body *felt* his presence.

His footsteps silent on the bare wood floor, he stepped into the room and tossed the hat onto the bed. Smoothing back his hair, his eyes still dark in the shadows, he leaned close to whisper, "You should never have run away from me."

Camilla's hand on the sponge tensed, sending fresh rivulets of water over the dark, puckered tips of her healing breasts. She held her breath as his gaze followed it down to the dark triangle at the juncture of her thighs.

She wanted to run, but the flicker of the lamplight highlighting his strong, dark features, kept her still. The hunger in his eyes sent liquid heat to her core while her heart beat fast in anticipation of his touch. Would he kiss her or kill her?

Finally, her mind surrendered to her body's betrayal. Naked, trapped in her room with the man she had once loved more than life itself, she didn't care if murder, lust, or love shone from his tortured gaze. So be it, she thought, and dropped the sponge.

Chapter Thirty

Patrick barely missed her again at the St. Charles hotel. The long-awaited desk clerk was late, but recognized the miniature. She'd left two hours earlier with a band of missionaries. *Missionaries?* Truly the sprite had an army of guardian angels watching over of her. A ten-dollar gold piece sharpened the clerk's memory enough to recall they were headed to St. Louis aboard the Robert E. Lee this same day.

Patrick knew the boat. He thought it a little conspicuous and lavish in its appointments for a young woman who, but for Lucy's quick thinking, would have been a hunted criminal. But hiding in plain sight with a band of missionaries? That was brilliant.

He'd made it to the docks in record time, finding a drayman resting on the back of an empty wagon just as the Bobby Lee's final boarding whistle blew. He showed the drayman the broach "I'm looking for this woman. She may be aboard the Robert E. Lee. Have you seen her?"

The big man looked at it, taking his time to answer. "Who wants to know?"

After several marathon days of chasing Camilla, Patrick's patience was spent. He lifted the corner of his jacket to reveal the revolver tucked into the waist of his trousers. "I can be a husband or the police," he growled. "You decide which. Either way I suggest you tell me the truth. Now!"

The drayman raised his arms and jumped down from the wagon. "Sorry, suh," he stammered. "Ah don' want no trouble with a man lookin' fo' his woman—or the police. Yes, suh, ah remember her. She be yonder, on the Bobby Lee, there." His arms still up, he nodded toward the boat pulling up the boarding plank.

He turned just as the boat pulled away, scanning the people crowding the railing, waving goodbye to their friends and family. For just a moment, his heart skipped a beat as a tiny, russet-haired woman dressed in black was shouldered aside by a man twice her size. He blinked and she was gone, making him doubt his sanity. But he believed his heart and the frightened drayman. Camilla was on that boat!

Unless the Bobby Lee stopped in Natchez, no steamboat on the river could beat it to St. Louis. His bad luck held as several inquiries told him it had no other stops planned. Fatigue and frustration threatened to overwhelm him, but he was too close and had more information now than when he left Langesford.

The smaller city of St. Louis had fewer decent hotels for western-bound travelers than New Orleans, and he knew her boat. Patience wasn't his strong suit, but a relaxing train ride upriver to St. Louis would still get him there a day or two ahead of the Bobby Lee. Knowing she was safe with a group of missionaries comforted him and put a spring in this step as he headed for the Louisville & Nashville railway station.

After pacing the waterfront for the arrival of the Robert E. Lee during the day, and haunting the taverns and alleyways for signs of Beecher at night, Patrick's heart quickened at the sight of Camilla with the missionaries. He'd have to remember to thank them one day.

He also thanked the saints of coincidence when he recognized the couple who had tried in vain to convert the wayward Leon to ways of the Lord at Redfern Plantation. He even spoke with them once or twice about the boy's penchant for lying and laziness. They'd come to Anthony's funeral, standing behind the former slaves to pay their respects.

New Englanders. Carter, he thought was the Reverend's name. He smiled as fortune finally turned in his favor. It would be easy enough to find their hotel, and he'd put money on the Planter's. All self-respecting pioneers stayed at the Planter's.

He lit a cheroot, adding another gray plume to the sooty air hanging over the newly industrialized city. The Reverend's wife's name was Judith, he recalled. She'd seemed kind enough, though a little unnerving. Her eyes seemed able to see through his very soul. And that was one thing he did *not* want anyone to see.

Still, he'd noticed the bond between the two women on the dock, surprised that after such a short acquaintance, Camilla would trust a stranger—a Yankee at that. Then he watched them embrace and noted their sadness as they parted.

What the Hell? Why would Camilla leave their protection? Of course. She was protecting them from the danger surrounding her. From the New Orleans police, from Beecher—and since she'd bought Beecher's tale hook, line, and sinker, from him.

He dropped the cheroot and ground the toe of his boot into it, hoping it would crush the pain of her lack of faith in him, as well as his fear for her life. He'd kept his silence to protect her memory of her father and brother. But he'd waited too long. Apparently, silence was *not* always golden.

As much as he wanted to rush to her, to confess everything and carry her back home where she belonged, they both still had cause to be wary. With Beecher on the loose, anyone close to her was in danger, including the good missionaries. And while he'd be only too happy to relieve the world of Arty Beecher's presence, he grieved at the possibility of Camilla choosing a life without him.

He'd waited until she left the pilgrims on the dock, then followed her to the River's Rest. It was one of the largest of the riverfront boarding houses for sailors, and one of the roughest. Longing to call out to her, he again kept his distance. If he could follow her, so could Beecher, and he could almost smell the stench of Andersonville Prison above the rancid odors of the waterfront.

He watched for the next several days, his arms aching to hold her. She looked tired. Thin, wearing somber gray or faded calico, she worked like a slave for Hiram Woods, hiding her riotous hair under a muslin head wrap as she trudged between her clapboard shack and the boardinghouse at dawn, returning well-past sunset.

How he marveled at her strength. *Indomitable.* Though her back must have ached, her shoulders were square, her head unbowed as she smiled and nodded to the adoring loungers along the boardwalk. She was a queen among paupers, and not one of them treated her with disrespect.

But now and then, when she stopped to take a ragged breath or rest against the trunk of an ancient oak, his temper raged over his inability to replace her haunted, wary glances, with the sparkle of mischief. To once again see that defiant chin. He was about to throw caution to the wind and approach her when a young sailor attached himself to her like a lovesick puppy.

Avoiding the comparison to himself, he settled in at the Planter's Hotel, sleeping during the day while she worked, and watching her house at night until the boy's boat went back down river. He also did some detective work on the sailor called, "Sandy" Sutcliff.

It seemed the handsome lad had a reputation for playing the "protector" to unescorted women, widows mostly, gaining their trust and companionship—only to swindle them out of their meager savings and leave them stranded at one of his many ports of call. One villain at a time, Patrick told himself. He knew only too well how Camilla could take care of herself. Compared to Arty Beecher, and Delmont Marchaud, young Sandy was an amateur.

So he watched and waited. The Bobby Lee was loaded and leaving at dawn. Camilla had managed to dodge the boy's advances so far, but as one man watching another court a beautiful woman, Patrick knew the sailor would have to play his card this night or lose the game. He waited in the shadows by her house for them to come down the deserted street, prepared to step in when the sailor forced himself on her.

It happened quickly, but before he could react, Camilla efficiently dispatched the boy with an elbow and a well-aimed knee. He smiled *That's my Cammy!* Though he'd given her ample opportunity—and cause, he was grateful she'd never used her elbows and knees like that with him.

Keeping to the shadows, he heard Sandy's oath as he hobbled down the street. Once Camilla was safely inside, her siren-song drew him to the parlor window, and finally her tiny bedroom.

She stood in the circle of lamplight, her moisture-laden body shimmering like a mirage on the desert—or a Banshee, drawing him to his own death. But this was no mirage or Irish harbinger of doom. He knew Camilla's body as intimately as his own. She'd become a part of him he couldn't live without.

He heard his voice, but not his words as he stepped from the shadows toward the heat of her body, the sweet scent of lavender on her skin. Then she turned to him, and froze, terror reflecting from those exotic green eyes, her lips frozen in a surprised, "O." He dropped his hat to reach out to stroke the soft line of her cheek. But at his touch, his dream of happiness collapsed in front of his eyes.

~ * ~

It was still dark when Camilla moaned and stirred. The sheet felt warm on her bare skin, and a gentle hand caressed her forehead with a cool, damp cloth. She opened her eyes to see Patrick leaning over her, his jacket off, shirt unbuttoned to the waist. His eyes were unfathomable in the shadows cast by the lantern behind him, but instead of choking the life out of her, he kissed her forehead lightly. "It's all right, darling," he whispered. "You'll be fine now I've found you. You're safe."

If I'm dreaming, she prayed, don't let me wake up. She closed her eyes again and raised her arms to encircle his neck, guiding his lips to her hungry mouth to taste him. "Darling," she whispered, hoping it wasn't a dream.

He waited until she spread her hands against his chest, opening his shirt wide. At her nod, he shed it and his trousers to join her under the sheet. His touch was gentle, cautious, as if she might shatter at any moment. But she didn't want him to be gentle. She wanted to feel him deep inside her. To breathe to the rhythm of his breath, move to the touch of his fingers, his lips, and his tongue. She'd felt like the walking dead since Beecher came to her. Now she begged Patrick to bring her body to life—if only until he handed her to the hangman.

They made love and slept in each other's arms until a shaft of sunlight through the closed curtains coaxed her eyes open. A warm, comfortable weight on top of her kept her from moving. She felt Patrick's head again nestled against her shoulder, his strong, tanned arm stretched across her breasts, legs wrapped around hers.

So it wasn't a wonderful dream. But mornings had a way of turning happy dreams into sad memories. She nestled closer to him. *Perhaps reality can wait a little while.* But her movement woke him and he rolled off to the side. "Good morning, Mrs. O'Grady." He smiled. "Or should I say Mrs. Lange?"

Sarcasm. All too quickly, the dream began to dissolve. She pulled

231

the thin sheet up to cover her breasts and stared at the water-stained ceiling. "You tell me, Mr. O'Grady. If indeed it is *your* real name."

He shifted to hover above her, his breath tickling her skin, his passion rising as it touched her thigh. She saw the truth in his eyes when he said, "I never lie about who I am."

He peeled back the cover then, frowning at the fading bruises from Delmont's hands and teeth. "I won't ever let this happen to you again," he whispered, kissing every pink scar and faded purple bruise, making her forget who he was and what she was.

Relaxed in each other's arms again, she spoke first. "I thought you were going to kill me."

His tongue tickled her earlobes, "Only with love, my dear. When I get you back to Langesford."

Langesford. He spoke of love, but couldn't call it home. *He's still using me.* She threw the sheet aside and reached for her clothes. "What if I don't want to go?"

She felt him watching her, studying her every move until she fastened the last button of her dress and turned to him. "I'm late. I have to go to work," she said, as if her whole life weren't crumbling, and this was just a normal conversation between husband and wife. Before he could touch her again, she reached for her shawl and left the room.

Patrick had just stepped from the bedroom when a knock sounded on Camilla's door. "Miz Carrie," a voice called in a pitch only young males can manage. Then it cracked into a deep masculine tone. "You all right? Hiram's worried."

Camilla pushed Patrick into the tiny back room, out of sight of the door. But when she opened it, he stepped up next to her.

A boy stood on the other side of the threshold, his eyes downcast, feet shuffling nervously. He spoke to his shoes. "I'm sorry if I bothered you, Miz Carrie. Hiram, sent me. Said you better get your...I mean go to the Rest right away or..." He blushed, still studying the bare toes sticking out here and there from the worn-out fisherman boots.

"I...well, I think he's just worried. I got breakfast on all right. It's just...well he don't much like Sandy...an' you ain't never been late before."

"There's always a first time," Patrick answered, "and I must say I share the man's opinion of the sailor."

The boy's head shot up at the stranger's voice. "Who...?"

"Jesse," Camilla interrupted and stepped between them. *What poor Jesse must think!*

Patrick smiled broadly at the boy's now-closed face. "Well now, Jesse, is it?" he beamed. "I can't tell you how relieved I am that my dear *sister's* employer is concerned for her welfare. No worries though, her tardiness is entirely my fault. Please come in."

Camilla held her breath, stunned at Patrick's support of her secret identity. Suspicious too. *What new game is he playing?* At her nod, Jesse stepped across the threshold.

Patrick ignored Camilla's heated stare and flushed cheeks, as well as Jesse's suspicious gaze. "Allow me to introduce myself," he chatted in the open doorway. "The name is Sean O'Sullivan, late of the Georgia 5th Regiment. I am *Carrie's* brother."

He guided Jesse into the tiny parlor, motioning for them both to sit down while he took center stage. "Unfortunately, my service to my beloved country ended with a minié ball in the leg. The fall from my horse caused me to lose my memory. I recuperated in a Yankee prison and after the war, I wandered aimlessly in search of my past."

Jesse and Camilla both sat spellbound as he wove just enough facts into his fiction to make it believable. They both jumped when he suddenly dropped to his knees in front of her. "You see, until only a few short months ago I had no idea where I belonged. Then I stumbled onto what I knew was my home and it all became clear to me."

He reached up to take her hand. "But I'd been gone too long. The only person I loved in this world had fled. I've been searching for her ever since." He smiled tenderly at Camilla. "But now I've found her. My dear *sister*, Carrie."

He dropped her hand after a dramatic pause and slapped his leg before standing. "Who would imagine I'd find her in St. Louis?"

Camilla pressed a hand to her forehead while Jesse frowned. "You don't look alike."

Smiling at the boy's keen eye, Patrick covered, "No. It seems the males in our family too closely resemble our black Irish forebears." He lightly touched a burnished curl near Camilla's earlobe. "But the saints blessed Carrie with our mother's fair coloring and gentle manner."

He shrugged and smiled. "Why, it is even possible that my children could resemble her, and hers me."

Camilla blushed at the hope in his eyes that they'd test the theory soon. *Not until I know I can trust him, as well as love him.* With Patrick now slouching by the window, she took a deep breath and turned to Jesse. "Yes, imagine my surprise when he appeared at my…door just last night."

"I nearly frightened her to death," Patrick helped her. "But after she recovered from her shock, I'm afraid we stayed up all night talking about the misinformation she received about my demise on the battlefield, and how wonderful it is to be a family again."

Again, looking only at Camilla, he added, "She is all I have in this world. I think no one never appreciates what they have until they risk losing it."

He blinked and coughed. "But enough jawboning here." He reached out a hand to help Camilla up. "You both have jobs to get to and I am famished. You won't mind if I accompany you, will you? I understand the River's Rest serves the best meals around."

He winked at Jesse. "I'm not surprised. She learned from the best cook in Louisiana. You do remember Flora, don't you, Carrie?" he asked over Jesse's shoulder. "She's as anxious for your return as I am."

Sudden tears stung her eyes at the mention of Flora. *Not now!* Now, she had a room full of hungry rivermen waiting for breakfast. She tossed the light shawl over her shoulders and snapped, "I'd never forget Flora. And you may accompany us, but you'll have to pay. Only Jesse and I get free meals."

Jesse's grin split his face when she smiled and tucked her arm through his, making Patrick follow behind them on the narrow walk.

Chapter Thirty-One

She introduced him to Hiram as her long-lost brother, Sean O'Sullivan, noting that lies seemed to come easier the more she practiced. It didn't please her. The burly innkeeper, who cared less about her family tree than feeding his boarders, harrumphed a grumpy, "Don't look much like kin," before ushering her into the kitchen.

Hoping Patrick would leave, she looked over her shoulder, disappointed when he straightened the revers of his white jacket, scanned the room, and took a seat at a table in a corner by the door. His sly smile as he lit a cheroot made her wonder again what he was up to.

She kept a wary eye on him between cooking and serving. He ate two thick stacks of flapjacks covered with fresh butter and syrup, and downed a tankard of milk before leaning back and pushing the plate away.

"I'd forgotten how good my sister's cooking is," she overheard him tell Jesse while he cleared the dishes away. "When is she finished?"

Jesse answered, "After we clean up breakfast, and get dinner on the stove, she goes up to clean the rooms. Then there's supper to be started."

Camilla listened from the other side of the kitchen door, afraid Patrick would sit there all day, watching her with those hungry eyes, smiling his secret smile, and sending shivers to places she didn't have time to think about. Thankfully, Jesse stopped the direction of her wayward thoughts by answering, "But today we're way behind. She won't likely be out until after supper's done."

She peeked through a crack in the door, breathing a sigh of relief when Patrick looked at his pocket watch. "Well, when exactly will supper end? I don't want her going home unescorted."

Feeling his gaze directed toward her, Camilla ducked back when Jesse replied, "'Round nine o'clock usually, if we ain't...aren't...too busy. Otherwise, more like ten, like last night."

Patrick whistled low. "A long day. Well, I have one or two errands to run. Tell her I'll be back by nine o'clock to see her home."

She barely escaped a bruised nose when he pushed the door open to announce, "Carrie, I'll be looking up a friend at the Planter's Hotel. If you need me, send Jesse."

The afternoon both sped and crawled as she worked like a demon in the kitchen, never turning out so many meals in such a short time. When Jesse couldn't wash dishes fast enough, she sank her arms into the giant sinks with him. Then she feverishly set about cleaning and chopping vegetables for supper; cutting meat, sharpening knives and polishing cutlery. All the while, waiting for—and dreading, nine o'clock.

He'd want to talk then, and she'd be hypnotized by his eyes and soft, lilting voice. And if he touched her, she'd surrender as completely and shamelessly as she had last night. She shuddered at the memory, or was it a shiver of excitement?

Still, they had to talk, she supposed. *About Beecher.* She wondered what would happen then, not knowing if the sudden knot in her stomach came from her fear of being near him, or of losing him—again.

She jumped when the old ship's clock struck nine, and searched the immaculate kitchen to find some small, important task left undone. But the sparkling white tiles only grinned back at her. It was time to face him. Slowly, like a soldier preparing for battle, she folded her apron, smoothed her skirt and removed her head wrap. Catching a glimpse of herself in the gleaming surface of a serving tray, she sighed. Maybe he wouldn't be interested in the haggard drudge she'd become.

Hiram watched closely when Patrick encircled her shoulders with one arm and kissed her lightly on the cheek. "My poor, tired, little sister," he whispered. "Let me get you home for a good night's rest."

Involuntarily, she sagged against him, taking comfort from his strong arm and soft voice. Then she realized what he'd said. *I can't spend another night in the same house with him.* She pulled away under the pretense of fetching her shawl. "Really, Sean," she said with her back to him. "You don't have to see me home. I'm quite safe, and often walk

236

home alone," she lied.

She answered his protest before it came. "Besides, you would just have to walk back here alone. Hiram's been kind enough to rent you a room until you return to…" Her throat closed at the thought her lost home.

"But my dear Carrie," he said with a smile, "after being lost to each other for so long, I planned to spend time with you. To convince you the danger you fled doesn't exist. That it's safe to come home again."

She couldn't play the game. "I'm afraid, there isn't anything you can say that will convince me of that. Too much has…happened." She pretended to brush a curl from her eye. "I've begun a new life…here. I'm afraid I won't be good company tonight. Perhaps we can talk tomorrow. I have only brunch to prepare on Sundays."

But Patrick had much more experience at the game. "Nonsense. The fresh air will perk you right up." He pulled her arm back through his, patting her hand affectionately. "We've so much to catch up on and so many plans to make. Now I've found my sister, I'm not going to lose her to hard work."

She couldn't pull away without creating a scene, so fell into step with him. "Please, Patrick, don't do this," she whispered at the door when he took her key from her. They both knew she couldn't fight him, and once inside, she wouldn't want to.

The key turned easily in the lock and the door yawned open. He touched her cheek. "Camilla, I can end this little charade any time and claim my full rights as your husband without anyone giving it a second thought."

The threat stiffened her spine and raised her chin. "Then, why haven't you?"

"Because I am not accustomed to forcing my company on a woman." Then his voice lowered and he laid his ace on the table. "And because I know about Delmont Marchaud."

Her starched collar suddenly felt like a noose. He'd come for the map after all, and would use her crime to get it from her. "I…I had no choice. He would have killed—" She stopped when he put a finger to her lips and peered into the darkness down the street.

"Never mind him," he whispered and pushed her inside.

She followed him into the front room, hugging her shawl close while he lit a lamp on the tiny shelf above the coal stove. When he gestured toward one of the two faded arm chairs on either side of a small round table, she obediently sat.

"Don't try to run," he warned, leaving the room to return with two empty jelly jars. He put them on the table beside her and pulled a silver flask from his pocket, filling each jar half-full of a shimmering, gold liquid. Holding one out to her, he said, "Drink up. You need to stay calm."

The hard edge of his voice convinced her to accept it. Following his example, she downed the fine brandy in one gulp, surprised at the pleasant, slightly sweet flavor, and how smoothly it went down. Its warmth spread through her whole body, relaxing her muscles, one by one, down to her fingers and toes.

No wonder Maman liked it so much. She bet enough of it could make any problem seem small, any enemy seem a friend. Despite the risk, she held the jar out for more.

But instead of filling it with more of the heavenly nectar, Patrick took it from her, gently placing her fingers against his lips. She sighed at his touch and closed her eyes, waiting to taste the brandy on his tongue, to give herself to him as she knew she would—one last time.

Instead, he placed her hand back in her lap. "Flora told me Beecher came to the house after I left for Savannah."

The unaccustomed warmth spreading through her seemed to have melted her bones until she dared not try to rise. Resigned to whatever whim fate intended for her, she nodded.

He cleared his throat. "Let me guess what he said to you."

Caressing the back of her hand, her fingers, her palms, as if memorizing them, he said, "Beecher told you that Brent and your father were thieves and traitors. That they conspired to rob the Federal government of millions in gold and cheat the failing Confederate government by hiding it until after the war."

His warm hand crept up to massage her bare arm beneath a rolled-up sleeve, relaxing it on the outside as the brandy had on the inside. His voice grew softer and she leaned closer to hear him.

"Then he demanded the map they were discussing when you found him in your room."

Her nod loosed scalding tears to fall on their entwined fingers.

"And he told you I was a Federal agent assigned to the robbery. That I hadn't given up the search because I wanted the gold for myself."

His eyes darkened, but he held her arm securely, even when she tensed and tried to pull away. "He also said I married you after Anthony died to get the map." He stood, his voice no longer gentle. "And you believed him, didn't you, Camilla."

"Yes," tore from her soul and she sobbed into her hands. When she finally raised her head, her shoulders heaved with the struggle to breathe.

Like a prosecutor, pressing for a confession, he leaned down, next to her ear, and whispered, "What made you believe him? His good looks and trusting manner?" He answered his own question. "No, you found the map, didn't you?"

But she just sat in the chair, wringing the little linen handkerchief until it began to rip. Finally, he grasped her shoulders. "Tell, me, you little fool. We both know it's true. And so does Beecher. The minute you left Langesford, you confirmed it. And when I came after you, we may as well have painted a sign on our backs saying, 'Follow us to the mythical 'Rebel Treasure'."

Exasperated with her continued silence, he knelt in front of her, taking her now ice-cold hands in his. "Don't you realize if I can find you, chances are Beecher already has, and is just biding his time to catch you alone? Trust me...please. Did you find the map?"

The word trust broke the spell. *How dare he expect me to trust him?* She rose suddenly, nearly knocking him off his heels. Her swollen eyes clear of tears now, she snapped, "Yes! Yes, yes, yes, I believed him. He knew so much about...what happened that night...during the ball. And about...you."

Her strength renewed, she paced around him this time. "Why else would you invest in a half-dead plantation? Why else would you marry a ragged country bumpkin like me?"

She pointed at him, charging, "You came from Chicago, traveled the world, wore silk shirts with pearl buttons and knew beautiful women like Papa's nurse, Miss Watson. How stupid you must think I am."

She stopped, hands on her hips. "But I'm not stupid, Patrick. I knew there had to be something more than me to keep you on after Papa died. But I didn't want to believe it." He flinched when she jabbed him in the chest with her finger, and finished, "When I found the map, I couldn't stay and be used by you...by anyone...any longer."

"What did you do with it?"

Her last ounce of strength spent, she collapsed back into her chair. Hatred, the other side of love, rose like bile from the pit of her stomach. Patrick's darkened eyes showed her the color of his soul, and his clenched jaw told her that Beecher was right about his intentions. Bracing for the violence she knew lay just under the surface of his smooth manners, she said, "I burned it."

Patrick thought about her answer for a long moment. It was true he'd spent four years dreaming about the gold, risking his own money and Dr. Johnson's savings to gamble on Anthony Langesford. But all that ended at the hot spring, with their first kiss.

What troubled him was that if she'd found the map, she'd read it. And she never forgot anything she read. His patience had finally paid off. Burned or not, she knew the location of A lost treasure in gold. *Your last chance to redeem your reputation as an investigator. To finally be something besides a bastard and a spy. To finally live your dream.*

And what dream is that? he wondered. A bigger set of rooms in Chicago? Finely tailored suits? Beautiful women on his arm? *Shallow, vacuous women whose beauty was only skin deep.*

He'd never put a hoe to earth in his life before becoming Anthony's partner. Never seen a seed he'd planted grow to maturity. Never felt the love of a woman who couldn't lie. Until he met Camilla.

Images of her kneeling in the dark Georgia clay; sitting with her chin on her knees at the hot spring; laughing with Cato on the trail; wearing the mauve gown like a queen, and the tips of her breasts teasing him until he thought he'd burst, ran through his mind. He knew she loved him enough to tell him about the map; but the set of her chin told him he'd never see her again if he asked. *Do you love her enough to let the treasure of a lifetime go?*

Finally, he sat with a thump onto the chair next to hers, pouring two more drinks. He offered her one as though they'd just had a lovers' spat. She took it, but neither drank until he said, "Good."

Chapter Thirty-Two

Camilla woke alone in her bed the next day. Her clothes and bed covers were hardly mussed and she felt more rested than she had in weeks. She closed her eyes, remembering that the second brandy had soothed her ragged throat and stopped her trembling. The memories blurred after the third, or maybe the fourth, glass of heavenly nectar.

No matter, they'd finally addressed the map and Beecher. Patrick believed she destroyed the paper map and never asked about the one still in her head. And she believed he loved her over the lost gold.

They moved on, laughing over Otis' attempts to handle the high-spirited Jupiter and how Flora secretly let Scar into their room at night. They also celebrated the profits from their crop that far exceeded their modest expectations. Profits already safety set aside in their New York bank account. But most of all, she remembered his warm, brandy-flavored lips on hers and his strong arms lifting her from her chair. After that, she remembered nothing.

"Well, well, Sleeping Beauty finally awakes," came from the doorway. Patrick lounged comfortably against the wall, a cup of coffee in his hand.

His smile took her breath away. She stretched, licking her dry lips. "How much did I drink?" she asked, "I must have slept like the dead. Even now I don't want to move a bone."

"Smart," he answered. "I wouldn't rush into moving if I were you. You're not used to brandy's punishment." He stepped away, returning a moment later with a steaming, chipped, tea cup she hoped held coffee.

He sat on the edge of the bed. "Just raise your head slowly and take a few sips of this. You'll be good as new."

Instead, she bolted up. "Really, I feel fine. Wonderful. Better than I have been in...Oh." She fell back as pain stabbed from the front of her head to the back, making the room spin and her stomach lurch.

He caught her shoulders, laughing. "Stubborn woman. Why do you insist on never listening to me?"

She didn't have the strength for a biting retort and leaned forward to sip his magic elixir. She was grateful it was coffee, but it also carried the flavor of something bittersweet, and familiar, though she couldn't place it. She felt better with each sip.

"You're a witch doctor," she accused as the lead hammer inside her head stopped beating her temples.

"It's just coffee." He rose to refill her cup and winked. "And Dr. Johnson's Indian Blood Syrup."

The flying pillow missed him by inches, and his deep, rich laughter filled the tiny house. "You're out of practice, Cammy."

When she recovered, he sat with her on the bed, holding her hand as he explained what he and Lucy had done with Delmont's body. They'd never been lovers, he told her. Rather, were partners—and friends. To be anything more would have threatened both their lives.

As the hideous elixir strengthened Camilla, she probed further. "You know everything about me," she said. "But I know nothing about you. If we are to be...more than partners, I must know the whole truth about you.

His kiss was soft and slow, but he pulled away before it was too late. "You drive a hard bargain, Mrs. O'Grady," he said rising to pace the room. In the bright morning light, he described his shadowed life as the secret child of Dr. William Stainsby in Boston. She wept as he recalled his innocent mother's love for him and her tragic, lingering death.

No more secrets, he promised, offering to seal it in blood, if she wished. Instead, she kissed him.

Finally, she sat up, doubt and fear suddenly gripping her. "Will we have to go back to New Orleans to return...home?" Her fingers bit into his hand. "Even with the danger passed, I don't think I can look at the city again."

No, he assured her. They'd go by train with their own sleeping compartment, and be home in just a few days.

Feeling oddly refreshed, as well as restless, she stood, steady on her feet and ready to face the day. He left her to her preparations and she took her time washing before slipping on a new pale green frock he'd brought the day before and tied her hair back with a yellow ribbon.

There was no need to pinch her cheeks for color. The flush came naturally when she entered her tiny kitchen to see the table set for two, plates of fresh croissants and butter, and more coffee perking on the stove.

He smiled like a little boy. "While you were sleeping, I found a bakery." He nodded toward the table. "Sit down. Your *pure* coffee will be ready in a minute."

She curtsied like the lady of the manor she was bred to be and settled on a three-legged stool. He bowed elaborately, sitting opposite her on an up-turned milk bucket.

Patrick cradled his own steaming cup of black coffee between his hands, watching her pick daintily at her fluffy croissant. Now and then, he reached out to touch her hair. "So how soon can you be ready to leave?" he asked, his fingertips caressing her cheek.

She leaned into his caress. He'd convinced her he was no longer the man Beecher described, if indeed he ever was. She believed his promise to abandon the quest for the gold, calling her his, "Rebel Treasure." But most of all, she believed he wanted to go back to Langesford, their home—forever. And with Delmont—gone, she had no reason to stay away from where she belonged. She moved her lips to meet his palm. "Soon."

"Wonderful." He stood, leaning down to kiss her. "Leave the Rest today. I'll get train tickets for tomorrow and tonight we'll have dinner at the Planter's Hotel. I'd like to introduce you to an old friend staying there."

She put a hand on his arm. "But what if word about Delmont, and my real name has reached St. Louis? I…"

"Stop," he interrupted. "Don't worry about Marchaud. He was a degenerate blackguard who made his money from brothels, gaming dens, and blackmail. The people who wanted him dead are too many count, if anyone ever tries. Trust me when I say he disappeared without a trace. Try to forget about him."

He kissed her forehead. "It's over. The past is dead."

She doubted it. Like Flora and Judith, she knew the past never died. But she couldn't risk losing him to tell him the secret of her bloodline. Instead, she forced her mind to stay in the present. "But what about Hiram and Jesse? I've only just started."

"From what I can see, the boy is ready to take your place now. He knows more than either you or his father give him credit." Smiling at her surprise, he winked. "Reading people has kept me alive this long. Besides, there's more of Hiram Woods on the outside of him than Indian. Time will tell what's on the inside."

His assessment of her young friend pleased her. Jesse had learned quickly, and each day, pride showed a little more in Hiram's eyes. They'd be fine without her. She nodded and changed the subject. "I have friends staying at the Planter's Hotel too. They're going west. I've lost track of time, but soon, I think. Tell me about this old friend of yours."

"We go back a long way," he said with a faraway look in his smoky eyes. "I owe him my life many times over."

Her smile turned to concern. *I know so little about him.* "Tell me about him."

"Oh, he's quite the character all right. I can't wait to see the look on his face when he meets you."

He scooped up her wrap, handing it to her. "If you're going to tell Hiram, there's no time like the present." His lips brushed over hers with a promise of more to come. "Ready?"

She nodded and took his arm. "Ready."

Hiram's bushy eyebrows raised when they came through the newly-mended screened door. Patrick's arm circled Camilla's waist, and her head rested against his shoulder in a most un-sisterly way. Then she left him to hug Hiram and kiss his hairy cheek. "Mr. Woods, I have good news and bad news."

His black eyes sparkled with humor as he stroked his side whiskers and curled his massive mustache between his thumb and forefinger. "Don't tell me. This man ain't your brother an' you're runnin' off with him." His eyes narrowed. "An' I'm losin' the best cook and cleaner I ever had. What's the good news?"

She covered one of his huge hands with both of hers. Tears softened the image of the rugged man's features. "The good news is I'm not running away anymore." Turning to Patrick, she announced, "And this is my husband, Patrick O'Grady. We had a…misunderstanding, but we've cleared it up and I'm going back home to Georgia with him."

The clock struck ten o'clock. Jesse would already be heating up the stove and cracking eggs. She answered Hiram's raised eyebrows, "It's a rather long, boring story and I have to help Jesse."

Hiram smiled at her and then frowned at Patrick, "She's a witch fer sure to do what she did with this place and my…boy," he said. Then he waved a ham-sized fist in front of Patrick's nose to warn, "You better not make her regret goin' back with you, or so help me God you will suffer fer it the rest o' yer short life, after I git ahold o' ye."

"I don't make the same mistake twice, Mr. Woods," Patrick soothed the beast, knowing all too well there were an infinite number of mistakes to be made in a lifetime. With nothing more to say to each other, he shrugged. "Well, she has a meal to prepare for you and I have errands to take care of before we leave. With you and Jesse, I know she'll be safe."

At Hiram's nod, Patrick turned to Camilla. "I'll be back around five o'clock. Will you be done by then?"

It gave her plenty of time to clean up and say goodbye to Hiram and Jesse privately. "I'll be ready," she answered, trying not to sound too anxious for Hiram's sake, or too reluctant for Patrick's.

The day seemed to fly until finally, her work finished, Camilla carefully untied her apron and hung it on a peg near the kitchen door. She turned a slow circle in the center of the room, taking in the gleaming kitchen tools, each hanging on the proper hook—so different from the chaos she'd found just a short time ago.

"Harrumph." Hiram cleared his throat behind her.

She turned quickly, blinking away tears. "Oh, Mr. Woods," she sighed, "I guess I'm finished here."

"Aye, I guess so."

Jesse broke the uncomfortable silence. "My…Hiram has something for you."

"Oh. Yeah." The big man swiped at a speck of dust in the corner of his eye. "Yer pay." He held out a huge palm holding a Liberty Head half-eagle five-dollar gold piece. More than a month's wages for less than two weeks' work.

Camilla took it from him and sobbed, "Oh, Hiram," into his barrel chest. "I'll miss you so. I'll never forget your kindness in giving me a job and a place to stay, even though I wretched into your spittoon." She pulled away, and they both laughed through their tears at the memory.

"Well," he huffed. "Ye held up yer side of the bargain. Ye did clean the place up." He nodded in Jesse's direction. "And a whole lot more, I'm glad to say." He cleared his throat. "Promise you'll be happy with the Irishman."

"I promise," she said solemnly, as if making her marriage vow. Then she turned to Jesse, put the coin in his palm and wrapped his fingers around it. "This is yours. It's part of my agreement with Hiram. He pays me and I pay you."

"But you worked so hard," Jesse protested.

She hugged him so tight he blushed. "No harder than you. And I just gave you a raise." Seeing the pride in Hiram's smile as he looked at his son, she pressed, "And I know Hiram would like you to have my house."

"What?" they both shouted. Hiram frowned at the lost rent while Jesse grinned.

Camilla put her hands on her hips. "Really, Hiram, the house sat empty long before I came here. It needs a caring hand. And you can't have your new manager living in the attic, can you?"

She stood firm while his face turned from beet red to purple, and back again. "Now, you know there isn't anyone more qualified. It's as if he was born to it." Then, appealing to his cash box again, she bargained, "You wouldn't want the Planter's to steal him."

Hiram scowled at the truth in her words. "You really are a witch," he finally grunted and slapped Jesse on the back. "Agreed. But I'll take half of what I pay you for the lost rent on my house." He pointed a finger in Jesse's face. "And you better take care of it too, you hear...son."

Jesse pumped Hiram's hand. "I will...Father. Thank you. Thank you," he repeated to Camilla.

They all jumped and laughed when the old clock chimed. *Three o'clock.* Two hours yet before Patrick came to collect Camilla for their dinner at the Planter's Hotel.

"Well, I can't just stand around here doing nothing." She fanned herself with her straw hat. "I think I'll take a little walk, maybe do some shopping."

"Please let me go with you." Jesse wrung his small cap in his hands, looking anxiously at Hiram for support. "You—I mean a lady like you, shouldn't be out alone." At Hiram's nod, he added, "And I'd like to talk to you about my work. Please."

Such a long speech for Jesse, she thought. He'd come so far so quickly it would be cruel to disappoint him. "Well, if I'm to have a protector, there's no one I'd rather have." She linked her arm with his. "Shall we go?"

The day had warmed nicely under the late summer sun and they joined other couples strolling at an easy, unhurried pace, looking in the windows of the closed shops. They were in the heart of the Mercantile Exchange when Jesse finally spoke. "Let me go with you, Miz Carrie. I'm grateful for all you did for me here, but I don't think I can do it." He lowered his gaze. "They know me here. What I am."

"Dear Jesse." She kissed his cheek. "I understand better than you know, but believe me, running away is not the answer. This is your home, and whether he says so or not, Hiram needs you. Your dream is of one day finding your mother and giving her a nice home to come back to, not to follow me to a cotton plantation."

They stopped in front of a display of hats in a millinery shop window and she spoke to their reflections. "I tried to run away from my life, but it wouldn't let me go. When Patrick found me, I realized my life is with him. Langesford is *my* home, Jesse, not yours. But don't worry, one day you'll find yours."

He nodded and they moved on to admire a bridal display. The bride's dress, a confection of silk and lace, with mother-of-pearl doves along the hem, as if holding the heavenly creation to the earth. Camilla sighed at what her wedding might have been, and raised her gaze to the veil. Suddenly, she gasped and clutched Jesse's arm, staring with wide, terrified eyes at the window.

His hand covered hers, his voice cracked with concern. "Miz Carrie? What's wrong?"

But she couldn't tell him she'd seen her husband enter the alley across the street with a shorter, limping figure who could only be Arthur

Rebel Treasure

Beecher. She'd blinked to clear her vision, but they were still reflected in the glass, and if she turned, she'd see Patrick in deep conversation with the man he'd said he despised.

A wave of her hand silenced Jesse so she could whisper, "Get behind me, and block me from the view of the alley. When he started to turn, she hissed, "Don't look. We can cross down the block."

Jesse dutifully followed her orders until they crossed the street two buildings down from the bridal shop. "Are you sick, Miz Carrie?" he asked when they stopped and she let out her breath. "You look like you seen a ghost."

She took in another deep breath and shook her head. "I only wish it were so. No. I saw someone in the alley who is an enemy of mine. I have to find out what he's up to."

Jesse stretched to his full height, more than a head taller than she. "An enemy? I'll protect you." The fierce look in his eyes told her he'd die doing it if she asked him.

"No, no. I don't want him to know I'm here." She looked over her shoulder and pushed him into a shadowed alcove. "Stay here. I'll go listen and be right back."

Keeping to the shadows, she tiptoed her way to the corner. Then, clinging to the brick building and holding her breath, she heard an angry voice she'd never forget.

"You greedy bastard," Beecher accused in his unmistakable whine. "You want it all—" The rest of his words were garbled by a choke as if he'd been grabbed by the collar.

Then Patrick's familiar deep voice snarled, "You know better than to call me a bastard, you twisted piece of scum." Then it turned sly. "Besides, I already have everything I need. Camilla is..."

An idiot, she finished the sentence in her mind. She didn't bother to wipe away the tears threatening to spill from her eyes. They meant she still lived. Still had feelings. She wanted to run, but stayed still, hoping to hear something to prove her wrong. Something to prove her husband loved her more than the gold.

But Beecher spoke instead. "Now, Paddy, you'd think since we're such old friends, and partners too, for such a long time, you'd be willing to share. The gold is worth millions."

249

"I know how much it's worth, 'old friend,'" Patrick answered. "And you'll not see a penny of it. Now, get out of my way."

The sound of a body thumping against the wall told Camilla the conversation had ended badly for Beecher. *How stupid of me to believe him! Again.* Bitterness overcame her shame and she thanked God she'd found out before they'd gone back...home. Once there, she'd never have the chance to escape again. Patrick would force her to reveal the contents of the map and then leave her on her debt-ridden farm, probably pregnant with his child. The vision felt so real she touched her stomach to dispel it.

At least Beecher had openly threatened her for what he wanted. And Marchaud, who had been lied to and cheated by her family. Of them all, Patrick was the cruelest. He'd used her innocence and trust to destroy what little pride she had left.

Recognizing Beecher as the "old friend" Patrick planned to take her to in a scant hour's time, she thanked the twist of fate that allowed her to see their ghostly forms on the glass. Apparently, there had been a falling out between the greedy thieves. Now she could escape them both and thwart their evil plan.

Patrick's angry footsteps, normally silent on any surface, crunched on the gravel in the alley and Camilla dove for the cover of the nearest doorway. When the sound faded in the direction of the Rest, other, more halting ones, receded in the opposite direction. If she wanted to elude them both, she'd have to hurry.

She rushed back to Jesse, trembling and talking so fast he couldn't follow until she slowed down and repeated, "You have to help me." Searching his face for the depth of his feelings for her, she pleaded, "If you are truly my friend, you will do this and ask no questions."

He nodded without hesitation. "What do you want me to do?"

"Thank you," she breathed and swallowed hard. She'd escaped Patrick and Beecher before. She could do it again. "Go back to the Rest. When Patrick comes to fetch me, you must tell him I left you to run an errand and I'll return within the hour."

At his eager nod, she added, "You must keep him there as long as possible, understand?"

"But he is your husband. He can help you."

Her fingers dug into his arms. "Jesse, you promised not to question. Just believe me." Shame over her own stupidity kept her from telling him of Patrick's treachery. "He can't help me. Please Jesse, every moment counts. You must know a shortcut to the Rest. Hurry."

As if he felt her fear, he answered, "Yes, I know a good shortcut and I can run like the wind." He touched her cheek. "For you." Then he sprinted off to another alley where he dodged trash and jumped fences to get back to the Rest before Patrick.

When he was out of sight, Camilla walked to her house as quickly as a lady could without being noticed. Once inside, she again took down her little bag and stuffed it with all her worldly belongings.

Missing the five dollars she'd given Jesse, she pulled Flora's last two double eagles from her reticule. She'd take no more charity from Judith Carter, and if she caught them in time, she'd pay for her own passage. A wry smile curved her lips. It seemed she would be dining at the Planter's Hotel this evening, after all. But not with Patrick and his "old friend."

Chapter Thirty-Three

Patrick returned to the Rest to find Camilla gone. First, his gut wrenched in fear for her safety. Then Jesse told him she'd run an errand and would return soon. Suspicious of Jesse's shaky voice and averted eyes, he gave them both the benefit of the doubt. After nearly an hour passed without her return, Patrick pulled Jesse to the chair beside him. "Where is she?"

The boy ran his hands through his newly shorn hair, a sure sign something was terribly wrong. Patrick sat opposite him employing every interrogation tactic he'd learned from Allen Pinkerton, short of torture, to get him to tell truth, but Jesse's Comanche blood kept him stoic as a statue and silent as a stone.

Finally, Hiram interrupted. "The man's her husband, boy. And this ain't like her. Somethin's wrong. Tell 'im what he wants to know...son."

Jesse's eyes widened at Hiram again calling him son. He hung his head. "I gave my word," he mumbled. "And I don't know what she was doing."

Wanting to throttle the lovesick boy, Patrick was careful to keep his voice even. "Tell me everything you did from the moment you left here with her. Don't leave out any detail and I won't hurt you."

Jesse's black eyes finally met Patrick's. "I ain't afraid o' you mister. And I don' never lie. It's like I said, nothin' happened. We jest walked and talked. Then she got all aggravated, like the vapors or somethin' and tol' me to tell you she had to go someplace."

Tears suddenly filled his eyes. "She tol' me she wanted to surprise you and wouldn't be long." Raising his hands, he shouted to both men, "She promised. She jest prob'ly lost track o' time," he offered with less

252

enthusiasm this time.

"You're lying!" Patrick's chair hit the floor when he jumped up. Pleased to finally see doubt flicker in Jesse's eyes, even for a moment, he bent over the boy. "*Something* happened, Jesse. Or she would be here now. We all know it."

He picked up the chair and straddled it, leaning over the slatted back, his face inches away from Jesse's. "Think hard. What did you say? What did you see? What did you hear? What did she say? How did she say it? Every detail of the hour you spent with her is important. And every minute wasted is a minute lost."

Jesse's voice cracked as he described the people they saw, the items in the shop windows. Cringing from Hiram, he admitted to begging Camilla to take him with them, and her reasons for refusing him, but he paused when he came to their stop in front of the bridal shop.

Patrick picked up on it. "Then what?"

"I can't tell you."

Again, the chair upset, but this time Jesse rose too, his arms raised defensively. "I have to show you."

They sprinted to the shop. "The sun was high then," Jesse said. "She looked at the window, at the dress, for a while, and then she got all upset. She told me to walk behind her to block her from the alley."

Patrick moaned. Standing exactly where Camilla had stood, staring into the shop window as Camilla had done, he swore, "Holy mother of God." He turned then and faced the alley where he and Beecher had argued a little more than an hour ago. It was shadowed now, but clearly reflected in the shop window behind him.

Feeling dead inside, he asked one more question. "What did she do next?"

Jesse confirmed his worst nightmare. "She went down a couple stores, crossed the street, and snuck back to the corner over there."

Turning back to the happy wooden bridegroom next to his equally happy wooden bride, Patrick swore, "Damn." Would she never trust him?

He sighed, admitting she had no reason to trust him or any other man, Jesse the one exception. It would take more than a few brandies and the tale of his pitiful childhood to convince a woman as smart as she that he was an honest man. *No, an honest Yankee.*

He suddenly felt ancient, the weight of the world resting upon his shoulders. "Thank you," he choked. "There's no point in looking further. She must have changed her mind about going home. You go on now, back to the Rest. I'll be leaving for Georgia in the morning."

But Jesse ran after him. "No, you ain't. I seen you two together and I know you ain't leavin' without her. If she's in trouble, I helped put her there. An' if you're goin' to look for her, I'm goin' with you."

Patrick knew enough not to argue this time. *Young love.* And when it came to finding Camilla, he could use all the help he could get. "All right. First we'll check her house and make sure she isn't there taking a nap."

As he suspected, the house was empty, the little carpetbag gone. He touched the dress he'd bought her spread across the bed. *A goodbye note to him and her old life.* Now he just had to figure out what other "new" life she had in mind. Then it struck him. "The missionaries!"

Jesse frowned. "I don't think a man o' the cloth would do anything to her, sir. An' I ain't seen a whole lot o' miracles lately."

Patrick chuckled, slapping Jesse on the back. "On the contrary my young friend. A man—or woman, of God is exactly what we need. In fact, I'm having dinner with both this evening."

Indians weren't allowed in the Planter's, so Jesse paced up and down the busy boardwalk while Patrick went inside to meet his old friend Marcus Williams and his employers, Charles and Judith Carter.

But Marcus sat alone at the table for four. "Where's yer surprise guest?" he asked Patrick.

"Where are your employers?" he countered.

Marcus shrugged. "The Mr. left ahead. An' his wife took sick. Vapors prob'ly. Maybe second thoughts."

Patrick shook his head. He'd met the woman and doubted the word vapors was in her vocabulary. "Strange," he muttered. "It seems my guest may be overcome with the same malady."

"What you mean?" Marcus asked after the waiter took their orders for prime, Kansas beef steaks.

"My guest was—is, Camilla Langesford. She has it in her head I married her to get my hands on the Denver gold. Beecher's got her convinced we're partners."

Marcus rubbed the gray fringe on his chin. "Well, that sounds like the God's own truth to me, boyo. The fey little bastard did give you the tip on Langesford. And you took the bait hook, line, and sinker. "'Cept for the marriage part. Didn't think you the type to marry for money."

Patrick hated it when Marcus pointed out his flaws. His fist hit the table. "It was Langesford's offer that sealed the deal for, me" he said. "It was time to start a new line of work and Beecher's tip just added to the potential."

"And the girl?"

The nearly raw steaks arrived, but Patrick's went ignored as he explained, "Things changed when I saw the plantation. The promise it held. Then I met Camilla. And her father died. I couldn't leave her all by herself, so I married her. Then I fell in love with her."

He raised a hand when Marcus' jaw dropped. "I'll explain later. The point is, while I was in Savannah selling our crop, Arty found Camilla and told her we were partners. She took off before I could explain. Then I found her again in New Orleans, but she slipped away with the missionaries.

"I caught up with her here and last night I thought we were straight, but she caught me rousting Beecher this afternoon. Now she's gone and he's sure as Hell followed her.

Marcus shook his head, drank a big swallow of beer, and helped himself to Patrick's beefsteak. "Yer losing yer touch, boyo. Looks like love's done addled yer brains. An' as usual, ya don't know when to call it quits. Maybe the chit jest don' want to be with you."

Patrick took his steak back but didn't touch it. "I suppose I deserve that and I can live with it, but she won't live long if Beecher gets her alone. She has the map to the gold in her head."

"What!" caused other diners to look at them—again.

"Never mind the map." Patrick dismissed his friend's shock to pull out the locket, handing it to Marcus. "This is her. I think she might be on your wagon train."

His old friend squinted closely at it and ran callused fingers through his bristly beard. "Sorry, Paddy. I met all the folks on the train just a couple hours ago. Believe me, I'd remember her face."

She's really gone then. From St. Louis, she could have gone nearly anywhere—by train or boat, even wagon train—in any direction. With her pilgrim clothes and the little carpetbag, she'd blend in like a gopher on the desert. But he wouldn't give up—yet.

Patrick, Marcus and Jesse split up to cover the waterfront, train depot, hotels, and boardinghouses—even brothels. Nothing. He began to believe his mother's stories about wraiths sent to haunt humans. First, they grant their victim's wish, then they wrench it away, along with the poor person's heart. This time, the cold, empty place in his chest told him Camilla was gone for good.

After saying goodbye to Marcus, he and Jesse went back to the Rest to see if she'd come to her senses and gone back there. *No luck*. He walked alone back to the house to spend the rest of the night sitting in the little armchair, filling the old jelly jar with cheap rye whiskey time and again.

I'm finished chasing her around the countryside, he told himself. *And tired of chasing rainbows and lost treasure*. The only treasure he really wanted was truly lost. All he had left was Langesford.

The jelly jar broke at contact with the horsehair plaster wall. "I have a plantation to run," he told the empty room. *In case she ever decides to come home*. But would he take her back? His head told him no, but his heart overruled the verdict. *Yes! Even if it took a lifetime*.

At dawn, Patrick washed his face with cold water and didn't bother to shave the dark shadow along his jawline. He opened the door, turning back one least time to whisper, "Good luck, Cammy. My love."

Chapter Thirty-Four

Camilla nearly ran the whole way to the Planter's Hotel, stopping only when she entered a lobby no less grand than the St. Charles in New Orleans. Breathing hard, she stared as western adventurers, trappers, and simply-dressed pioneers mingled among business magnates and socialites. If St. Louis was the wheel of the nation's Westward movement, surely the Planter's Hotel was its hub.

"My dear Carrie," Judith exclaimed when she opened her door to Camilla's timid knock. Then soft, comforting arms folded around her shoulders and she pulled Camilla into another overly furnished room, including a deep green velvet arm chair.

"It's so wonderful to see you again," she exclaimed, her wise eyes taking in Camilla's agitation—and the familiar little satchel. "Once again you found me in the nick of time before we depart for the territories. Please sit. Tell me what has happened since we parted."

Again, Camilla protected Patrick, or was it her own pride? Instead, she blamed Sandy Sutcliff's ill-timed advances as her reason to leave St. Louis—before he came back and made good on this threat.

The older woman politely shook her head. "How tragic. He seemed such a nice young man."

Camilla couldn't look at her. "Well, in my experience, present company excluded, people are rarely what they seem."

Judith's laugh cheered the heavily-curtained room. "Rarely so in mine as well," she agreed. "But God does work in mysterious ways. And he seems determined to merge our paths. As I said, there is always a place for you with us. In fact, we'd be honored if you would join us on our grand adventure."

At Camilla's nod, Judith poured a cup of tea and handed it to her, offering a toast. "To the beginning of a new life."

They chinked their teacups together, repeating, "A new life." Camilla wondered how many new lives God would allow her before calling her sins and the sins of her family due.

After only a sip of the fresh Earl Gray tea, Judith took up Camilla's bag. "You'll spend the night here of course, with me. Charles is spending the night on the boat, with a few men to guard our supplies. I confess I pled illness to avoid dining alone with our wagon master. He's a fine man," she explained, "but a little...off-putting. I much prefer your company this evening."

How like Judith, Camilla thought. To make giving sanctuary seem like a favor from the one receiving it. She didn't deserve such a lovely guardian angel.

The aroma of steaming coffee woke her the next morning. This time she met the day filled with enthusiasm. This would truly be the first day of her new life. The life she had begged her father to share with her. She'd been played for a fool, beaten to within an inch of her life, and nearly led to slaughter; and now she was about to venture into Indian Territory, but she'd never felt so alive—so strong.

Her, "Thank you," to Judith couldn't begin to pay the debt she owed the woman. Nothing could, and she knew Judith would never ask for repayment.

The missionary patted her hand and clucked. "Sakes girl. You're helping me. I'm so disorganized, you'll have your work cut out for you." Then her humor turned to concern. "I meant it when I said you nearly missed us. We embark for Independence this morning. Can you manage?"

Camilla choked on her coffee. *What if I'd come tomorrow?* But there would have been no tomorrow. Patrick and Beecher would have forced her to redraw the map, and as sure as the sun had just risen, she'd either be dead, or a prisoner of their greed. She nodded. "Of course."

The older woman patted Camilla's hand and rose. "Well then, it's time to go."

She produced a large-brimmed bonnet from a trunk beside the bed. "Put this on. If you tuck your hair up inside, it will be just what you need to protect you from..." She winked mischievously. "The sun."

She introduced Camilla as the widow, Carrie Lange, to the small group of pilgrims who had joined the last wagon train of the season to cross the prairie. Judith explained that while they weren't part of the mission, numbers meant safety on the trail.

At hearing Camilla's name, Little Sam Pruitt pulled away from his mother to run boldly up to her and peek underneath her bonnet. "You came!" he squealed, hugging her knees so tight they nearly buckled.

"I knew you wouldn't leave us," he stated with a young boy's certainty that all things would go his way.

She bent to return his hug and kiss. "How could I leave after you proposed to marry me?"

Emma pulled Sam away and embraced her new friend and traveling companion. "I'm so glad you changed your mind. You'll finally meet Jim. And I'm as happy as my son about traveling together."

The St. Louis riverfront was nearly as busy as New Orleans, but instead, the ships holds were filled with supplies for farmers, families, and adventurers setting out on the great sea of grass, the desert, and the mountains between them and the riches of California. Unfortunately, Camilla spend most of the trip in Emma's cabin, suffering from motion sickness as the smaller boat fought unexpected rough water. The rest of the time, she watched over young Sam while Emma attended meetings.

But watching him was no easy task. Having stored up enough energy for three children on the cramped little boat, he soon tired of stories and toy soldiers, insisting they leave the security of the cabin to play a game of hide and seek. Camilla would be "it" while he hid among the many boxes, crates and bales on the broad, cargo deck.

Looking forward to some fresh air when the river's choppy current quieted, she agreed and gave him the rules of the game. "Stay close to me. Stay away from the assembly rooms. Keep away from railings and cargo, and walk on the deck, don't run."

It didn't surprise her when he shot off toward the forbidden stern. "Samuel Pruitt," she called after him. "You mind what your mother said about those wheels and be care—" The word caught in her throat when she saw what Sam didn't.

Careening full speed down the corridor, he turned his head to answer, "Don't worry," and tripped on a carelessly coiled rope. His feet left the deck, sending him flying toward certain death in the churning paddlewheels.

She screamed and rushed to the rail, praying he'd landed on one of the massive support beams attached to the boat. Without a thought to her own danger, she gripped the top of the rail and struggled with her skirt to climb over it, screaming, "I'm coming Sam!"

She'd nearly made it when a strong, weathered hand caught her arm and pulled her down. Then a deep, gravelly voice asked, "You lookin' for somethin' ma'am?" as if she'd dropped her parasol.

Struggling against the iron fist keeping her from saving Sam's life, she heard, "Carrie," in a little-boy voice. "Sam?" she whispered like a prayer and pulled her gaze from a grizzled frontiersman's faded blue eyes to see Sam step out from behind him.

Tears of fear turned to joy as she alternately hugged and shook him by the shoulders. "I told you to be careful. What if you'd fallen?" she cried into his wild hair, nearly smothering him in her embrace.

"I'm fine." He pulled away to look up at the giant in a faded Stetson hat who had caught him in mid-air. He danced around them both, waving his arms like a bird. "You should have seen, missus. I *flew!*" he screamed, stretching his arms as high as they could reach. "*This high!*"

Hero-worship shining from his eyes, he looked up at the man's brown beard, flecked heavily with gray. "An' he caught me, just like in the circus I saw once." He pulled on the lanky man's leather vest. "Could we do it again Mr.?"

"Sam!" Camilla recovered. "Stop! We could have both been killed." To help him understand what killed really meant, she took him by the arm and led him to the railing above the noisy paddles. She picked up a small oar lying on the deck with the other. When she threw it over, the massive machinery broke it like a toothpick, bouncing pieces from blade to blade until they were swallowed up by the tumbling river. "Promise me you won't *ever* run on the deck again."

The boy stared at the last pieces of the oar sinking into the river and looked back at Camilla. As if suddenly aware of the difference between life and death, he hugged her. "I'm sorry. I didn't want to hurt nobody. I just wanted to find my hiding place fast."

They turned away from the frothing water to find the frontiersman watching them closely. She smiled her thanks to him and he tipped a finger to the brim of his hat. "You got quite a boy, there, ma'am."

"Oh, no," she answered, embarrassed without knowing why. "He's not my son. I'm just watching him while his mother is in prayer meeting."

A three-colored eyebrow raised. "You one of them missionaries?"

"Oh my," she stammered, "I've totally forgotten my manners. I'm Cam...Carrie Lange. She'd been using the name for weeks, why did she stumble on it now? "And no, I'm not a missionary. I'm traveling with the Carters to New Mexico—as Mrs. Carter's secretary."

Hush up! But she couldn't. Something about this man made her want his trust. "When we arrive in Santa Fe, I'll look for other work, though I suppose I could teach," she rambled, suddenly liking the idea of staying in New Mexico.

His kind eyes, as faded as the denim pants he wore, crinkled at the edges when he smiled, reminding her of—*No!* "Oh, I'm so sorry," she fumbled. "I've rambled like a magpie and don't even know your name. Please forgive me."

He settled back on his stool to light a match with his thumbnail and rekindle a stubby cheroot. "Marcus Williams, ma'am," he told her through a cloud of smoke. "I'm the Carters' wagon master." He nodded toward a wandering Sam. "Glad to be of service."

She followed his nod to see Sam rolling a barrel that could have been filled with gunpowder for all she knew, down the narrow corridor. "No!" she yelled at Sam, and, "I thank you, sir," to Marcus before taking off after the wild, red-haired sprite.

~ * ~

Independence wasn't the dusty frontier town Camilla expected. From the docks, she saw a brick court house and store-lined streets supplying emigrants on their journey west. Where the shop windows in St. Louis had displayed fashions from Paris, Independence featured calico dresses with canvas-lined yokes for warmth and strength, and curious looking slat bonnets with wide, stiff brims to protect a woman's face from the fierce prairie sun.

Doris M. Lemcke

She caught the excitement of their great adventure as the party unloaded their provisions to begin assembling their caravan. "If you don't need me right now, Judith," she said, "I think I'll browse in the shops and get a few things for the trail."

Judith looked up from her bill of lading to nod. "Of course, dear. You run along. We'll still be here at midday. Meet us here when you're finished shopping."

Camilla enjoyed the warm sunshine, as well as solid earth beneath her feet. She felt strong now, her steps firm on the boardwalk. She didn't know which shop to enter first. And after seeing so many things displayed as absolute essentials for the trail, she became discouraged. Forty dollars wouldn't go far.

Finally, she wandered up and down the narrow aisles of one of the smaller shops, noting the prices were a bit more affordable here. Cooking utensils, weapons, food, tools, and medicines were already communal property on the train, but she drew the line at depriving others of their scant supply of clothing.

She priced a sturdy looking calico dress and sunbonnet for daytime, along with boots, heavy socks, and a wool coat for the cold, prairie nights. Suddenly the cost of those and the myriad of other things, such as a rain slicker and wool pantaloons to keep insects and other more loathsome creatures from crawling up her skirts, made her panic at the expense of her undertaking.

After carefully comparing the quality and prices between the male and female garments, she purchased a pair of boy's long johns, denim trousers, and a flannel shirt, along with a pair of ugly-but-sturdy work boots and a coat. And instead of the expensive slat bonnet, she chose a wide-brimmed Stetson capable of standing up to both rain and wind. Though she'd set some female tongues to wagging at dressing like a boy, she managed to leave the shop with one coin left in her purse—for a rainy day, she told herself.

Struggling with her packages, Camilla dropped the boots three times between the counter and the door. She blushed from the scrutiny of the storekeeper and several unsavory loungers by the tobacco counter when she bent to pick them up. Then a thin young man with a pock-marked face stepped out of the shadows to scoop them up. "I'll help you carry

262

those," he said, tucking them up under his left arm.

She smiled. "Thank you for your help. I'm going back to the docks to meet my party. It's just a short way."

"I know where the docks is." He didn't offer to carry anything else, keeping his right hand in his pocket. Lame, she assumed when he nudged her with his elbow. Still, she was grateful for any help she could get. But at the end of the block, before stepping off the boardwalk to cross the alley, something sharp pressed against the small of her back.

"I don't want to hurt you, lady, so do exactly what I say," whispered so close she felt the moisture from his tobacco-tainted breath. Believing him, she nodded.

He nudged her toward the alley. "Go in there. Do it real quiet like, and ain't nothin' goin' to happen to you."

She wanted to scream, but her throat constricted and her muscles refused to obey her desire to run for her life. Instead, she stood rooted to the spot, clutching her purchases, her eyes searching for someone—anyone, to help her. But the busy travelers were bent on their own business. No one even looked her way.

Again, fetid air blew into her ear. "Go! Now!" he pushed her with the blade. The sharp end of the knife again bit through her clothing until she felt the heat of her own blood soaking through the back of her dress. She squeezed back tears of pain and helplessness to focus on the blind alley ahead of her.

Shadows enveloped them after only a few steps, along with the stench of garbage from nearby restaurants and chamber pots from backstreet rooming houses. Her eyes adjusted quickly to the gloom, making out the shadow of a stooped figure facing her, leaning on a cane. She moaned. *Beecher.*

"Good work, Jimmy," the familiar voice told her abductor. He tossed a coin in the young man's direction. The boy dropped the knife as he dove for the money and ran from the alley.

Camilla tried to run too, but Beecher's cane tripped her. She fell on top of the now-harmless knife. Her fingers closed around it when Beecher grabbed a handful of hair and pulled her to her knees, the cold muzzle of a pistol pressing against her temple.

Beecher bent over her, spittle from the gaps in his teeth splashing her cheek. Don't move even a muscle, you little bitch. And what's this?" he keened. "Tears?"

He put his horrid face close to hers, repeating, "Tears from a high and mighty Langesford? What will you do next? Plead?" The gun moved along her jaw to press against her throat. "Go ahead, beg for your life."

But instead of breaking her spirit, his taunts gave her strength. She'd faced death before. Be it Yankee soldiers, Delmont Marchaud, or Beecher, she would *not* go out of this life on her knees with tears streaming down her face.

She realized Patrick was right about Beecher following her, but if he wanted her dead, he'd had ample opportunity. No, he needed her. He'd let her live so long as he thought she could lead him to the gold. The knowledge gave her power.

Staring into his soulless eyes, she forgot the burning pain in her back to clench her teeth. "What do you want?"

The gun barrel slammed against her jaw. "You know what I want, slut."

Stars swimming in front of her eyes, she spit blood from her cut lip onto his evil face. "I don't know where the gold is."

He stepped back as if her blood had soiled his filthy clothing. "You're lying. Admit it."

She stared into the eyes of death. "I admit nothing."

He seemed to enjoy the game, pressing the gun against her forehead this time, and running a misshapen finger along the length of the ragged, red scar on his own cheek. "Then why did you run away from your precious *husband* right after our little conversation?"

"To get away from you," she shouted, risking a bullet in the brain. "And your partner." It surprised him enough for her to thrust the knife at him. But instead of bringing him down, it bounced off his wooden leg and clattered onto the stones.

Staring at the impotent knife now out of reach, Beecher's convulsive laughter told her she was already dead. "You stupid, stupid girl. You *believed* me. I guess the fruit doesn't fall far from the tree. Your pathetic *Maman* believed everything I told her—including that she was beautiful, and I loved her."

His voice turned cold then. "Stupid little cunt, Patrick O'Grady's

264

persistent presence in your life is the only reason we haven't had this conversation sooner."

He circled her like an insane court jester. "Oh, yes, Miss High and Mighty Langesford. When I told you the truth, you didn't believe me, and when I lied, you did."

"Stupid, stupid, stupid," echoed in the alley. "But four years in prison taught me to be patient. I followed you—everywhere. To Savannah and New Orleans, even to the doors of the Opera House." He shrugged. "Of course, they wouldn't let me in. I almost had you at the market, but you whored yourself out to the little whore and her lawyer. And in St. Louis, you charmed the sailor boy."

He stepped closer. "When you chased him away, I would have had you—if O'Grady hadn't appeared out of nowhere."

His insane laughter faded into the background as she realized she'd misjudged Patrick—again. He'd never forgive her for running from him this time. Suddenly, the emptiness of death seemed welcome. *But not at the hand of this lunatic.*

As if he'd read her thoughts, Beecher tilted his head. "But then you stupidly left him. And now I finally have you. When O'Grady married you, I knew he'd struck out on his own." He raised his free hand, punching the air above his head. "He had no right! The gold is mine and I won't let any interfering government agent stop me just because he's happy in her ladyship's bed."

Her voice barely above a whisper, Camilla said, "But you...and Patrick were together in St. Louis."

He grimaced to nod. "Bastard! Oh, how he hates to be called what he really is. But a fact is a fact. He found me behind the boardinghouse, waiting for you to come out with the garbage. He caught me and dragged me to an alley a few blocks away." Beecher knocked on his wooden leg. "As you see, I'm not as fast as I used to be."

Disgust lowered his voice. "I offered to split the treasure with him, but he'd already gone soft. The romantic fool said *you* were his treasure. Seems he just wanted to go back to the plantation and raise cotton and brats for the rest of his life." His disfigured face turned grotesque when he smiled. "Unfortunately, we don't always get what we want."

"What do you mean?" She didn't know who, or what, to believe.

"What I mean, stupid slut, is that he wouldn't agree to my terms so I had some friends dispose of him." He chuckled when she moaned. "Don't worry, he didn't suffer. Much." He bent over then, distracted by his own insane laughter.

Dead? Patrick is dead? Camilla no longer felt fear, anger, or pain. But her heart refused to believe it. *He can't be dead while this scum continues to walk the face of the earth. Or while I draw breath.*

Beecher read her face. "Yes, your knight in shining armor will no longer come to your aid, my dismal damsel. So just tell me where the gold is and I may—or may not—let you live."

They both knew neither would happen. She would never reveal her knowledge of the map and he would never let her live. In fact, she was dead already. Her body just didn't know it.

His gun no longer frightened her. She'd caused the death of the only person worth living for. A bullet from Beecher's gun would only release her from this horror of a life. She stood and spat at Becher's face. "Damn your hide to Hell. We'll both rot there before I tell you a thing, you piece of filth. Shoot me or don't. It matters not to me."

Her surprise assault made him step back. She took advantage of the gap between them to turn her back. Picking up her packages, she put one trembling foot in front of the other, waiting for his bullet to cut her down.

Instead, his voice shot through to her heart. "I know what you did to that fancy-pants lawyer, and the little secret about your nigger grandmother. I'll follow you for the rest of your life if I have to, but I'll get the gold. It's mine. And I mean to have it."

Chapter Thirty-Five

Flora collapsed in Patrick's arms when he told her Camilla had disappeared without a trace. From that moment on, they both became shadows in the dark and lifeless house, the sound of their footsteps haunting the empty rooms during sleepless nights.

Nearly two weeks after returning to Georgia, Patrick sat behind the half-empty partner's desk, lost in reading the tattered journal he'd found beneath Delmont Marchaud's body. He'd forgotten it in his haste to find Camilla—only to lose her again—twice.

He'd learned to both speak and read French from one of his father's maids. The skill had served him well in New Orleans, during the War. What he read explained so much, but he was the last person in the world to judge someone for something they couldn't control. If only Camilla could believe that.

He waved a hand when Flora appeared at the door to announce a visitor. "I'm busy. Tell them to make an appointment."

But the old woman stayed, ramrod straight, hands folded neatly over her apron. Just as she had the first night he arrived. "He says his name is Jesse," she said quietly. "And he's a friend of Cammy's."

"Jesse!" he shouted in disbelief, nearly upsetting his chair to cross the room. Hands still folded, tears rolling down her cheeks to stain the spotless apron, Flora's eyes glittered with hope and she smiled the way Camilla had smiled when he convinced her to come home.

It wasn't the first time he'd caught an expression, a gesture, a tilt of the head that reminded him of Camilla. And it was true. This woman had sacrificed her freedom to raise her daughter as a White. But how they both came to be at Langesford was a mystery for another time.

Doris M. Lemcke

Why didn't I guess? he chided himself. But what reason would he have had to? *And does it matter?* Not a goddamned bit, both his mind and heart agreed as he rushed past Flora to greet Jesse.

She walked with him to the veranda where Jesse, dressed in western gear paced the shell drive.

"Jesse!" Patrick called out, leaping off the steps and crossing the lawn. "What in this Hell on Earth are you doing here?"

"A telegram," Jesse shouted back before Patrick caught him in a bear hug.

He stepped back. *No good news ever came from a telegram.* His smile turned to a worried frown while Jesse fumbled for something inside the pocket of his leather vest.

Staring at the red clay covering his boots, Jesse held it out to Patrick. "I read it."

Patrick forced himself to take the wrinkled piece of paper but couldn't open it—yet. "You came all this way for a telegram? Why didn't you just send it on?" he asked, his chest tightening at the delay in receiving what he was certain was news of Camilla's death.

"Too much talk," Jesse interrupted. He nodded at the tattered document in Patrick's hand. "Read."

The smudged teletype print told him it had been sent from Independence the day after he left St. Louis. At the pressure of Flora's hand on his arm, he read aloud, "Paddy. Stop. Mrs. O'G with my train. Stop." He strained to read the next line. "Beecher too. Stop. Headed for Fort Dodge. Marcus."

Patrick grinned, grabbed and twirled Flora, nearly crushing her frail ribs. "We've found her!" Then his joy turned to despair. *And so did Beecher.*

Suddenly, he didn't care if Camilla believed him to be a thief who married her to find the legendary Denver Mint gold. He didn't mind she'd run away from him twice, or even if she hated him and never came back home. He couldn't let Beecher hurt her.

Forgetting Jesse, he crumpled the wire in his fist and ordered Flora, "Pack my bag with the trail clothes from my trunk." And to Otis, standing in the shadows, "Saddle Jupiter with the Western gear. I'm leaving as soon as he's ready. As an afterthought, he looked at Jesse's

268

exhausted rented mount. "And see this one is taken care of."

Jesse caught his arm. "I'm going with you."

Patrick exploded, "You fool! You wasted nearly a week because you wanted to run away from home? Even by mail, I'd have received this sooner and *maybe* have had a chance to find her before she disappeared into the prairie. Does Hiram know you took off?"

Jesse clenched his fists. "Yes! Hiram sent me because he didn't trust you. And I came because if you don't go after her, I will."

The boy's defiance struck a familiar chord. Patrick's eyes narrowed. "I see, Mr. Hero. And if I don't go, just how do you plan to not only find her, but rescue her, AND bring her home—especially if she doesn't want to? You may be half Comanche, but have you even seen a real one, in his own territory?"

"Well," he shuffled his feet. "I don' know exactly. Just that I'd head to Fort Dodge and bring her back to where it's safe. Somehow."

"Somehow," Patrick repeated, his arms folded across his chest. "Do you even know where Fort Dodge is?" He thumped a fist against Jesse's shoulder, nearly knocking him down. "Even if you did, you'd never get there. The desperados and Mexicans would eat you for supper."

He fought the urge to throttle the boy then and there for his delay. But the determination in Jesse's face told him he had a partner whether he liked it or not. Jesse confirmed it by stepping up to point his own finger at Patrick. "You can't stop me, even if I have to ride in your shadow. And I *will* find her.

"So be it," he gave in. "I'll give you time for a quick meal before we leave. I travel light and I travel fast. Keep up or go back to St. Louis. *Somehow.*"

A look at the old nag Jesse rode in on told them both he'd never keep up. "Otis," Patrick called. "Ready Master Langesford's gelding with the same gear as mine."

Otis' eyes bulged. "You mean Cap'n, sir?" The handsome gray hadn't been ridden since Anthony's death and the veteran war horse could be dangerous under an untrained hand. "Ain't nobody—"

Patrick interrupted. "Cap'n is the best mount in the stable besides Jupiter. The boy's an Indian. He can ride anything." He challenged Jesse. "Right, boy?"

Though it was obvious to everyone standing there that he'd never ridden anything besides the rented nag, Jesse nodded enthusiastically.

They saved a day's travel going to Atlanta by train and on to Independence from there. Without bothering to eat or find a room, they had the horses re-shod for the trail and Patrick inquired about a wagon train led by a lanky old mountain man named Williams.

The sweating blacksmith wiped his face with a dirty sleeve and laid down his hammer. "Les' see. Yep, nigh on two weeks it was. Had to rim a couple wagons for 'em," he recalled, then paused to crank the bellows. "Good man, Williams. Seen him afore a time or two."

Holding the red-hot horseshoe up for inspection, he eyed Patrick in his fringed buckskins, and Jesse in his new wool trousers and flannel shirt. "You a friend o' his?"

Patrick knew the game, and Jesse knew enough to keep silent. "Yup," he grunted. "Wanted to join up with him but got delayed when the boy here got sick on me."

The smithy looked at the healthy young man Jesse was becoming, then at Patrick. "Looks like a breed to me."

"Yup," Patrick answered again, spitting a wad of chew onto the ground. "Ma's a Comanche. Did laundry at Fort Dodge. When she ran away, my sister raised him back East." He paused and appraised Jesse. "But he's a man now, and wants to go back to his people."

"Heard them Comanche don't cotton much to visitors." Now the smithy spit onto the straw-covered mud. "Even half-uns."

"It's not my problem. I'm on my way to the gold fields after I dump him. Figured to hitch up with Marcus on the way."

"'Pears you missed yer chance."

"'Pears so." Then, as an afterthought, Patrick mused, "A big train wouldn't take us too long to catch up. Those big ones move slower 'n molasses."

"Yep, ten miles is a good day."

They'd only be about a hundred miles ahead, Patrick calculated, pleased with the information.

The smithy dunked another horseshoe in water, talking through the steam. "But this one only had six—no, eight wagons is all, after the Michigan folks and the crippled fella joined up. Could make fifteen, even twenty miles a day," he speculated. "Have to, leavin' so late and all. Grass'll be gone on the prairie afore long."

He patted Jupiter's withers before picking up his foot to shoe it. "But with a couple fine animals like these, you could cover twice that without workin' up a sweat." Then he loaded up his mouth with nails and set about his work, while Patrick settled on a stump, chewing on an unlit cheroot.

When they paid up, Patrick posed one last question. "Might give catchin' up to Marcus a try. You know which trail they took?"

The smithy nodded. "Head'n fer New Mexico, I heard. Said somethin' 'bout cuttin' off fer the Santa Fe Trail at the Blue River crossing."

Patrick tipped his hat. "Much obliged." Jesse copied him and they mounted up.

They rode hard, sleeping in the saddle, eating beef jerky and hard tack on horseback through torrential rains to reach Westport in two days. There, they rented a room, had a bath and a good meal, along with a warm, dry bed for the night.

More inquiries as to recent trains passing through told them they were now only seven days behind Camilla. They were doubling the speed of the wagons and should reach them in three days, if the weather straightened out.

It didn't. They lost a day at the Blue River crossing where the Santa Fe Trail split from Oregon Trail, heading southwest into Texas and New Mexico. After the rains, the river ran swift and deep. None of the ferries were operating.

Freight wagons, coaches, and Conestoga wagons as well as horsemen, waited impatiently for the Missouri River to go down to its normal level. Patrick paced the riverbank, swearing under his breath at each mile he knew Camilla and Beecher were putting between them. Two days later, again fighting to make up lost time, they crossed into the vast, "Sea of Grass."

Jesse's voice showed his faltering hopes. "With this grass so tall and no landmarks anywhere, we could pass within a mile of them and never know. How can we be sure they crossed here?"

Patrick chuckled. "Looks like you're Indian in name only, boy. To you there's no landmarks, but to me and anyone who's come this way before, there's a trail. Since the Donner Party disaster out in California, Marcus takes no chances with his people. He always sticks to the trail.

He pointed at deep ruts worn in the hard-packed earth. "And this one's over a hundred years old. It'll take more than a summer shower to wash it away."

Other markers came and went as they pushed on from sunrise to long past moonrise. So long as they had light to see, they followed the Santa Fe Trail, passing by crude graves testifying to the toll it took on early pilgrims. Grandfather clocks, bureaus, trunks, even four-poster beds stood as silent sentinels in the waving grasses as they alternately walked and rode their strong mounts. By the morning of the seventh day, the gates of Fort Dodge loomed in the distance.

Jesse let out a whoop when he saw it and made ready to spur Cap'n into a gallop. "Whoa, boy." Patrick caught the reins, nearly unseating him. Our horses are about done in, and things out here are a lot farther than they look. We've got a day's ride or two days' walk to the fort. From the looks of our mounts, we better take the walk."

Jesse looked closely at Cap'n and Jupiter. Their ribs were showing from their diet of only grass and sparse water. Their withers were mated and covered with dust, proud heads hanging low with fatigue.

He dismounted and patted Cap'n on the neck. "Sorry, friend, I forgot." He quoted Patrick's lecture on the care of his mount. "On the prairie, your horse is your life." As if he understood, Cap'n nickered his forgiveness and both horses perked up their ears as if sensing the end of the trail.

Chapter Thirty-Six

Camilla and her fellow pilgrims rose before dawn, traveled under clear skies and slept under stars brighter than she'd ever imagined. There, under the open, cloudless sky, she reconnected with constellations she'd known as a child. And each passing night, she became acquainted with new ones from the vast Western wilderness.

By day, the routine of cooking, tending the animals, and riding or walking to the pace of horses and oxen offered some comfort for her tormented soul. And each day, the prairie stretching in front of them renewed her spirit. If I must live, she reasoned, where better than in this wild, free land where you survived by your labors, regardless of parentage or tradition. *And maybe here I can forget my family's shame and heal the guilt of causing Patrick's death.*

Only one thing kept her painful memories alive. Arthur Beecher had held to his threat to follow her, posing as a wounded war veteran seeking the warmer climate of the southwest. Against Marcus' advice, Reverend Carter had welcomed him and his burly driver, along with two families from Michigan. Three more wagons and six more guns helped even the odds in case of an attack by renegade Indians or raiders, he argued.

Now, two weeks into the trip, Tom Nickerson, the latecomer from Saginaw, Michigan, ran up to the Carter wagon, breathing hard, terror shining from his eyes. "Miz Carter," he gasped. "It's little Jenny. She's terrible sick. She screams when we move her. We must stop the train and tend her until she's well."

Marcus rode over, curious as to why Judith had stopped her wagon. When Nickerson explained, he shook his head as if deeply regretting what he had to say. "This train is already over a month late, son. Even one day's delay makes crossing the prairie more dangerous. Water and grass are drying up as we sit here jawbonin', an' snow's coming in the mountains. If we stop ever' time a young'un gets a bellyache, we'll all end up dinner for the vultures."

Nickerson ignored the frontiersman to turn back to Judith. "We can't go on, Miz Carter. Just one day, please. She's in such pain."

Judith couldn't override Marcus. Nearly thirty lives were in his hands. But as a Christian, she also couldn't ignore the poor man's plea for help. She offered a compromise. "Marcus, a large train travels slower than individual wagons, does it not?"

He shook his head warily, pulling the brim down on his hat against the bright sun. "What you gettin' at ma'am?"

"Well, I have some medical experience from the war. We, the reverend and I, could stay behind with the Nickersons to tend their little girl. We can catch up to the rest of you in a day or so."

She ignored his shaking head to assure him. "We won't tarry longer than two days, I promise. But we're the only people here who can help them. We can't call ourselves Christians and leave them alone."

Reverend Carter came quietly around the wagon to stop in front of Marcus. Looking up at the mounted wagon master, his dark eyes bored into Marcus' light ones. "She's right, Williams. We can't endanger the entire train," he admitted, allowing Marcus his dignity. "But we will stay with the Nickersons for forty-eight hours if necessary, and then follow your trail. If we don't find you in four days, send someone back for us."

At Marcus' doubtful expression, he hefted his rifle. "Don't worry, with God's help and this carbine, the girl will recover quickly and we'll be safe." He turned to Camilla who sat next to Judith in the box. "You can travel with the Pruitts. If the fair weather holds, it won't be too crowded." He winked. "And Emma can always use the help with Sam."

Camilla peeked around Judith to face Marcus, whose piercing blue eyes had studied her from across the fire in the evenings. Her throat dry from eating the dust of the wagon in front of them, she swallowed hard. "No, I'll stay here with you. My home served as a hospital more than once during the war. I may be of some help."

The reverend beamed and answered before Marcus could argue. "Marvelous! We're grateful for your help." He looked at Marcus. "Will you agree, Mr. Williams?"

"Hell no," he bellowed. He pulled off his Stetson and slapped it on his thigh before spitting a wad of chew onto ruts carved by the hundreds of wagons before them. "But yer the boss. Suit yerself," he conceded. "Two days, Reverend. Not four. And on the third day, I'm comin' back for ye myself."

"Agreed." Carter nodded. "Judith, bring your bag while Camilla turns the wagon. We'll see to young Jenny."

Tom Nickerson cried with relief, repeating over and over, "Bless you. Bless you all."

Word spread quickly and more volunteers came forward to stay with them, but Reverend Carter wouldn't have it. They reluctantly followed his orders to push on. All of them except Beecher.

"I'm not in your party, Reverend," he pointed out, oozing concern for the ailing brat. "I'm alone, except for my driver. Perhaps we can provide some protection, if needed."

Rather than argue with the strange, crippled man who watched them all as if they were infinitely amusing to him, the reverend accepted his offer of help.

They found Susan Nickerson cradling her four-year-old daughter in her lap, sponging her fevered forehead and humming while the child moaned and coughed blood into a handkerchief. The fear in Susan's eyes told them what they already knew. Jenny was dying. If her father couldn't accept it, her mother knew.

"It's—" Judith began.

"Consumption," Camilla whispered. "My father died of it a short while ago."

Judith nodded, opening her bag for whatever could ease the child's suffering before God welcomed her home. She and Camilla sat with them all day and night, doing what they could to keep little Jenny comfortable while the reverend and the other men stood guard.

Shortly after midnight the next night, Jenny Nickerson died. Judith and Camilla washed her tiny body and wrapped her in a bright quilt. Then Susan Nickerson closed her daughter inside a cedar "hope" chest. After a short prayer service led by Reverend Carter, they buried the child on the trail, driving the wagons over the freshly dug grave to keep it safe from scavengers.

The nearly three day old tracks of the main train were easy to follow until the ground became hard and the landscape barren. For many miles, the tracks were barely visible. And while the Reverend strained to follow them, the tiny group looked in vain for a source of water to make camp. Beecher's driver noticed a low fringe of trees on the horizon and they turned off the trail toward it.

They made camp on the edge of a small stand of cottonwoods and a shallow stream. Tom Nickerson, whose grief kept him from sleeping, stood watch. In the morning, he told Reverend Carter, "I tell you I heard a rifle shot. This may be Indian country."

The reverend patted him on the shoulder. "Now, now, son. You're so tired you'd jump at a snapped twig. He gestured at the trackless prairie surrounding them. "See for yourself. There's nothing as far as the eye can see." Tom couldn't deny it and left to hitch up his wagon.

At the end of the day, Camilla heard the alarm in the reverend's voice when he told his wife, "Young Nickerson thinks he heard rifle fire last night. And I'm sure I saw Injun sign yesterday."

"Oh, Charles, are you sure?" she whispered.

Camilla felt like a spy crouched behind the rear wagon wheel, her blood chilling when he answered, "No, I'm not sure, my dear, but if it is true, we have two serious problems."

"Two?"

"Yes. We seem to have lost the trail. It must have happened when we traveled after dark last night."

His wife waited a silent a moment before offering a solution. "Well can't we just retrace our trail back to where it diverged from the main one and then resume our course?"

"And lose an entire day's travel? Not to mention requiring Williams to come and fetch us like straying children? No. I'm sure we veered northward of their course. We'll set out southwesterly and intercept them along the way."

"But Charles, what if—"

"There's no 'what if' about it, woman. It's exactly what we'll do."

Camilla agreed with Judith, but in the morning the group chose to follow Reverend Carter's orders to travel steadily southwest. At noon, with still no sign of the trail, they stopped for a meal and a short rest. As they cleaned up, Sue Nickerson's brother-in-law Bill, who had scouted ahead, rode up with good news. "The reverend's right. There are mounted men ahead. It must be Williams."

A cheer went up as they all looked forward to the safety of the larger group. When they saw the horsemen turn north, away from them, they fired their guns and made as much noise as possible while Bill rode out to meet them.

"Look!" Camilla pointed. "They've seen us."

The group of riders halted, wheeled around and galloped toward the wagons as Bill raced back, this time shouting, "Indians!"

Reverend Carter shouted, "Circle the wagons and unhitch the horses!"

Beecher's driver moved with amazing speed, unhitching and tying the horses, mules, and oxen to each other and to the wagons as a shield. Following his lead, the travelers took cover under their wagons behind the animals.

"You women get under the lead wagon," Charles ordered, pointing to boxes heaped around the opening for protection.

Judith led a hysterical Susan to safety while Camilla went unnoticed in her male clothing. When the reverend realized she wasn't with them, it was too late to stop her. She already had a rifle in her hand and the attack began.

The savages could have overtaken them by sheer force of numbers, but when they saw the sun reflecting from the white men's weapons, they slowed from a full gallop to a moderate lope, then a walk, finally halting just out of range, holding council.

"Be certain of your mark," the man of God cautioned. "If possible, shoot only one rifle at a time. And be prepared for a sudden rush."

They crouched in their positions, watching as the Indians finished their council. Soon, about ten warriors spread out from the main body, single file, roughly fifty paces apart, forming their own circle around the three wagons.

"Damn," the reverend cursed. "Surround. Keep your eyes clear. Don't fire until I give the word."

He took a moment to explain the Indians' strategy. "They'll ride by us fast in a circle, shooting arrows and trying to draw our fire. When our ammunition is spent, the rest will rush in." As if unafraid of facing certain death himself, he smiled. "Unless you're ready to meet your maker, don't waste a shot."

Suddenly, savage cries seemed to come from all around them, drawing closer and closer. The settlers stood back to back behind the horses. Even Beecher held his pistol ready to take aim at the attackers. But as soon as they came in range, the Indians disappeared behind the bodies of their horses, a hand grasping the withers and only a hint of a grinning painted face showing beneath.

"Don't shoot the horses, Carter ordered. "It's what they want. After we spend our bullets on the animals, they'll finish us off." So they stood their ground in silence, watching arrows fly around them, hitting the animals who were so tightly tied together they remained standing, even in death.

After the fifth circle, one pony stumbled, throwing its rider. Reverend Carter's bullet struck him in the head. "God rest his soul," he whispered what would be his last words. An arrow hissed though the air and he sank to the ground with a groan as it entered his brain through the right eye.

In the few moments of hesitation while the remaining eight people realized their leader lay dead, the Indians advanced in a living tide, fighting hand to hand until Tom Nickerson and his brothers-in-law were covered with wounds. Their death shrieks rose above the sounds of the battle. Beecher lay unconscious by his wagon. It took three arrows into his driver's chest to bring him down. And Susan's father lay in a pool of his own blood, gut shot.

The Comanche ignored Camilla to focus on the larger, more threatening opponents. Dressed as boy with her hair tucked under the Stetson hat, her blows were met with kicks and laughter. But she fought anyway, with her teeth, her fists, and her boots, until something struck her from behind and her world turned black.

Chapter Thirty-Seven

When she woke up, Camilla tried to run, but made only a few steps before being tackled by what felt, looked and smelled like a grizzly bear. Her hat fell off and her hair tumbled to her shoulders. She lay still, with a moccasin on her belly and the point of a lance pressed against her chest. For a long moment, obsidian eyes glinted in the sun, watching her from a painted head cocked to the side like a curious crow. Then the warrior's knee replaced the lance on top of her. Smelling of horse, and smiling with broken teeth, he bent low to touch her hair.

With his hot breath on her face and his filthy, blood-stained fingers testing the strength of her scalp, she twisted beneath him, managing to raise her own knee to connect with his crotch. He howled, his hands now clutching himself, releasing the pressure of his knee just enough for her to roll over. She was almost on her feet when a blood-curdling yelp filled the air and she was once again pulled to the ground. This time, she felt the entire weight of a man's body along the length of hers, his knees pinning her legs together, her arms outstretched and trapped in his big hands. It was all she could do to draw air, let alone fight him off.

Determined to face her murderer, she lay still, willing him to see her courage, not her fear. One side of his face was painted all in red, the other unpainted, with a ragged, white scar running the length of his dark cheek. The mark of a black hand covered his entire chin and mouth, long fingers pointing through the red die to his hate-filled eyes. Eyes that told her she belonged to him, for as long as he chose to allow her to live.

Without a word, he slung her over his shoulder and tossed her onto his mustang's back. He mounted behind her and tied her to his naked chest with rawhide thongs. Leaving her fellow travelers' mutilated bodies lying where they fell, the band rode for hours, to camp in another grove of cottonwoods.

Her captor tied her to a tree outside the main camp where fires were lit. At dusk, when the Indians had eaten their fill of a fresh-killed mule deer, he returned to thrust a charred piece of meat at her, his hands still covered in her friends' blood. She veered away in disgust and received a brain-jarring blow for her defiance. Then he roughly pulled her from the ground to a clearing where the main party had assembled.

She screamed and ran to Judith, where they cried in each other's arms. When they finally separated, she saw Beecher cowering in the shadows. He grinned, jumping up and down within the confines of his bonds, repeating in Spanish and then English, *"Mi hermana.* My sister, my sister," as if the Indians cared about his blood relations.

What they cared about was Camilla's fiery hair and fair skin. They clustered around her to paw her hair, her face, and feel the strength in her arms. Their attention only made Beecher more determined to be noticed.

Finally, substituting English words for those he didn't know in Spanish, he screeched, "She knows *el secreto del oro.* Mucho oro."

That caught the leader's attention. He grabbed the front of Camilla's shirt to throw her on the ground at Beecher's feet. With a wave of his hand, the glade quieted, and he listened as Beecher pointed at her, repeating, *"Mucho oro. Mucho dinero."*

At the Indians' lack of response, he pantomimed, "Buy rifles. Shoot whites," Again, he pointed to Camilla, saying, *"El secreto del oro."*

While the other Indians laughed, jeered, and poked at Beecher's strange body and wooden leg, her captor made the connection between gold, rifles, and her. She shrank from the hate in his black eyes, shook her head, and tried to scramble away. But he caught her by the ankle and again tied her to a tree, along with Judith and Beecher.

The next morning, she and Judith were each tethered to a warrior's horse, forced to keep, up no matter what the pace. Beecher rode a mule as they traveled through rough canyons where only an occasional clump of sagebrush or foul-smelling wild pita plants could survive.

Through Judith and Beecher's spotty Spanish, they learned they were prisoners of a Comanche raiding party returning home after their yearly raids into Mexico during the Mexican Moon. Rich with plunder, scalps and slaves, they'd turned when Bill Nickerson rode out to them, mistakenly thinking they were Marcus Williams' search party.

This was a smaller band, led by Mah-to-chee-ga, a second chief of the Comanche nation and Camilla's captor. In camp, he rarely took his eyes off her and her "brother."

She lost track of the days before they reached the main camp and Mah-to-chee-ga threw her into a circular lodge about thirty feet at the base, narrowing up to a smaller opening at the top. A framework of poles driven into the ground held it up and a fire burned in a depression at the center of the circle. Five woven mats lay neatly around the walls.

Two mats were screened by curtains of dressed skins with bead and paint ornamentation. The largest was reserved for her captor, Camilla surmised as she struggled to her feet. The weapons arranged around his bed and the display of enemy scalps showed him to be immensely powerful, as well as brutal. Low moans came from behind another mat, screened from view.

She'd just gotten to her feet when sunlight flooded the shadowed interior and a fiendish looking man painted red and blue from head to toe, rushed in. He threw the deerskin curtain aside to reveal a young woman on a blood-soaked blanket in the throes of childbirth. He performed a hideous dance, prodding her belly and shouting into her face. When she screamed against another contraction, the monster squatted between her legs, rose and shook his head at the chief.

Breech. She'd seen it a few times when she helped slaves and neighbors give birth. But Flora always took charge, and more often than not, delivered a healthy child. Now, without understanding his words, she agreed with the medicine man. The girl, as well as her child, would die if someone didn't help them soon.

Her own peril suddenly faded in the face of this woman's imminent death, Camilla conjured what little Spanish she remembered from a Mexican house slave and called to an older woman sitting serenely next to the young mother.

Using Beecher's ploy of a blood relationship, she pointed at Judith, standing in the brutal sun outside the lodge. *"Mi madre,"* she kept repeating. *"Mi madre es doctor."*

Neither the woman nor the girl responded, so Camilla tugged the chief's hand to point at Judith and repeat, *"Mi madre es doctor de gran alcance."* She emphasized the word for powerful and pointed to the girl who lay dying with his child in her belly.

The room went silent, either from shock that she'd dared touch *and* raise her voice to their chief, or someone understood her. *Which?*

In frustration, Camilla gestured as wildly as Beecher had the night they were captured. She abandoned her halting, and no doubt faulty Spanish, to again point outside the lodge at Judith. With tears streaming down her face, she pantomimed rocking a baby in her arms and pointed to Judith, pleading, *"Judith puede ahorrar a la y al niño."*

Finally, the older Comanche woman's weathered features softened. She rose to stare into Camilla's eyes a long moment, then with just the slightest of nods, muttered something to the chief.

He followed her outside, where the woman's voice raised in opposition to his growled responses. But all Camilla heard were the dying girl's screams. They tore at her heart until she pushed the medicine man aside to kneel beside her and take her golden-brown hands in her white ones. The man behind her, covered in furs and feathers, raged at her in a language she didn't understand until she turned slowly to look up at him.

Her lips barely moved as a stranger's voice came from deep within her. "Don't...you...dare...touch...her," she growled as fiercely as any she-bear protecting her cub. The shaman stared at her, his rattle raised, threatening to crush Camilla's skull, while her gentle fingers gently massaged the girl's belly to relax her muscles.

"Alto!" came from the opening of the lodge, full of authority—and power, breaking the gruesome tableau

"Judith," Camilla whispered to avoid disturbing the girl's fitful slumber. At a nod from his Chief, the shaman lowered his weapon and Camilla stood when Judith entered, carrying her ever-present medical bag. How she'd managed to keep it would be a question for later—when the girl and the child were safe from death's door.

Judith knelt on the other side of the young mother. "Cammy," she whispered, dropping the pretense of using her alias. No one in the camp cared if she even had a name. "I feared those screams were yours."

Camilla whispered back. "If we can save this girl, they might treat us better and allow us a chance to escape, or at least survive until..."

The shaman cuffed the side of her head with a hand covered by a bear's paw and made a guttural sound that said, "Silence," in any language. Still, she refused to show weakness by touching her ear that burned like Hell's own fire.

Don't get your hopes up, dear," Judith risked a response. "This poor child looks near gone. If she dies, it could cost our lives." She took a deep breath. "But we have to help her. She can't be more than fifteen years old and her baby is obviously too big for her to birth. It may even be breech."

As Judith turned her attention to the plight of the young woman on the deerskin pallet, Camilla, the shaman, and the squaw, sat cross-legged in a tight circle. The claw-covered hand raised again at their whispers, only to be stopped by the woman who had convinced the chief to let Judith inside. At her one sharply-spoken word, he and the others who had wandered in, left the tepee.

Judith ordered Camilla to boil water and opened what was now an empty medical bag. Frowning, she stood to pull off one of her underskirts, ripping it into strips before crossing to the chief's pallet and removing a small bone skinning knife from its sheath.

"Boil these together for five minutes," she ordered Camilla. But before she could do more than nod, the older squaw snatched both the knife and petticoat, leaving them alone and empty-handed.

"Don't worry," Judith addressed Camilla's panic that both their throats would both be slit by the end of the day. "She'll be back. Now help me get the girl's legs up onto my shoulders. It'll take the pressure off her back."

Her heart breaking at the girl's panic and pain, Camilla followed the orders to the letter while Judith checked the position of the baby. "Yes, breech," she confirmed without looking up.

The girl screamed when her legs settled on Judith's shoulders, then sighed when her pain lessened. A few minutes later, the older woman returned with a leather pot filled with hot water, the knife wrapped in a strip of freshly laundered Irish linen.

Camilla gasped when Judith plunged her hands into the near-scalding water and held them up for Camilla to wipe with the newly boiled strips of her underskirt. The Comanche woman's obsidian eyes bored into Judith's clear blue ones before she reached her own hand into the pot to produce another bone. With a nod, she placed it between the young mother's teeth.

The stick kept the girl from biting, or swallowing her tongue, and the other woman's hold on her shoulders kept her down when Judith pushed her hand inside her body to change the baby's position. Within the hour, Chief Three Feathers' young wife grunted with the last ounce of her strength and Judith called out, "*Es nino*. It's a boy!"

She handed the bloody, screaming and writhing little human being to Camilla, along with the bone knife, motioning for her to cut the cord and clean him up while she attended to the spent woman on the pallet. First, she pressed her ear to the girl's chest and felt for a pulse in her limp wrist. A long moment later, with tears in her eyes, Judith answered all their fears. "She's alive," she said in English. Meeting the Indian woman's gaze squarely, she added, "Barely."

As if understanding, she nodded and lowered the girl's head to the brightly-colored blanket beneath her head. Then she pulled on the end of a long string of deer sinew at the edge of the now-cooling water bag, and handed it to Judith. Because the end had dried, Judith didn't need a needle and began sewing the tears the woman's flesh while she was at peace.

By the time Judith finished, Camilla had successfully knotted the severed life cord and handed the child over to be presented to the father. Peeking out of the deer hide flap, she stifled a scream as the woman who had worked so hard to bring the boy into the world, marched directly to the nearby river and immersed him in the swift, cold mountain water.

Her return with the tiny, mottled body squalling blood-curdling cries, heralded cheers and laughter from the village. They quieted when she returned to the tepee, emerging moments later with the child swaddled in a gleaming white doeskin blanket, suitable for a prince of any nation. Darkness fell by the time the three women buried the placenta near the entrance to their tepee, offering prayers to their own gods for the child's protection and a long, good life.

With a new fire warming the encroaching evening chill, and the baby suckling at his mother's breast, the two white women watched the un-named woman who had saved their lives twist the child's life-cord into a tight circle. Then with great ceremony, she placed it into an ornately-beaded leather pouch gleaming with amethyst, turquoise, and aquamarine stones.

The ritual completed, the woman ignored Camilla to say in barely-accented English to Judith, "Three Feathers is pleased. This is his first wife. And he is happy to welcome a man-child to his lodge." Her gaze narrowed as she again reached into Judith's soul through her eyes.

"It is rare to find a woman with powers such as yours. You have value beyond your golden hair. You will now go to the shaman's lodge where you will help him increase his power. He is Wakometkla. You will teach him and he will teach you."

Before Judith could rise to obey her, Camilla cried out, "No! Don't send her away. We helped save the Chief's wife and child. Let us stay together." Tears filled her eyes when Judith shook her head. "Have faith. It will give you strength." She turned then, to follow the squaw to the medicine lodge.

Camilla sat helplessly on the hard-packed earth, staring at the fire until a shadow rose on the other side of the flames. The Comanche woman who spoke English looked down at her through the flames. Though her expression was soft now, she said nothing when she sat down, picking up the bone knife to sharpen it on a nearby stone.

Camilla collected her emotions to acknowledge the obvious. "You speak English."

She answered without looking up. "Yes. I was a slave among the whites for many years."

Thrilled to be able to communicate in her native tongue, Camilla barely heard the word "slave" and ventured, "I'm Camilla O'Grady." She'd no longer lie about her name. Patrick had died because of her. She would honor the name he'd given her. "Please tell me, what can I call you?"

The crackling fire and soft snores of the exhausted young mother, were the only sounds for so long, Camilla wondered if she was somehow trapped in purgatory, with this woman guarding the gates of Heaven—or Hell.

Afraid to speak again, she watched the fire. Flames, shooting up toward heaven, then cowering low, as if afraid to be judged. The struggle between joy and sorrow, courage and cowardice, mesmerized her until she seemed to float just above the lodge, observing the tableau of three women and a child. So different; yet so alike. She leaned closer to the flames that would free her of her prison on earth, welcoming the heat into her soul.

A brown hand caught her shoulder, pulling her from her dream. The woman sat beside her, also staring into the dancing flames. She seemed to speak to them when she said, "I am *Taabe Huutsu.* In your language it means Morning Bird, but the whites called me, "Squaw. The same as whore."

Camilla's eyes widened at the cruelty of her own race as she listened quietly to Morning Bird's story. "I lived for a time in one of your great cities. I was a slave to a man and to the men he served. It has been two full cycles of the moon since I escaped and returned to The People. To my brother. In your tongue, his name is Three Feathers."

Still thinking only of herself, Camilla pleaded, "Then you understand how I feel. Please help me escape."

The flat of Morning Bird's hand across her cheek answered her. "Stupid. We are little different, your people and mine. Wanting only to be free, even if we must enslave each other to believe it. Once I was a slave to the whites and now you are a slave to the Comanche. What is, is."

She rose in one fluid motion, pointing to a colorful blanket lying on thick mat of rushes a few feet from the fire. "This is where you sleep. You must tend the fire at all times. And the needs of Zoe and her son during her laying-in time. My brother will not enter the lodge or see his wife and son for three days."

A moment later a chilly draft from the tent flap replaced Morning Bird's unsettling, but somehow comforting, presence. Camilla stole a glance at the sleeping mother and child. Three days, she thought. Three days before Chief Three Feathers announced her fate.

She remembered Morning Bird's conversation with her brother. They spoke a mixture of their own dialect and Spanish, but she'd recognized the words, *gringa, oro,* and *armas de fuego.* White woman, gold and guns!

Beecher had convinced the chief she could lead him to gold that would buy guns. *He'll find out soon enough I can't.* Then what? Chills wracked her body at the answer. *After coming so close to death so many times, am I really ready to die?*

But Three Feathers didn't wait three days to enter his home. At dusk the next day, he stepped into the tepee, barked a few orders and the new mother who had been at death's door only the day before, retreated outside with her babe. When Camilla tried to follow, he caught her arm, squeezing it until her hand went numb from lack of blood.

She bit her lip to avoid crying out and looked up at the now-unpainted face of her captor. He looked younger without his war paint, with an aquiline nose testifying to an ancient Aztec bloodline. Just below a strong brow line, almond-shaped eyes accented by high, chiseled cheekbones, assessed her. But what would have been a handsome face was marred by the jagged scar running along his right cheek, causing one side of his mouth to droop in a permanent scowl.

His ink-black hair, once stained red with the blood of her friends, had been washed and plaited with feathers and beads. Today, instead of deerskin leggings, a loincloth barely covered the strong thighs that guided his horse without benefit of saddle or reins. She held her breath and shrank from the sheer, violent power radiating from him.

"*Oro,*" he finally spoke in a deep voice accustomed to giving orders. "*Donde esta?*"

She didn't have to know Spanish to understand him. "I don't know," she answered in English. When his brow furrowed, she said in Spanish, "*No se.*"

With her next heartbeat, she realized her error. *Instead of saying I didn't know, I should have called it a lie.*

Both his hands bit into her shoulders as he pulled her against his bone breastplate. With one arm holding her to him, the other produced the knife Morning Bird had sharpened the night before. He pressed it against her throat. "*Donde esta?*" thundered into her ears.

But she remained silent, praying for him to just kill her. As if he'd heard her prayers, he let go of her enough to rip the ragged flannel shirt from her body. His knife quickly accomplished the same with her loose-fitting trousers and the long underwear she wore beneath them. Soon, she

287

stood naked in front of him with only the fire pit behind her.

Knowing the moment of death was approaching, she felt no shame. She met his gaze with her own, judging his resolve as he judged hers. She also felt no fear for her highly over-rated feminine virtue, for hate burned brighter than lust in his eyes.

Instead of cowering before him, she stood still as a statue, even as the tip of his knife ran the length of her cheekbone to her lips, and pressed against the throbbing pulse along her neck. Nor did she blink at the touch of the dull side of the blade as it circled her breasts. And though her mind screamed in terror, she refused to bend to his will. She would leave the world as she was told she entered it, naked and without a whimper.

His patience short, he howled like a wolf at the moon and spit on the ground at her feet. His hammer-like blow across her jaw sent her to the mat beneath them, a bright light blinding her to the source of the weight crushing her body.

"Donde? Donde, Donde," accompanied each blow that batted her head from side to side. And each time, choking and spitting blood, she answered, *"No se."*

When battery failed, he turned to what every white woman feared most in the world. His knees spread her legs apart and he rose above her, his manhood raised like a spear for her to fear. But though her life depended on it, she refused to allow him into the part of her that belonged to Patrick. She kicked, bit, bucked and writhed to avoid him, but he was too strong and the moment he crouched down to enter her, she raised her head and vomited onto the proud Chieftain's breastplate.

He leaped up with a howl of disgust at the stinking bile dripping from the ornate, ceremonial bone and feather ornament. She curled into a ball, atop a mixture of her own vomit, blood, and his seed. With one last blow to the side of her face, the world went black.

She woke to the feel of soft buckskin on her skin and the warmth of sunlight above her. Something cool and wet lay across her forehead, but when she tried to open her eyes, they wouldn't obey. And when she tried to speak, her mouth wouldn't open. "Muerta?" she heard through the drumming in her ears. *Am I dead?*

She hoped so, but knew it couldn't be true. Death was the end of pain, or so she'd been told. To test the theory, she again struggled to open her eyes and raise her head. The pain of being alive shot through her entire body as she fell back with only a glimpse of Morning Bird and the new mother called Zoe.

Their eyes were sympathetic, their voices soft as they whispered in their native tongue, washed her wounds, and spread an ointment that smelled like fresh grass, over her body. As if in response to their touch, her throbbing pain eased and they helped her sit up to pull on a nearly pure white, doeskin dress.

Her blurred gaze shifted in the direction of the fire pit, where she saw her bright yellow and blue blanket stained dark with what could only be her own blood. She tried to speak again, but her mouth wouldn't form the words.

"Hush," Morning Bird whispered. "Do not try to move. The blood is from the blows to your face and head. Your wounds will mend quickly. You should rest now. You must be well enough to build the evening fires tonight, or he will kill you."

Once dressed, Camilla lay back onto a rolled-up blanket, grateful her eyes could open even a little. Morning Bird stood over her, arms crossed over her chest. "You should have told him what he wanted to know."

"I don't know where the gold is," Camilla moaned through swollen lips. "Do you think I would have endured this to keep it a secret? If I knew, he'd be welcome to it—if only to leave me alone."

Tears further shrouded her vision. "What will happen to me now?" Surely nothing could be worse than what she'd already endured at his hands.

A long moment later, Morning Bird answered, "My brother will decide your fate. For defying him, you could be killed. But because you were brave and did not cry out, he may let you live. Either way, no one will touch you again. You belong to Three Feathers. And to him, you are unclean."

She tried not to show her joy at being pronounced unfit for the man's attentions. "When will I know his decision?"

"Each morning you see means you will live another day," she answered while Zoe stared in uncomprehending silence.

Doris M. Lemcke

Morning Bird allowed Camilla to do the inside work, such as tending the fire, the baby, and the cooking pots for two days; while Three Feathers basked in the sun like a dog outside the lodge, smoking the native tobacco they called, "k'neck k'nick", in his pipe. Now and then, he blocked the sun at the door to watch her, but he didn't touch her again.

Beecher had not fared so well. Because he was already horribly misshapen and scarred, torture offered no entertainment. Instead, they turned him loose in the desert with no food or water, to die from exposure, dehydration, starvation, or wolves. For the Comanche, and for Camilla, Arthur Beecher no longer existed.

Chapter Thirty-Eight

Patrick's heart raced at the sight of several Conestoga wagons corralled outside the walls at Fort Dodge. He strained to see a familiar trim figure with chestnut hair among those milling around the wagons. His jaw set, he also scanned the area for Beecher's misshapen form, but no one fit either description. And there were only five wagons.

The smithy had said there were eight. Worry threatened his sanity as he asked directions to the suttler's store, a combination officer's club and information center, as well as mercantile. If Marcus had come through there, the suttler would know.

"Stay with the horses," he told Jesse, and entered the long, low building. He made a few small purchases and was about to ask about the train outside the gates, when a familiar voice boomed, "I'm tellin' you folks to wait fer the next train and hook up with 'em. I ain't leadin' five wagons out into Injun country to get kilt. I got enough souls on my conscience."

Marcus! Patrick frowned. He sounded drunk. Wondering what would have sent his old friend back to the bottle after so many years, he stepped inside the small barroom in the back of the building. As he approached, a calmer voice insisted, "We paid you to take us to Santa Fe."

"Paid, hell." The chinking sound of coins rolling onto the plank floor was followed by Marcus' roar. "Here, ye can take yer blood money. Go get kilt if ye've a mind to, but leave me be."

Patrick waited outside until a young man with spectacles on the end of his nose and a tiny woman with flame-red hair came out. They approached the storekeeper. "We seem to have lost our guide," he said with a disappointed sigh. "To whom do we speak about bringing our wagons inside until we can find another one?"

The accent sounded familiar. 'Bama, Patrick thought. Planter class from the way he phrased his question. And New England educated. Putting off his reunion with Marcus, he lounged against the chinked log wall and lit a cheroot.

The storekeeper shook his head, combing thick fingers through his beard. "No guides left I know about," he muttered. "Won't be back 'til Spring. Ye'd be best off followin' yer driver's advice."

"Come, Jim," The woman said, tugging his arm. "Let's find the commander and then have a meeting with the others. We must trust in God to show us the way. It's what Charles and Judith would want." Her voice cracked when she said, "Carrie too."

Carrie? Patrick's head snapped to attention as they walked by. The tears in the woman's eyes made his heart sink like a brick in his chest. *No!* He wouldn't accept what his mind told him was true, and went into the barroom.

Marcus was slumped over his table muttering, "Shoulda stayed, shoulda forced 'em to go." He looked up when his glass of whiskey rose from the table to disappear from his sight.

Patrick downed it in one gulp, then grimaced at the taste. "Thought you gave this up, boyo," he said with his old Irish lilt.

Marcus squinted in the dim light. "Paddy? Is it really you?" At Patrick's nod, he shrugged. "Good. You can kill me now."

"And why would I want to waste a bullet on you?" Patrick asked, pulling up a chair opposite the poor shadow of the man he'd idolized for twenty years.

But Marcus refused to look at him. "Because I want you to, and because I saved your life—more than once. You owe it to me. It's the code."

Patrick noted Marcus wasn't so far gone with drink to want to die. Something else ate at him. "Not good enough, old friend."

The older man turned bloodshot eyes on him. "Well then, how 'bout because I left yer wife behind in Injun country and got her kilt?"

The table between them flew across the room and Patrick pulled Marcus to his feet by his buckskin shirt. "You what?" he shouted,

Rebel Treasure

striking his oldest friend hard enough to knock him to the floor. He straddled Marcus, his hands around the frontiersman's throat.

"Tell me exactly what happened to Camilla, or you just may get your wish," he growled with enough resolve to discourage the few pilgrims and soldiers who came in to break up the fight.

Marcus shook his head to clear the fog from too many cheap whiskeys and tainted tequilas. "Outside, Paddy," he croaked. "Let's go outside."

Patrick nodded and stood, letting Marcus disengage himself from the wreckage of the table, bottles, glasses, and chairs. He barely made it to the steps before doubling over the hitching rail and losing most of what he'd drunk into the horse trough.

With a moan, Marcus rested with his hands on his knees shaking his head of the cobwebs from his week-long binge. Then he finished the trip to the dusty street and dunked his shaggy head in the cleaner trough. Shaking his head like a wet dog, he dropped onto the warped boardwalk step.

Patrick sat next to him. "Tell me, Marcus, or I'll make your wish to die come true right here, right now, and to Hell with the consequences."

Bloodshot eyes rolled heavenward. "'Bout two, no, closer to three weeks back, the Nickerson girl took sick. The Carters, yer wife, and the Beecher fella stayed back 'til she got better or went on to..." He blinked at the bright, cloudless sky. "...Yonder."

"Beecher?" roared into his ear as Patrick pulled Marcus to his feet dragging him into the dusty yard. He shook the older man like a rag doll. "You let him near her? You left her *alone* with him? *In Indian country?*"

Marcus didn't bother trying to fight for his life. Rather, he nodded within Patrick's chokehold. "Weren't much I could do. Guides don't have the power we used to. And we were close to the fort, off the normal path o' the hostiles. The reverend was hell-bent on staying, and I said I'd come back if they didn't catch up in two days."

Terrified of what he'd say next, Patrick released his old friend to sit on the bottom step. He pulled off his hat and wiped a dusty sleeve across his sweaty forehead. "Go on."

But his old friend had no more excuses as he sat down too, covering his face with his hands. "Two days to the button, like I said, we...Pruitt,

293

Andersen and me, we went back. Only they weren't nowhere on the trail. Had to go all the way back to where we left 'em to find out."

"Find out what?" Patrick whispered. Hope still lived in his heart. Camilla couldn't be dead because there was no god cruel enough to take her while he continued to draw breath.

"The little girl musta died," Marcus rambled. We found a little grave crossed over by the wagons." He swallowed hard. "It musta happened quick an' they took after us, followin' the trail like they said. Woulda made it too, if they hadn't split off at Rocky Creek." He shrugged. "Maybe they tried travelin' at night. I told that stubborn bastard NOT to travel at night. But he didn't listen. They never listen."

He wiped his eyes. "It looked like they crossed south of us to water and rest and then headed southwest again, straight into Apache and Comanche territory." The seasoned soldier and Indian fighter sobbed into his hands. "When we found what was left of them, they was all dead, Paddy. Or are by now."

"By now?" Patrick punched him in the arm, repeating "By now? Sober up, man. Who died and who didn't?"

Marcus swallowed hard. "We recognized the bodies of the reverend, young Nickerson and the men in his family. But the others were in bad shape. We figured the big one was Beecher's driver, but..." he hesitated, "...we only found the body of one woman inside a burned wagon. A young one."

Patrick held his breath, unable and unwilling to ask the question.

Hope lifted his head when Marcus said, "Don't know who she was fer sure. Maybe young Miz. Nickerson. Miz Carrie, she favored boy's duds, but there weren't no clothes around and the body was...burned."

Shaking his head as if to erase the image from his brain, he soldiered on, "We buried 'em on the trail. Couldn't find a trace of Mrs. Carter, Beecher, or...the other woman."

As if it would help, he said, "Those pilgrims put up one hell of a battle, but they didn't have a chance against the Comanche. We found five Injuns and a pony dead outside the circle. Left 'em fer the wolves."

Patrick let out his long-held breath. Camilla would never have cowered in the wagon. She'd have fought like a she-devil with the men and would have been surrounded by dead Indians. The body belonged to

Mrs. Nickerson.

He stood over his old friend. "Then there's a chance Camilla is alive. I won't rest until I know for sure. I'm setting out to find her, Marcus, with or without you."

"But they's Comanche! You know what they do to women prisoners. She may as well be dead." The crack of bone on bone sent Marcus rolling down the step to land against the water trough he'd soiled earlier.

When he sat up to massage his jaw, Patrick squatted in front of him. "And don't you *ever* say death is better than life. No matter what happened to her, she's my wife, and if she's alive, by God, I'll find her. If it takes the rest of my life—and yours."

He glared at the man who had saved his life more times than he could count. "I depended on you to keep her safe and your stupidity got her into this. You're coming with me."

Sober as a judge now, Marcus stood, straightening his dirty buckskin shirt. "Dammit, Patrick. How could you think I wouldn't? The preacher lady was—is, a fine woman. I owe it to the reverend. 'Sides, I quit my job."

"No, you didn't."

"What?"

"You can't let them down too. They don't have any place else to go and won't make it through the winter on their own. We'll see them safely to Santa Fe and scout around the tribes along the way. If it's a Comanche trading party, they might be heading south to sell their plunder." *And if they sold her, Camilla will be lost forever.*

He knew that even it if took a lifetime of searching, and he found Susan Nickerson instead of Camilla, he could never go back to Langesford before he knew for sure. The search would keep him sane until then.

~ * ~

After dropping the tiny party of leaderless, would-be missionaries in Santa Fe, Marcus, Patrick and Jesse set out to continue their search. As days turned into weeks with no word of new white captives among the tribes, Patrick's hopes grew as cold as Camilla's trail. But he wouldn't give up haunting the dusty New Mexico towns and canyons.

When weeks turned into months, their minds all echoed with the question none of them had the courage to ask out loud. *Could she survive nearly eight months as a prisoner of the Comanche?*

Finally, Patrick admitted he couldn't keep Marcus and Jesse prisoners of his grief and guilt any longer. When they stopped in Salinas on their way back to Santa Fe, he went to the nearest cantina and ordered tequila.

It came in a dirty glass with a dead fly floating on top. He fished it out and downed the burning liquid in one swallow. What now? echoed in his brain. When no answer came, he ordered another and spent the afternoon in quiet, drunken desperation.

A sudden slap on his back woke him from his stupor on the dirty bar. "Ain't gonna find yer little lady in a bottle boyo," Marcus mimicked their reunion nearly a year ago and sat on the filthy stool next to him.

But Patrick only rolled his head on the bar. "It's no use, Marcus, ol' frien'," he slurred. "She's gone. Vanished into the desert. If she ever existed at all. A wraith, she is, o'l man. A spirit sent to haunt me the res' o' my days."

He raised his head from the drunken tears wetting the bar, to look at Marcus. "You were right. If she survived the attack, she could be dead by now, or sold to any one of the tribes from Montana to Mexico."

He waved an arm at nothing in particular. "You go on. An' take Jesse. Boy's got a life to live. I'll move faster alone. May hook up with some miners and prospect a while."

"Still givin' the orders eh, Cap'n?" Marcus sneered. "Well, I ain't takin' 'em. Fer once you'll be listenin' to somebody else—if'n you shut yer waggin' tongue long 'nough to hear what the boy here has to say. You'll be the better for it. I promise."

Patrick wearily raised his head and squinted through the afternoon haze at Jesse. "What?"

Jesse cleared his throat and puffed out a chest grown wide and strong during his months in the West. "Well, I was drinkin' a little tiswin with some of the Comanche scouts passin' through here with the soldiers. About the time Miz Carrie disappeared, they made a big raid in Mexico. They took a different way home to fool the soldiers. Swung way north," he said. "Took some white captives."

The news didn't cheer Patrick. "Could be anywhere by now."

Jesse ignored him to talk to Marcus, "A scout who left the band told me it was a cocky sub-chief named Three Feathers who led the raid. One captive was a crippled man who kept screaming his sister knew where to find gold to buy guns."

"The hell you say," Patrick swore, upsetting his stool. He'd have fallen on his face if Marcus hadn't caught him under the arms and set him right, leaning against the bar.

Patrick fought against his steadying hands to shout, "Beecher! The bastard has nine lives." Almost sober now, he grabbed Jesse by the collar. "What about Camilla? What did they do to her? Where is she?"

Jesse nodded with a wide grin. "The scout said they were headed to their summer camp in the Sierra Madres. He had a falling out with Three Feathers and left the band to join the blue coats."

"Mrs. Nickerson had yellow hair," Marcus noted.

After a moment of respectful silence for those who didn't survive, Jesse continued. "Nantaje still smarts after his beating from Three Feathers over a captive with chestnut hair wearing men's clothes. Says he wants revenge."

"It's her!" Marcus shouted and thumped Jesse on the back. "She's alive. What about Judith—I mean Mrs. Carter?"

Jesse nodded. "He said they took an old woman too, but didn't put much stock in her value as a slave. They were both alive when he left Three Feathers."

"Were," the melancholy Irishman spoke up. "Nearly a year ago. If they believed Beecher about the gold and she couldn't show them where it is, they could have killed both women."

"But we don't know do we?" Jesse and Marcus said at the same time.

Dumping his new tequila onto the dirt floor, Patrick stood up. "So where is this scout of yours?"

Jesse translated while Nantaje told them he didn't have any better idea of where to find Camilla than they did. The Comanche seldom stayed in one place long, and ranged through Mexico, Arizona, Texas, and as far north as Kansas. It seemed hopeless.

In the quiet of the evening, Patrick sat alone in the darkness of their camp, mulling over what Nantaje had told them about Three Feathers. The Comanche sub-chief had a maniacal thirst for power. He hated whites, but in truth, hated anything or anyone who stood in his way of becoming a first chief, namely, his uncle, Red Wolf.

Smoke from his last cheroot circled his head in the still, night air. If Three Feathers believed Beecher, and he would if it meant enough money to buy weapons, he'd take Camilla to his camp and try to force the information from her. His stomach tightened with the knowledge of Comanche methods of persuasion. But Camilla was smart and didn't care a whit about the gold. If it meant staying alive, and finding a way to escape, she'd take them to it.

His mind focused only on finding his love, Patrick reacquainted himself with the four-year-old gold robbery that had blackened his stellar career as a detective. He'd combed all the logical routes open to Langesford and his band, and came up empty. Alan Pinkerton had dismissed the only other possible route as too rugged and too dangerous for a small group of raiders on the run with a wagon of gold. Then the war ended. Life went on, and the mystery of the Rebel Treasure faded into legend.

Now the wild plan leading straight through Indian country made perfect sense. To a sane person, it seemed like suicide, but to an invincible young Southern officer determined to save his country, it would be the shortest and fastest route into Confederate Texas. To hell with the Indians. He was on a mission from God.

"Thank you!" he addressed a deity he'd denounced decades before and jabbed the stub of his spent cheroot into the sand. "Jesse, Nantaje," he called. "Get the gear together."

He waved at Marcus to meet him at the stream and weighted a worn map of the territories to the ground with rocks. By the light of the moon, he pointed at two marked lines east to Kansas and north to Canada, explaining, "I tracked these routes when I looked for the gold back in '62 and '63."

Using a pencil stub from his pocket, he drew a line in a southeasterly direction from Denver, cutting through northern New Mexico, into Texas, and across the Gulf to Louisiana. Then he stabbed

Taos, New Mexico with the pencil.

"I never figured they'd try this route, and sure wasn't fool enough to go through there alone. But it's the perfect hiding place. The mountains surrounding Rancho de Taos are riddled with old pueblos and caves. They're sacred to all the plains Indians. They believe if they make war there, their souls will wander the earth forever."

He smiled at his old friend. "If the Rebs made it there, they'd hide out before going on. And if I were Three Feathers and thought there might be gold in there, I'd say hang the ghosts and head for it."

Marcus played devil's advocate to Patrick's overconfidence. "But does the Mrs. know any of this?'

Feeling closer than ever to her now, Patrick refolded his map. "She saw the map."

Chapter Thirty-Nine

Camilla's son entered the world in a Comanche camp in New Mexico's Sangre de Christo Mountains. Judith, now well-respected as Wakometkla's assistant, along with Morning Bird, helped her during the long labor in a birthing hut along the Rio Grande River.

She gave birth the Comanche way, crouching to let the baby ease its way down through her womb. But she insisted Judith catch the child, rather than letting it fall into a bed of leaves beneath her. After his baptism in the mighty Rio Grande river, Camilla took him to her breast and told them, "Three Feathers has a strong and healthy son today."

She wore a white, beaded doeskin dress she'd made to present her child to the sub-chief on his third day of life. But before the boy was one day old, Three Feathers arrived at the hut and took him from her breast. He inspected the hungry child closely, his fierce black eyes looking for signs of himself in the tiny infant's eyes.

Camilla had long since learned that Three Feathers understood much more English than he spoke, and complimented him on his fine, strong son. But he only grunted, handing the boy back to her in disgust, saying, "White."

She knew he'd only let her live because Morning Bird noticed her signs of pregnancy shortly after his attack. Zoe's child had suffocated under her body during the night a few weeks later and Camilla's pregnancy offered him the chance for another son. Though she couldn't be sure, Camilla knew in her heart he'd failed to plant his seed that horrible night. But her only hope for both their lives depended on her ability to make him believe he'd succeeded in raping her.

"No," she called after him. "He is a chief's son. See his thick black hair and red skin." Knowing his skin was reddened from the effort of feeding, and would soon fade if she was right that she'd conceived in St Louis with Patrick, she prayed for Three Feathers to believe her.

Curious, he returned to stare at the now-howling child's red and mottled skin. Then he pointed a tawny finger at the baby's dark, gray eyes. "White eyes."

Camilla begged Patrick's departed soul to forgive her lie. "You have come too soon. A new child's eyes turn dark in the days after birth. They were light when he was born but already have turned the color of stormy skies. And he has the raven black hair of his father, the great warrior...Three Feathers.

Just as she'd hoped, the flattery made him pause. She pressed, "And he is strong. Though he was born more than a month early, he has the strong body of Three Feathers and his ancestors."

He scowled, but took the babe again, this time seeing what he wanted to see. Proudly, he held him above his head and pronounced him, Mah-ho-te. Storm Cloud, after the wintery color of his eyes. With a satisfying look of victory on his scarred face, he pushed her away to give his son to Zoe to nurse.

Camilla's mind snapped. She sprang to stand between them, shouting, "No," causing even more wails from the hungry newborn. "It is my babe." She again faced her captor, defiantly staring into his hate-filled black eyes.

He sneered as if she were an annoying pest, waved an arm, and knocked her weak body to the ground. She could only watch as her child was given to another woman while her own breasts ached from the weight of her milk.

As if from outside her body, she defied Three Feathers to shout, "If you want to see the gold, give me back my child."

Three Feathers turned slowly to face her, death in his eyes. White slaves didn't bargain with a second chief of the great Comanche nation and expect to live. But Camilla wouldn't back down and watched the dawn of understanding flush his disfigured face. His paralyzed cheek distorted into an evil grin. "Oro?"

She nodded and took her child from Zoe, placing him at her own breast, rocking gently back and forth to calm his gasps and her own quaking limbs. Knowing Three Feathers wouldn't wait long, she struggled to recall the intricate lines on her father's map.

"We need Morning Bird," she stalled, and out of greed, Three Feathers obeyed the tiny white captive to fetch his sister.

The three of them sat on the packed earth in the center of the tepee, near the fire. Camilla drew the map on the dirt with a stick. Speaking to Morning Bird, who relayed the information to her brother, she said, "I only saw the map once. On my son's life, I swear this is all I know of the gold. If you know this place, it will be there."

Three Feathers leaned closer to the crude drawing, slowly running a finger along one line and then the other until he declared, "Taos," and planted a fist on the "X."

His sister surprised them both to obliterate the sand drawing with her own closed fist.

Morning Bird and Three Feathers argued animatedly in their own tongue while Camilla watched in horror. *Is he going to kill us both now he has his information?* She crept to Storm Cloud's blanket, prepared to steal away to Wakometkla's lodge for protection. Then, as quickly as it erupted, the discussion ended.

Three Feathers stomped from the lodge and Morning Bird turned angrily, pointing a brown finger at Camilla. "You have caused the ruin of our tribe. We will all perish and our souls wander the earth for eternity."

Camilla's eyes stung with tears at her only friend's accusation. "I had to tell him," she argued. "He would have killed my son." She looked at the kicked-up earth. "I don't even know what any of it means."

Anger turned to resignation in the Indian woman's eyes. "My brother's hatred of whites and lust for this gold has brought you to us. Your map is of the meeting of the Rio Grande, Gila, and Colorado Rivers. It is the ancient land of our people, a place of holiness, solitude, and peace."

She sat then, and took the child from Camilla, cooing softly to him until his tremors stopped and he slept in her arms. "The towers of Taos are sacred to us," she explained. "All who enter with bloodshed in their hearts will perish. Now my brother will defy the spirits of our ancestors and go there to find gold to buy weapons and kill whites. I can do nothing. The great spirit has spoken." She handed the boy back to

Camilla.

A hasty council with all the sub-chiefs and warriors formed in the center of the camp. The women were banished to the lodges and Camilla nursed her newborn to the sounds of angry voices outside her door. But Three Feathers never returned to the lodge to kill them.

They broke up the village the next morning, heading east through the desert toward Santa Fe—toward Camilla and Judith's original destination. Nearly a year late, and so changed, she thought. Then she looked at her son and wondered about little Sam Pruitt, praying he and his parents survived the journey that had changed all their lives.

Chapter Forty

"We head North to Taos," Patrick announced to a puzzled Jesse and a sullen Nantaje. The scout argued against heading toward the Pueblos, unwilling to risk the anger of the ancients who guarded the sacred land.

Nantaje crept soundlessly under the full moon to Marcus' bedroll, his dagger poised over the blanket. Suddenly from behind, a hand covered his mouth and a hoarse voice whispered, "This is one old scalp no Injun's gonna dangle on his belt." It was the last thing the Comanche who killed Reverend Carter heard.

Marcus dragged Nantaje's body over to a nearby ravine and rolled him off the ledge, to land hundreds of feet below them, a small blemish on the desert floor. Then he tethered the horses Nantaje had planned to steal near his bedroll.

"The boy ran off," Marcus answered Patrick's raised eyebrow at Nantaje's sudden desertion. Neither Patrick nor Jesse asked why he'd left his horse behind.

Nearly a week later, Jesse rode back to Patrick and Marcus at breakneck speed, even for Cap'n. "Whoa, there," Marcus warned. "One gopher hole and yer both goners."

But Jesse didn't hear. "Comanche," he gasped. "Over the next rise. A whole village."

Patrick fired questions, one after another. "Where exactly? Are they moving or making camp? How many warriors? How many women? Did you see any white captives? Did they see you?"

Jesse answered them in one long breath. "About two miles north in a box canyon. They're making camp. I don't know how many, just a lot of them. No whites as far as I could see. And no one saw me."

Patrick nodded. "Wrap the horse's hooves to keep the dust down. We'll walk to the mesa and see where they post their sentries."

They waited all afternoon in the hot sun as Patrick scanned the group with his spyglasses. The women all wore nearly identical buckskin dresses, their dark hair coiled or braided. Then a tall white woman with blonde hair piled on top of her head stepped out of a tepee.

Marcus had told him about Judith Carter, calling her a, "right robust and formidable woman." This woman, though blonde, appeared strong, with a trim body, not the plump matron Patrick remembered.

He handed the glasses to Marcus. "Look here," he said, pointing slightly west. "Over there at the medicine lodge. Is she your lady friend?"

Marcus uttered an oath Judith wouldn't have appreciated when he nodded. Grinning from ear to ear, he boasted, "Ain't she a fine lookin' woman, even in that Injun getup?" He coughed to suppress his joy at finding the woman whose husband had died under his own watch, and gave the glasses back to Patrick. "I mean, looks like she held up all right."

Patrick put the glasses back up to his tired eyes, putting all his hope, and whatever faith he still had in God on the line to pray Camilla was still in the camp. The sun was high when he caught a glimpse of a small white woman leaving the largest lodge. He ignored the angle of the sun to raise his head and feast his eyes on her thick, russet braids and white doeskin dress with a bright beaded belt circling her tiny waist.

Suddenly, she raised a slender arm to look up, shading her eyes with one hand. He gasped as she looked directly at him, but couldn't move to take cover. Her face was tanned by months in the western sun, but her smooth skin was mercifully free of tattoos.

He put the glasses down and wiped his eyes before raising them again, careful now, to avoid the sun's reflection. Below him, Camilla had turned away and he saw a baby board strapped to her back with a tiny, black-haired child inside. He moaned when she gently removed the cradle board, lifted the child out and kissed a tiny cheek before laying it on the ground by her. The glasses hit the dust with a thud and Patrick swore, "Holy Mary Mother of God."

"Didn't yer ma teach you better'n that," Marcus joked. His smile faded at the shock on Patrick's face when he said, "She has a child."

They waited out the cold desert night with no fire as they planned a way to rescue two women and a baby from an armed Comanche camp in a box canyon. It seemed hopeless and Jesse voiced what they all thought. "They ain't just makin' camp, are they? With the warriors painted and all, they got somethin' else on their minds."

"It's time, Paddy," Marcus said, nodding toward Jesse. "We could die out here. The boy needs to know what's goin' on."

Patrick sighed. Marcus was right. The boy had proved himself time and again over the last months. He was smart, strong and loyal. All a man could hope to be. "They're after gold," he said, explaining the robbery and Camilla's link to it. "They think it's hidden in one of the old caves in the Taos Pueblo."

Jesse's eyes widened at the talk of hidden treasure. "Is it really there?"

Patrick stared at the dry sand under his boots. "The only question that matters, is if Three Feathers think it is." With a nod to the canyon, he said, "And it looks to me like he does."

At dawn, they again crept to the edge of their mesa and Patrick watched his wife perform the duties of a slave to the Comanche. With the child on her back, she gathered fuel for the fire and began the outdoor cooking pots, making *tasajo* cakes for the trail.

His blood boiled when a tall, sinewy, half-naked brave emerged from the lodge and stood over her to eat his fried corn cake filled with buffalo meat, leaving only crumbs for her.

Knowing that to rush down and pluck her from them would kill them both, he was willing to try, until an older woman offered her a meatless piece of bread.

A short while later, the young buck roused himself to shout orders. Instantly, the other lounging warriors sprang to their feet and mounted their horses. Minutes later, they rode out of the camp in a cloud of dust, toward the foothills of the Sangre de Christo Mountains.

Patrick's lips curled into a smile and he scratched the dark beard he'd neglected to shave for months. "Must have got impatient," he muttered, handing the glasses to Marcus.

He looked at a camp now populated by old men, women and

children. "Looks like he evened up the odds a bit fer us, boyo," Marcus smiled. "What say we quit sunnin' ourselves and go fetch our ladies?"

They rode into the camp disguised as traders. Patrick passed for a Mexican with his dark beard and tanned face, while Jesse's half-blood opened the gate for them. The tribes already knew Marcus as a trapper and trader, and with Nantaje's trophies, they had plenty to sell.

They used his pony as a pack horse and entered the camp amid barking dogs, to stop in front of Camilla's fire pit. Marcus made a big show of spreading a blanket and displaying his wares, and Jesse invited the village to join them. Soon, women and children, and even a few of the younger braves came out of their lodges to take part in the trading.

Patrick tethered the unpacked pony behind Three Feather's tepee. When Camilla didn't come out with the other women, he lifted the bottom of the skin wall and slipped inside. She was bent over a cooking pot while the babe slept on a mat close by.

He crept up without a sound to cover her mouth with his left hand while his right pinned her arms to her sides. But instead of screaming and fighting like the banshee he once knew, she froze. The wildly beating pulse along the soft skin of her throat showed him her fear, but she didn't cry out.

The long, dusty ride and his emotions made his voice gritty when he whispered, "Cammy, it's me."

But instead of relaxing in his arms, she stiffened. He knew if Beecher had poisoned her mind against him and he let her go, she could get them both killed, but took the chance. "I'm here to help you. Can I let you go?"

At her nod, he loosened his hold and she turned to him. She gasped as if she'd seen a ghost and stepped back, nearly upsetting the pot. Without a word, he pulled her into his arms, kissing her tenderly at first, then hungrily, as they convinced themselves they were still alive—for the moment.

"Beecher said you were dead," she whispered into his lips, his eyes, his cheeks.

He reluctantly pulled back, his hands framing her face. "I told you not to believe a word from him," he whispered back. He forced himself to ignore his rising passion for this woman who, even in an enemy tent,

Doris M. Lemcke

dressed in animal skins, made him forget his instinct for survival. "Hurry," he said.

But she didn't move. "My baby," she whispered.

If she wanted it, he'd carry it to Hell and back, but he gave her the choice. "It's Comanche. Another woman will raise it."

He finally saw a glimmer of the old Camilla in the set of her chin. In the dim light of the tepee, her eyes looked huge and dark. Without denying the babe was the issue of a Comanche, she told him, "He is my child and his name is Storm Cloud. I won't leave without him."

Without hesitation, Patrick scooped up the sleeping child and his board. Camilla grabbed a buckskin bag and followed him through the back of the tent where he strapped the board to her and slipped the child inside. Then he lifted them both onto the pony. "Go now, while we have their attention. Meet us on the mesa to the south."

"But Judith."

He frowned. "Marcus will take care of her. Now go!" he ordered as he slapped the pony's rump.

When she was far enough away, Patrick made his way over to the trading area and shouted, "Thief!" Then he jumped Jesse and they scuffled in the dust, giving the Comanche tremendous delight to watch one of their own wrestle a White. "They're mine," Patrick roared. "From a Mexican desperado. Kilt the man myself."

"Liar," Jesse gasped, pulling out from Patrick's stranglehold. "You gave them to me."

They wrestled to give Camilla enough time to escape, but not too long to bore their audience. Allowing Jesse to flip him into a chokehold, and then flipping the boy back onto the ground, Patrick finally let go and dusted off his dirty leggings. "Well fought son," he laughed, spitting blood from a split lip. "What say we split 'em?" He pulled Jesse up to offer him one of a pair of fancy, Mexican spurs.

Jesse held up his trophy and turned in a slow circle to show it to his cheering brethren. Then suddenly, he dropped it in front of the lone woman standing silent in front of him.

"Wah-ho-ne," Morning Bird whispered and Jesse answered, "Mother."

Patrick rested his hand on the hilt of his knife, braced for alarm

308

when Morning Bird led them into the lodge. Her intelligent gaze swept the empty interior, but instead of screaming when she discovered her slave missing, she picked up Camilla's cooking tools and offered them food.

She welcomed her son to his true home with The People and spoke of how happy her brother, Three Feathers, would be when he returned from his hunting trip at sundown. Then she explained slowly and clearly, exactly where he had gone, how many men had gone with him, and when they expected him to return.

Without knowing her reasons for offering the information, Patrick appreciated her help. They didn't have much time. They had to get Judith and be out of the canyon before Three Feathers came back at dusk. A look at Marcus told him he felt the same.

After a few bites of venison, Marcus cleared his throat and spoke to Morning Bird in her tongue. "You have a white captive here, at the medicine lodge. A fine lookin' woman. Would ye be willing to sell her to me?"

It was a reasonable request. Comanche were well-known slave traders. It didn't matter if the slave was White, Negro, Mexican, or a member of other tribes. Like horses, good strong people unfortunate enough to cross paths with the Comanche, were valuable merchandise.

Though Judith had become nearly as powerful as Wakometkla in the village, Morning Bird nodded and said a few words to Zoe, who had also kept her silence about Camilla's absence.

A few minutes later, Zoe returned with Judith and Wakometkla. Patrick saw Judith miss a step when she recognized Marcus, but she kept her gaze on the ground during the negotiations over her selling price.

She was very helpful, the Shaman insisted through Morning Bird's translation. Her price would be high. They offered all the proceeds from the sale of Nantaje's treasures, but still fell short of his price. When Marcus looked ready to spring for the man's throat, Jesse put his hand on the old scout's arm.

"Keep your money, my friend," Jesse told the man who took him under his wing when Patrick was lost in his black Irish moods. "It is time for me to repay you…both, for the kindness you have shown me."

He turned to Wakometkla. "My horse, Cap'n, is a finer mount than any in this camp. Worthy of only a chief or a medicine man as powerful as you." Hiding a smile at the flattered shaman's interest, he bowed his head. "Now I am home, it is far too great a horse for me to ride."

He avoided Patrick's stare to propose, "I offer him to the great Wakometkla in exchange for the white woman."

The man behind the blue and red paint smiled at the offer of the fine gray gelding, agreeing it would rival the sub-chief's own powerful steed. Before the boy could change his mind, he shoved Judith toward Marcus, who caught her by the shoulders.

Patrick rose and bought a horse for Judith with Nantaje's money, but Jesse refused to leave. He took Patrick aside. "It is finished. You have your wife, and Marcus, I think, will have Judith for a long time. And I am with my people."

He shook Patrick's hand. "Go quickly and give Miz Carrie my love. I owe her my life."

Morning Bird's warning frown told them to hurry. They mounted quickly and rode fast out of the canyon. Though Judith's Indian pony was sure-footed and swift, it could never match Jupiter, so Patrick rode on ahead to the mesa.

He found Camilla looking as calm and serene as the Madonna herself, nursing her child in the shade of an ancient boulder. He dismounted and walked slowly up to her, memorizing the details of the moment. To his dying day, he knew he would never forget this vision of her in the white doeskin dress, her tumbling, russet hair, the child held close to her full breast. He also knew he'd never love her more than at this moment.

He knelt on one knee beside her, silently watching the baby suckle. Its eyes were closed and a full head of black hair surrounded a round face, dark with the effort of feeding. Patrick blinked away the image of the man who had created this child, while thanking all the saints in heaven for the babe who had kept his love alive.

When young Storm Cloud finished his feast, Camilla laid him over her knees on his stomach, covered herself and patted his back until a satisfied belch escaped the tiny lips. Then she thrust him into Patrick's awkward grasp, saying, "His Indian name is Storm Cloud because of the color of his eyes, but I call him Sean Patrick. Before we go further, you must decide which name it is to be."

Patrick looked closely at the little face, returning the toothless grin directed at him. When a tiny finger held tight to his, he thought, I'm white, but my skin is darker than his. Then gray eyes with green flecks fixed on his as if they recognized him. *Mary O'Grady's eyes.*

Tears clouded Patrick's vision when he looked up to see the hope in Camilla's face. "Sean O'Grady will do nicely," he said. "We can decide on his second name on the way home."

"Home!" Camilla's happy cry accompanied the sound of Marcus and Judith's approach.

Chapter Forty-One

Camilla knew this day would always be the happiest day of her life. Patrick was alive! And he'd accepted her child as his own without question. Dear Marcus had once again saved her and a child from certain death. And Judith, her angel, her champion, her rock, would no longer be alone. Their futures looked bright, but first, they had to escape a gold-crazed monster who intended to kill them all.

With precious minutes flying by, she and Judith embraced. "Come with us back to Santa Fe," Judith urged. The nod from Marcus told them his wagon train days were over.

Patrick looked to Camilla, giving her a last chance to choose her "new" life. But there was no choice to be made. Her heart made the decision the moment Patrick found her. She gave both Judith and Marcus one last embrace and shook her head. "No. My life is with Patrick and our son."

Feeling whole for the first time in her life, she melted into the circle of her husband's arms. "And our life at Langesford. The *new* Langesford we will build together."

The sudden cry of an eagle taking to the air broke the joyful reunion that had turned somber. "Something disturbed it." Patrick observed. "We've no time to waste."

He turned to Marcus. "We have to split up. "You two can travel faster. Head south to make them think we're going to Santa Fe, but cut over to Fort Union and alert the cavalry."

He squeezed Camilla's shoulder. "We'll follow the river to Rancho de Taos and take the Mountain branch north to Bent's Fort. After that, it's a cakewalk back to Fort Dodge. I hear the Union Pacific Eastern spur is close to Junction City. We'll take the train from there."

Camilla smiled at his optimism, knowing it was for their friends' benefit. Both she and Judith had walked the trail as prisoners and knew it wouldn't be as easy as Patrick presented it, even on horseback.

They rode steadily without overtaxing the horses. Even the child sensed their joy at being together and fretted little after spending hours on Camilla's back. But ever cautious of being followed, they ate sparingly of the few corn cakes and jerky in Patrick's saddlebag. And without a fire at night, they huddled under their horses' blankets, the child between them.

Two days later, they were in the heart of the magnificent Taos mountains riddled with caves hewn by the ancient and mysterious Anasazi people. They camped on the desert floor near Rancho de Taos, hoping to barter for supplies in the sleepy little village of peaceful Pueblo Indians and Mexicans.

As the sunset turned the golden rock cliffs to blood red, Patrick put his arm around Camilla. "I wonder," he thought out loud.

She pulled back. "No!"

But he held her close. "No. I've found my rebel treasure. And I'm taking it home."

Satisfied, Camilla murmured, "Home."

They made love for the first time since their reunion on a blanket over the hard-packed earth, savoring the moment to remember when they returned to their four-poster bed with a feather mattress. One day, they promised, they would tell Sean and their other children of their journey into golden mountains that glowed red at sunset. One day, Camilla thought, after the horrors of her captivity faded.

Just after sunrise, Patrick saw clouds of dust rising from the south. Four horses, closing fast and headed for the Pueblo. Moments later, they turned their own horses away from it, picking their way carefully along the steep climb, toward the safety of the mysterious holy place. But they both knew they couldn't outrun or out-climb a Comanche pony. The wild mustangs were bred in the mountains and could climb like goats.

Patrick halted high above the desert floor, near the maze of hollowed-out rock homes that looked older than time itself. A distant plume of dust told him they'd only gained a little time. He dismounted, telling Camilla, "Looks like they found out we weren't in the Pueblo. And Three Feathers isn't afraid of ancient curses. We'll have to stand and fight."

He nodded to a narrow ledge ringing the caves above them and handed Jupiter's reins to her. "He won't make it up there with me on his back. And he's too good for the Comanche. Take the gear and let him go. Yours will handle you and the babe. Take cover in one of the caves while I try to pick them off."

He tossed her a pistol and a loaded gunbelt. "Open fire when you can. A cross-fire will help."

She'd outgrown her need to question orders and turned her sure-footed Indian pony toward the steep incline, a nervous Jupiter in tow. An infant on her back, a rifle in her lap, and a stallion behind her, she let the pony guide them all to safety.

With each terrifying step, she searched the mesa for a cave deep enough to shelter the horses and give her a view of Patrick in the craggy ravine. Only one ancient home was large enough, with niches in the walls for their gear and stone benches for sleeping above the ground.

With the horses put away, and Sean asleep on an ancient rock shelf at the back of the cave, she crouched just inside the entrance to load the gun. Her perch near the clouds allowed her to watch Three Feathers and his braves climb agilely up the rocks, perilously close to Patrick's hiding place. She ached to call out a warning, but to do so would threaten his life, as well as hers and little Sean.

Her dress blended into the rock and sand cliff as she lay on her stomach, praying to be able to pick off one of the braves before he saw Patrick.

"Closer, closer, just a few more steps," she whispered to Black Bear, her finger aching to gut-shoot the monster who had kicked her and ate her food, even while he thought she carried his chief's baby. But he turned away from her as the sun blinked off Patrick's rifle. Before either could shoot, he leaped behind a boulder. Fortunately, she was behind Black Bear when he stood to aim his bow. Her shot helped even the odds.

Suddenly caught in a cross-fire, Three Feathers and his two other braves took cover blending into the desert canvas as easily as a chameleon. For long moments, only the cry of an angry hawk deprived of its midday meal disturbed the eerie quiet. But while Comanche footsteps were silent to a white man's untrained ears, Camilla recognized her captor's tread on any surface. She heard it now, below her, climbing ever closer to Patrick.

She had to warn him. She pushed loose rock and soil over the edge with her free hand. When Three Feathers broke his cover, Patrick's shot glanced off the rocks above his head. But when Red Dawn sprang up to return fire, her second shot sent him to his death. Her third ended Bended Bow's short life on earth.

Patrick raised his head from beneath a narrow rock outcropping to scan the rocky terrain scattered with sagebrush and late-blooming desert flowers. Without shrubbery or trees, the steep cliff walls were worn smooth by the weather. But an Indian could blend into the tawny landscape like a mountain lion, unnoticed until his teeth sunk into his unwary prey.

He couldn't hear his pursuer's steps, but he could smell his scent in the thin mountain air. A shadow floated across the sun-baked rock above him and Patrick fired blindly. A howl of pain told him he'd hit his mark. But where? And who? Then a shot rang out from the same direction, followed by a searing pain in his arm.

His rifle fell onto the ledge below. He ducked into a crevice in the rock wall, pulling his knife from his boot and holding it between his teeth. With blood flowing down his arm, he pulled the sleeve off his shirt, using his good arm and teeth to wrap it above the gushing hole near his shoulder. Then he pressed his palm against the bandage to staunch the flow, sliding down the wall to wait for three Feathers to check his kill.

Minutes seemed like hours as he fought to stay conscious and keep the pressure on his wound. Then a stone dislodged near his hiding place. He hid the knife beneath his thigh and dropped his head to play dead.

The smell of bear grease, sweat, and blood told him the Comanche stood over him. Through half-closed eyes, he saw a trail of blood running down Three Feather's naked leg, confirming his hit. As he'd hoped, the frugal Comanche seemed reluctant to waste a bullet on a dead enemy. In that moment of hesitation, Patrick opened his eyes and raised his weapon.

Loss of blood made him slow, but the surprise was enough to stab another hole in Three Feathers' wounded leg. He went down to his knees, dropping his Army-issue Remington rifle.

For long moments, the one-armed man and his one-legged opponent fought with fists, teeth, and the weight of their own bodies on the narrow precipice. When Three Feathers slammed a fist into Patrick's wounded shoulder, he lurched sideways, ramming his knee into the Comanche's still-bleeding leg. They teetered there a moment, locked in a bloody embrace as both men struggled to retain their footing. When Patrick's booted foot kicked Three Feathers' ankle, he faltered, grabbing what was left of Patrick's shirt and pulling them both over the cliff to the ledge where Patrick's rifle lay.

Camilla was nearly within reach of her wounded husband when Three Feathers found Patrick. Too far away to help him, she could only watch their deadly struggle, hoping to get a shot without killing her husband. When then they fell over the ledge, locked in combat, her scream joined the scavengers already diving on Black Bear's corpse.

She knew, for her child's sake, she should run back to the cave, but she was no longer Camilla Langesford, or Camilla O'Grady. She was Wild Fire, a name bestowed on her by the Comanche, because of the color of her hair and her fierce battle at the wagon train. She ran to the edge of the outcropping where both men lay still. Three Feathers was on top of Patrick, their blood co-mingling as it flowed down to the canyon floor.

Her gun pressed against the back of Three Feathers' head, she rolled him over to find Patrick's hunting knife sunk to the hilt in his painted chest. One more shove and his body rolled off the ledge. She dropped to her knees above her still and pale husband. "Nooooo," she keened to her God and the mountain spirits who punished all trespassers on their sacred land.

"I'm fine," sounded like a sigh from God.

"Patrick?" she whispered back and he smiled before he passed out.

Her ear on this chest told her his weak heart was still beating beneath her blood-soaked fingers. Tears of joy and love streamed down her face as she tore the unconscious man's shirt off to assess his wound. The bullet had gone through his shoulder, missing the bones. Her lips taut, she held the shirt tightly to the wound until the thick, homespun fabric stiffened under her fingers. Satisfied the bleeding had stopped, she pulled away and stood.

"Stay quiet," she warned when he moved his head. "I need to clean the hole and close it for good. Promise me you won't move." His blink told her he probably couldn't if he tried. For good measure, she placed a rock where her hand had been to keep the pressure on the wound. "I will only be a moment," she whispered as if leaving the parlor to refill his brandy.

Within minutes, she returned with Sean on in his backboard, and Patrick's canteen to clean his wound. Closing it with the catgut thread in his kit, she sacrificed a sleeve of his spare shirt to bandage the wound. When he could stand, helped him climb back down to the base of the trail leading to their aerie.

With Patrick's strength used up and a steep climb facing them, they stopped to rest in the shade of a boulder, dislodging an iguana from his afternoon shade. A sudden snort made them both jump and Camilla turned toward the sound, the rifle at her shoulder. There, at the base of the Anasazi trail, Jupiter bowed to his knees for his wounded master to mount.

Patrick had misjudged his strong and faithful mount. Following Camilla's lead, the big horse carefully picked his way up the narrow trail. By sunset, they were finally safe in the cave with their son.

She risked a small fire in the ancient pit to roast a jack rabbit drawn to the cave by the cooing child. Patrick ate sparingly, taking the occasional swig of whiskey from a flask in his saddlebag to ease his pain. When he fell asleep, Camilla felt his forehead for signs of fever and kissed a stray lock of black hair.

"It's over, my love," she whispered, gathered Sean into the pouch made from Patrick's serape wound around her neck. Then she left to gather more mesquite bushes for fuel.

~ * ~

While Patrick regained his strength, Camilla settled into cleaning their temporary home with a broom made from the versatile mesquite bush. She also retrieved supplies from the Indian ponies before freeing them to return to the wild mustangs in the valleys below.

On the second day, she left him with Sean to look for game. "I can go," Patrick protested, still unsteady on his feet, and fighting the dizziness and nausea still plaguing him from the loss of blood. She smiled. "So I see. Maybe tomorrow." Taking the rifle and their canteens, she kissed them both and carefully picked her way down the now familiar cliff path.

The sun had just begun its descent when she stooped to re-enter the pueblo, three rabbits hanging on her belt. "It must be going to rain," she announced. "They were running around like mad. I had my pick."

When Patrick didn't answer, gooseflesh rose on her warm skin. She turned slowly to face the contorted, scarred face of Arthur Beecher. He laughed, pointing Patrick's pistol at her. "Quite the little hunter now, aren't you?"

She froze. *No! It can't be.* Patrick lay unconscious on the cave floor, a fresh stain on his shoulder, and a gash on the side of his head.

"What's the matter, Princess Squaw?" Beecher taunted. Ragged clothes hung on his emaciated frame and the stench of months without bathing filled the cave. He'd lost more teeth, his skin covered with sores. "Cat got your tongue? Or has your awe at seeing me alive made you dumb?"

"What do you want?" she asked, staring into bulging, glazed eyes. *And how did you possibly survive the banishment?*

"What do you want? What do you want?" he mimicked, laughing at her cry when he poked the pistol barrel into her fussing baby's chest.

"What do you think I want, Indian-loving whore?"

"The gold," she whispered.

"Bright girl. Now don't you just wish it was so simple. Stay right there," he threatened when she tried to reach her baby.

"What do you want me to do?" She wouldn't beg for her life but would do anything for Sean and Patrick. "Just don't hurt my child."

Patrick moaned and Beecher planted a foot on his wounded shoulder, transferring the gun barrel to the barely conscious man's head.

He nodded toward the now-crying child. "Shut it up or I'll blow both their heads off."

She scooped Sean into her arms. "He's hungry," she, turned from Beecher to face the wall.

"Don't turn your back to me, bitch," echoed in the stone cavern, punctuated by another moan. "Show yourself to me."

She straightened her back. "No."

"No? Do you want to see your precious husband die? Right now?"

She covered herself and the baby with the serape and faced him. "Do you want the gold?"

"Ah so you know where it is. I knew it! Where?"

Her voice lowered. "If you want to see the gold before you die, you'll let Patrick up. I can take you to it, but he must be able to see to the child. It's a long walk and it'll be dark soon."

Knowing greed would overrule Beecher's distrust, she pressed. "It's so close I'm surprised you can't smell it, even above your own terrible stench. Just do as *I* say and I'll take you there now."

Beecher slowly removed his foot from Patrick's shoulder and the gun from his head, ordering, "Move slow now. I'm real nervous on this trigger."

Patrick obeyed, rising slowly, his eyes taking in Beecher's shaking hands and twitching face. He nodded when Camilla told him, "He's too clever for us, Patrick. He survived the banishment."

"How?" Patrick, rasped. A ploy to keep him talking, Camilla hoped.

"Beecher's shrill laugh sent roosting bats to flight. "Why Paddy," he sneered. "I'm resourceful. And Indians are lazy louts." He laughed at his own cleverness. "I was never far from the camp, and stole food and water at night."

He turned to Camilla. "I heard the old bitch tell the little bitch here, what the lines on the map meant. Then I stole a pony and got a head start for the best seat in the house to watch Three Feathers kill you."

He frowned at Camilla. "But it seems you're resourceful too. That needs to stop." With a nod to her, he ordered, "Throw the rifle over the ledge." Then he prodded her with the pistol. "And you go first."

With a warning nod to Patrick, she did as he asked, Beecher following close behind her on the cliff walk—but not close enough for her to knock the gun away without being shot. So she kept climbing, praying for a sign. She stopped short when they rounded a curve onto a mesa with several caves lining a wide trail to another canyon floor.

Beecher grew impatient as the sun dipped between the twin mountain peaks. He poked her in the ribs with Patrick's gun. "Don't stall any longer, girl. Where is it?"

As the sun continued to descend, she pointed at the glow across the ravine. "There," she cried, "There is your Rebel gold, you bastard. Go get it."

He followed her gaze, his disfigured face rapturous as he stared at the red rocks now reflecting the golden sunset. Then a shot rang out and he straightened, dropping his gun. His eyes glazed in surprise, he fell silently to the canyon floor.

Camilla dropped to the stone ledge, trying to identify the direction of the shot. To get a glimpse of the one who had saved her life. Or had they aimed for her, shooting Beecher instead? Long moments passed without another sound, as she crawled to where Beecher had stood, staring down at the tiny dark stain on the rocky ground hundreds of feet below her.

"Please, God," she prayed in the dying light. "Let it finally be over. Let the killing stop." She turned away from the rock that had glowed golden for Beecher, and moments after his death, returned to the dusky color of blood.

Still afraid of the unknown person with a rifle, she followed the last rays of sun toward the opening in the rock wall behind her. But instead of a long-abandoned cave dwelling, she found a human skeleton. The tragedy of violent death no longer shocked her as she approached the rotted shreds of a soldier's uniform clinging to bones picked clean by scavengers.

"Who are you?" she asked, hesitating as if waiting for an answer. With only the sounds of scuttling bats as her response, she stepped inside as a last flash of sunlight winked from…something in the skeletal hand. She knelt beside the body, telling herself it was the sudden cry of a hawk that made her heart race before reaching toward the harmless fingers.

A locket. It fell open in her hand, revealing two tiny portraits of a woman and young girl. The woman had delicate, aristocratic features, perfectly coiffed white-blonde curls and bright blue eyes. The girl's emerald eyes and russet hair framed a heart-shaped face.

Tears streaming down her face, she collapsed beside her brother's bones. The cry ripping from her soul echoed through the endless canyons, sending eagles screeching from their mountain aeries. Coyotes responded to her keening with their own mournful appeals to the rising moon. When the echoes died, day surrendered to night, mercifully shrouding her pain in darkness.

~ * ~

Patrick abandoned his one-armed struggle with his son's backboard at the sound of a rifle from the direction Beecher and Camilla had gone. How could that be? His rifle was at the bottom of the canyon. And Beecher had his pistol. Was one of Three Feathers' men still alive?

He retrieved his serape and followed Camilla's movements to create a sling for his son. Ignoring the pain in his skull, dizziness, and his throbbing shoulder, he steadied himself with the mesquite broom and set out on the path she and Beecher had taken.

As the setting sun turned the blood red stone of the Sangre de Cristo mountains to gold, a woman's cry, followed by what sounded like the echo of angels singing the Comanche death song, filled the canyon. He'd only gone a short way when a veil of clouds parted from the full moon, revealing a dark spot on the sand below. His heart constricted, but the cloud mercifully returned before he could see if the broken body wore a white, doeskin dress.

"Cammy!" bounced off the canyon walls. "Where are you?" He inched his way along the narrow, crumbling mountain path with only the spotty moonlight to lead him. One wrong step and he and Sean would join the body on the desert floor. But with each hesitant step, he called her name.

It was her child's cry that brought Camilla's mind back from the day she'd pressed the locket into her brother's hand and said goodbye from the Langesford veranda. Even then, she knew she'd never see him again. "In here," called to her future.

Steadying Sean with his good arm, Patrick again braced his back against the cliff wall, following her voice. He found her standing motionless in the mouth of the cave, shafts of moonlight shimmering off her white dress and pale face. "Holy Mary Mother of God," he whispered, wondering again if she was a ghost beckoning him to join her in the afterlife.

She held out the locket in her hand. "It's Brent," she said. "I…I gave this to him when he left Langesford." Her tears spent, she stepped out of the cave to embrace her husband and child.

Patrick held her until her trembling stopped. With Sean once again settled against his mother's breast, he stepped inside the cave. "What happened here?" the detective in him asked.

The moonlight revealed Brent Langesford, forever guarding the entrance to the cave, but the interior was black as pitch. Using a rock as a flint, Patrick set the mesquite broom on fire and stepped inside. An old torch lay near the opening, and he transferred the flames from the nearly spent bush to the old, oil-soaked rages. The three of them entered the void together, stepping over the bones of three other Confederate soldiers to approach a knee-high pile of…something, covered by a tarp.

"You do it," she told him, though they both knew what lay under it.

He pulled the rotted canvas off, revealing several stacks of gold bars bearing the imprint of the Denver mint. His low whistle circled the cavern. "They nearly did it." he said. "They took thirty bars. Worth more than a half-million dollars." He turned to her. "It looks like we're missing two."

She stepped up next to him, facing of the obscene alter to the god of war. "Brent left with six men," she said. "Only two came back. Mason and Samuel Berens." Is it true, she wondered? Samuel Berens' story about stealing Yankee gold? And what Mason said? Was he one of them?

"But they look heavy. How could they get them out of Denver and up a mountain?"

He shrugged. "About fifty pounds a bar. Near as we could figure, they lined the bottom of manure wagon and drove it right down Main Street. A couple strong horses and good map could get them this far. But we're a long way from Denver. The other two could have helped themselves to a bar and taken off for Mexico, or anywhere between here and Denver." He raised an eyebrow. "Does it matter?"

Yes, she thought. If Sam Berens killed her brother for a gold brick, she'd see to it he never spent a dime. She'd been well-educated by the Comanche, and could make him believe it. "No," she lied and watched him replace the shroud before turning to examine the bodies.

One lay with arrows still imbedded between his bones. Dark stains on the blankets beneath him attested to his slow, agonizing death. Another had a fractured skull. Brent and the last one lay facing each other, Brent's body with a bullet on the ground beneath his chest cavity, the other a hole in the center of his skull.

Other than Brent, none of them had anything that could identify them. *Poor, brave and gallant fools,* she thought. Only God knew what brought them to their deaths. But she knew their names. And she promised they would all remain heroes of the battle of Chickamauga.

Patrick took her hand, leaving the stench of death, rot, and greed behind them to step into the clean, dry, desert air. Putting the locket around his own neck, he wrapped his good arm around her shoulder saying, "It's over. We'll send someone back so you can take Brent home. But who killed Beecher? he wondered out loud."

"Shush." she held a finger to his lips. "Listen."

The night sounds stilled as a woman's voice rose high and mournful, from God's own amphitheater below them, singing the Comanche death song. Patrick recognized the voice as the one he'd followed to Camilla. He cupped her chin in his hand, staring into her eyes once. "It wasn't you...before?"

She shook her head. *Morning Bird.*

They listened to the woman's plaintive cry to the Comanche gods, seeking forgiveness for her dead brother's sins. Even without knowing the words, they understood her plea for the spirits to take him to the hunting grounds of their ancestors. To a place where no white man dared trespass, and their people lived in peace. In the silence afterward, Camilla said her own prayer for Three Feathers and Arthur Beecher to wander the underworld forever, enduring the same suffering they inflicted on so many.

Chapter Forty-Two

They found Morning Bird on the canyon floor at dawn, securing her brother's body to his horse for burial outside the ancient tombs. She stopped at Camilla's approach and for a few moments, they stood together overlooking where Beecher's body still stained the earth.

Already, birds of prey were cleaning up his mess until soon, the fragments of his remaining clothing would become part of another scavenger's nest. Camilla looked away from the gruesome scene to see Three Feathers' rifle on the Indian woman's horse. "You saved our lives," she said. "I will owe you into eternity."

Morning Bird handed the gun to Patrick and grasped Camilla's hand. "No, you saved *my* life. You brought my son back to me. Jesse will become a strong leader. As foretold by the ancients, the white tide has come to overtake us. Only a leader who can walk the way of the White man, with the spirit of the People in his heart, will save us."

Her grip suddenly tightened, her gaze hard. "But violence has been done in this sacred place and atonement must be made. Go now, while the spirits sleep."

"What about you?"

The older woman looked up at the cloudless sky. "I am theirs now." She smiled and repeated what she'd told Camilla after Three Feathers attacked her. "Each morning I see means I will live another day."

She squeezed Camilla's hand one last time, her brown eyes bright, as if seeing into the future. "Others will come. And I must protect the secrets." Then she turned her back to lead her brother's body down to the canyon floor, and Camilla showed her the respect she deserved by not looking after her.

Two days later, they met Marcus, Jesse, Judith, and a small platoon of soldiers in the foothills. When the hugs and tears were finished, and their camp laid, Judith told them, "Jesse saved our lives. He left the Comanche to warn us and helped fight them off."

Her face glowed with love for the young 'half-breed'. "Then we went on to get the soldiers in Santa Fe and he fetched his mother. Where is she?"

Camilla fought back tears of gratitude—and grief, knowing her happiness had come at the expense of Morning Bird's life with her son. She told Judith, "Morning Bird saved *our* lives. She's chosen to live among the ancient Anasazi. To guard the Pueblos."

Tears filled Judith's eyes and she bowed her head to pray for all those who had suffered from hatred and war. She held Camilla's hand a moment longer, then rose to retrieve her tattered medical bag, forcing Patrick to sit near the fire.

"I'm sorry, but this is going to hurt," she apologized before removing the shirtsleeve now crusted onto his wound.

With a new bandage and his pain eased with an old bottle of Bulleit Bourbon, she addressed the new sorrow in Camilla's eyes. "What can possibly be the matter now?"

"We found Brent...and the gold," she whispered.

Marcus overheard and thumped Patrick on his good shoulder while Jesse fairly danced with excitement. Patrick caught Camilla's hand before she could run away and they rose together to find a private place by the horses.

She stood with her back to him, gazing up at the diamond-studded night sky. "I never meant to keep the gold, Cammy," he said. "but I'm honor-bound to turn it over to the Federal Government."

He took her stony silence as agreement and explained, "When an investigation is unsolved for three years, it transfers to public domain and carries, basically, a salvage fee. "There is a $50,000 reward." He stepped in front of her to pull her to him and kiss her lips. "We're rich, Cammy!"

Her entire body stiffened in his embrace and he pulled away, searching her face. "What's the matter? I can pay Dr. Johnson for his investment and we'll own Langesford outright, with enough left over to fulfill both your father's and my dream of building a breeding stable. You should be pleased."

She stepped from him, her beautiful features distorted by more than the horror beyond finding her dead brother in a cave with a pile of stolen gold. Echoing Morning Bird, she hissed, "The Pueblo has cursed the gold. It has already taken the lives of my entire family. I can't live with any part of it." The cry of an eagle punctuated her final words. "Or with you, if you accept it."

"But—"

"I won't!" She backed away. "It is the evil spawn of the lies that began at my mother's birth. The price of the sins of the fathers," she rambled, repeating Delmont Marchaud's words. "Give it to the army and never speak of it again in my presence!"

Nearby soldiers stopped eating to watch her frantic pacing until Patrick pulled her close. "Think about what you're saying, Cammy. I don't want the gold. Just the reward. It can ensure our future. Sean's future."

He winced when she pushed his injured shoulder "The third generation. No. Please God, no."

Seeing, but not understanding her horror, he conceded. "I have to take the commander at Fort Union up there to inventory it. After that, the Army will decide how to get it out. I'll bring your brother back."

She clutched his good arm. "No! Brent—and the others, are part of the pueblo now." Then, more slowly, "Go back once more if you must. If only to bury the men and rid the sacred mountains of the gold's vile presence. Take only the commander and Jesse. Stay only as long as you need. Morning Bird will protect you."

Her eyes wide and filled with tears, she repeated her warning. "But take nothing with you. Promise me—on your mother's grave."

Holding her close, he rested his chin on the top of her head. "Very well,"

At Fort Union, Patrick shook Marcus and Jesse's hands. They were staying in Santa Fe with Judith to continue Reverend Carter's work by opening a school in his name. With a glance at Camilla and Judith saying their goodbyes, he pressed an envelope into Marcus' hand. "We owe you our lives, old friend. Inside is a letter that names you, Judith, and Jesse as guardians for Sean if something happens to us."

In answer to the question in his old friend's eyes, he added, "It also authorizes you to claim the reward for the gold and put half of it in the bank at Santa Fe under the name of Sean C. O'Grady. The rest of the money is yours and Judith's. Use it for the school and make a difference if you can."

"But Paddy," he argued. "I thought the missus didn't want any part of it."

Patrick shook his head. "She's not thinking straight. She's been through too much because of it, but she'll come around eventually. I'm only asking for the finder's fee. It's the only way we can leave something for our son if things don't go well at Langesford—and if they go well, she'll never need to know."

Marcus nodded, but cautioned, "You sure 'bout this? What about the boy?"

Annoyed at his old friend's faultless logic, he snapped. "When Sean is old enough, we'll both tell him about...everything, including the reward."

He turned to his wife bidding goodbye to her dearest friend. "She's my Rebel Treasure, and the only one I'll ever need."

About the Author

A native Michigander whose great-grandmother was a member of the Saginaw Ojibwa tribe, Doris is fascinated by American history and Native American culture. Sources for this book included first-hand accounts from early Western pioneers and from the Civil War and Reconstruction eras.

Now retired in Southeast Michigan, Doris loves spending time with family, friends and other writers while writing and researching fast-paced historical and contemporary novels about strong, intelligent women caught in the web of, *Love, Lies and Family Secrets.*

Author Contacts
www.dorislemckebooks.com
www.facebook.com Doris Lemcke Author
www.LinkedIn.com
email: Doris@DorisLemckeBooks.com

Other Works by the Author:

Legacy of Lies
– The Truth Can Trap As Well As Set You Free